Critical acclaim for David Baldacci's novels

'Baldacci inhabits the skin of his creations –
tripping us up with unexpected empathy
and subtle identification'
Sunday Express

'Compelling . . . finely drawn . . .
a page-turner worth losing sleep over'
USA Today

'As expertly plotted as all Baldacci's work'
Sunday Times

'Baldacci cuts everyone's grass – Grisham's,
Ludlum's, even Patricia Cornwell's – and
more than gets away with it'
People

'A plot strong enough to make
the bath go cold around you'
Independent on Sunday

'Yet another winner . . . The excitement
builds . . . The plot's many planted
bombs explode unpredictably'
New York Times

'As usual, Baldacci delivers the goods in
fine style, with thrills and spills aplenty'
Independent on Sunday

First Family

David Baldacci is the internationally acclaimed author of eighteen bestselling novels. With his books published in at least 45 languages, and with over 90 million copies in print, he is one of the world's favourite storytellers. His family foundation, the Wish You Well Foundation, a non-profit organization, works to eliminate illiteracy across America. Still a resident of his native Virginia, he invites you to visit him at www.DavidBaldacci.com, and his foundation at www.WishYouWellFoundation.org, and to look into its programme to spread books across America at www.FeedingBodyandMind.com.

Novels of David Baldacci

The Camel Club series

The Camel Club
The Collectors
Stone Cold
Divine Justice

Sean King and Michelle Maxwell series

Split Second
Hour Game
Simple Genius
First Family

Shaw series

The Whole Truth
Deliver Us From Evil

Other novels

Absolute Power
Total Control
The Winner
The Simple Truth
Saving Faith
Wish You Well
Last Man Standing
The Christmas Train
True Blue

DAVID BALDACCI

First Family

PAN BOOKS

First published 2009 by Grand Central Publishing, USA

First published in Great Britain 2009 by Macmillan

First published in paperback 2009 by Pan Books

This edition published 2012 by Pan Books
an imprint of Pan Macmillan, a division of Macmillan Publishers Limited
Pan Macmillan, 20 New Wharf Road, London N1 9RR
Basingstoke and Oxford
Associated companies throughout the world
www.panmacmillan.com

ISBN 978-1-4472-2654-3

1 3 5 7 9 8 6 4 2

A CIP catalogue record for this book is available from
the British Library.

Printed in the UK by CPI Group (UK) Ltd, Croydon, CR0 4YY

To my mom,
and my brother and sister,
for all the love

PROLOGUE

Her footsteps were unhurried. Down the street, making one left, a two-block straightaway, and then a slight right. There was a pause at one intersection, a longer stop at another. Just from habit, really. The radar in her head showed no danger and her pace picked up. There were people around though the hour was late, but they never saw her. She seemed to ease by like a breeze, felt but never seen.

The three-story cinderblock building was right where it had always been, stuck between a high-rise on the left and a concrete shell on the right. There was security of course, but it was basic, not the best. A typical package, it would slow down a journeyman for a few minutes, a pro for much less.

She selected a window in the back of the building instead of breaking in the front door. These entry points were almost never wired. She popped the swivel latch, slid up the window, and wriggled through. The motion detector was handled with ease; she was humming as she did it. Yet it was a nervous hum. She was getting close to it, what she was here for.

And it scared the hell out of the lady. Not that she would ever admit that.

The file cabinet was locked. She cracked a smile.

You're really making me work here, Horatio.

Five seconds later the drawer slid open. Her fingers skimmed over the file tabs. Alphabetical. Which left her smack in the middle of the pack, something she'd never considered herself to be. Her fingers stopped skipping and curled around the file. It was a thick one; she'd never doubted it would be. She obviously wasn't a mere ten-page head case. A lot more trees had fallen because of her. She pulled it free and glanced at the copier on the worktable.

Okay, here we go.

Horatio Barnes was her shrink, her mind guru. He'd convinced her to enter a psych hospital a while back. The only mystery that voluntary incarceration had solved was one that did not involve her problems at all. Later, good old Horatio had hypnotized her, taking her back to her childhood, as any shrink worth his sheepskin invariably does. The session apparently had revealed many things. The only problem was that Horatio had decided not to fill her in on what she'd told him. She was here to correct that little oversight.

She slid the pages in the feeder and hit the button. One by one the events of her life whooshed through the heart of the Xerox machine. As each fresh piece of paper was catapulted into the catch bin her heart rate seemed to increase by the same single-digit measure.

She put the original file back in the drawer, popped a rubber band around her copy, and held it in both hands. Constituting only a few pounds, its weight still threatened to sink her right through the floor. Out the same way her boots made a clunking sound as they kissed asphalt. She walked calmly back to her SUV, a breeze again, invisible. Nightlife going on all around here; they never saw her.

She climbed in her ride, revved the engine. She was ready to go. Her hands played over the steering wheel. She wanted to drive, always loved to rip her eight cylinders down some new road to where she didn't know. Yet looking through the windshield, she didn't want new, she desperately wanted things to be the way they were.

She glanced at the file; saw the name on the first page.

Michelle Maxwell.

For a moment it didn't seem to be her. In those pages was someone else's life, secrets, torments. Issues. The dreaded word. It seemed so innocuous. Issues. Everyone had issues. Yet those six letters had always seemed to define her, breaking her down into some simple formula that still no one seemed capable of understanding.

The SUV idled, kicking carbon into an atmosphere already bloated with it. A few raindrops smacked her windshield. She could see people start to pick up their step as they sensed the approaching downpour. A minute later, it hit. She felt the wind buffet her sturdy SUV. A spear of lightning was followed by a long burp of thunder. The storm's intensity forecast its brevity. Such violence could not be sustained for long; it used up too much energy far too fast.

She couldn't help herself. She cut the engine, picked up the pages, ripped off the rubber band, and started to read. General info came first. Birth date, gender, education, and employment. She turned the page. And then another. Nothing she didn't know already, not surprising considering this was all about her.

On the fifth page of typed notes, her hands began to tremble. The heading was "Childhood—Tennessee." She swallowed once and then again, but couldn't clear the dryness. She coughed and then hacked, but that only made it worse. The swells of saliva had solidified in her mouth, just like they had when she'd nearly killed herself on the water rowing to an Olympic silver medal that meant less and less to her with each passing day.

She grabbed a bottle of G2 and poured it down her throat, some of it spilling on the seat and the pages. She cursed, scrubbed at the paper, trying to dry it. And then it tore, nearly in half. This made tears creep to her eyes, she was not sure why. She pulled the rent paper close to her face though her eyesight was perfect. Perfect, but she still couldn't read the script. She looked out the windshield and couldn't see anything there either, so hard was the fall of rain. The streets were empty now, the people having scattered at the first bite of water bent nearly horizontal by the wind.

She looked back at the pages but there was nothing there either. The words were there of course, but she couldn't see them.

"You can do this, Michelle. You can handle this." Her words were low, sounded forced, hollow.

She refocused.

"Childhood, Tennessee," she began. She was six years old again and living in Tennessee with her mother and father. Her dad was a police officer on the way up; her mom, was, well, her mom. Her four older brothers had grown and gone. It was just little Michelle left at home. With them.

She was doing fine now. The words were clear, her memories also crystallizing, as she crept back to that isolated wedge of personal history. When she turned the page and her gaze flickered over the date on the top it was as though the lightning outside had somehow grounded right into her. A billion volts of pain, a shriek of anguish you could actually see, and feel, as it pierced her.

She looked out the window, she didn't know why. The streets were still empty; the rain now racing to earth so hard the drops seemed to be connected, like trillions of strings of beads.

Yet as she squinted through the downpour she saw that the streets weren't empty. The tall man stood there, no umbrella, no overcoat. He was soaked right through, his shirt and pants melted to his skin. He stared at her and she did the same right back. There was not fear or hatred or sympathy in his look as he eyed her through the walls of water. It was, she finally concluded, an underlying sadness that easily matched her own despair.

She turned the key, put the SUV in drive, and hit the gas. As she raced past, she glanced at him as another thrust of lightning cracked and briefly made night into day. Both their images seemed solidified in that blast of energy, each of their gazes frozen onto the other.

Sean King never attempted to speak and didn't try and stop her as she roared by. He just stood there, his waterlogged hair in his face, yet his eyes as big and invasive as ever she'd seen them. They frightened her. They seemed to want to pull her soul right out of her.

An instant later he was gone as she turned the corner and slowed. Her window came down. The bundle of pages was hurled out, landing squarely in a Dumpster.

A moment later her SUV was lost in the punishing face of the storm.

1

Birthday balloons and submachine guns. Elegant forks digging into creamy goodies while toughened fingers coiled around curved metal trigger guards. Gleeful laughter as gifts were unwrapped floated into the air alongside the menacing *thump-thump* of an arriving chopper's downward prop wash.

The facility was officially designated by the Defense Department as Naval Support Facility Thurmont, yet most Americans knew it as Camp David. Under either name, it was not a typical venue for a preteen's birthday party. A former recreation camp built by the WPA during the Great Depression, it was turned into the presidential retreat and named the U.S.S. Shangri-La by FDR, because it was essentially replacing the presidential yacht. It had acquired its current and far less exotic moniker from Dwight Eisenhower, who named it after his grandson.

The hundred-and-thirty-acre property was rustic and had many outdoor pursuits, including tennis courts, hiking trails, and exactly one practice hole for presidential golfers. The birthday party was in the bowling center. A dozen kids were in attendance along with appropriate chaperones. They were all understandably excited about being on hallowed ground where the likes of Kennedy and Reagan had trod.

The chief chaperone and planner of the event was Jane Cox. It was a role she was accustomed to because Jane Cox was married to Dan Cox, also known as "Wolfman," which made her the First Lady of the United States. It was a role she handled with charm, dignity, and the necessary elements of both humor and cunning. While it was true that the president of the United States was the world's ultimate juggler of tasks, it was also a fact that the First Lady, traditionally, was no slouch in that department either.

For the record, she bowled a ninety-seven without gutter bumpers while wearing patriotic red, white, and blue bowling shoes. She clamped her shoulder-length brown hair back into a ponytail and carried out the cake herself. She led the singing of "Happy Birthday" for her niece, Willa Dutton. Willa was small for her age, with dark hair. She was a bit shy but immensely bright and wonderfully engaging when one got to know her. Though she would never admit it publicly of course, Willa was Jane's favorite niece.

The First Lady didn't eat any cake; Jane was watching her figure since the rest of the country, and indeed the world, was too. She'd put on a few pounds since entering the White House. And a few pounds after that on the hell-on-a-plane they called the re-election campaign her husband was currently engaged in. She was five-eight in flats, tall enough that her clothes hung well on her. Her husband was an inch shy of six feet and thus she never wore heels high enough to make him look shorter by comparison. Perception did matter and people liked their leaders taller and more robust than the rest of the population.

Her face was in decent shape, she thought, as she snatched a look in a mirror. It held the marks and creases of a woman who'd given birth multiple times and endured many political races. No human being could emerge unblemished after that. Whatever frailty you possessed the other side would find and stick a crowbar in to lever every useful scrap out. The press still referred to her as attractive. Some went out on a limb and described her as possessing movie-star good looks. Maybe once, she knew, but not anymore. She was definitely in the "character actress" stage of her career now. Still, she had progressed a long way from the days when firm cheekbones and a firmer backside were high on her list of priorities.

As the party continued, Jane would occasionally glance out the window as serious-looking Marines marched by on patrol, weapons at the ready. The Secret Service had of course traveled up here with her, but the Navy officially ran Camp David. Thus all personnel, from the carpenters to the groundskeepers, were sailors. And the bulk of the security duties fell to the permanent barracks of Marines deployed here. In truth, Camp David was better protected than 1600 Pennsylvania Avenue, though you wouldn't find many who would admit that on the record.

Security wasn't uppermost in Jane's mind as she watched in delight while Willa blew out the dozen candles on her two-tier cake and then helped hand out slices. Jane moved forward and hugged Willa's mother, Pam Dutton, who was tall and thin with curly red hair.

"She looks happy, doesn't she?" said Jane to Pam.

"Always happy around her aunt Jane," replied Pam, patting her sister-in-law's back affectionately. As the two women stepped apart Pam said, "I can't thank you enough for letting us have the party here. I know it's not, well, it's not the norm, what with Dan, I mean the president not even being here."

Not being a blood relation, Pam still found it uncomfortable calling her brother-in-law by his first name, whereas the president's siblings, and Jane herself, often called him Danny.

Jane smiled. "The law provides for joint ownership of all federal property between the president and the First Lady. And just so you know, I still balance our personal checkbook. Danny's not that good with numbers."

Pam said, "It was still very thoughtful." She

looked at her daughter. "Next year she's a teenager. My oldest a teenager, hard to believe."

Pam had three children. Willa, John, who was ten, and Colleen, seven. Jane also had three children, but all of them were older. The youngest was a nineteen-year-old son in college and her daughter was a nurse at a hospital in Atlanta. In between was another young man still trying to figure out what to do with his life.

The Coxes had had their family early. Jane was still only forty-eight while her husband had just celebrated his fiftieth.

Jane said, "Based on my own experience, boys will mess with your heart and girls with your head."

"I'm not sure my head's ready for Willa."

"Keep the lines of communication open. Know who her friends are. *Gently* insert yourself into everything that's going on around her but pick your battles cautiously. Sometimes she'll pull back. That's only natural, but once you've laid the ground rules it'll be okay. She's very intelligent. She'll get it pretty quickly. She'll be glad of the interest."

"Sounds like good advice, Jane. I can always count on you."

"I'm sorry Tuck couldn't make it."

"He's supposed to be back tomorrow. You *know* your brother."

She shot an anxious glance at Pam. "It'll be okay. Trust me."

"Sure, right," the woman said quietly, her gaze on happy Willa.

As Pam walked off, Jane focused on Willa. The girl was a curious mix of maturity coupled with frequent flashes of the preteen she still was. She could write better than some adults and discourse on subjects that would befuddle many folks far her senior. And she possessed a curiosity about things that was not limited to issues common to her age group. Yet if one watched her, one would see that she giggled impulsively, used "like" and "wow" liberally, and was just starting to discover boys with impulses of both disgust and attraction typical of the preadolescent girl. That reaction to the opposite sex would not change much when Willa became an adult, Jane well knew. Except the stakes would be far higher.

The party ended, goodbyes said. Jane Cox stepped on board the chopper. It wasn't designated as Marine One because the president wasn't riding on it. Today, it was strictly ferrying the B-team, Jane knew. And that was perfectly fine with her. In private, she and her husband were equals. In public, she walked the obligatory two steps behind.

She strapped in and the door was swung shut and secured by a uniformed Marine. Four stoic Secret Service agents shared the ride with her. They lifted off and a few moments later she was staring down at Camp David, or the "Birdcage," as the Secret Service had code-named the retreat, where it was cradled in the Catoctin Mountain Park. The chopper turned south and thirty minutes from now she would land safely on the lawn of the White House.

In her hand she held a note that Willa had given her before they'd left the party. It was a thank-you letter. She smiled. It was not unusual that Willa already had one prepared. The note was written in a mature voice and said all the right things. Indeed, some of Jane's staff could have taken a page from her young niece's etiquette handbook.

Jane folded the letter and put it away. The rest of the day and night would not be nearly as pleasant. Official duty called. The life of a First Lady, she had quickly learned, was one of a frenzied perpetual motion machine buffered often by bursts of tedium.

The chopper's skids touched grass. Since the president wasn't on board there was little fanfare as she made her way to the White House. Her husband was in his working office near the ceremonial oval one. She had made few demands on him when she'd agreed to stand by him in his run for the nation's highest office. One of them was that she could enter his inner sanctum without announcement, without being on the official visitor's list.

"I'm not a visitor," she'd told him at the time. "I'm your wife."

She approached the president's "body man," officially known as the Special Assistant to the President. He was at that moment looking through the peephole in the door to the Oval Office prior to going in and breaking up a meeting that was running behind. He was the person charged with keeping her husband on schedule and functioning at maximum efficiency. He did so by rising before dawn and devoting every moment of his waking life to whatever the man needed, often by anticipating these needs even before the president. In any place other than the White House, Jane thought, the "body man" would be simply called a wife.

"Get 'em out, Jay, because I'm coming in," she told him. He moved with alacrity to do just this. He had never once "peeped" her. And never would if he wanted to keep his job.

She spent a few minutes with the president and told him about the birthday party, before going to their living quarters to freshen up and change her clothes for a reception she was hosting. As darkness fell a few hours later she returned to her "official" home, tugged off her shoes, and drank a much-needed cup of hot tea.

Twenty miles away, newly twelve-year-old Willa Dutton screamed.

2

Sean looked at Michelle as they drove along. A brief look, a sizing-up glance. If she felt it, she didn't comment. Her gaze stayed straight ahead.

"When'd you meet them?" she asked.

"When I was in protection. Kept in touch. Really nice family."

"Okay," she said absently, staring out the windshield.

"Have you seen Horatio lately?"

Michelle's hand tightened around her cup of Starbucks coffee. "Why did you follow me down to his office?"

"Because I knew what you were going to do."

"Which is what exactly?"

"Break in to try and find out what you told him when you were hypnotized."

Michelle remained quiet.

"*Did* you find out?"

"It's pretty late to be going over to someone's house."

"Michelle, I think we need to talk this—"

"What you need to do, Sean, is not go there."

Sean stared out at a night that seemed to be closing in on him.

"You didn't answer my question," she said.

"You didn't answer mine either," he said in an annoyed tone.

"So about going over to their house this late?"

"It's not my call."

"I thought you were dropping off a birthday present?"

"I bought the present *after* she phoned. I suddenly remembered it was her birthday today."

"Why then?"

"It might have to do with a job for us."

"Your really nice family needs a private investigator?"

"And she didn't want to wait."

They turned off the winding country road and pulled into the long drive, passing trees on both sides.

"Boondocks," muttered Michelle.

"Private," Sean amended.

The next instant the large house came into view.

"Nice place," she said. "Your friend obviously does well."

"Government contracting. The Feds apparently throw money at people."

"Wow, what a surprise. But the house is dark. You sure you got the time right?"

Sean eased the car to a stop in front.

Michelle put down her coffee and pulled out her pistol from its belt holster. "That was a woman's scream."

"Wait a minute. Don't go off half-cocked," he said, putting a restraining hand on her arm. The crashing sound from inside the house made him reach in the glove box for his own weapon. "Let's confirm before calling the cops."

"You hit the back, I got the front," Michelle said.

He climbed out and hustled to the rear of the brick colonial, skittering next to the side-load garage and stopping for a few moments to scan the terrain before heading on. After doing her own recon of the area, Michelle was next to the front door a minute later.

No more screams or crashes. No other vehicles in sight. She could call out, see if everything was okay. Only if it wasn't she might be giving some bad guys a warning. She tried the front door. Locked. Something made her pull her hand back, she wasn't quite sure what, only she was glad she had.

The bullet blast ripped through the door, sending shards of painted wood spinning into the air. She could actually feel the slugs race past before they riddled Sean's car.

She leapt off the front porch and did a roll, coming up and hitting full sprint two steps later. Her hand dug into her pocket and her fingers drilled 911 on the keypad. The dispatcher's voice came on. Michelle was about to speak when the garage door blew open and the pickup truck cut a tight turn and bore down on her. She turned, fired at the tires, then the windshield. Her phone flew out of her hand as she catapulted to the side and rolled down an embankment. She landed in a pile of leaves and mud at the bottom of a runoff ditch. She sat forward and looked up.

And fired.

Her aim, as usual, was unerring. The bullet hit the man dead in the chest. There was only one problem. Her jacketed 9mm round didn't drop him. He staggered back, then brought his weapon up, took aim, and fired back.

The only thing that saved Michelle Maxwell that night was that she deduced her attacker was wearing body armor, and then was nimble enough to roll behind a monster oak before the MP5 rounds headed her way. Dozens of slugs slammed into the tree, shredding its bark and sending pieces of oak tailings whipsawing away. Yet wood that thick always won out, even over submachine gun bullets coming in waves.

She didn't pause, because it only took a practiced hand seconds to eject and then slap in another clip on the MP. She jumped out, both hands on her pistol grip. This time she would aim for the head and drop him for good.

Only there was no one there for her to kill.

Mr. MP5 had pinned her down, then fled.

She cautiously made her way up the slope, her pistol pointed straight ahead. When she heard the truck start to race off she scrambled up, pulling at roots, branches, and vines. The pickup was out of sight by the time she reached the driveway. She hustled toward Sean's car thinking she would take up pursuit, but stopped when she saw steam rising from under the hood. Her gaze drifted to the bullet holes in the sheet metal. They weren't going anywhere.

They?

"Sean," she screamed. "Sean!"

"In here!"

She sprinted up the steps, kicked open what was left of the shattered front door, and barreled into the living room, her gun making precise grid arcs.

Sean was kneeling on the floor, hovering over the woman. She was lying on her back. Arms and legs spread-eagled like she was frozen in a jumping jack. Her eyes were open but hard and flat because she was dead. The red hair touched her shoulders. It was easy to see what had killed the woman. Her throat had been shredded.

"Who is she?"

"Pam Dutton. The woman we were going to be meeting with."

Michelle noticed the writing on the woman's bare arms. "What's that?"

"I'm not sure. It's just a bunch of letters." He leaned closer. "Looks like they used a black Sharpie."

"Is anybody else in the house?"

"Let's find out."

"Can't screw up the crime scene for the cops."

He countered, "And we can't let someone die who we could otherwise save."

It only took a few minutes. There were four bedrooms on the top floor, two on each side of the hall set catty-cornered from one another. There was a young girl in the first bedroom they reached. She was unconscious but with no apparent injuries. Her breathing was steady and her pulse weak but steady.

"Colleen Dutton," said Sean.

"Drugged?" Michelle said as she gazed down at the little girl.

Sean lifted the girl's eyelid and noted the dilated pupil. "Looks to be."

In the second bedroom lay a young boy in the same condition as the girl.

"John Dutton," said Sean as he checked the child's pulse and pupil. "Drugged too."

The third bedroom was empty. The last bedroom was the largest. It wasn't empty.

The man was on the floor. He had on pants, a T-shirt, and was barefoot. One side of his face was swollen and badly bruised.

"It's Tuck Dutton, Pam's husband." Sean checked

his pulse. "Knocked out but his breathing's okay. Looks like he took quite a blow."

"We really need to call the cops." Michelle grabbed the phone off the nightstand. "Dead. They must've messed with the outside box."

"Use your cell phone."

"I lost it when they tried to run me down."

"When *who* tried to run you down?"

"A driver and a guy with a submachine gun. Didn't you see anybody when you came in?"

He shook his head. "I heard gunfire, then I came in the back door. Then another loud sound."

"That was them crashing through the garage door. Looks like I had all the fun tonight."

"Pam dead. Tuck knocked out. John and Colleen drugged."

"You told me they had three kids."

"They do. Willa's apparently gone. Her bedroom was the empty one."

"In the truck? Kidnapping?"

"Can't be sure. What'd you see?"

"It was a Toyota Tundra, double cab, dark blue. Didn't see the plates because I was busy trying not to die. Driver and a shooter. Both guys. Oh, and there's at least one bullet hole in the windshield."

"Did you see them well enough for an ID?"

"No, but one of them was wearing some serious body armor, like military level. Took a jacketed round from my Sig with no problem. And he was wearing a black ski mask, which made an ID problematic."

"And no sign of a twelve-year-old girl in the truck?"

"Not that I saw. Probably drugged her too."

Sean used his cell to call 911 and relay all the information. He slipped it back in his pocket and looked around.

"What's that?"

Michelle strode across the room to check out the piece of luggage that was sticking out of the closet. "Garment bag, half open." She bent lower. "It has a tag on it. United Airlines Flight 567 into Dulles with today's date on it." She used a washcloth snatched from the bathroom to cover her hand while she slid the zipper open a few inches and peered inside. "Men's clothes. Must be Tuck's."

Sean looked down at the unconscious man's bare feet and his T-shirt. "He gets home, probably sees Pam, heads up here to drop his bag, starts to change, and wham."

"Something is bugging me. That Tundra that came out of the garage. Either it belongs to the Duttons or the bad guys drove their own vehicle in there."

"They might have done it so no one would see them put Willa in it."

"In the boondocks? At this hour? You can't even

22

see another house from here. I'm not even sure there *is* another house."

"And why take Willa and not one of the other kids?"

"And why would they kill the mom and leave everyone else alive?"

Sean tried to rouse Tuck, but got no response.

"Better leave him alone. He might have some internal injuries."

They walked back downstairs and then Sean veered toward the kitchen and through it into the garage. There were three garage doors. In one bay was a late-model Mercedes four-door sedan. In another bay was a Chrysler minivan. The third bay was empty.

Michelle pointed to the destroyed garage door. "Truck was parked in this space, obviously. Do you know if the Duttons owned a blue Tundra?"

"No. But the odds are it was theirs."

"Because the bay is clear?"

"Right. Just about every garage is packed with all sorts of crap, sometimes even including a car. The fact that all the bays were clean meant they had three vehicles, otherwise the third bay would be used for storage."

"Wow, you really are a detective."

Sean put his hand on the hood of the Mercedes. "Warm."

Michelle ran her finger over one of the car's tires.

"Tread's wet. We had some rain this evening. Must be Tuck coming from the airport."

They walked back to the living room and stared down at Pam Dutton. Sean used his elbow to flick on the light switch, pulled out his notepad, and copied down the letters on the woman's arm.

Michelle bent lower and examined Pam's hands. "Looks like she's got some blood and skin under her nails. Most likely defensive trace."

"Noticed that too. Hope they can trip something on a DNA database."

Michelle said, "But shouldn't there be more blood?"

Sean examined the body more closely. "You're right. The rug should be covered. Looks like they severed her carotid. She would've bled out pretty fast."

Michelle saw it first, the plastic piece protruding out from under the dead woman's elbow. "Is that what I think it is?"

Sean nodded. "It's an empty vial." He glanced over at his partner. "Did they take her blood with them?"

3

Talbot's was having a sale. Diane Wohl had left work at four to take advantage. A new dress, a few blouses, maybe some slacks, a scarf. She'd just gotten a raise at work and wanted to put it to good use. There was nothing wrong with pampering yourself every once in a while. She parked her car in the shopping mall garage and walked about four hundred feet to the store. She left two hours later after trying on several outfits and buying two bags full of clothing, doing her patriotic duty to stimulate an otherwise lousy economy.

She hopped in the car after tossing her bags in the passenger seat. She was hungry and was thinking about picking up some Chinese take-out on the way home. She had just put the key in the ignition when she felt the small circle of metal against her head. A strong odor made her forget about kung pao chicken with all white meat and egg drop soup. It was a mixture of gun oil and cigarettes.

"Drive," the voice said quietly but firmly. "Or you're dead."

She drove.

An hour later the suburbs had disappeared. The only thing visible was lined asphalt, a harvest moon, and walls of trees. Not another car, not another person. Diane Wohl was completely alone with whatever monster was sitting in the back of her Honda.

He spoke again. "Turn off here."

Her gut tightened and stomach acid driven by fear heaved up her throat.

The car bumped along the dirt road for a few minutes. The mass of trees seemed to swallow up the car.

"Stop."

Diane slid the gearshift lever to park. As she pulled her hand back the woman eyed her purse with a sideways glance. Her cell phone was in there. If she could somehow turn it on. Or her keys. She had a big wad of them. She could pull them; gouge him in the eyes like she'd seen on TV shows. Only she was so terrified she couldn't. Her entire body was trembling like she had Parkinson's.

The monster of few words said, "Out."

She didn't move. Her throat was crusted dry but she managed to say, "If you want my car and my money you can have them. Just please don't hurt me. Please."

The monster was not persuaded. "Out." He

wedged the gun muzzle against the back of her head. A piece of her hair caught against the bump of the gunsight and was pulled out root and all. Tears trickled down the woman's cheeks as she confronted the last few minutes of her life. It was like all the warnings had said:

Know your surroundings. Be alert. It only takes a second.

From Talbot's to death on a lonely strip of dirt.

She opened the car door and started to slide out, her hand clutching her purse. She gasped and let go when the gloved fingers closed around her wrist.

"You won't need that."

She closed the door behind her.

Her hopes sank when he joined her outside the car. She had been praying that he would merely climb over the front seat and take her Honda, instead of stealing her life.

He was older, with thick, longish white hair that looked sweaty and dirty. And his face appeared carved from solid rock with rivulets running all over the surface. He was older, but he was also a big, tall man, well over two hundred pounds with broad shoulders and huge, veined hands. He towered over the petite Wohl. Even without the weapon she had no chance against him. His gun was pointed right at her head. The fact that he wasn't wearing a mask terrified her; she could clearly see his face.

He doesn't care. Doesn't care if I know who he is. He's going to kill me. Rape and then kill me. And leave me out here. She started to sob.

"Please don't do this," she said as he took a step forward and she took a step back, bracing for the attack.

She never noticed the other man come up behind her. When he touched her shoulder, she shrieked and turned. He was smaller and wiry, his Hispanic features clearly defined. Yet she never saw this because he held up the canister and the dense mist hit her squarely in the face.

Choking, Diane took a deep breath to clear her lungs. It didn't work; her senses quickly leaving her, she slumped in his arms. They put her in the back of a rental van parked nearby and drove off.

4

The law enforcement army was here in full, splendid force. Sean and Michelle watched from one corner of the pine needle-strewn yard as cops, techs, and suits swarmed over the stricken Dutton home like ants on a carcass. In certain important respects that analogy was exact.

The ambulances had come and taken the living members of the Dutton family to the hospital. Mrs. Dutton was still inside enduring the swarm. The only doctor she would be seeing later was one who would cut her up even more than she was already.

Sean and Michelle had been questioned three times by uniforms and then tie-and-jacket homicide detectives. They methodically gave detailed answers and notebooks were filled up with their descriptions of the night's horrific events.

Michelle's attention turned to two black sedans skidding into the driveway. When the men and women popped out she said to Sean, "Why's the FBI here?"

"Didn't I mention? Tuck Dutton is the First Lady's brother."

"The First Lady? As in Jane Cox, wife of President Cox?"

Sean just gave her a look.

"So that means her sister-in-law was murdered and her niece was kidnapped?"

"You'll probably see the news trucks pull up any minute," he said. "And the answer would be, 'No comment.'"

"So Pam Dutton wanted to hire us. Any idea why?"

"No."

They both watched as the Fibbies talked to the local detectives and then marched inside the house. Ten minutes later they came back out and headed toward Sean and Michelle.

She said, "They don't look too happy about us being here."

They weren't. It was clear after the first three minutes that the FBI agents were having a hard time believing that the two had been summoned by Pam Dutton but didn't know why.

Sean said for the fourth time, "Like I said, I'm a friend of the family. She called me and said she wanted to meet. I have no idea why. That's why we were coming tonight. To find out."

"At this hour?"

"She set the time."

"If you're so *close* to them maybe you have an idea who could have done this," one of them said. He was a medium-sized guy with a thin face, buffed shoulders, and an apparently permanent sour expression that made Michelle think he was either plagued by ulcers or had jumpy intestines.

"If I had any idea I would've told the county suits when they asked me. Any sign of the truck? My partner here put a round through the windshield."

"And why does your *partner* carry a gun?" Sour Face asked.

Sean slowly reached in his pocket and pulled out his ID. Michelle did the same along with her concealed weapons permit.

"Private detectives?" Sour Face managed to make it sound like "child molester" before handing the IDs back.

"And former Secret Service," Michelle said. "Both of us."

"Good for you," Sour Face snapped. He nodded at the house. "In fact, the Secret Service might take some heat for this one."

"Why?" Sean asked. "Siblings of the First Family don't qualify for protection unless there's been a specific threat. They can't guard everybody."

"Don't you get it? It's perception. Mom slaughtered, kid snatched. It won't play well in the papers. Particularly after the Camp David party today. First Family goes safely home. Last Family gets run over by a freaking tank. Not a great headline."

"What party at Camp David?" Michelle wanted to know.

"I'm asking the questions," he shot back.

And for the next hour Sean and Michelle again went through what they'd seen and done in minute detail. For all of Sour Face's irritating characteristics, they both had to admit the man was plenty thorough.

They ended up back in the house staring down at Pam Dutton's corpse. One forensic photographer was snapping close-ups of the blood-spatter patterns, the death wound, and the trace under Pam Dutton's nails. Another tech was typing into a laptop the string of alphabet letters on the dead woman's arms.

"Anybody know what the letters mean?" Michelle asked, pointing to them. "Is it a foreign language?"

One of the techs shook his head. "It's not any language I've ever seen."

"It's more like random letters," suggested Sean.

"There's good defensive trace under her nails," Michelle pointed out. "Looks like she was able to scratch the perp up."

"Nothing we don't know," said Sour Face.

"How're Tuck and the kids?" asked Sean.

"Heading to the hospital now to get some statements."

"If they had to knock the guy out because he was fighting with them, he might have seen something," said one of the agents.

"Yeah, but if he did see something you wonder why they didn't give him the same treatment they gave his wife," said Michelle. "The kids were drugged, probably saw squat. But why leave an eyewitness?"

Sour Face looked unimpressed. "If I want to talk to you two again, and I probably will, I trust I'll be able to find you at the addresses you gave?"

"Not a problem," said Sean.

"Right," said Sour Face as he and his team trudged off.

Sean said, "Let's go."

"How? They shot up your car. Didn't you notice?"

Sean walked outside and stared over at his ruined Lexus before whipping around to glare at her. "You know, you could've told me that before."

"I've had so much time on my hands."

"I'll call Triple A, how about that?"

As they waited for the ride, she said, "So are we just going to leave it like this?"

"Like what?"

She pointed to the Duttons' house. "Like this. One of the pricks tried to kill me. I don't know about you, but I take that personally. And Pam wanted to hire us. I think we owe it to her to take the case and see it through."

"Michelle, we have no idea that what she called me about has anything to do with her death."

"If it doesn't I'd call that the mother of all coincidences."

"Okay, but what can we do? The police and the

FBI are involved. I don't see much room for us to operate."

"Never stopped you before," she said stubbornly.

"This is different."

"Why's that?"

He didn't say anything.

"Sean?"

"I heard you!"

"So what's different?"

"What's different are the people involved."

"Who? The Duttons?"

"No. The First Lady."

"Why? What does she matter?"

"She matters, Michelle. She just matters."

"You sound like you know her."

"I do."

"How?"

He started walking off.

"What about Triple A?" she called after him.

Michelle didn't get an answer.

5

Sam Quarry loved his home, or what was left of it. The Atlee Plantation had been in his family for nearly two hundred years. The property's footprint had once extended for miles with hundreds of slaves working it. It now had been reduced to two hundred acres with migrant laborers from Mexico doing the bulk of the harvesting. The plantation house itself had seen better days, but it was still sprawling, it was still livable, if one didn't mind the leaky roof, the drafty walls, or the occasional mouse scurrying across the brittle wooden floors. These were surfaces that had encountered the booted steps of Confederate generals and even Jefferson Davis himself on a brief stopover during the losing effort. Quarry knew the history well, but had never reveled in it. You didn't pick your family *or* your family history.

He was now sixty-two years old with a cap of thick snowy hair that seemed even whiter because of his sun-beaten skin. Long-boned and strongly built with a big, commanding voice, he was an out-doorsman both by choice and necessity. He made his living off the land but also enjoyed the rustic trappings of the hunter, fisherman, and amateur horticulturist. It was just who he was; a man of the earth, he liked to say.

He sat behind his cluttered and scarred desk in the library. It was at this same desk that generations of Quarry men had perched their behinds and made important decisions that affected the lives of others. Unlike some of his ancestors who'd been a bit freewheeling in their oversight, Sam Quarry undertook this responsibility seriously. He ran a tight ship as much to provide for himself as for the people he still employed here. Yet in truth, it was more than that. Atlee was really all he had left now.

He stretched out his six-foot-four-inch frame and settled wide, callused, and sun-reddened hands over his flat stomach. Gazing around at the bad portraits and grainy black-and-white photos of his male ancestors hanging along the wall, Quarry took stock of his situation. He was a man who always allowed the time to think things through. Almost nobody did that anymore, from the president of the United States to Wall Street barons to the man or woman on the street. Speed. Everybody wanted it yesterday. And because of that impatience the answer they got usually turned out to be wrong.

Thirty minutes went by and he didn't move. However, his brain was far more active than his body.

He finally hunched forward, slid gloves on, and under the watchful eye of the portrait of his grandfather and namesake Samuel W. Quarry, who'd helped lead the opposition to civil rights in Alabama, he started tapping the faded keys on his old IBM Selectric. He knew how to use a computer but had never owned one, though he did have a cell phone. People could steal things right off your computer, he knew, even while they were sitting in another country. When he wanted to use a computer he traveled to the local library. To get his thoughts from his Selectric, though, they would have to invade his domain at Atlee and he seriously doubted they would walk out alive.

He finished his two-fingered pecking and pulled out the paper. He read over its brief contents once more and then placed it inside an envelope, sealing it not with his saliva but with a bit of water from a glass on his desk. He was not inclined to give folks any way to track him down, from DNA in his spit or otherwise.

He slipped the envelope into his desk drawer and locked it with the turn of a nearly one-hundred-year-old key that still worked just fine. He rose and headed to the door, out to daylight to oversee his little crumbling kingdom. He passed Gabriel, a skinny eleven-year-old black boy whose mother, Ruth Ann, worked for Quarry as his housekeeper. He patted Gabriel on the head and gave him a folded dollar and an old stamp for his collection. Gabriel was a smart boy who had the ability to go on to college and Quarry was determined to help him try. He had not inherited any of the prejudices of his grandfather or those of his father, who'd hailed George Wallace, at least the unrepentant George Wallace, as a great man who "knew how to keep the coloreds in their place."

Sam Quarry believed all humans had strengths and weaknesses and they weren't tied to pigment type. One of his daughters had actually married a man of color and Sam had happily given his daughter away at the wedding. They were divorced now and he hadn't seen either of them in years. He didn't blame the breakup on his former son-in-law's race. The fact was, his youngest daughter was damn tough to live with.

He spent two hours going over his land, riding in a battered and rusted Dodge pickup with over two hundred thousand proud miles on it. He finally pulled to a stop in front of a dented decades-old silver Airstream trailer with a tattered awning attached. Inside the trailer was a tiny bathroom with toilet, a propane cook top, a six-cubic-foot under-the-counter fridge, a hot-water heater, a miniscule bedroom, and an air conditioner. Quarry had gotten the trailer in a barter exchange off a produce wholesaler short of cash one harvest season. He'd run an underground power line to it from a junction box cabled to the big hay barn, so it had electricity.

Under the awning sat three men, all members of the Koasati Indian tribe. Quarry was well versed in the history of Native Americans in Alabama. The Koasatis had inhabited parts of northern Alabama for centuries with the Muskogee, Creek, and Cherokee to the east and the Chickasaw and Choctaw tribes to the west. After the Great Indian Removal during the 1800s most Native Americans were expelled from Alabama and forcibly moved to reservations in Oklahoma and Texas. Nearly all who spoke the Koasati language now lived in Louisiana, but some had managed to return to the Yellowhammer state.

One of the Koasatis had come here years ago, long after Quarry had inherited Atlee from his father, and he'd been here ever since. Quarry had even given him the little trailer as his home. The other two had been here for about six months. Quarry wasn't sure if they were going to stay or not. He liked them. And they seemed to tolerate him. As a rule they did not trust white men, but they let him visit and share their company. It was technically his land after all, though the Koasatis had owned it long before there were any Quarrys or any other whites in Alabama.

He sat down on a cinderblock chair with an inch-thick rubber mat over it and shared a beer and some rolled cigarettes, and swapped stories with them. The one whom Quarry had given the trailer to was known as Fred. Fred was older than Quarry by at least a decade or so, small and stooped, with straight white hair and a face right out of a Remington sculpture. He spoke the most of the group, and drank the most too. He was an educated man, but Quarry knew little of his personal background.

Quarry conversed with them in their own language, at least as best he could. His Koasati-speaking skills were limited. They would accommodate him by talking in English, but only with him. He couldn't blame them. The white men had basically crapped all over the only race that could call itself indigenous in America. He kept this sentiment to himself, though, because they didn't like pity. They might kill a man over pity.

Fred cherished telling the story of how the Koasati had gotten their name. "It means lost tribe. Our people left here in two groups long ago. The first group left signs for the second group to follow. But along the Mississippi River, all signs from the first group disappeared. The second group continued on and met up with folks who didn't speak our language. Our people told them that they were lost. And in our language *Koasai* means 'we are lost.' So the folks wrote it down as my people being Koasatis, meaning the lost people."

Quarry, who'd heard this story about a dozen

times, spoke up. "Well, Fred, to tell the truth, in some ways, we're all lost."

About an hour later, as the sun blazed down on them, filling the flimsy awning with furnace-like heat, Quarry rose, dusted off his pants, and tipped his hat at them, promising to come back soon. And he would bring a bottle of the good stuff and some corn on the cob and a bucket of apples. And smokes. They could not afford but liked the store-bought cigs over the rolled ones.

Fred looked up at him, his face even more leathery and wrinkled than Quarry's. He took the homemade cigarette out of his mouth, went through a protracted coughing spell, and then said, "Bring the unfiltered ones next time. They taste better."

"Will do, Fred."

Quarry drove on for a long way over dirt trails that were so rutted they knocked his old truck from side to side; the man barely took note. This was just how he lived.

The road ended.

There was the little house.

Actually, it was not really a house. No one lived there, at least not yet, but even if they did, it would never really be a place where anyone could live for an extended time. It was really just a room with a roof and a door.

Quarry turned and looked in each direction of the

compass and saw nothing but dirt and trees. And the slice of Alabama blue sky of course that was prettier than any other sky Quarry had ever seen. Certainly nicer than the one in Southeast Asia, but then that horizon had always been filled with anti-aircraft fire aimed squarely at him and his U.S. Air Force-issued F-4 Phantom II.

He walked toward the structure and stepped up on the porch. He'd built the place himself. It wasn't on the Atlee property. It was several miles from there on a plot of land his granddaddy had bought seventy years ago and never done anything with, and for good reason. It was in the middle of nowhere, which fit Quarry's purposes just fine. His granddaddy must've been drunk when he bought this patch of dirt, but then the man had often been drunk.

The building was a mere two hundred and twenty-five square feet but it was large enough for his purposes. The only door was a standard three feet wide with no raised paneling and set on ordinary brass hinges. He used a key to unlock the door but did not go inside right away.

He'd built all four walls two and a quarter inches wider than was normal, though one would have to possess a keen eye to discern that construction anomaly. Encased behind the exterior walls were thick sheets of metal welded together, giving this little house incredible strength. He'd done the welding himself with his own acetylene Oxy-fuel welding flame torch. Each seam was a work of art. It would probably take a tornado landing right on top of the place to knock it over, and even that hammer of God still might not do it.

He let fresh air fill the place before he stepped inside. He'd made that mistake before and had almost passed out going from full oxygen on the outside to barely any on the inside. There were no windows. The floor was two-inch-thick wooden planks. He'd sanded the boards down fine; there wasn't a splinter anywhere. What there was, though, was an eighth-of-an-inch gap between each floorboard; again barely discernible to the naked eye.

The subfloor was also special. Quarry could say with great confidence that probably no other floor of any home in America had an underbelly such as the one he'd built here. The interior walls were covered in hand-applied plaster over chicken wire. The roof was tied down to the walls as tight as anything on an oceangoing tanker. He'd used incredibly strong bolts and fasteners to ensure strength and to prevent any settling or movement. The foundation was poured cement, but there was also a sixteen-inch-high wrapped-in-cement crawlspace that ran underneath the structure. That lifted the house up by the same amount, of course, but because of the porch it was hardly noticeable.

The furnishings were simple: a bed, a ladder-back chair, a battery-powered generator, and some other equipment, including an oxygen tank that sat against one of the walls. He stepped off the porch and turned to face his creation. Every mitered cut on the walls was perfect. He had often worked under the generator lights as he lined up the studs and joists on his sawhorses, his gaze a laser on the cut-line. It was hot, tiring work, but his limbs and mind had been driven with a determination wrought from the two strongest human emotions of all:

Hatred.

And love.

He nodded in appreciation. He had done good work. It was solid, as perfect as he was ever going to make it. It looked unexceptional, but it really was an extraordinary bit of engineering. Not bad for a boy from the Deep South who'd never even gone to college.

He looked to the west where in a tree shielded from both the burn of the sun and prying eyes was a surveillance camera. He had designed and built this too, because nothing he could afford was good or reliable enough. With a bit of careful pruning of leaves and branches the camera had a good sightline of all that needed to be seen here.

He'd notched out a hole and a long trench in the bark on the rear of the tree and run the cable feed from the camera down it, and then glued the bark strips back over it, concealing the line completely. On the ground he'd buried the cable and run it several hundred feet away from the tree, to a natural berm that also featured one man-made attribute.

There was another underground cable running from this same spot up to and under the little house inside a PVC pipe that Quarry had laid in before he'd poured the foundation. That cable line had a dual end splitter with more cable running in two routes off it. All of it was concealed behind lead sheathing he'd overlaid on the metal sheets in the wall.

He locked the door to the house and climbed back in his old Dodge. Now he had somewhere else to go. And it wasn't by pickup truck.

He looked up at that perfect Alabama sky. Nice day for a plane ride.

6

An hour later the decades-old four-seat Cessna raced
down the short runway and lifted into the air. Quarry
looked out the side window and down as the end of
his land raced by. Two hundred acres sounded like a
lot but the fact was it wasn't much.

He flew low, keeping an eye out for birds, other
planes, and the occasional chopper. He never filed a
flight plan so a good lookout was essential.

An hour later he dipped down, landed softly on
the tarmac of a private airstrip, and refueled the plane
himself. There were no fancy corporate jets here. Just
sheet-metal hangars with open fronts, a narrow strip
of asphalt for a runway, a windsock, and aircraft like
his, old, patched together, but looked after lovingly
and with respect. And as cheap as the plane had been
when he'd bought it thirdhand years ago, he couldn't
have afforded to buy it today.

He'd been flying ever since he'd joined the Air
Force and raced his sturdy F-4 Phantom over the
paddy fields and dense waterlogged jungles of
Vietnam. And then later over Laos and Cambodia

dropping bombs and killing folks because he'd been ordered to in a phase of the war that he only found out later hadn't been officially authorized. Yet it wouldn't have mattered to him. Soldiers simply did what they were told. He wasn't second-guessing anything riding that high up while people were shooting at him.

He climbed back in his little plane, throttled up, and once more lifted into the sky. He headed on, zipping into a forgiving headwind of less than five knots an hour.

A short time later, he pulled back on the throttle, pushed the yoke forward, and rode the thermals down. This was the tricky part, landing at his other property. It was set in the mountains and there was no runway, just a long strip of grass that he'd leveled and mown with his own sweat. It was firm and flat and yet the crosswinds and shears up here could be challenging. The balls of his cheeks tightened and his strong hands gripped the yoke as he swooped down, his landing flaps set on full. He touched, bounced, touched again and bounced up once more, the tiny plane's suspension system getting a nice quiver. When he came down the third time his wheels held to the earth and he pushed hard on the tops of the foot pedals with his heels to engage the front-wheel brake. That along with the landing flaps allowed the Cessna to come to a halt well short of the end of the makeshift landing strip.

He pressed the tops of the lower foot pedals with his toes to work the inner flaps and direct the plane back around so it faced in the opposite direction; then he cut the engine. Quarry climbed out after grabbing his knapsack and a set of roped-together triangular parking blocks that he carried in the aircraft. He placed them under the wheels of the lightweight plane to keep it stationary. Then his long legs ate up the rising, rock-strewn ground to the side of the mountain. He pulled a ring of keys from his coat pocket and flicked them around until he found the correct one. He stooped and unlocked the thick wooden door set into the side of the mountain. It was mostly hidden behind some boulders that he'd levered off an adjacent outcrop and then chocked down tight.

For decades his grandfather had worked the coal seams inside this mountain, or rather his crew of underpaid men had. As a child Quarry had come here with his ancestor. Back then they had traveled here by a road that had been accessible until a day ago when Quarry had blocked it off. It was by this road that the dump trucks had carted away the coal when the mine was in operation, and he had used the same route to ferry by truck all the supplies he'd needed up here. They wouldn't have fit in his little plane.

This chunk of mountain hadn't always been a mine. Cavernous rooms had been created over time by the corrosive force of water and other geological muscle. In these spaces, long before any coal was ripped out of it, imprisoned Union soldiers had slowly and horribly died here during the Civil War, eking out their final days without sun and fresh air as the flesh fell off their bodies, leaving only glorified skeletons on the day they stopped breathing.

The shafts were now set up with lights, but Quarry didn't use them unnecessarily. The power came from a vented generator and fuel was expensive. He used an old flashlight to see. The same one, in fact, that his father had used to hunt down "uppity" blacks— as his daddy had called them—at night in the swamps of Alabama. As a child he'd spied on his old man coming home at night, all giddy about what he and his comrades in hate had done. Sometimes he would see the blood of the old man's victims on his father's sleeves and hands. And his daddy would cackle as he sucked down his whiskey, in sick celebration of whatever it was he thought he was accomplishing by killing folks who didn't look like him.

"Old hateful bastard," Quarry said between clenched teeth. He reviled the man for all the misery he'd caused, but not enough to throw out a perfectly good flashlight. When you didn't have much, you tended to keep what you had.

He opened another door set against a rock wall off one of the main shafts. He grabbed a battery-powered lantern from a shelf and switched it on, setting it on a table in the middle of the room. He looked around, admiring his handiwork. He'd framed out the room with sturdy two-by-fours and put the Sheetrock up himself; every wall was plumb and painted a therapeutic light blue. He'd gotten all the materials for free from a contractor buddy of his who had supplies left over from jobs with no place to store them. Behind the walls was the solid rock of the mountain's innards. But anyone looking around the room would think they were in a house somewhere. That was sort of the idea.

He walked over to one corner and studied the woman who sat slumped in the straight-backed chair. Her head rested on her shoulder as she slept. He poked her in the arm, but she didn't react. That wouldn't last.

He rolled up her sleeve, pulled a sterilized syringe from his knapsack, and stuck her in the arm. That did drive her awake. Her eyes opened and then slowly focused. When they settled on him, she opened her mouth to scream, but the tape across it prevented this.

He crinkled a smile at her even as he efficiently filled two vials with her blood. She stared down in horror at what he was doing but the restraints held her tightly to the chair.

"I know this must seem strange to you, ma'am, but believe me, it's all for a good cause. I'm not looking to hurt you or anybody else, for that matter, really. Do you understand that?"

He pulled the syringe free, dabbed the wound with a cotton swab doused with alcohol, and carefully placed a Band-Aid over it.

"Do you understand that?" He gave her a reassuring smile.

She finally nodded.

"Good. Now, I'm sorry I had to take some of your blood but I really needed to. Now, we're going to feed you and keep you clean and all that. We won't keep you tied up like this. You'll have some freedom. I know you can see that was necessary at first. The tying-up part. Right?"

She found herself locking gazes with him and, despite the terror of her situation, nodding once more in agreement.

"Good, good. Now, don't you worry. It's going to turn out okay. And there won't be any funny business. You know with you being a woman and all. I don't tolerate any crap like that. Okay? You have my word." He gently squeezed her arm.

She actually felt the edges of her mouth curl up in a smile.

He put the vials in his knapsack and turned away from her.

For a moment she imagined him whipping back around and, with a maniacal laugh, firing a bullet into her brain or slitting her throat.

Yet he simply left the room.

As Diane Wohl looked around she had no idea

where she was, why she was here, or why the man who'd kidnapped her had just relieved her of some of her blood. She had gone shopping at Talbot's, he had been in her car with a gun, and now she was here, wherever here was.

She began to sob.

7

Sean King sat in the dark. The light blazing on made him lift a hand to shield his eyes and squint up at the intruder.

"Sorry, didn't know you were in here," Michelle said, though she didn't actually sound apologetic.

"I slept here," he explained.

She perched on the edge of his desk. "Going off in a pout? Refusing to answer questions? Sleeping at the office? Sitting in the dark? Do I sense a pattern?"

He slid a newspaper across to her. "Did you see the story?"

"Read it online already. Got most of the facts right. You seemed appropriately thoughtful in the photo."

"It's a file shot they pulled from my Secret Service days."

"I thought you looked remarkably youthful."

"Had a bunch of reporters calling. I kept hanging up."

"They're not just calling. They're parked out in front of our office. I came in through the back. I think someone spotted me, so that exit's probably covered now too."

"Great. So we're trapped in here."

He stood and paced, his long feet kicking out angrily.

"You want to talk about it now?" she asked.

He stopped, flicked a piece of carpet fuzz with his loafer. "It's a tough situation," he answered.

"Which part? Finding a woman cut up and a kid gone? Or something going on inside your head?"

He just started pacing again, his chin tucked to his chest.

"You said you knew the First Lady. How? You were long gone from the Service before Cox was elected. Come on, fess up."

He was about to say something when the phone rang. Sean turned away, but Michelle snatched it up. "King and Maxwell. We snoop so you don't have to." She stopped dead. "What! I . . . Oh, yeah, sure. Here he is."

She held the phone out.

"I don't want to talk to anybody."

"You will to this person."

"Who is it?"

"Jane Cox," she whispered.

Sean cupped the phone against his ear. "Mrs. Cox?" He listened and, giving a quick, embarrassed glance at Michelle, said, "Okay, *Jane*."

Michelle did an eyebrow hike and watched her partner closely.

"I know. It's truly a tragedy. Willa, yes, of course. Right. That's right. You understood correctly. Have you spoken to Tuck? I see. Of course, I understand that. What?" He checked his watch. "Certainly, we can make that." He glanced at Michelle. "She's my partner. We do work together, but if you'd rather . . . Thank you."

He hung up and looked at Michelle.

She snapped, "If you clam up and start pacing again I swear to God I'm going to pistol-whip you. What did she say?"

"She wants us to come by to see her."

"See her? Where?"

"At the White House."

"Why? What does she want us for? To tell her what we saw the other night?"

"Not exactly."

"Then what exactly?"

"I think she wants to hire us to find out who did this."

"The First Lady wants to hire us? Why? She has the entire freaking FBI."

"She doesn't want them apparently. She wants us."

"I'm not deaf. You mean she wants *you*."

"Do you think we can lose the reporters? I don't want them trailing us to Pennsylvania Avenue."

Michelle stood and tugged out her keys. "I'm offended you even have to ask."

8

Sam Quarry unlocked the door and peered in, saw her sitting at the table having a bowl of cereal. She snapped her head around, jumped from the chair, and drew back against the wall.

He kept the door open as he walked in. "Willa, there's nothing to be scared of."

"I'm not stupid. There's like everything to be scared of. Most of all *you!*"

Her cheeks quivered and fearful tears clustered at the corners of both eyes.

Quarry pulled up a chair and sat down. "I guess I'd be scared too. But I'm not going to hurt you. Okay?"

"You can say anything. How do I know you're not lying? You're a criminal. Criminals lie all the time. That's why they're criminals."

Quarry nodded. "So you think I'm a criminal?"

"You *are* a criminal. You kidnapped me. People go to jail for that."

He nodded again and then glanced at the bowl. "Cereal not too soggy? Sorry, but powdered milk is all we got."

She stayed flattened against the wall. "Why are you doing this?"

"Doing what? You mean bringing you here?"

"Under the circumstances, what else could I possibly mean?"

Quarry smiled at her blunt logic. "Heard you were smart."

"Where's my family? I asked the other man but he wouldn't say. He just grunted."

Quarry pulled out a handkerchief and wiped his face, concealing a look of profound disgust as he did so.

"Why are you wearing latex gloves?" she asked, staring at his hands.

"Heard of eczema?"

"Sure."

"That's what I got and don't want to give it to anybody else."

"I asked you about my family," she said earnestly. "Are they okay? Tell me."

"They're doing fine. But then if I'm a criminal, I could be lying."

"I hate you!" she screamed.

"Can't blame you."

"Is this because of my aunt?' she said suddenly.

"Your aunt?" he replied innocently.

"Don't treat me like I'm dumb. Jane Cox is my aunt. My uncle is the president."

"You're right. You're sure right about that."

"So is it about him?"

"I'm not gonna answer that. Sorry."

Willa raised the sleeve on her shirt, showing a Band-Aid near the crook of her elbow. "Then tell me what's this for?"

"I guess you got cut."

"I looked. It's just a little pinprick."

He eyed her bowl and spoon again. "You done with these?"

"Is this about my uncle?" she snapped.

"Let's get something straight right now, Willa. I don't want to hurt you. It's true I broke the law and brought you here, but I'd much prefer to see you walk right out that door and get on back home. But while you're here, it'd be real good if we can just try to get along as best we can. I know it's hard, but that's just the way it's got to be. Better for me." He stared intensely at her. "And better for you."

He scooped up the spoon and bowl, cradling them against his chest, and walked toward the door.

"Will you tell my mom and dad I'm okay?" she said in a softer tone.

He turned around. "I sure will."

This statement made his growing anger harden intractably.

After he left, Willa sat back down on a cot set up in one corner and slowly gazed around the room. She had spoken bravely to the man, but she didn't feel very courageous. She was scared and she wanted to see her family. She curled and uncurled her hands in anxiety. The tears began to slide down her cheeks as she considered one horrible scenario after another. She prayed and spoke out loud to her mom and dad. She told her brother and sister that she loved them very much, even if they did come in her room unannounced and mess with her stuff.

She wiped the tears away and tried to stay focused. She didn't believe the man about the gloves and the eczema or the mark on her arm. She believed it had to do with her aunt and uncle. What other reason could there be? Her family was pretty ordinary otherwise. She began walking around the room, singing softly to herself; it was something she often did when she was worried or scared.

"It'll be okay," she said to herself over and over after she couldn't sing anymore. She lay back down and covered herself with the blanket. But before she turned the light off, she looked over at the door. She rose, crossed the room, and stared at the lock.

It was a sturdy dead bolt, she noted for the first time.

And because of that, fear was suddenly replaced with a tiny spark of hope.

9

Quarry walked down the mineshaft, one hand idly playing over the black rock of the walls where the remains of old bituminous coal seams were still visible. He unlocked the door to another room. Inside he sat at a table and lifted out the vials of blood from his knapsack and labeled each with different numbers. On a shelf hung on the wall he pulled off a box and opened it. Inside were more vials of blood. Some belonged to Pam Dutton, who now lay in a morgue in Virginia, he knew. Others were blood he'd taken from Willa while she had been unconscious.

He labeled Pam's and Willa Dutton's vials with numbers and placed them all in a cooler filled with ice packs. Next, he slid Willa's bowl and spoon in a plastic baggie and put this inside another box.

Okay, the busy work's done. I got to get on with things.

He rose, unlocked a freestanding metal gun safe that he'd brought here on his truck. Inside were automatic and semiautomatic pistols, shotguns, rifles, scopes, two MP5s, and a couple of AKs and rounds of ammo for all of them. The cache represented several generations of the affection Quarry men held for the Second Amendment. He looked carefully over the selection and settled on a .45 Cobra Enterprises Patriot. His hand gripped the polymer frame as he slapped in an extended seven-round magazine filled with standard 1911 ordnance. It was a light gun, though with plenty of power, and took twelve pounds of force to pull the trigger. Because of its imbalance with a twenty-ounce frame and a .45 round, it wasn't the most fun pistol to shoot. But it was light to carry around and whatever you hit with it at close range dropped on the spot.

It was a nice, compact weapon for personal protection. But that's not what he'd be using it for. As his hand gripped the loaded pistol it began to sweat.

His magazine carried seven rounds, but in truth he only would need two. And it would give him no pleasure. Not one damn bit.

He trudged down the rock corridor preparing mentally for what needed to be done. His daddy and granddaddy had hunted down humans before, though he knew they hardly considered black folks human. Killed 'em probably without much thought, like they would a cottonmouth or a pesky mole. Yet that's where the son and grandson parted company with his male relations. He would do what needed to be done, but he also knew the scars would be deep and he would relive the killing moment over and over for the rest of his life.

He came to the spot and shone his light through the prison bars set in the opening of a large alcove in the wall. These were the same bars that had held back scores of Union soldiers, although Quarry had refinished the rusting metal and reseated the bars back into the rock.

Against the back wall two men crouched. They were dressed in Army fatigues, their hands cuffed behind them. Quarry looked over at the small, wiry man who stood next to him on the free side of the bars.

"Let's get this done, Carlos."

The man licked his lips nervously and said, "Mr. Sam, all due respect, I don't think we got to go down this road, sir."

Quarry wheeled around on him, towering over the little man. "Only one damn leader of this band, Carlos, and that's me. You got a chain of command here and that's just the way it's got to be. You're an Army man and you know that's the truth, son. Trust me, this is hurting me a helluva lot more than it'll ever hurt you. And it's leaving me shorthanded for what I got to do. A real pisser all around."

The cowed man looked down, opened the door, and with a hesitant wave of his hand motioned the two men to step out. Their legs were shackled together too, so they hobbled forward. When they came into the wash of light from Carlos's flashlight, the perspiration shone clear on their faces.

One of the men said, "I'm sorry. Jesus, sir, I'm sorry."

"I'm sorry too, Daryl. This doesn't give me any pleasure at all. None."

While Daryl was thickset the man behind him was tall and reedy. His Adam's apple bobbed up and down in his terror. "We didn't mean to do it, Mr. Quarry. But after we got the kid knocked out she came in and started screaming and fighting. Hell, look at Daryl's face, she damn near scratched it off. It was just self-defense. We were trying to knock her out too and get her with the syringe, but the lady just went nuts."

"What'd you expect a momma to do when you're taking her baby? We went over that scenario a hundred times and what you were supposed to do in every damn situation. Killing was not an option. Now I got a little girl who's never gonna see her momma again and it never should've happened."

Daryl's voice was pleading. "But the daddy was home. And he wasn't supposed to be."

"Don't matter. Planned for that too."

Daryl was not giving up. "She scratched me up good, dug a finger in my eye. I got real pissed. Lost my head. I just swung with the knife. Caught her right in the neck. I didn't mean for it to happen. She just died. We tried to save her. Nothing we could do. I'm sorry."

"You already told me all this. And if that had

made a difference you wouldn't be standing here right now and neither would I."

Daryl nervously eyed the Patriot. "We always been there for you. You know that. And we got the little girl for you. Not a bruise on her."

"One exception breaks the rule. When you agreed to help me do this, I told you there weren't many rules, but you broke the most important one. You swore me an oath and I accepted that oath. Now here we are."

He nodded at Carlos, who reluctantly gripped the men by their wrists and pulled them down to their knees.

Quarry stood over them. "Speak to your God, men, if you got one. I'll give you time to do that."

Daryl started mumbling what sounded like the fragments of a prayer. The thin man just started to cry.

Sixty seconds later Quarry said, "Done? Okay."

He placed the Patriot against the base of Daryl's skull.

"Oh, Jesus. Sweet Jesus," wailed Daryl.

"Please," screamed the other man.

Quarry's finger slipped from the metal guard onto the trigger. Yet he ended up pulling away the Patriot. He didn't exactly know why, he just did.

"Get up!"

Daryl looked at him in astonishment. "What?"

"I said get up."

Daryl stood on shaky legs. Quarry stared at the man's scratched-up face and the blood-red right eye, then he ripped open the front of Daryl's shirt. A large purplish bruise was revealed between the man's muscled pecs.

"You say it was a woman who shot you?"

"Yes sir. It was dark, but I could still see it was a girl."

"That *girl* was a damn good shot. By all rights you ought to be dead anyway, boy."

"Wore the armor like you told us," Daryl gasped. "I'm sorry she got killed. I didn't mean for it to happen. I'm sorry."

"And you say you *think* you left a vial behind?"

"Just the one. It was all rushed like after what happened, especially when the other folks showed up. We counted the vials up on the way back. But they gonna know we took the woman's blood anyway, when they cut her open and stuff."

Quarry looked uncertain for a moment. "Get the hell on, then."

"What?"

Quarry nodded at a relieved Carlos, who quickly unshackled Daryl. The man rubbed his raw wrists and looked at the thin man still on his knees. "What about Kurt?"

Quarry shoved the muzzle against Daryl's chest. "No more talking. Now get on before I change my mind. Kurt's not your concern."

Daryl staggered off, fell, picked himself back up, and stumbled onward into the dark.

Quarry turned back to Kurt.

"Please, Mr. Quarry," the condemned man mumbled.

"I'm sorry about this, Kurt. But what we got here is an eye for an eye, boy."

"But Daryl's the one what killed the lady, sir."

"He's also my *son*. I don't have much, but I got him."

He pointed the pistol at Kurt's head.

"But you're like a daddy to me, Mr. Quarry," said Kurt, the tears lapping down his cheeks.

"That's what makes this so damn hard."

"This is crazy, Mr. Quarry. You crazy," he screamed.

"Damn right I'm crazy, boy!" Quarry shouted right back. "Crazy as a mad hatter on crack. It's in my blood. No way to shake it."

Kurt threw himself sideways and tried to wriggle away, his clunky boots throwing up little clouds of coal dust. His screams swept down the shaft, like the Union soldiers before.

"Hold the damn light closer, Carlos," ordered Quarry. "I don't want him to suffer one second more than he's got to."

The Patriot barked and Kurt stopped trying to get away.

Quarry let the gun drop and swing next to his

side. He mumbled something incomprehensible while Carlos crossed himself.

"You know how pissed off I am about this?" said Quarry. "You understand my level of rage *and* disappointment?"

"Yes, sir," said Carlos.

Quarry nudged dead Kurt with his boot, stuck the heated Patriot in his waistband.

He turned and marched on down the shaft. To daylight.

He was tired of the dark.

He just wanted to fly.

10

Michelle left her pistol in her locked safe box in the SUV. She had no desire to sit in a federal prison for the next several years contemplating the error of her ways for trying to waltz into the White House with a loaded weapon.

They had lost the reporters hanging outside their office, although the effort had cost some rubber off Michelle's truck tires and one of the journalist's cars had banged into a parked van during the abbreviated chase. She had not stopped to assist.

They passed through the visitor's entrance. They expected to be led into the White House but were surprised when after they'd been wanded and searched one of the agents stationed there said, "Come on."

They were hustled into a Town Car waiting outside the entrance. It sped off as soon as the door closed.

Sean said to the driver, "Where the hell are we going?"

The man didn't answer. The guy next to him didn't even turn around.

Michelle whispered, "SS doesn't look too happy right now."

"Blame game's started," Sean whispered back. "And they might know why the First Lady has asked us here. And they probably don't like outsiders snooping around."

"But we used to be one of them."

He shrugged. "I didn't exactly leave on the best terms. And neither did you."

"So the FBI hates us and so do our own guys. You know, what we need is a union."

"No, what we need is to know where we're going." He was about to ask the question again when the car slowed and stopped.

"Out here, in the church," the driver said.

"What?"

"Get your ass in the church. The lady's waiting."

As soon as they stepped out of the car they realized their trip had been very short. They were on the other side of Lafayette Park from the White House. The church was St. John's. The door was open. They walked inside as the Town Car drove off.

She was seated in the front pew. Sean and Mich-elle sensed rather than saw the presence of the security detail around the room. When Sean sat next to Jane Cox, he couldn't tell whether she had been crying or not. He suspected she had, but he also knew she was not the sort of woman who showed her emotions easily. Perhaps not even to her husband.

He *had* seen the woman become emotional before, but only once. He had never expected to witness another such episode.

Under her black overcoat she wore a knee-length blue dress, along with sensible pumps and little jewelry. Her hair, though covered in a scarf, was in its trademark upsweep that many had compared, mostly favorably, to Jackie Kennedy. The woman had never been flash, Sean knew, just classy. Elegant. She never tried to be something she wasn't. Well, that wasn't exactly true, he concluded. A First Lady had to be many things to many people, and there was no way any single personality could accommodate so many different requests. So some role-playing was inevitable.

"This is Michelle Maxwell, Mrs. . . . Jane."

Jane smiled graciously at Michelle and then turned back to Sean. "Thank you for agreeing to meet with me so quickly."

"We thought it was going to take place at the White House."

"I thought so too, but then reconsidered. The church is a little more private. And . . . peaceful."

He leaned back in the pew and studied the altar for a moment before saying, "What can we do for you?"

"You really were there when it happened?"

"Yes. I was bringing a present for Willa." He went

on to fill in the details of the night's events, with-holding the more graphic elements.

"Tuck doesn't remember much," she said. "They said he'll be fine, no internal bleeding or anything, but his short-term memory appears to be impaired."

"That often happens with blows to the head," Michelle remarked. "But it might come back."

"The Secret Service is undertaking protection of the . . . extended First Family now," she said.

"Smart move," said Sean.

"The Achilles' heel finally exposed," noted Jane quietly.

Sean said, "The FBI is investigating. I'm not sure there's anything we can do that they can't."

"I threw a birthday party for Willa at Camp David. Pam was there, Willa's friends, her brother and sister. It was a very special day for a very special girl."

"She is special," Sean agreed.

"To think that on the same day of that wonderful celebration this . . . this horror would have hap-pened." She suddenly stared at Sean. "I want you to find Willa. And the people responsible for this."

He swallowed nervously. "It's a federal investi-gation. We can't get in the middle of that. They'll eat us for lunch."

"You helped me once, Sean, and I've never for-gotten that. I know I have no right to ask, but I desperately need your help again."

"But the FBI?"

She waved a dismissive hand. "I'm sure they're very good. But it goes without saying that because of Willa's relationship to me this will very quickly become a political punching bag."

"How could anyone make the murder of a mother and the kidnapping of her child political?" Michelle asked.

Jane gave her a smile that came awfully close to condescending. "We're in the middle of a re-election campaign. This town specializes in making the apolitical political, Michelle. There are no limits to the depths to which some people will go."

"And you think that might influence the FBI's investigation?" Sean said.

"I don't want to take the chance that the answer to that question is yes. I want people with only one agenda. Finding out the truth. Without smears. Without spin. Which means I want *you*."

"Do you have any idea why someone would have done this, Mrs. Cox?" asked Michelle.

"I can't think of anyone."

Sean suggested, "How about the usual suspects? A terrorist group? The First Family is too well protected so they go against a softer target."

"If so, we should hear some group taking responsibility then, or a demand of some kind," added Michelle.

"We might soon. What does the president think?" asked Sean.

"He's as worried and concerned as I am."

"I meant does he have any idea who might have done this?"

"I don't believe so, no."

Sean added in a delicate tone, "Does he know you're meeting with us?"

"I see no reason for him to know, at least not right now."

"With all due respect, your Secret Service detail knows, ma'am," said Michelle.

"I believe I can rely on them to be discreet."

Michelle and Sean exchanged a nervous glance. There wasn't a Secret Service agent alive who would intentionally hide anything from the president. That would be career suicide, discretion notwithstanding.

"Okay," said Sean. "But if we're going to look into this thing, our involvement may come out at some point."

Michelle interjected, "If it does we can claim we're just doing it because Sean is a friend of the family and was actually there when it happened. In fact they tried to kill me. So maybe we hang our hat on that."

Sean nodded and glanced at Jane. "We can play it that way, certainly."

"Good."

"We'll need to talk to Tuck and John and Colleen."

"I can arrange that. Tuck is still in the hospital. The children are staying at Pam's sister's house in Bethesda."

"And we'll need access to the crime scene."

Michelle added, "The FBI will have all the forensics evidence. We'll need to see that too if we're really going to get anywhere."

"I'll see what I can do. After all, this is my family."

"Okay," Sean said slowly, watching her closely.

"So you'll do it?" She laid her hand over the top of Sean's.

He looked at Michelle, who gave a quick nod. "We'll do it."

11

They left the church. The Town Car was not waiting for them.

"I guess we didn't pay for a round trip," muttered Michelle.

They were starting to walk across Lafayette Park when Sean said, "Hold on to your organs. Here they come."

The two men were marching with a shared purpose. One was Sour Face, the FBI agent. The other one Sean knew well, as did Michelle. He was Secret Service, higher-up Secret Service named Aaron Betack. The man's distinguished career at the Service had swiftly propelled him from the trenches to the power tower, and Sean noted he had quite the spring in his step right now.

They blocked Sean and Michelle's way.

Sean feigned surprise. "Hey, you guys out for a stroll too? Great minds and all."

Sour Face said, "We know where you've been and who you just talked to and we're here to put the kibosh on it right now. The last thing we need are two cowboys—" He paused and leered at Michelle. "Excuse me, and *cowgirl* screwing this up."

"I never did get your name," said Sean pleasantly.

"FBI Special Agent Chuck Waters, WFO."

"That's good to know," put in Michelle. "Because I've just been referring to you as *dickhead*."

"Maxwell," snapped Betack. "You show some damn respect."

"Show me something I should respect and I will," she shot back.

Waters inched closer to her and waggled a finger an inch from her nose. "You just back the hell off, little lady."

Since Michelle was nearly four inches taller than Waters, she said, "If I'm a *little lady* that must mean you're a dwarf."

"And just so you know, *Chuck*, this little lady here can kick all of our asses without breaking a sweat, so back off," said Sean.

Betack, who was the same size as the six-foot-two King with even broader shoulders, cleared his throat and gave his FBI colleague a cautious look and then a shake of the head. Waters's face flamed red but he did take a noticeable step back.

Betack said, "Sean, you and Maxwell are not investigating this case. Period."

"Last time I looked at my pay stub it didn't mention Uncle Sam."

"Nevertheless—"

"There's no nevertheless. We met with a prospective client. We have agreed to represent said client. This is America. They allow that sort of thing here. Now, we have a case to get working on."

"You're really going to regret this, King," barked Waters.

"I've regretted a lot of things in my life. And yet here I am."

He pushed past them and Michelle followed. She made sure to let her elbow impact with Waters's shoulder.

When they got back to Michelle's SUV she said, "I was really proud of you back there."

"Don't be. We just made enemies of two of the most powerful agencies in the world."

"Go big or go home."

"I'm serious, Michelle."

She put the SUV in gear. "So that just means we have to solve this thing fast."

"You really think that's even remotely possible?"

"We've cracked tough stuff before."

"Yeah, and none of it happened fast."

"Allow me to be cautiously pessimistic. Where to first? Tuck?"

"No, the kids."

As they drove along she said, "And what did you think of Jane Cox's story?"

"It seemed pretty straightforward."

"Oh, you think so?"

"And you didn't?"

"You never did tell me how you know the lady."

"How does anyone really know anyone else?"

"Cut the existential crap. I want to know how you know her."

"Why does that matter?"

"It matters because if your judgment is clouded—"

"Who the hell says my judgment is clouded?"

"Come on, I saw how she put her hand on top of yours. Did you two have an affair or something?"

"You think I was banging the president of the United States' wife? Give me a freaking break!"

"Maybe she wasn't the First Lady when you knew her," Michelle said calmly. "But I don't know that because you refuse to tell me, your *partner*, anything about it. Talk about a one-way street. I've bared my guts to you, I expect a little reciprocity."

"Okay, okay." He fell silent and looked out the window.

"Okay, what?"

"I did *not* have an affair with Jane Cox."

"Did you want to?"

He shot her a glance. "What do you care?"

Michelle, who'd been grinning at him, now looked flustered. "I, I don't care who you lust after. That's your business."

"That's good to know, because I'm really into lust privacy."

There was an awkward silence as they drove along.

Michelle was racking her brains for some other line of questioning and gratefully pounced on it. "But you were gone from the Service long before her husband ran for the Oval Office."

"He was also a U.S. senator before that."

"But what's the connection with the Service? Or did it not have anything to do with that?"

"It did. And it didn't."

"Great, thanks for clearing that up."

He remained silent.

"Sean, come on!" She slapped the steering wheel in frustration.

"This can go no further, Michelle."

"Yeah, I'm a real blabbermouth."

"I've never told anyone this. No one."

She glanced over at him and noted the grim expression. "Okay."

He settled back in his seat. "Years ago I was working presidential advance team duty in Georgia. I went out to have a late bite to eat with another agent. He left to get back on shift but I was off for the night. I took a stroll, scoping out the place, with an eye to doing some recon for trouble spots along the motorcade route. I'd been walking around for about an hour. It was maybe 11:30. That's when I saw him."

"Saw who?"

"Dan Cox."

"The president?"

"He wasn't president back then. He'd just been elected to the Senate. If you recall, he served a full term and then a couple years of his next before running for president."

"Okay, you saw him, so what?"

"He was in a parked car in an alley, dead drunk, with some chick going down on him."

"You're shitting me."

"You think I'd make that up?"

"So what happened?"

"I recognized him. He'd actually been at a briefing we did for the local officials in anticipation of the president coming to town."

"So what was he doing getting 'serviced' in an alley by a woman who wasn't his wife?"

"Well, I didn't know it wasn't his wife at the time, but it was still dicey. He was in the same political party as the president and I didn't want this to make waves before the man came down. So I knocked on the car window and flashed my shield. The chick jumped off him so fast I thought she was going to go right through the car roof. Cox was so wasted he had no idea what was happening."

"So what'd you do?"

"I told the lady to get out of the car."

"Was she a hooker?"

"Don't think so. She was young but not dressed the way you'd think a hooker would be. I remember she almost fell out of the car trying to pull her panties on. I asked her for some ID."

"Why?"

"Just in case this came back to bite me in the ass later, I wanted to be able to find the lady."

"So she just gave you her driver's license?"

"She obviously didn't want to, but I told her she had no choice. I bluffed her and told her if she didn't I was going to have to call in the police. She let me see her license and I wrote her name and address down. She lived in the city."

"What happened after that?"

"I was going to call her a cab but she just took off. I started to go after her, but then Cox began making noises. I hustled back to the car, zipped up his pants, pushed him into the passenger seat, got out his license to get his address, and drove him home."

"And that's where you met Jane Cox?"

"That's right."

"Boy, some introduction. Did you tell her everything?"

Sean started to say something, but then paused.

"Discretion the better part of valor?"

"Something like that," he said. "I just told her I'd found him in the car 'under the weather.' Although you could smell the perfume on him and there was lipstick on his shirt. I carried him into the house and upstairs to the bedroom. It was pretty awkward all around. Luckily their kids were asleep. I'd shown her my ID when I first got there. She was incredibly thankful, said she'd never forget what I'd done for her. And him. Then . . . then she sort of broke down crying. I guess this wasn't the first time this had happened. I . . . I sort of held her, tried to calm her down."

"You *sort of* held her?"

"Okay, I had my arms around her. What the hell was I supposed to do? I was trying to comfort the woman."

"Was that when you were lusting in your heart?"

"Michelle!" he said sharply.

"Sorry. Okay, you were sort of holding her. Then what?"

"When she stopped crying and composed herself, she thanked me again. She offered to drive me back to town but I didn't think that was such a good idea. So I walked for a bit and then grabbed a cab."

"That was it?"

"No, that wasn't it. She called me. I don't know exactly how to phrase it; we became acquaintances and then friends. I believe she was really grateful for what I'd done. If someone other than me had found him like that he probably wouldn't be president right now."

"Don't be too sure. Politicians aren't exactly known for their morality."

"Anyway, I knew the ins and outs of the town

pretty well and she picked my brain about it. I think she came to know the workings of D.C. better than her husband did."

"And that's how you got to know Tuck and his family?"

"Jane invited me to a few functions. I don't think Dan Cox even remembered me. Or remembered that night. I'm not sure how she explained my presence to him, but he never questioned it. After he was elected president I didn't really see that much of them anymore, for obvious reasons. Folks like me don't travel in those circles. And I was out of the Secret Service and out of D.C. by then. But she always sent me a Christmas card. And I kept in touch with Tuck and his family. When we moved here, they were some of the first ones to welcome me back."

Michelle looked surprised. "How come you never introduced me to them then?"

A grin eased across Sean's face. "Hell, I didn't want to scare them off."

"So here you come to the lady's rescue one more time."

"Like they say, déjà vu all over again."

"Yeah? Well, let's hope we live through it. They almost got me the other night and I'm using up my nine lives at an alarming rate hanging around you."

"Yeah, but it's never dull either."

"No, it's never dull."

12

Sam Quarry drove on rutted roads back to Atlee. The Patriot he'd used to kill Kurt sat on the truck seat next to him. He pulled up in front of his pre-Civil War pile of hand-formed bricks and local stone, as the Alabama dust swirled around the truck's tires, looking more like simmering heat than dirt fists of the Deep South. He didn't move for the longest time. He sat there, hands on the wheel, staring at the twenty-ounce Patriot with its firing pin safety mechanism. He finally flicked a thumb across one of its grip pads, trying to shove from his mind what he'd done, by touching the very instrument with which he'd done it.

He'd nearly crashed the Cessna on the flight back. He'd started shaking uncontrollably right after take-off. Then at barely two hundred feet up he'd caught some wind shear and his wings had rotated nearly vertical. Later, he figured he'd come a few seconds from losing lift altogether before regaining control and soaring upward as the aircraft claimed its buoyancy.

He'd always kept Daryl close to him when his son was growing up. The boy had never been too special in the brains department, his father knew, but he loved him anyway. He was loyal, that boy was. Did whatever his daddy told him to. And what he lacked in intellect he more than made up with dogged determination and attention to detail; attributes he shared with his father. Those traits had worked well for him in the Army. He, Kurt, and Carlos had signed up and fought in Iraq and Afghanistan, earning eight combat medals among them and surviving the worst that the enemy could throw at them, including dozens of IEDs.

Then the trouble had started. Quarry had come down one morning to find the three men eating breakfast in the kitchen at Atlee.

"What you boys doing here?" Quarry had asked. "Thought you had orders to ship back out to the Middle East."

"Got homesick," Daryl mumbled, his mouth full of grits and fat bacon, while Kurt just nodded and grinned while he slurped Ruth Ann's strong coffee. Carlos, always the quiet one, had just stared nervously down at his plate, pecking with his fork at the food.

Quarry slowly sat down in a chair across from them. "Let me ask a stupid question. Does the Army know about this?"

The three men snatched a glance before Daryl

said, "Expect they will before too long." He chuckled.

"So why'd you boys go AWOL?"

"Tired of fighting," Kurt said.

"Hotter in I-raq than it is in Alabama. And then colder than the moon in winter," added Daryl. "And we been there four times already. Shot al-Qaeda all the hell up. And the Taliban too."

"Towelhead freaks," added Carlos as he fingered his coffee cup.

"But they keep coming back," said Kurt. "Like Whack-a-Mole. Smack one, nuther muther pops up."

"Kids come up to you asking for candy and then blow themselves right up," added Daryl.

"Damndest thing you ever seen, Mr. Quarry," added Kurt. "Tired of it. That's the God's honest truth."

Daryl had put his fork down and wiped his mouth with the back of his meaty hand. "So we all decided it was time to come on home to Alabama."

"Sweet home Alabama," added Kurt with a sly grin.

The MPs had shown up the next day.

"Haven't seen 'em," Quarry told the stern-faced soldiers. They talked to Ruth Ann, Gabriel, and even Indian Fred. But they learned nothing from any of them. Family took care of family. He didn't tell the MPs about the old mine, though, because that's where Kurt, Carlos, and Daryl were hiding out. He'd flown the men up there the night before.

"It's a federal crime to harbor AWOL soldiers," the little Hispanic sergeant had told Quarry.

"I served my country in 'Nam, Mr. Sergeant Man. Killed me more men than you ever will even in your dreams. And got me a couple Purple Hearts and not even a thank-you from Uncle Sam for my troubles. But I did get a kick in the ass from my country when I got home. No parades for the 'Nammers. But if I see my son, I'll sure do the right thing." Quarry had given them a little salute and then shut the door in their faces.

That had been two years ago and the Army had come back twice in that time. But roads in and out of this area were few and Quarry always knew they were coming long before they got to Atlee. After that, the Army never came back. Apparently they had more things to worry about than three Alabama boys tired of fighting Arabs seven thousand miles from home, thought Quarry.

Kurt had been like a son to him, almost as much as Daryl. He'd known the boy since he'd been born. Taken him in when his family was wiped out in a fire. He and Daryl were a lot alike.

Carlos had just shown up on his doorstep one morning over a dozen years ago. He hadn't been much older than Gabriel was now. No family, no money. Just a shirt, a pair of pants, no shoes, but a strong back and a work ethic that didn't have quit in it. It seemed Quarry had spent his whole life picking up strays.

"Whatcha doing there, Mr. Sam?"

Quarry left his thoughts behind and looked out the truck window. Gabriel was watching him from the front steps. The boy had on his usual faded Wranglers, white T-shirt, and no shoes. He had on an old Atlanta Falcons ball cap Quarry had given him. He wore it backward so his neck wouldn't get sunburned, or so he'd informed Quarry one day when he'd asked.

"Just thinking, Gabriel."

"You sure think a lot, Mr. Sam."

"It's what adults do. So don't grow up too fast. Being a kid's a lot more fun."

"If you say so."

"How was school?"

"I like science a lot. But I like reading best of all."

"So maybe you'll be a science fiction writer. Like Ray Bradbury. Or that Isaac Asimov."

"Who?"

"Why don't you get on and help your ma? She's always got something to do and not enough help to do it."

"Okay. Hey, thanks for that stamp. Didn't have that one."

"I know you didn't. Otherwise I wouldn't have given it to you, son."

Gabriel walked off and Quarry put the truck in gear and drove it into the barn. He stepped out and slipped the Patriot in his waistband and took the ladder up to the hay storage area above, his boots slipping against the narrow rungs as he arm-pulled himself along. He popped the hayloft doors and looked out, surveying the remains of Atlee. He came up here several times a day to do this. As though if he didn't check all the time it might disappear on him.

He leaned against the wood frame, smoked a cigarette, and watched the illegals working in his fields to the west. To the east he could see Gabriel helping his mother Ruth Ann tend the kitchen garden where more and more of their food came from. Rural Alabama was right on the cutting edge of the "greening" of America. Out of necessity.

When people are losing their ass in the land of plenty, they do what they have to do to survive.

Quarry carefully put out his smoke so it wouldn't ignite the dry hay, skipped down the ladder, grabbed a shovel off the rack, marched to the south for nearly a half mile, and came to a stop. He dug the hole deep, which was hard because the soil was so compacted here. But he was a man accustomed to working with his hands and the shovel bit deeper and deeper with each thrust. He dropped the Patriot into the hole and covered it back up, placing a large stone over the disturbed earth.

It was as though he'd just buried someone, but he didn't say a prayer. Not over a gun, he wouldn't. Not over anything, actually. Not anymore.

His mother would not have been pleased. A lifelong Pentecostal, she could speak in tongues without the least provocation. She'd taken him to services every Sunday since his brain had worked out the process of memories. As she lay dying one night in the middle of an Alabama gully-washer she'd spoken in tongues to her Lord. Quarry had only been fourteen at the time and it'd scared the shit out of him. Not the tongues, he was used to that. It was the dying part coupled with the screaming in a language he could never understand. It was like his mother knew she was leaving this life and wanted the Lord to know she was coming, only he might be deaf so she had to really belt it out. He thought Jesus was going to drop into his mother's bedroom any second just to get the poor woman to shut the hell up.

She hadn't talked to him in her last hours, though he'd sat right beside her, fat tears running down his thin cheeks, telling her he loved her, waiting with all his heart for her to look at him, say something like, "I love you, Sammy." Or at least, "Goodbye, boy." Maybe it was somewhere in the tongues, he couldn't be sure. He'd never learned that language. And then she'd let out one more scream and just quit breathing and that had been that. Not much fanfare, actually. It had amazed him really, how easy it was to die. How straightforward it was to *watch* someone die.

He'd waited a bit to make sure she was actually dead and not merely resting in between screams to the Lord, then shut her eyes and folded her arms over her chest like he'd seen them do in the movies.

His daddy hadn't even been there when she'd passed. Quarry found him later that night drunk in bed with the wife of one of his farm workers who was laid up in the hospital after having a reaper tear up his leg. He'd carried him out of the woman's house over his shoulder and drove him to Atlee. Even though Quarry was only fourteen he was already two inches north of six feet and farmer strong. And he'd been driving since he was thirteen, at least on the back roads of early 1960s rural Alabama.

He'd pulled the old car into the barn, cut the engine, and grabbed a shovel. He'd dug a grave for his father close to where he'd buried the Patriot. He'd walked back to the barn. On the way he'd contemplated how best to kill his old man. He had access to all the guns at Atlee, and there were a lot of them, and he could fire every single one of them with skill. But he figured a blow to the head would be far quieter than a gunshot. He certainly wanted to murder the old adulterer, but he was smart enough not to want to trade his life for the privilege either.

He'd dragged his father out of the car and laid him

facedown on the barn's straw-covered floor. His plan was to deliver the killing blow to the base of the neck, like you would an animal you were planning to do in. As he was readying the sledgehammer to strike his father had abruptly sat up.

"What the hell's going on, Junior?" he'd slurred, staring at his son through the blur of drunken eye slits.

"Nothing much," Quarry had said back, his courage fading. He might've been as tall as a full-grown man, but he was still only a boy. One look from his daddy was all it took to remind him of that.

"I'm hungry as all get out," said his father.

Quarry had put down his murder weapon and helped his old man up, supporting him as they made their way to the house. He fed his father and then half carried him upstairs. He kept the light off in the bedroom, undressed the man, and laid him in bed.

When the man woke up the next morning next to his cold, dead wife, Quarry could hear the screams all the way to the milking barn where he sat pulling cow teats for all he was worth. He had laughed so hard, he'd cried.

Quarry walked back to Atlee after burying the gun. It was a fine evening, the sun ending its stay in the sky with a glorious burn right down into the foothills of the Sand Mountain plateau on the southern big toe of the Appalachians. Alabama, he thought, was just about the prettiest place on earth, and Atlee was the finest part of it.

He went to his study and lit a fire though the day had been hot and the night was muggy with the predator mosquitoes already on the prowl for blood. *Blood.* He had lots of blood in those coolers. He'd locked them up in the big safe his granddaddy had kept for important documents. It was in the basement next to the old clattering furnace that was rarely needed in this part of the country. The safe had a spin dial that as a child he'd whirled as hard as he could, hoping it would land on the right numbers and reveal its contents. It never had. His father's last will and testament had finally given Quarry the proper numerical sequence. The thrill just hadn't been the same.

The fire building up fine, he took the poker, dipped it into the flames, and got it good and hot. He sat back in his chair, rolled up his sleeve, and placed the reddened metal against his skin. He did not cry out, but just about bit through his lower lip. He dropped the poker and looked down at his throbbing arm. Gasping with the pain, he bent his mind to studying the mark the heated metal had left behind. He had made one line with it, a long one. He had three more to go.

He unscrewed a bottle of gin he kept on his desk and drank from it. He poured some on the mark.

The blistered skin seemed to swell more with the bite of the alcohol. It looked like a tiny mountain ridge forming after a million-years-ago hiccup of the earth's bowels. The gin was cheap, all he drank anymore, mostly grain with other crap piled in, locally bottled. That's all he did anymore: local.

He hadn't been lying to poor Kurt. There *was* madness in his family. His daddy clearly had it, and his daddy before him too. Both men had ended up in the state mental hospital where'd they'd finished their days babbling about stuff nobody wanted to hear. The last time Quarry had seen his father alive the man was sitting naked on the dirty floor of a room, smelling worse than an outhouse in August and jabbering on and on about damn LBJ the traitor, and the coloreds, though he had not used such a polite term. It was right then that Quarry had decided his father was not insane, just evil.

He sat back in his chair and studied the flames popping and hissing back at him.

I might be some sorry-ass redneck from nowhere, but I'm gonna get this done. I'm sorry, Kurt. I'm truly sorry, son. One thing I promise you, you won't die in vain. None of us are gonna die in vain.

13

They traveled to Tuck's sister-in-law's house in Bethesda, Maryland, where the kids were staying. John and Colleen Dutton were still in shock and knew very little. Michelle had sat with seven-year-old Colleen and tried her best to coax something out of the girl, but mostly to no avail. She'd been in bed in her room that night. The door had opened, but before she could look, someone grabbed her and then she felt something on her face.

"Like a hand or a cloth?" said Michelle.

"Both," said Colleen. Tears welled up in her eyes when she said this and Michelle decided not to push it. Both children had been given a relaxant to help keep them calm, but it was obvious that the kids were still in the grips of numbing grief.

Ten-year-old John Dutton had been sleeping in his room too. He had awoken when he felt something near him, but that was all he could remember.

"A smell? A sound?" Sean had suggested.

The boy shook his head.

Neither of them knew for sure where Willa had been in the house. John thought with his mother downstairs. His little sister believed she remembered hearing Willa on the steps going to the second floor a few minutes before Colleen was attacked.

Sean showed them a copy of the markings that had been on their mother's body but neither of them knew what they meant.

The usual questions of strangers lurking around, odd letters in the mail, or weird telephone calls had gotten them nowhere.

"Would either of you have any idea why your mom might want to see me? Did she talk to you about that?"

They both shook their heads.

"How about your dad? Did either of you see him last night?"

"Daddy was out of town," said Colleen.

"But he came back last night," noted Michelle.

"I didn't see him," said John and Colleen at the same time.

The little girl desperately wanted to know if they would get Willa back.

"We'll do everything we can," Michelle said. "And we're pretty good at what we do."

"Now what?" said Michelle as they drove away from the stricken family.

"I got a message from Jane. Tuck will see us."

"We can talk to everybody, but if we don't have

access to the crime scene and the forensics we don't have much of a shot at this thing."

"What happened to my little miss sunshine?"

Michelle glanced in the rearview mirror. "It got burned off back at that house. Those kids are devastated."

"Of course they are. But they'll be even more devastated if we don't find Willa."

Two Secret Service agents were outside Tuck's hospital room, but they had been notified of Sean and Michelle's visit and the pair was quickly allowed in. Tuck was sitting up in bed looking groggy. An IV stand was next to the bed with a unit of meds hanging on it and a line running to Tuck's arm.

Sean introduced Michelle and put a hand on the man's shoulder. "I'm so sorry about Pam," he said.

Tears slid down Tuck's face. "I can't believe it. I can't believe she's gone."

"We just saw John and Colleen."

"How are they?" Tuck sat up straighter in his anxiety.

"As best as can be expected," Sean said diplomatically.

"And Willa? Any news?"

Sean glanced at Michelle and pulled up a chair and sat down next to the bed. "No. What can you tell us about that night?"

Michelle drew closer. "Just take your time. Don't rush it."

As it turned out, Tuck could not tell them that much. He'd been in the bedroom when he'd heard a scream. He'd rushed to the door and then something hit him in the head hard.

"Docs say I have the mother of all concussions but no permanent damage."

"What time did it happen?"

"I'd gone upstairs to change. I'd been at a meeting out of town. I got home late."

"How late?"

"A little bit after eleven."

"We got there at 11:30," said Sean.

Tuck looked confused. "You were there?"

Sean took a minute to explain. "Where were you coming in from?"

"Jacksonville."

"You drove home in your Mercedes?"

"That's right. How'd you know?"

"You drove straight home? No stops?"

"Yeah, why?"

"Well, if someone were following you, you might have noticed something if you stopped."

"Why would someone be following me?"

"Sean's point is that whoever attacked your family might have followed you home."

"You mean it was random?"

"They see somebody in a late-model Mercedes, it's not unheard-of Tuck."

Tuck put a hand over his face. "Jesus, I can't believe this."

"You mind my asking what the meeting was about?"

Tuck slowly removed his hand. "Nothing too exciting. You know I'm a defense contractor. We have a small office down in Jacksonville. My company is a subcontractor on a team working on a biodefense proposal for Homeland Security. We were just polishing our submission."

"And you got back right in time to get your head crunched," said Michelle.

Tuck spoke slowly. "They told me about Pam. How she died."

"Who? The police?"

"Guys in suits. FBI, I think they said. Head's still not working right. Sorry."

They asked him the same questions that they had the children and got the same unhelpful answers.

Tuck smiled weakly. "It was a great day for Willa. She got to go to Camp David for her birthday. How many kids get to do that?"

"Not many," agreed Michelle. "Too bad you had to miss it."

"First time I ever missed one. And Camp David too. I've never been there."

"It's pretty rustic," said Sean. "So the First Lady has played a big part in Willa's life?"

"Oh yeah. I mean to the extent she has time. Some days I still can't believe she's married to the president. Hell, I can't believe that I'm his brother-in-law."

"But you two have always been close?"

"Yeah. I like Dan too. Even voted for him." Tuck managed a smile before choking back a sob. "I can't understand why anyone would do this, Sean."

"There's one elephant in the room on that, Tuck," he said.

"You mean that it's connected to Dan and Jane?"

"Folks know you're family. You're a much easier target."

"But if that's the case what do they want? If it's money the president can't just dip into the Treasury and pay a ransom."

Sean and Michelle exchanged another glance as Tuck looked from one to the other. "I mean he can't, right?"

"Let's just focus on the facts, Tuck. There'll be plenty of time for speculation."

"We don't have time, Sean. What about Willa? They've got Willa. She could be . . ." He sat up in his agitation.

Sean gently pushed him back down on the bed. "Look, Tuck, the FBI is all over this and we're going to do everything we can too. What we need now is for everybody to remain calm and just tell us what they know."

Sean pulled out the copy of the markings on Pam's arms.

"Do you recognize this?"

"No, why?"

"The FBI didn't ask you about it?"

"No. What the hell is it?"

"This stuff was written on Pam's arms with a black pen."

"Oh my God. Is it some sort of cult thing? Is that what this is?" Tuck's expression changed from anger to terror. "Has some kind of modern-day Charlie Manson freak with a beef against the government got Willa?"

The nurse came in the room and said sternly, "I'm going to have to ask both of you to leave. You're clearly upsetting him."

Michelle started to protest but Sean said, "Right, sorry." He gripped Tuck's arm. "You just focus on getting well. John and Colleen really need you, okay?"

Tuck gave a quick nod and sank back on the bed.

A few minutes later Sean and Michelle were climbing in her SUV.

"Got one question," said Michelle.

"Just one? I'm impressed."

"Why was Tuck out of town at a meeting on the day of his daughter's birthday at Camp David? I mean, the polish meeting in Jacksonville couldn't wait? Or you couldn't do it by video conference? And was it just me or did he really seem to want to know if the president could pay a ransom from the U.S. Treasury?"

"He jumped on the cult thing a little too quickly too. That's why I didn't ask him about Pam wanting to meet with us, because it could be she wanted to meet with us about *Tuck*."

"So you suspect him?"

"I suspect everybody. That's why I didn't mention it to Jane Cox either."

"I liked your tactic in nailing down that he drove straight home. But do you think this really was just a random thing?"

"No, I don't."

"Then do you think this is really tied to the First Family?"

"I did until Tuck said it."

"Said what?"

"That he was working on a big biodefense project for the government."

14

Later that evening they drove near the Duttons' home but didn't pull down the road they lived on because it was closed off to traffic by portable blockades. In front of the barriers police cruisers and FBI SUVs sat slant-parked. Behind the temporary walls, the road was still clogged with police and forensics vans.

Beyond the barrier zone they could see eager journalists running around with fat microphones clutched in hand, while their videographers trotted behind. News vans with electronic masts raised to the heavens were parked up and down the road. Gawkers were out in force as well, trying to get a peek of what was going on and becoming fodder for the reporters who had little else to do but seek out inane comments since the authorities weren't talking.

"Okay, so much for tripping through the forensics evidence," said Michelle.

Sean wasn't listening. He was staring down at the piece of paper on which he'd written the letters found on Pam Dutton's arms. He was trying to assemble them in a way that made sense.

"*Chaffakan. Hatka* and *Tayyi*?"

"*Chaffakan*? Like in Chaka Khan? Maybe they're fans of pop singers with cool names."

"Will you get serious?"

"Okay, *Tayyi* sounds like Japanese or Chinese. Either a martial art or a relaxation technique."

"Or how about a code?"

"If so we don't have the key."

Sean pulled out his phone and pecked on the digital screen.

"What are you doing?"

"What everybody does these days, I'm Googling it."

He waited for the search request to load and then started scrolling down the responses. He didn't look too confident.

"*Hatka* is either an actress or an entertainment company. And *Tayyi* has something to do with Arabs in the sixth century, apparently some tribal groups."

"Some terrorist thing?"

"Doesn't feel right. I'm going to try a few more combinations with these letters." He pecked at the digital keys and got more results until another entry caught his attention.

"*Yi*."

"What about it?"

"I typed in *Yi* instead of *Tayyi* and here's what it

says." Sean read off the screen. "The Yi Syllabary's origins are lost in time but are thought to be influenced by the Chinese writing system. Each character represents one syllable. It was used mainly for religious and secret writings. It's spoken by millions of people in the Chinese provinces of Yunnan and Sichuan."

"So a secret Chinese religious society with a weird language is responsible for all this?" Michelle said skeptically. "But the letters are from the English alphabet, not Chinese."

"I don't know. I'm just trying to cop a lead." He punched in a number and held up a hand when Michelle started to say something.

"Hey, Phil, it's Sean King. Right, yeah, it's been a long time, I know. Look, I'm back in D.C. and I've got a question about a language. Right. No, I'm not trying to learn one, I'm trying to see if something is a language or not. Yeah, I guess I'm not making much sense. Look, do you know anyone at Georgetown who's familiar with a language called Yi? From China?"

Michelle tapped her fingers on the steering wheel while he talked.

"Yeah, I know it's not one of the major ones. But could you check and see if anyone in your department might know? Thanks, I owe you." He gave Phil his number and clicked off.

When Michelle looked at him questioningly he

said, "Buddy of mine who's in the foreign language department at Georgetown. He's going to check and get back to me."

"Yi-pee."

He stared at her crossly. "You got any better ideas?"

She was about to answer when his phone rang. "Yeah?" He straightened up and then glanced out the window. "Now? Right, okay."

He clicked off and then looked puzzled.

"Who was it?"

"FBI Special Agent Waters. We've been officially invited to participate in the investigation."

Michelle slid the gearshift lever to drive. "Wow, Jane Cox really lived up to her billing."

15

Waters met them at the front door. It was quite obvious that the FBI agent had been put on a short leash with a choke collar and didn't like it one bit. He had them put on elastic booties and instructed them to walk only where he walked. He was obviously taking great pains to sound polite, but it all came out as a near growl.

"It must be nice to have friends in high places," he said as they headed up the stairs to the bedrooms after passing the outline of Pam Dutton's body on the living room rug.

"You should try it, but then you'd have that whole 'getting friends' challenge to overcome," snapped Michelle. Sean elbowed her in the side as they stopped at the door to one of the bedrooms. Waters pushed it open. Sean and Michelle looked around as they stood just inside the doorway.

This was Willa's room, the one that had been empty when they'd searched the house before. It was neat and clean. There were shelves full of books and a slender silver Mac on her desk. The words "Willa

Land" were written out on one wall that was actually a black chalkboard.

"John Dutton said he thought Willa was downstairs with their mother when it happened. But Colleen said she thought she heard Willa on the stairs," said Sean.

"The same thing they told us," Waters said curtly.

"Could you tell which version was right?"

"If Willa was attacked on the stairs there's no trace left there. What she might have heard on the stairs were the kidnappers."

"Any sign of forced entry?"

"We think they gained access through the back door. It wasn't locked. There's a rear stairs to the upper level from there." He pointed to his left. "Just down that hall."

"So is the idea that the attackers came in via the unlocked door in the rear and worked their way through the house, room to room, back to front?" said Michelle.

"Drugged Colleen, then John, knocked out Tuck, and then killed Pam and took Willa?" finished Sean.

"That's one theory," said Waters.

"Why not drug Tuck too? He told us he opened the bedroom door and something hit him."

"He's a big guy, not a kid. Maybe they didn't want to take a chance with the drugging part. Blow to the head was better."

"What drug did they use?"

"The docs took some samples from residue on the kids' faces. Looks to be a liquid form of general anesthetic."

Sean said, "And is your theory that Willa was the intended victim all along?"

"Not necessarily. It might just be that they ran into Willa first and grabbed her. Pam Dutton comes in the room, sees what's going down, and starts fighting to protect her daughter. Only natural. They kill her and take the kid."

Sean shook his head. "But the living room is in the *front* of the house. If they came in the back like you think they did and worked their way through the rooms, they would have come on Tuck first, John next, then Willa's room, and Colleen last. And only then gotten to the front. And if Willa had been in her bedroom they would've got her before Colleen. And I can't believe they would have killed Pam first and then taken the trouble to knock out Tuck and drug the other kids."

Michelle added, "And when we drove up we heard a scream. Probably Pam's dying one. The bad guys were already in the living room by then. Tuck and the other kids were already taken out."

Sean said, "So Willa probably wasn't in her bedroom at the time. She was maybe in the living room. She was the oldest, it was her birthday; Mom let her stay up late, or got her up when Dad got home so he could wish her a happy birthday."

Michelle picked up the train again. "Mom leaves the room, maybe goes to the kitchen for something, Tuck goes upstairs to change. Maybe the other kids are already drugged. They knock out Tuck, hustle to the living room, grab Willa, Mom comes back, sees what's happening, fights, and it costs the lady her life."

"But the point is," added Sean, "that Willa was the intended target. They would have already had access to the other kids."

From Water's expression the man had clearly not thought any of this through yet. He said, with as much confidence as he could muster, "It's early yet."

Michelle's face telegraphed her opinion of this answer. *Lame.*

"Did the ME say how much of Pam Dutton's blood was missing?"

"More than could be accounted for by the wound leakage and what we found on the rug."

"Who's the ME on this?"

"Lori Magoulas. You know her?"

"Name rings a bell. Any idea why they would take her blood?"

"Maybe they're vampires."

"How about the trace under the fingernails?"

"We're processing it," he said tersely.

"Prints? How about on the vials?"

"They must've worn gloves. They were good."

Sean said, "Not that good. They lost control of Pam and had to kill her, at least it looks that way."

"Maybe, maybe not," Waters said evasively.

"Did you find the Tundra?"

"It's registered to the Duttons. We found it in some woods about a mile from here. They'd driven the damn thing down into a ditch. Probably for concealment."

"Any signs of where they went from there?"

"Still checking the truck out for trace. They must've had another vehicle nearby, but we didn't find any evidence of that. We're canvassing, see if anybody saw anything. No hits yet." He eyed Michelle. "You sure it was *two* guys?"

"One submachine gunner, one driver. I saw the wheelman through the windshield. Tall. Definitely a guy."

Sean checked his watch. "With the time she's been missing and calculating driving radius in all directions you're looking at thousands of miles they could have covered, easily."

"By private jet, they could be anywhere in the world," added Michelle.

"I take it no ransom note has been received?"

Waters turned to face Sean. From the expression on the man's features it was clear that the short leash had just come off. "You know, I did some digging on you. Does it still hurt that you were thrown out of the Service on your ass for screwing up and costing a guy his life? That must be some serious shit to have to deal with. Ever think about eating a round because of it? I mean, it'd be understandable and all."

"Look, Agent Waters, I know this is an awkward situation. And I know it seems like we've been crammed down your throat—"

"Nothing *seemed* about it, you *have* been crammed down my throat," he declared.

"Fine. I'll make a deal with you. If we crack something or get onto a lead, we'll provide it to you to run with. I could give a shit about nailing any headlines from this. I just want to find Willa, okay?"

Waters took a few seconds to think about this, but then finally put out his hand for Sean to shake. But when Sean reached for it, Waters pulled it back and said, "I don't need you to *provide* me with anything about this case. Now, something else you want to look at while I'm babysitting you and your *partner*?"

"Yeah, how about your brain?" snapped Michelle. "Where is it, still stuck up your ass?"

"This pissing contest isn't getting us any closer to finding Willa," Sean pointed out.

"That's right," agreed Waters. "And the longer I have to deal with you two, the less time I have to actually work *my* case."

"Then we won't waste any more of your time," said Sean.

"Thanks for nothing."

"Mind if we look around a bit before we leave?" When Waters looked ready to refuse, Sean added, "I want to make sure my report to President Cox is complete. And I'll be certain to inform him of how helpful you've been."

If Waters had gone any paler the forensic techs on site would've slipped him into a body bag. "Hey, King, wait a minute," he said nervously.

Sean was already heading down the stairs.

When Michelle caught up to him she said, "Guys like that make me so proud to be an American."

"Forget him. You remember Tuck's bag, the one with the airline tag on it?"

"Garment bag, navy blue, standard lightweight polyester. Slightly ragged. Why?"

"Carry-on size?"

"Considering that these days people schlep packing crates the size of my SUV onto a plane? Yeah, definitely carry-on."

Sean whipped out his phone and punched some numbers. He let the screen load and then worked through several more layers. "United Flight 567 into Dulles from Jacksonville?"

"Right."

He stared at the tiny screen. "That flight routinely gets in at 9:30 p.m. He deplanes, goes to his car, and drives home. How long do you reckon that would take him?"

"Depends on which terminal it came into, because

that determines if he had to use a people mover to go to the main terminal. Terminal A he could just walk."

Sean made a quick phone call. He clicked off. "It gates at Terminal A."

"So no people mover two-step. And not much traffic that time of night. I'd say thirty minutes tops to get home."

"So say it took him fifteen minutes to get to his car and get out of the airport, plus the drive time, that would be 10:15. Round it to an hour to be safe, 10:30."

"If the plane landed on time."

"We'll have to check that. But if it did, there's thirty minutes that Tuck Dutton is unaccounted for if we believe him that he got home around 11:00."

"Do you?"

"The blood was crusted on his face by the time we found him, so yeah, I do."

"Wonder what the man was doing?"

16

Sam Quarry drove to a local UPS drop-off receptacle and mailed the box containing the labeled blood vials. They were being shipped to a lab in Chicago that he'd found using an online service at the local library. There was a prepaid return mailer packet inside.

After that he'd driven one hundred miles east, actually crossing over into Georgia. He pulled off the highway and into a truck stop. He had six packages with him but only one that mattered. He parked and walked across the truck stop to the U.S. mailbox. After making certain there were no surveillance cameras to record him doing so, he dropped all the boxes in the mailbox. The only package that mattered was being sent to an address in Maryland. In it were the bowl and spoon Willa had used, and the letter he'd typed earlier. He had no idea if the authorities could track exactly from where a parcel had been dropped off, but he had to assume they could. Thus the other boxes were just red herrings in case anyone was watching who could later talk to the police about someone dropping off *one* box here. Well, that wouldn't be him. He'd simply look like a long-haul trucker sending multiple packages home.

He drove back to Alabama, stopping once to get a bite to eat before heading on. When he got to Atlee the only light on was in Gabriel's room.

Quarry tapped on the door. "Gabriel?"

The little boy opened the door. "Yes, Mr. Sam?"

"What you doing up this late?"

"Reading."

"Reading what?"

"Reading this." Gabriel held up a book. Quarry took it and looked at the title. "*The Absolutely True Diary of a Part-Time Indian?*"

"It's real good. Makes you want to laugh. And cry sometimes too. And it's got some grown-up language in it, if you know what I mean. But I love it."

"But you're not an Indian."

"That's not all it's about, Mr. Sam. It's got stuff for everybody. Lady at the library told me about it. I wanta write a book one day."

"Well, Lord knows you got enough words in your head, because they come out faster than I can listen to them sometimes." Quarry handed the book back. "Your ma turned in?"

"About an hour ago. We wondered where you got to."

"Had some business needed taking care of." Quarry leaned against the doorjamb, struck a match against the wood, and lighted up a cigarette. "You seen Kurt 'round lately?"

"No sir."

He eyed Gabriel from under his thicket of eyebrows. "Think he might've moved on."

Gabriel looked surprised. "Now why would he do that? Where's he got to go to?"

Quarry tapped his cigarette against the door and ash drifted to the floor. "Everybody's got somewhere to go. Just takes some folks longer to figure out where to."

"I guess you're right."

"Anybody asks, I guess that's what we tell 'em. Damndest thing, though. He was like family. Now don't you go off like that without talking to me first, okay?"

Gabriel looked stunned by the very suggestion. "If I ever leave, Mr. Sam, you'll be the first to know, right after my ma."

"Good boy. Keep on reading, Gabriel. Got to be prepared. The world will give you a chance, but that's all. The rest comes from you. You blow it you blow it."

"You been telling me that long as I can remember."

"Good advice worth repeating."

Quarry trudged off to his room. It was set on the top floor and had once belonged to his mother and father. Tidiness had never been one of Quarry's strong points, though Ruth Ann and Gabriel did their best to keep the growing mounds of stuff at least orderly.

Quarry's wife, Cameron, had been dead for over three years. The greatest loss of his life, and he had suffered through several of them. After she'd passed, Quarry had not slept in their bed. He used a long, ragged, hundred-year-old couch set against one wall of his bedroom. He'd kept many of his wife's things in the bathroom, and Ruth Ann would dutifully dust them even though they would never be used again.

He could've and perhaps should have sold Atlee a long time ago. But that was not an option. Cameron had loved the place and parting with it would mean, for Quarry, finally parting with her. He could not do that, no more than he could kill his own son. Though it frightened him how close he'd come to doing just that. It was the Quarry insanity streak. Day by day, year by year, it kept growing stronger, like the tentacles of a tumor creeping murderously through his brain.

He settled down on the couch and reached for his bottle of gin. Yet before he took a drink, he changed his mind, rose, slipped on his boots, and grabbed the truck keys off a wobbly-legged table.

Two minutes later he was back on the road, staring up at a sky punctured with so many stars that night almost seemed turned into day. He rolled down the window, cranked up some tunes, and drank his gin.

The heat of a southern night hit him in the face. He hated air conditioning. Atlee had never had it, nor any vehicle he'd ever owned. A man should sweat. Running away from sweat was akin to running from what made you human.

His old truck ate up twenty miles, veering from dirt to gravel to macadam, and then bouncing onto asphalt heated slick from the hot day.

And then he was there. Been here a thousand times before. Each visit was the same and also different.

He knew everyone by first name. Visiting hours were long since over but they didn't care. This was Sam Quarry. Everybody knew Sam Quarry because everybody knew Tippi Quarry. They'd named her after the actress. Cameron Quarry had loved the movie with all those crazy birds. Their youngest daughter, Suzie, the one who'd married and divorced the black fellow, now lived in California doing something, only her father didn't quite know what. He was pretty sure if he *did* know he'd disapprove. Daryl had been the baby.

Only my damn baby just killed a mother of three children.

Yet neither of them had ended up like Tippi. She had just turned thirty-six last month. She'd been here for thirteen years, eight months, and seventeen days. He knew that because he marked the time off on a mental calendar like he was scratching off his remaining days on earth. And, in a way, he was doing that too. She had never once set foot outside the cinderblock walls of this place. And she never would.

Quarry's long legs directed him automatically to his oldest child's room. He opened the door just as he had so many times before. The room was dark. He scooted over to the chair that his butt had graced so often he'd worn off the paint. The trach was in her neck, the way they did it for long-term usage, because, for among other reasons, it was easier to keep clean than when it was down the throat. The attached ventilator was pumping away, keeping her lungs inflated. The vitals sign monitor beeped away. One end of an oxygen tube ran to the central line in the wall, and the other end was inserted in his daughter's nostrils. An IV drip with a computerized distribution device was hooked up to her and kept a flow of drugs and nutrients running to a central entry point cut into her skin near the woman's collarbone.

Quarry had a little ritual. He'd stroke her hair that wound around her neck and lay against her shoulder. How many times had he wrapped that hair around his finger when Tippi had been a little girl? Then he'd touch her forehead, a forehead that had crinkled up when he'd given his infant daughter a bath. Then he kissed her on the cheek. As a child the skin and lump of bone underneath had been smooth and pleasant to the touch. Now it was withered and hard long before it should have been.

His ritual complete, he took her hand in his, sat back down, and started talking to her. As he did, his mind wandered through the phrases the doctors had given him and Cameron when it had happened.

Massive blood loss.

Oxygen deprivation in the brain.

Coma.

And finally: *Irreversible.*

Words no parent would ever want to hear about their child. She was not dead, but she was as close to dead as one technically could be while still breathing with the aid of a machine and expensive drugs. He slipped the book from his jacket pocket and started reading to her by the small light on the nightstand he clicked on.

The book was *Pride and Prejudice.* Jane Austen's most famous novel had been his daughter's favorite, ever since she had plucked it off the library shelves at Atlee as a high-spirited teenager. Her profound enthusiasm for the story had led Quarry to read it as well, in fact several times. Before Tippi had ended up here, Quarry had always seen his daughter as a real-life version of Elizabeth Bennet from Austen's tale. Elizabeth was the intelligent, lively, and quick-to-judge main protagonist. However, after Tippi had come to this place Quarry had re-evaluated his daughter's alter ego in the story and decided she was actually more like the oldest daughter, Jane Bennet. Sweet but timid, sensible but not as clever as

Elizabeth. However, her most distinctive trait was to see only good in others. It had led to happiness for Jane in the story, but it had been devastating for Tippi Quarry in real life.

An hour later he rose and said what he always said. "You rest easy, honey, Daddy'll be back soon. I love you, baby."

He drove back to Atlee. As he lay on the couch with his gin, his last fleeting image before he fell asleep was Tippi young and smiling at her daddy.

17

The United Airlines flight Tuck Dutton had been on had not arrived late. In fact, it had arrived twenty minutes *early* due to a straight-in approach at Dulles and an early pushback from the gate in Jacksonville.

Michelle said, "So he had at least fifty minutes free instead of thirty. Maybe over an hour."

They were sitting over a cup of coffee the next morning at a café in Reston near their office. To get the press off their backs, Sean had given a statement that hadn't said much, but was enough to give them some breathing room. But they had not gone back to the office, and were staying at a hotel just in case the reporters got the primal itch to attack again.

"That's right."

"You think he was in on it?"

"If he was, why not just stay out of it? Why come back and get your head busted in?"

"To throw off suspicion."

"Motivation?"

"Husbands kill their wives with astonishing regularity," said Michelle. "Which is all the *motivation* I need never to walk down the aisle."

"And Willa?"

Michelle shrugged. "Maybe that's all part of the plot. Kidnap Willa but we'll find her somewhere safe and sound."

"Presumably this would all cost money. There must be a record of that."

She said, "It would be good if we could get a look at Tuck's financials."

"I know where his office is."

"We going there now?"

"After we see the ME. I talked to her. She just finished with Pam Dutton's post."

"So you *do* know the lady?"

"I'm just a friendly guy."

"That's what scares me."

Lori Magoulas was about forty-five years old, short and stocky with bottle-blonde hair tied back in a ponytail.

After Sean introduced Michelle, Magoulas said, "Surprised to hear from you, Sean. Thought you'd gone to lose yourself at that lake of yours."

"D.C. just has that pull, Lori."

Lori looked skeptical. "Right. I can't wait to get out of here and find *my* lake."

She led them down a tiled floor corridor where other people in baggy hospital scrubs hovered over the dead. They stopped at one stainless steel table where Pam Dutton lay, her body permanently marked by the slashed throat as well as the standard Y-incision Magoulas had carved into her.

"What did you find?"

"She was in good health. Would've probably led a long life but for that," she said, pointing at the woman's mangled neck.

"What about the blood levels?"

Magoulas pecked on a laptop situated on a desk next to the steel table, and studied some figures that appeared on the screen. "As best as I can figure, taking into account what was left on the rug and on her clothes, she's missing about a pint."

"Presumably they took it with them?"

"The wound dissected the carotid sheath, slicing open the left common carotid artery and the left jugular. She would've bled out in a few minutes."

"What's your best guess of how it went down?" asked Michelle.

"Judging from the angle of the stab wound and the trace under the nails, I'd say she was grabbed from behind and her throat was cut. She might have reached back and gouged her attacker in the face. We found a good deal of tissue and blood under her cuticles. She must have ripped the guy pretty good. Probably didn't improve his mood."

"Certain it was a guy?" Sean said, drawing a scowl from Michelle.

"We also found beard stubble with the blood and tissue."

"Just confirming," Sean said to his partner.

"So if the *left* jug and carotid were cut, that means the assailant was probably right-handed if he struck from behind," said Michelle.

"That's right." She picked up a small plastic bottle. Inside were several strands of a black material.

"Found some of these under her right thumbnail and left index finger and another caught in her hair."

Michelle squinted at the evidence. "Looks like nylon."

"From a mask?" Sean opined.

"The guy I saw wore a black mask," said Michelle. "Pam reaches back, gouges at his face with her hands. She gets the nylon under her nails."

"Did you see anything else?" asked Magoulas.

"Not really. I'm pretty observant, but the guy was shooting at me with an MP5. Came within an inch of shredding me instead of a tree. I decided it was smarter to stay alive than to get a positive ID on the shooter."

Magoulas looked at her wide-eyed. "Works for me."

"Anything on the letters on her arms?" Sean asked, as he indicated them on the body. They were harder to read now because of the discoloration of Pam's decaying skin. The dead flesh seemed to be absorbing the permanent ink. Rather than letters, they now appeared to be some sort of skin disease, or else the symbols of some insane human cataloguing process.

"I'm a pathologist, not a linguistics expert. It's black ink, probably from a broad-tipped pen like a Sharpie, written in block letters, and the penmanship, in my humble opinion, isn't great. I'm fluent in Spanish, but that's not Spanish. It's not any other Romance language. It's obviously not Chinese or Russian. Wrong alphabet."

"Maybe an African tribal language?" suggested Sean.

Michelle said, "But like Russian and Chinese I don't think they'd be using an English alphabet. Maybe it's just gibberish to throw us off."

"Okay, anything else of interest?" Sean asked.

"Yeah, that's some serious red hair the lady had. I've cut up lots of redheads, but she takes the cake. I almost needed sunglasses to do the post."

"And how is that relevant to the investigation?" asked Michelle.

"He didn't ask for *relevant*, he asked for *interest*." She added with a grin, "Hey, even MEs need to lighten up every once in a while. Otherwise, it could get depressing around here."

"Okay," said Sean. "I'll play along. Anything else of *relevance*?"

"Lady's had kids."

"We know that."

"Two C-sections." She indicated the old suture

127

tracks on Pam's belly paralleling the Y-cut. They looked like faded zippers.

"And the third vaginally," added Sean.

"Impossible," said Magoulas.

"What?" Sean said sharply.

"The visual exam showed her pelvic bones were unusually configured and her birth canal was abnormally narrow: The X-ray film confirmed those conclusions. And while it's hard to tell at the autopsy level, she appears to have had an SI joint dysfunction; she was probably born with it. Bottom line, no ob-gyn would've gone the vaginal route with the lady unless they wanted to lose their malpractice insurance; way too risky. She'd have to deliver by C."

She glanced at Sean and Michelle, whose gazes were locked on Pam Dutton's savaged belly, as though the answers they craved would float from there and into them.

"Is that relevant?" asked Magoulas, looking at them inquisitively.

Sean finally pulled his gaze away from the old surgical scars and the more recent incision. "You could say it's of interest."

18

An hour later they pulled into the parking lot of a two-story building at an office park in Loudon County.

"How'd you know where he worked?" asked Michelle.

"I'm a friend of the family." He paused. "And I snitched a business card from Tuck's bedroom."

"So one of the kids was not Pam's? Only which one?"

"Pam's a redhead and Tuck has blond hair. Willa has really dark hair. The other two kids are towheads."

"So even though it's a recessive gene maybe the red hair *was* relevant."

"And of interest."

Inside, Sean and Michelle strolled up to the receptionist's desk.

"I'm Sean King. This is my partner, Michelle Maxwell. We're representing Tuck Dutton in this awful business with his family."

The receptionist, a young woman with short

brown hair and wide sad eyes, said, "Oh, God, I know, we've all heard. It's horrible. How is he doing?"

"Not that well, actually. He asked us to come by his office and pick up some things."

"I hope he's not concerned about work at a time like this."

Sean leaned in closer. "I think it's the only thing keeping him going, actually. We just came from the hospital."

"You say you're representing him?" the woman said slowly. "Are you lawyers?"

Sean flashed his credentials. "Private investigators. We're working to find out who did this and also to get Willa back."

"Oh, God, I wish you luck. Willa came in here a few times. What a super little girl."

"Absolutely," said Michelle. "And in kidnapping cases time is of the essence. That's why Tuck wanted us to look at anything he was working on that might tie into the case."

She looked uncomfortable. "Oh, I see. Well, a lot of things Mr. Dutton's working on are sort of, well, confidential. You know, proprietary stuff."

Sean smiled. "I understand that completely. He told us as much. Maybe there's someone here who can help us?"

The woman smiled, obviously grateful to pass the

situation on to someone else. "Absolutely. Let me call Mr. Hilal."

She picked up the phone and a few minutes later a tall, thin, balding man in his forties came into the lobby. "I'm David Hilal. Can I help you?"

Sean explained why they were there.

"I see." Hilal rubbed his chin. "Come on back and let's discuss this."

They followed him to his office. He closed the door and sat across from them.

"How is Tuck?"

Sean answered. "Physically, he'll recover. The emotional part is a different story."

"It was horrible. I couldn't believe it when I heard."

"I know your firm is involved in some sensitive biodefense work. Tuck said you were in the middle of trying to get a big government contract in that field?"

"That's right. We're a subcontractor on the bid. But if we win it, it'll be huge for us. Several years' worth of business. Tuck was devoting a lot of time to it. As we all were."

"And that's why he was down in Jacksonville on the day it happened?"

"That's . . . right," Hilal said hesitantly.

Michelle added, "Well, was it or wasn't it?"

Hilal looked uncomfortable. "This is really Tuck's company. I'm only his partner."

"We're working with Tuck," said Sean. "We just want the truth to come out. And we want to find out who killed Pam Dutton. And we want to find Willa. I assume Tuck wants that too."

"This is awkward," said Hilal. "I mean, it's not really my place."

Michelle leaned forward and tapped her finger on the man's desk. "We're talking about a little girl's life."

Hilal slumped back in his chair. "Okay, I think Tuck was down in Jacksonville with someone."

"Someone? He said he was down there at the office the company maintains to work on the project. Is that not right?"

"No, we do have an office there. It's staffed with only one person, though. A woman."

Sean and Michelle exchanged glances. "This woman have a name?" he asked.

"Cassandra. Cassandra Mallory. She was working on the proposal. We hired her about six months ago. She has incredible contacts at DHS. Lots of people wanted her."

"Because she could help get them business?"

"Government agencies are like anything else. Winning contracts is built on relationships and trust. The Feds like comfort and familiarity. Cassandra being part of our proposal would help us immeasurably."

"And Tuck was down there with her. Are you saying in something other than a professional way?"

"She's a very attractive woman. Very bright. Blonde, nice tan, favors short skirts," Hilal added in an embarrassed tone. "She and Tuck really hit it off. Her expertise wasn't on the technical side, it was in sales. And the lady could sell. Pretty much anything."

Sean leaned forward. "Was Tuck having an affair with this woman?"

"If you're asking if I have any proof, I don't. It's just little things. Like him going down there so often. Things I've heard."

"So nothing concrete?" asked Michelle.

"There were some credit card charges that came through about a month ago. I'm sort of the unofficial CFO here. I review the bills, sign the checks."

"What were the charges?"

"It was just something weird about Tuck's expenses down there."

"Some flowers, candy, or lingerie for sexy Cassandra?" Michelle asked.

"No, you misunderstand me. It wasn't what he charged, it's what he *didn't* charge."

"I'm not following," said Sean.

"He didn't have a charge for a hotel room on his corporate card."

Sean and Michelle exchanged another glance.

"Maybe he used another credit card," suggested Michelle.

"He always uses the corporate card. In government contracting you have to be very meticulous with expenses and charges. We only use that card for work. Plus Tuck gets all his points on that card. He uses it for plane tickets, upgrades, we all do." Hilal hurried on. "And he always stays at the same place down there. It's a nice hotel, but not too expensive. And he gets all the point perks with that chain. But this time he was gone for three nights and had no hotel charges on his credit card."

"And Cassandra has a house down there?"

"A condo right on the water. I *hear* it's very nice," he added hastily.

"And there wasn't anyone else Tuck would've stayed with?"

"He didn't know anybody else down there. The only reason we opened that office was because Cassandra lived there and didn't want to make the move up here and didn't want to work out of her home. I think there were covenants in her condo building docs that precluded that. Plus, Jacksonville is a big defense area and we might want to go after other work down there. So it made sense to have a footprint."

Sean sat back in his chair. "What did you really think when you'd heard about what happened to his family?" he asked. "Truthfully."

Hilal let out a long sigh. "It's no secret that he and

Pam weren't the closest couple in the world. He had this business and she kept the home fires burning with the kids. But murdering his wife and kidnapping his own daughter? Tuck's no saint, but I can't see him doing something like that."

"Do you think Pam suspected something was going on?"

"I honestly don't know. I didn't have that much interaction with her."

"If he wanted out of the marriage there're easier ways to do it," Michelle pointed out.

"Right. Why didn't he just divorce her?" asked Sean.

Hilal tapped his fingertips against the desk. "That might've been problematic."

"Problematic how?"

"I said that we hired Cassandra about six months ago. Before that she'd been working for the Department of Homeland Security in their contracts department. That's the same agency we're trying to win the contract from. That's what I meant when I said she had great contacts."

"So if Tuck tried to divorce Pam then maybe the affair would become public?"

"In the world of government contracting the Feds don't like even the *appearance* of a conflict of interest. If the prime contractor we're subbing found out about an affair with a former employee of DHS, it would be a big problem. Maybe not enough to kill the relationship under normal circumstances, but this isn't a normal circumstance."

"What do you mean?" asked Sean.

"Tuck is the president's brother-in-law. Everyone is already edgy about an appearance of preferential treatment because of that. And the government might even think there was hanky-panky going on between the two *before* she left the agency and maybe they'd start checking past contracts awarded to us. It gets complicated real quickly. It's tough enough as it is to win these types of bid competitions. The other side will exploit any gaffe."

"You realize that you've just built up a very plausible scenario for Tuck to have orchestrated this whole thing," Sean said.

"I still can't believe he would've done something like that to his family."

Sean gave Michelle a subtle look that she still immediately translated.

She said, "We've got some more questions, Mr. Hilal. But do you have any coffee around here? You could probably use a cup too."

Hilal rose. "I sure could." He looked at Sean. "Would you like one?"

"No, but if you can just point me to the men's room."

Hilal led them down the hall and directed Sean to the restroom while he and Michelle headed to the lunchroom.

Instead of hitting the john, Sean doubled back and slipped inside the office two doors down from Hilal's and which they had passed on the way in. This was Tuck Dutton's turf, helpfully indicated by his name being stenciled on the door.

The space was large but cluttered and clearly showed a person juggling many things at once. Sean didn't waste time but went right to the computer on the desk. He pulled a small USB thumb drive from his pocket. Loaded on it was a unique program used by law enforcement to extract forensic evidence from computers without turning off the machine and seizing it. Sean had managed to snag one from a buddy of his at the FBI.

He inserted it into the slot on the keyboard, performed some mouse clicks, and the program from the thumb drive uploaded onto the screen. There was password protection on Tuck's database, of course. The software on the USB had password override programs that would take some time, so Sean decided to opt for a shortcut. He went through several attempts before it hit him.

He typed in the name "Cassandra." Nothing. Then he tried "Cassandra1."

The digital gates parted and with a few commands from Sean the software started dumping select parts of Tuck Dutton's hard drive onto the thumb drive.

19

As the young Secret Service agent carried the mail up from the box, his attention flickered to the package. There was no return address and the writing on the shipping label was done in block script. He relayed this information to his superiors and within thirty minutes a bomb squad truck lumbered down the street.

The explosives experts worked their magic and fortunately the neighborhood did not disappear in a nuclear fireball. Still, the contents were rather unusual.

A small bowl with the remains of hardened cereal and milk at the bottom.

A spoon with the same crusty residue.

And a sealed envelope containing a typed letter.

After the techs concluded there were no fingerprints or other useful traces on the box, envelope, or letter, the agents turned their attention to the contents of the letter.

Check the fingerprints on the bowl and spoon. You will find they belong to Willa Dutton. We have her. She is safe. We will contact you soon.

The box had been mailed to Pam Dutton's sister's house in Bethesda where John and Colleen Dutton were staying under Secret Service protection.

When the prints were run and compared with a set taken from Willa's bedroom there was a clear match.

They immediately contacted the Postal Service in an attempt to track from where the package had come. The matter was given the highest priority. However, the closest they could narrow the target to was Dalton, a town in northern Georgia. At least that's where the package had been processed.

Later that afternoon Sean and Michelle were contacted and told to come to the Treasury Department, which was located on the east side of the White House and had a statue of Alexander Hamilton out front. They were escorted down into the underground belly of the massive building where they entered a long tunnel that ran due west and connected with the White House next door. Sean had been down here before while pulling White House protection duty; however, it was a first for Michelle. As they passed by closed doorways along the long corridor, he whispered to her, "The stories I could tell about what went on in some of these rooms."

"I see London, I see France," Michelle murmured back.

The First Lady received them in her office in the East Wing. She had on black slacks, a pale blue sweater, and her black pumps lay underneath her desk. She looked far more tired than the last time they'd seen her.

Sean was surprised to see Aaron Betack hovering in the background. No, *cowering* was more like it, Sean assessed. The man didn't look like he wanted to be there. Yet what the First Lady wanted, she usually got.

"These are the times I regret giving up smoking," Jane said as she motioned them into chairs across from her.

"Weren't you just on the campaign trail in Connecticut?" Sean asked.

She nodded absently. "I flew back early after they told me about the box. I asked Agent Betack to be here so he could answer any questions you might have on behalf of the Service."

Sean and Michelle both looked at Betack, who didn't appear remotely interested in telling them even what time it was. Yet he nodded and attempted a smile that came out as though he had really bad gas.

Jane said, "I have heard that the FBI has been somewhat less than cooperative with you. I trust that has been taken care of and that you have met with no resistance from any *other* agency?"

There was only one other agency really involved and it was represented by the big man standing behind her, his face reddening slightly with her words.

Sean said quickly, "Everyone's been very cooperative. Particularly the Secret Service. It's been a stressful time for everyone, but they've been there for us the whole way."

"Excellent," said Jane.

Betack stared at Sean for a long moment and then gave a slight nod, silently thanking Sean for the cover he'd just provided.

Jane Cox sat down behind her desk and took a few minutes to explain what had happened. Betack filled in the more technical parts on the box's delivery and contents.

Michelle said, "So someone does have her. They say she's safe and will contact us later."

Jane said sharply, "We have no idea if she is really safe. She could be dead."

"It's troubling that they knew where to send the letter," Sean said.

Betack nodded. "We're theorizing that they might have researched the family and knew the aunt was local. Even if the kids weren't staying there the box would have eventually reached us."

"Or it could show the kidnappers have some inside info," said Sean. He glanced sharply at Betack. "I'm not suggesting that's coming from the Service, but there could be other leaks."

Betack said, "You're right. We'll cover that end."

"So what do we do now?" Jane wanted to know.

Sean said, "Can they determine where it was mailed from?"

Jane said, "Dalton, Georgia. At least that's what the FBI director told me."

Betack confirmed this with a nod.

"Okay, that's something. If it was at a specific processing center then there's a certain radius of postal pickups that are delivered there. That narrows the search down. It'll require a lot of manpower but they can canvass the area."

"FBI's already on it," said Betack.

Michelle said, "But if I'm the kidnapper I'll know that and I'll drive a long way from where I'm holding Willa to make the drop."

Sean added, "Dalton is in northern Georgia. It's in relatively easy driving distance from Tennessee, Alabama, and North and South Carolina."

"Which makes it hard but not impossible," noted Betack. "And it's one of the few leads we have."

Sean looked over to see Jane staring at a photo she held in her hands. She turned it around for them to see. It was a picture of Willa on a horse.

"She'd just turned six. She wanted a pony, of course. I guess all little kids do. Dan was still in the Senate back then. We took her to a little farm out near Purcellville in Virginia. She got right up on that animal and we almost couldn't get her off. Most kids would've been scared to death."

She slowly put the photo back down.

"A brave girl," Sean said quietly.

Jane said pointedly, "She is brave and capable, but she's still a little girl."

"Does the FBI have any thoughts on motive?" asked Michelle.

"Not as far as I know."

She looked at Betack, who merely shook his head.

"We talked to Tuck and went by his office."

"Did you find anything useful?"

Sean squirmed slightly in his chair before glancing uneasily at Betack. "This might get personal."

Betack looked at the First Lady. "I can leave, Mrs. Cox."

She thought for a moment. "Fine. Thank you, Agent Betack. The president and I want to be made aware of any developments without delay."

After Betack left she said, "What do you mean by personal, Sean?"

"Did Pam ever talk to you about any problems in the marriage?"

"Why do you ask that?" Jane said sharply.

"Just covering all the bases," said Sean. "So was there anything?"

Jane sat back and made a steeple with her hands while she slowly nodded. "It was at the party at Camp David. We were talking about Tuck not being there. That he was away on business. It was really nothing. But—"

"But what?"

"It just seemed that she wanted to say something, but then didn't. She made a casual comment about Tuck being Tuck. And that he'd be back the next day." She looked between the pair. "What is it?"

Sean and Michelle had both snapped forward in their chairs. "Tuck was supposed to come back the day *after* the kidnapping happened?" Sean asked.

Jane looked unsure. "That's right. I believe that's what she said. But he was there the night it happened." Jane leaned forward too. "What is going on?"

Sean glanced at Michelle. "Tuck might have been having an affair."

Jane stood. "What?"

"You had no idea?"

"Of course not, because it's not true. My brother would never do that. What proof do you have?"

"Enough to make us want to investigate it further."

Jane sat back down. "This is . . . incredible." She glanced up. "If you think he had an affair, you're not implying that . . ."

"Jane, I can't answer that question. At least not right now. We've only been on this thing for a short time. We're doing the best we can."

"And our priority has to be getting Willa back safe," added Michelle.

"Of course that's our goal. It's the only reason I

asked you to help." Jane put a shaky hand up to her forehead.

Sean could easily read her mind. "When you start an investigation you really can never be sure where it's going to lead. Sometimes the truth does hurt, Jane. Are you prepared for that?"

The First Lady placed a cool, rigid gaze on him.

"The truth is, at this point in my life nothing surprises me anymore. You just find Willa. And let the chips fall."

All three turned when the door swung open. Sean and Michelle reflexively leapt to their feet as President Dan Cox strode into the room, winged by a pair of veteran Secret Service agents. He smiled and put out his hand.

Cox was about Michelle's height, several inches shorter than Sean, but his shoulders were burly and his face, at age fifty, retained more vestiges of youth than it did the toll of middle age. That was somewhat remarkable considering his years under the unrelenting gaze of the world.

Sean and Michelle took turns shaking the man's hand.

Jane said, "I'm surprised to see you."

Cox said, "I canceled the rest of my appearances for today. My people weren't thrilled, but the president does get a few perks. And when you're up by twenty-five points in the polls and your opponent agrees with you more than he disagrees with you, a free day every once in a while is allowable. And even if I were behind in the race Willa's safety comes first."

Jane gave him a grateful smile. "I know you've always seen it that way."

Cox walked over and gave his wife a peck on the cheek and rubbed her shoulder gently before turning to his two Secret Service agents; his gaze flicked almost imperceptibly to the door. Within moments the men were gone.

Sean, who had watched this little exchange, thought, *How many times has a president done that very same eye flick with me?*

Cox said, "Jane's told me what you two are doing. I welcome your experience and input. We have to do everything we can to get Willa back safely."

"Absolutely, Mr. President," Sean said automatically.

Cox perched on the edge of his wife's desk and motioned for the pair to retake their seats. "I was briefed on the flight about the package. I pray that will lead to something positive." He paused. "Politics should not become involved in this and I'll do everything possible not to allow that to happen. However, the opposition controls the Congress so I clearly don't have *absolute power* there." He gazed at his wife and smiled tenderly. "I don't even have it in my own house, which is a good thing since my better half is smarter than I'll ever be." His casual smile melted. "But officially the FBI leads this investigation. Some of my advisors don't think I can play favorites here, but I've told FBI Director Munson that this case gets maximum priority. I'll deal with the political fallout later. My wife trusts you with this, so I trust you. However, while you will continue to be provided access to the investigation, remember that your role is that of a private consultant. The FBI runs the show."

"We understand, Mr. President."

"They've been very cooperative," Michelle added, without a trace of the sneer she was undoubtedly feeling coming on.

"Good. Have you made any progress?"

Sean shot a quick glance at Jane Cox. Her features were imperturbable yet somehow Sean was able to read them still. "It's early yet, sir, but we're working as hard and as fast as we can. It seems like they got a bit of a break with this package. Hopefully, as you said, that will lead to something else. Those things often do. The bad guys communicate and they let something slip."

"All right." Cox stood and so did Sean and Michelle.

"I'll talk to you later, honey," said the president.

Moments later he was gone, with no doubt his silent guards once more bracketing him.

Outside the White House the few square feet

around the president demanded maximum protection, and some agents, using a football analogy, referred to it as the "red zone," meaning that this was where the defense could never allow a score. That meant layers of perimeter walls rolling outward like the multiple skins of an onion. To get to the next depth, the intruder had to wipe out the layer above. The red zone was the last wall before you ran smack into the leader of the free world's flesh and bone. It consisted of top agents who'd been excruciatingly vetted to get to this level, positioned hip and flank in the form of a diamond. A hard diamond. And every single one of those agents would automatically fight to the death and take a lethal round for the man, without question. That was the one layer that could never be breached, because it was the last one.

Yet even in the White House, the Service was always within a foot of the man save for one place: the First Family's private quarters. In the field of presidential protection, you could never assume that you always knew where your enemies were, or whether your friends were really friends.

A few minutes later, Sean and Michelle were in the tunnel heading back to the Treasury, a Marine in full dress uniform leading the way.

"I've always wanted to meet the president," Michelle said to Sean.

"He's an impressive guy. But . . . ."

Michelle's voice sank to a whisper. "But you'll always see him in that car in the alley with that woman?"

He grimaced but didn't answer her.

"Why didn't you ask Jane about the two C-sections and three kids?"

"Because my gut told me not to. And right now my gut is scaring me to death."

20

Sean yawned, sat back, finished off his coffee, and rose to get some more while Michelle stared intently at the computer screen. They were at her apartment near Fairfax Corner. While outside cars and patrons streamed through the popular upscale shopping area, the two of them had been sequestered in Michelle's cluttered home office staring at digital liquid on her Mac. Sean returned and handed her a fresh cup of coffee. It had taken a long time to sift through Tuck Dutton's computer files. But some interesting information had been gained by the effort.

The *man* had been scheduled to come home the morning following the kidnapping attempt. Cassandra Mallory's cell phone had been listed in his contacts. Sean had called it. A woman had answered and then he'd hung up. Her address was also in Tuck's records.

"We might have to pay the woman a visit," Michelle said.

"If she's still around."

"You think she was in on it?"

"Hard to say. I have no doubt they had something

150

going on. You don't use a *coworker's* name as your computer password. But whether she knew about this, or whether Tuck was actually involved . . ." He shrugged.

She gave him a confused look. "I didn't think Tuck's involvement was an open question. If he *wasn't* involved it was a helluva coincidence, don't you think?"

"But we did a quick look at his financial account. There's no movement of cash out that isn't accounted for. So, what, they did this for free?"

"Maybe he has another account somewhere. The guy's in government contracting. You telling me folks like that don't have slush funds all over the place?"

"But if he decided to be at the house it apparently was a spur-of-the-moment thing. I checked with the airline. The reservation change was made at the last possible second."

"Like we discussed before, he might have thought about it and decided it was better cover to be there than not."

Sean looked out the window. "I feel like we're spinning our wheels. Maybe the trace under Pam's fingernails will get a hit on a database somewhere."

Michelle said excitedly, "Wait a minute, what if the ransom *is* the payment? That way Tuck doesn't have to cough up a dime and there's no money trail for the FBI to follow."

"So these guys do all this on the come? You know the kidnapping business sucks. The payoff is always problematic. Even with electronic transfers, there's always some trail to follow. You get your money and then the FBI knocks down your door." Sean drew a breath. "And we still have no idea why they took blood from Pam Dutton."

"So how do we play this with Tuck?"

"Question him some more, but don't tip our hand."

"His buddy Hilal might do that for us. Meaning tip off Tuck."

"Don't think so. His primary concern is not to let this contract blow up. And he doesn't want to fall in this mess with Tuck if he is guilty. I think he'll keep his distance."

"So if Pam wasn't Willa's birth mother who could it be?"

"It might not matter."

"But you said earlier that you thought Willa was the adopted one. So I thought you meant it was tied into this somehow."

"Willa is twelve. If it is tied to her it's taken somebody a long time to come around to it."

"Do you remember them ever talking about Willa being adopted?"

"Never. I just assumed all three kids were theirs."

"Okay, how about Jane Cox?"

"What about her?"

"She knows about our suspicions. What if she tips off her brother?"

Before Sean could answer, Michelle's phone rang. "Hello?"

"Oh, hey, Bill. I . . . what?" Michelle paled. "Oh my God. When? How?"

Michelle didn't say anything for about a minute, but her breath kept coming in accelerating bursts as she listened. "Okay, okay. I'll catch the next flight out." She clicked off.

"Michelle, what is it?"

"My mom's dead."

21

The sturdy wheels of the Cessna bumped against the compacted dirt with the grass topper, slowed, and came to a stop. Sam Quarry taxied down the make-shift runway, worked the foot pedals, and expertly spun the plane around. He climbed out and slung a knapsack over his shoulder. After blocking the plane's wheels, he unlocked the outer door of the old mine. He walked down the tunnel, his path illuminated by his flashlight and the dull glow of the overhead lights.

A few minutes later he met up with Carlos and Daryl.

"Did you take care of Kurt's body?" he asked solemnly.

Daryl looked down but Carlos said, "We buried it on down the south shaft. Said a prayer over him and everything. Real respectable."

"Good." Quarry glanced over at his son. "You learn anything from this, boy?"

Daryl nodded stiffly. "Don't never lose control." His tone didn't imply that he had actually learned anything. This was apparently not lost on Quarry.

He clapped his son on the back and then his strong fingers dug into the younger man's skin. "Every time you think about losing your temper, you think about the price Kurt paid. You think about that real good. 'Cause let me tell you, I could've easily let Kurt be the one walking away. And him and Carlos could've been saying the Lord's Prayer over *your* hole in the dirt. You hear me?"

"I hear you, Daddy. I hear you."

"Little piece of me died with him. Maybe more than a little. I've damned myself to hell for all eternity by doing that. You think about that too."

"Thought you didn't believe in God," Daryl said quietly while Carlos looked on, his features inscrutable except for the fact he was slowly rubbing the St. Christopher's medal he wore around his neck.

"I might not believe in God, but I sure as hell believe in the devil."

"Okay, Daddy."

"I don't make many rules, but the ones I do make I expect to be followed. Only way any of this shit works. Okay?"

"Yes sir," said Carlos, who'd stopped stroking the medallion and slipped it back under his shirt.

Quarry left the men and continued on. A minute later he was sitting across from Willa, who was dressed in corduroy pants and a wool shirt Quarry had provided.

"Got everything you need?" Quarry asked.

155

"I'd like some books," said Willa. "There's nothing else to do so I want to read."

Quarry smiled and opened his knapsack. "Great minds, you know." He lifted five books out and passed them over to her. She studied them carefully.

"You like Jane Austen?" he asked.

She nodded. "She's not like my absolute favorite, but I've only read *Pride and Prejudice*."

"That was my daughter's favorite book."

"Was?"

Quarry stiffened slightly. "She doesn't read anymore."

"Is she dead?" Willa asked with the bluntness of youth.

"Some might call it that." He pointed to the other books. "I know you're real smart. So I didn't bother with crap you're probably way past. But you let me know what you like or not. I got plenty."

Willa slid the books aside and studied him carefully. "Can I have some paper and a pen? I like to write. And it would take my mind off things."

"Okay, that's not a problem."

"Did you talk to my parents? You said you would."

"I sent out a message, yep. Told 'em you were okay."

"Are you going to kill me?"

Quarry flinched back like she'd sucker-punched

him, and maybe she had. He found his voice. "Where the hell did that come from?"

"Sometimes kidnappers don't give the person back. They kill them." Her wide eyes remained steadfastly on his. She was obviously not interested in retreating off this subject.

Quarry rubbed his jaw with a callused, weathered hand. Then he glanced down at it, as though he was seeing it for the first time. It was the same hand that had ended Kurt's life, so maybe the girl had something. *I am a killer, after all.*

"I appreciate that. I can see where you're coming from, sure. But if I were planning on killing you, I could just lie and say I wasn't going to. So what does it matter?"

She was ready for him in this little logics duel. "But if you tell me you *are* planning on killing me it's probably the truth, because why would you lie about that?"

"Damn, I bet sometimes people say you're too smart for your own good, don't they?"

Her bottom lip trembled just a bit as she transformed from Einstein to the frightened preadolescent she was. "I want to go home. I want to see my mom and dad. And my brother and sister. I didn't do anything wrong." Tears spilled from her eyes. "I didn't do anything wrong, and so I don't understand why you're doing this. I just don't!"

Quarry looked down, unable to confront the wide, wet eyes and the terror they held. "This isn't about you, Willa. Not really. It's just . . . it's just that this is the only way it'll work. I thought it through a lot of different ways and this is the only one that made sense. It's the only chance I had. The only cards I had to play."

"Who are you mad at? Who are you trying to get back at?"

He rose. "You need any more books, you just let me know."

He fled the room, leaving Willa to cry alone. He had never felt more ashamed.

A few minutes later Quarry was eying Diane Wohl as she sat on her haunches in the far corner of her "cell" from him. He should have felt sympathy for her too, but he didn't. Willa was a child. She hadn't had a chance to make choices. And mistakes. This woman here had done both.

"Can I ask you a question?" Wohl said in a shaky voice.

Quarry sat down at the small table in the middle of the room. Part of him was still dwelling on Willa. But he said, "Shoot."

"Can I make a phone call to my mother? To let her know I'm okay?"

"Can't do that. These days they can trace anything. Government eye in the sky. Sorry. Just the way it is."

"Well, then can you let her know I'm okay?"

"I might be able to do that. Give me her address."

He handed her a pencil and a slip of paper. Her brow furrowed as she wrote it down and then handed him back the paper. She asked, "Why did you take my blood?"

"I needed it for something."

"What?"

Quarry looked around at the small space. It wasn't a fancy hotel, but Quarry had lived in worse. He had tried to provide everything the woman needed to be comfortable.

I'm not evil, he told himself. If he kept thinking it, maybe he'd start believing it.

"Can I ask *you* a question?"

She appeared startled by this but nodded.

"You have any kids?"

"What? No, no, I never did. Why?"

"Just wondering."

She drew nearer to him. Like Willa she had changed into fresh clothes. Quarry had brought along the outfits she'd purchased from Talbot's. They fit nicely.

"Are you going to let me go?"

"That depends."

"On what?"

"On how things turn out. I *can* tell you that I am not by nature a violent man. But I also can't predict the future."

She sat down at the table across from him and clasped her hands together.

"I can't think of one thing I've done in my life that would make you do this to me. I don't even know you. What have I done? What the hell have I done to deserve this?"

"You did one thing," said Quarry.

She looked up. "What? Tell me!"

"I'll let you think of it yourself. You sure got some time to do that."

22

It was early morning as the puddle-jumper bounced along the tops of the grayish clouds lingering from a storm that had already passed over the Smoky Mountains. Later, as the plane descended into the Nashville airport, Michelle continued to do what she had done the entire flight: stare at her hands.

When the plane door opened she wheeled her bag out, grabbed a rental, and was on the road within twenty minutes after arriving at the gate. However, her foot was not mashing the gas pedal to the floor as usual. Instead, she drove at a sedate fifty miles an hour. Michelle had no desire to rush toward what she had to face.

According to her brother Bill, their mother had woken up in good spirits, eaten a bowl of cereal for breakfast, and worked in the garden. Later she had played nine holes of golf at a nearby course, returned home, showered, gotten dressed, warmed up a casserole for her husband, watched a show she had earlier recorded, and was heading out the door to meet with some friends for a late dinner when she collapsed in the garage. Frank Maxwell had been in the bathroom. He had gone into the garage a bit later and found his wife sprawled on the floor. Apparently, he believed Sally had been dead before she'd hit the cement.

They weren't sure what had killed the woman—stroke, heart, aneurysm—but dead she was. As the trees on either side of the road flew by, Michelle's mind raced even faster, from her earliest memories with her mother to the last few encounters, none of which had been particularly memorable.

An hour later she had talked with her four brothers, two of whom lived relatively close by their parents, and one, Bobby, who lived in the same town. The fourth, Bill Maxwell, who resided in Florida, had been driving to see his parents for a visit when he'd gotten the news barely an hour out. Michelle was the last to arrive. She had next spent several hours with her father, who was equal parts mute and staring off, before erupting from his malaise periodically to take control of the funeral arrangements.

Frank Maxwell had been a cop most of his life, ending his career as a police chief. He still looked like he could jump out of a patrol car and hoof it after someone and do something with the person once he caught him. It was from her father that Michelle had gotten her physical prowess, her drive to succeed, her sheer inability to ever finish second with a smile on her face. Yet as Michelle watched from a distance, catching her father in unguarded moments, she glimpsed an aging man who had just lost everything and had no idea what he was supposed to be doing with the time he had left to live.

After absorbing all she could take of this, she retreated to the backyard where she sat on an old bench next to an apple tree weighed down nearly to the ground with fruit, closed her eyes, and pretended her mother was still alive. She thought back to her childhood with them both. This was tough to do because there were blocks of her youth that Michelle Maxwell had simply eliminated from her memory for reasons that were obviously more apparent to her shrink than to her.

She called Sean to let him know she'd arrived okay. He had said all the appropriate things, was supportive and gentle. And yet when she hung up, Michelle felt about as alone as she ever had. One by one her brothers joined her in the backyard. They talked, cried, chatted some more, and cried some more. She noted that Bill, the biggest and the oldest, a tough beat cop in a Miami suburb that could reasonably be classified as a war zone, sobbed the hardest.

Michelle found herself mothering her older brothers, and she was not, by nature or inclination, a nurturing type. And the close, grief-stricken company of her male siblings started to suffocate her. She finally left them in the backyard and returned to the house. Her father was upstairs. She could hear him talking on the phone to someone. She eyed the door to the garage accessible from the kitchen. She hadn't gone in there yet. Michelle didn't really want to see where her mother had died.

Yet she was also one to confront her fears head-on. She turned the knob, opened the door, and stared down the three unpainted plywood steps leading to the two-bay garage. A car was parked in the nearest bay. It was her parents' pale blue Camry. The garage looked like any other. Except for one thing.

The splotch of blood on the cement floor. She drew closer to it.

Blood on the cement floor?

Had she fallen down the steps? Hit her head? She eyed the door of the Camry. There was no trace there. She gauged the space between the rough steps and the car. Her mother was a tall woman. If she had stumbled forward, she *had* to have hit the car. She really couldn't have fallen sideways because the stairs had half-walls on both sides. She would have simply ended up slumped there. But if she had stumbled because she'd had a stroke? She could have bounced off the car and then hit her head on the floor. That would account for the blood.

That *had* to account for the blood.

She turned and almost screamed.

Her father was standing there.

Frank Maxwell was officially six foot three, though

age and gravity had stolen more than an inch from him. He had the compact, dense muscle of a man who had been physical his entire life. His gaze flitted across his daughter's anxious face, perhaps trying to read all the content there. Then it went to the spot of blood on the floor. He gazed at it as though the crimson splotch constituted an encrypted message he was trying to decipher.

"She'd been having headaches," her father said. "I told her to go get them checked out."

Michelle slowly nodded, thinking that this was an odd thing to open the conversation with. "She could have had a stroke."

"Or an aneurysm. The neighbor down the street, her husband just had one. Nearly killed him."

"Well, at least she wasn't in any pain," Michelle said, a bit lamely.

"I don't think so, no."

"So you were in the bath, Bill said?"

He nodded. "Showering. To think that she was lying there while I . . ."

She put a hand on his shoulder and clenched it tightly. It scared her to see her father like this. Right on the edge of losing it. If there was one thing her father had always been, it was in control.

"There was nothing you could have done, Dad. It happens. It's not fair. It's not right, but it happens."

"And yesterday it happened to me," he said with finality.

Michelle removed her hand and looked around the garage. The kids' things had long since been purged from her parents' lives. No bikes or wading pools or T-ball bats to clutter up their retirement. It was clean, but stark, as though their entire family history had been washed away. Her gaze went back to the blood as though it was the bait and she was the hungry fish. "So she was going to see some friends for dinner?"

He blinked rapidly. For a moment she thought he was going to dissolve into tears. She suddenly recalled that she had never seen her father cry. As soon as this thought fully formed in her head, she received a jolt somewhere in her brain.

I have seen my father cry, but I just don't know when.

"Something like that."

His vague answer made her mouth dry up and her skin feel like someone had just burned it.

She slipped past her father without a word and grabbed her rental car keys off the kitchen counter. Before she drove off she snatched a glance at the house. Her father was watching her through the picture window in the living room. His face carried a look that not only couldn't she decipher, she didn't want to.

A cup of coffee from a Dunkin' Donuts in hand, she drove the streets of the Nashville suburb where her parents had built their retirement dream home with financial help from their five kids. Michelle was the only unmarried and childless one, so she had contributed disproportionately to the cause, but never regretted it. Raising a large family on a cop's salary was no easy thing, and her parents had sacrificed much for them. She had no problem paying that debt back.

She pulled out her phone and called her eldest brother. She didn't even let him get the hello all the way out before she pounced.

"Bill, why the hell didn't you tell me about the blood in the garage?"

"What?"

"The blood on the damn garage floor!"

"She hit her head when she fell down."

"Hit her head on what?"

"Probably the car."

"You're sure about that? Because there wasn't a mark on the car that I could see."

"Mik, what the hell are you suggesting?"

"Are they doing an autopsy?"

"What?"

"An autopsy!"

"I . . . I don't know that for sure. I mean, I suppose they might have to," he added uncomfortably.

"And you didn't mention this to me when you called because why?"

"What would have been the point? They'll do the autopsy and we'll find out she had a stroke or a heart attack or something like that. She fell, hit her head."

"Yeah, the head again. Did the police come?"

"Of course. And the ambulance. They were here when I got here."

"Which of you four were there first?"

Michelle thought she knew the answer. Her brother Bobby was a police sergeant in the town where their parents lived. She listened to a mumbled conversation as Bill apparently consulted with his brothers.

He came back on. "Dad called Bobby and he was here like within ten minutes even though he lives on the other side of town."

"Great. Put Bobby on!"

"Jesus, what the hell are you getting so pissed off—"

"Put him on, Bill!"

Bobby's voice came on a few moments later. "Mik, what is up with you?" he began sternly.

"Dad called you. You came over. Were you on duty?"

"No. I had yesterday off. I was at home helping Joanie with dinner."

"What did Dad tell you?"

Bobby's voice rose. "What did he tell me? He told me that *our* mother was dead. That's what the hell he told me."

"Were the police there when you got there?"

"Yeah. Dad called 'em. They got there maybe five minutes before I did."

"And Dad told them what exactly?"

"Well, he was in the shower, so he didn't know *exactly* what had happened. He found Mom and he called 911 and then he called me."

"And what did the cops say after they looked over things?"

"They said it looked like she'd fallen and hit her head."

"But they didn't know *why* she'd fallen."

"They wouldn't know that. If she just stumbled and hit her head, okay. But if something popped in her body to make her fall, the ME would have to determine that." He added fiercely, "And it's making me sick to think of them having to cut Mom up."

"Did you see blood on the Camry door when you went into the garage?"

"Why do you want to know?"

"Because, Bobby, she had to hit her head on *something*."

"Like I just said, she could've stumbled down the stairs, bounced off the car, knocked her head on the floor. Or maybe on the stair wall. It has a sharp edge. You hit a spot just right, it's all over. You know that."

Michelle tried to imagine her mother catching her heel on the unfinished riser—maybe on a nail head that had popped upward over time—stumbling forward, hitting the car without making a dent in it, falling sideways, and smacking her head with such force on the floor that it had drawn blood. Yet if the autopsy revealed a reason for her death?

"Mik? You still there?"

She snapped back. "Yeah."

"Okay, look, we don't know where you're heading with this but—"

"Neither do I, Bobby. Neither do I." She clicked off, stopped the vehicle next to a small park, hopped out, and started to sprint.

She was having thoughts that were terrifying her. And all she could do right now was try and outrun them, even as the image of her father watching her from the window, his face seized into a solid mask of what she didn't quite know, chased her all the way.

23

While his partner was in Tennessee trying to confront family demons, Sean was finishing up some Italian take-out in his office and still studying the reams of paper he'd printed off the computer. He was hoping that buried in here somewhere was a clue that would tell him if Tuck Dutton had had his wife killed and his daughter kidnapped for reasons yet unknown.

The ringing phone interrupted his thoughts. It was Jane Cox.

She said, "I want you to meet me at the hospital. Tuck wants to talk to you."

"About what?" he asked warily.

"I think you know."

Sean pulled on his jacket and walked down to his rental. His car was in the shop with about eight thousand bucks' worth of damage and his insurance company was telling him that a bullet barrage was not covered under his policy.

"Why not?" he'd argued.

"Because we consider it a terrorist act and you

171

don't have a terrorism rider," replied the insurance grunt, somehow managing to convey this denial in a cheery tone.

"It wasn't terrorism. It was a criminal act and I was the victim."

"There were thirty-seven bullet holes in your car, Mr. King. Under our policy guidelines that is not a criminal act, it's terrorism."

"You go by the number of bullet holes! How the hell does that make sense, lady?"

"You can always appeal the decision."

"Really? What do your *guidelines* say the odds are of me winning that appeal? Less than zero?"

Miss Cheery had hung up on him after thanking him for his business.

He started up the car and was preparing to back out when someone tapped on his window. He looked around. It was a woman, early thirties, blonde hair, shapely, too much red lipstick, and with the dried-out skin of someone forced to undergo pancake face paint on a daily basis to fight the high-def cameras. She was holding a microphone with a built-in digital recorder like it was a grenade she was about to heave.

He glanced behind her and saw the news truck ease into view and block his exit.

Crap.

Sean rolled down the window.

"Can I help you?"

"Sean King?"

"That's right. Look, I gave the media pool guy a statement. You can piggyback off him."

"Developments dictate a fresh angle."

"What developments?"

"Did you steal confidential records from the office computer of Tuck Dutton?"

Sean's stomach gave a heave and part of his veal picatta got bumped up into his throat.

"I don't know what you're talking about. Who told you that?"

"Do you deny going to his office?"

"I'm not admitting or denying anything."

"Tuck Dutton's firm is a government contractor working on highly classified matters for DHS."

"So are you a reporter or a company spokesperson? I can't tell."

"Do you realize it's a crime to steal someone else's property? And if you're found to have stolen classified information for purposes of espionage you could be charged with treason?"

"Okay, now you sound like a lawyer wannabe. I happen to be the genuine article. So if you don't get your buddy back there to move his van, I'm going to see how far I can push it down the street with my wheels. And then I'll pull him out of the van and start to 'assault and battery' him. But I'll just call it self-defense. It's less of a prosecutable offense that way."

"Are you threatening us?"

"I'm one second away from calling the cops and charging your ass with unlawful detention, harassment, and slander. Go look those up in your *Black's Law Dictionary* while you're cramming for the LSATs."

Sean gunned the motor and slammed the car into reverse.

The woman jumped back and the news van driver nailed the gas just in time to avoid getting T-boned by Sean's ride.

A half hour later Sean was walking to Tuck's hospital room and his mood was growing darker with each stride. Of course he had taken the information, not because he was a spy but because he was trying to determine if Tuck was involved in his wife's murder. It had left him legally exposed, but it wasn't the first time he'd pushed the envelope. That wasn't why he was ticked off. Someone was setting him up to take a fall. And he wanted to know who and why.

He held out his ID to one of the wall of Secret Service agents stationed in the hallway. Because the First Lady was here they took extra time frisking and wanding him and then ushered him into the room. Tuck sat in a chair next to the bed. Jane Cox stood next to him, her hand supportively on her brother's shoulder.

Two agents parked themselves against a wall until Jane said, "Please wait outside." One burly agent gave Sean a piercing look as he and his partner edged to the door. "We'll be *right* outside, ma'am." He closed the door behind him. Sean turned to face the sister and brother.

"Thank you for coming," Jane said.

"You made it sound like it was important. I hope it is."

His brusque manner seemed to catch the woman off-guard. Before she could respond, Sean turned his attention to Tuck. "You look like you're feeling better. The mother of all concussions healing nicely?"

"It still hurts like hell," said Tuck defensively.

Sean pulled up a chair and sat down across from the pair.

"I just got smacked out of left field by a TV reporter on a witch hunt." He glanced at Jane. "Know anything about that?"

"Of course not, how could I?"

"I don't know." He settled his gaze back on Tuck. "Okay, Tuck, time is of the essence so why beat around the bush? Cassandra Mallory?"

"What about her?"

"Who is she to you?"

"She's an employee of my company."

"That's all?"

"Of course it is."

"That's not what your partner thinks."

"Then he's wrong."

Sean rose and peered out the window. Down

below was the motorcade waiting for the First Lady to finish her visit. Life in the bubble. Sean knew it well. Every move treated to the closest scrutiny, sucking the breath right out of you. And yet some spent hundreds of millions of bucks and devoted years of their life to getting to that bubble. Was that insanity, narcissism, or elements of both hidden under the excuse of public service?

He turned back to them, thinking rapidly. If he admitted he knew that the password to Tuck's computer was Cassandra, he'd be confessing his own guilt in hacking into the guy's database. Instead he said, "You willing to take a polygraph on that?"

Tuck started to say something, but Sean saw the First Lady's fingers tighten on his shoulder and no words came out.

"Sean," she began, "why are you doing this?"

"You asked me to investigate this case. That's what I'm doing. I can't help where it might lead, even to places you don't want it to go. You told me to go for it while sitting in the White House. I'm sure you remember. It wasn't that long ago. I believe the exact phrase was, 'Let the chips fall.'"

"I also recall that I asked you to find Willa."

"Well, I can't very well do that if I don't find out who took her and why. And killed Pam in the process." He glared at Tuck when he said this last part.

"I had nothing to do with this," Tuck snapped.

"Then you won't mind taking a polygraph."

"You can't make me take one," he shot back.

"No, but if I go to the FBI and tell them what I've found out, they'll start looking in places you don't want them to look. If you pass the polygraph, I won't do that. That's the deal."

Jane said calmly, "So you talked to his partner, David Hilal?"

"I didn't think you were that familiar with your brother's work."

She continued imperturbably. "Did Hilal also tell you that he's been desperate to buy Tuck out? That he wants the company for his own?"

Sean looked at Tuck. "Is that true?"

"Absolutely true. I won't lie. I've had some financial reversals. David knew I needed money. He wants to buy me out, but at a price that does not reflect the value of the contract with DHS we're working on. It would mean millions of extra dollars."

"So you see, it's in Hilal's interests to implicate Tuck in this. If Tuck goes to jail, Hilal will get everything for pennies."

"Not necessarily," said Sean.

"But I'd be forced to sell at that point, just to pay the lawyer's bills," Tuck pointed out. "He would get it for next to nothing. And I built that company."

Jane added, "Sean, you may want to redirect your attention away from Tuck and onto a more plausible suspect."

Sean took a moment to process this. "You think Hilal orchestrated a kidnapping and murder just so he could blame it on Tuck and get the company? That's a bit of a stretch, don't you think? And why kidnap Willa?"

Jane came around and perched on the edge of the hospital bed. "I'm not going to try and reconstruct the mindset of what may be a psychopath. Yet it's no more of a stretch than thinking my brother would have his wife murdered, his beloved daughter kidnapped, and suffer a blow to his head that could have easily killed him, simply because he was *allegedly* having an affair."

Sean looked out the window again, his hands stuffed in his pockets. What she was saying did make some sense. He might have jumped to conclusions about what Hilal had said without corroborating it. And yet the computer password? Something jolted him. What if someone had changed the password and made it "Cassandra1"? What if Hilal had done it, thinking that Sean would try to break into the hard drive, guess the password, and conclude beyond doubt that the lady and Tuck were having an affair?

That, he concluded, was about as likely as his insurance company paying for his *terrorist* damage.

He whipped around. "Tuck, what's the password on your computer at work?" Sean snapped his fingers to push the man's answer along. "Come on, what is it?"

Tuck hesitated just enough. "Carmichael."

Jane said quickly, "That's Pam's maiden name, isn't it?"

Tuck nodded, as he lifted a hand and wiped a tear from his right eye.

You are both lying to me. They know somehow that I hacked the computer. They sent the reporter chick after me. To scare me off.

Tuck's prevarication was not surprising. The First Lady going along with it struck Sean as very odd. He obviously had a lot more digging to do.

"Okay, I'll check out Hilal."

"Good." Jane rose, gave Tuck a peck on the cheek and a hug.

As she walked toward Sean, she said, "I appreciate your continued cooperation on this."

"Right." He ignored her outstretched hand and walked out of the room.

24

Sam Quarry wiped the streaks of sweat from his brow, angled his aching back just so and received a gratifying *pop* as pressure was released from his over-worked spine. He was surveying his farmland from the highest point at Atlee, an anomalous rock mound that jutted about fifty feet in the air with access gained to the top by a series of stone steps worn smooth by the boots of his ancestors. It had been known, at least for as long as Quarry could remember, as Angel Rock. As though it were the stepping-off place to heaven and ostensibly a better life than the one granted to the Quarry family on plain earth. He wasn't a gambling man, but Quarry would've bet a few bucks that almost none of his male ancestors had successfully made the journey.

Atlee, for all its historical significance was, at bottom, a working farm. The only things that had changed over the last two hundred years were *what* was grown and *how* it was grown. Diesel engines had replaced mules and plows and a variety of crops had taken the place of cotton and tobacco. Quarry was not wedded to any particular crop and would try something different so long as it could be profitable with small farms like Atlee had become. Like most efficient farmers he obsessed over every detail, from the soil composition, to rainfall, to harvest times down to the minute, to predicted frost levels to yield per acre in relation to expected market prices, to the precise number of hands to do the picking, tractors to do the hauling, and bankers to extend the credit.

He was too far north in Alabama to grow kiwifruit but he had taken a stab at raising canola because a milling plant had finally opened not too far away that could turn the collard-like plant into "value-added" canola oil. It was a good winter crop and produced more income per acre than the staple winter wheat. He also grew traditional produce like cabbage, pole and snap beans, corn, okra, squash, pumpkins, tomatoes, turnip greens, and watermelons.

Some of it fed the people who lived at Atlee with him, but most was sold to local companies and stores for income that was desperately needed. He also carried twenty hogs and two dozen head of forage-fed cattle and had found willing markets in Atlanta and Chicago that used the beef in *churrasco* cooking. They also kept some for their own consumption.

Farming was a risky proposition under even the best of circumstances. Folks who toiled in the dirt could do everything right and a drought or an early freeze could come and wipe them out. Mother

Nature never apologized for her divine and sometimes disastrous intervention. He'd had his share of
good and bad years. While it was clear that Quarry
would never become rich doing any of this, money
just as clearly wasn't the point. He paid his bills, he
held his head up, and he was fairly certain a man
shouldn't expect more than that out of life unless he
was corrupt, overly ambitious, or both.

He spent the next several hours toiling with rented
help in the fields. He did this for at least two reasons.
First, he liked to work the land. He'd been doing it
since he was a boy and saw no reason to stop simply
because he was fast becoming an old man. Second,
his workers always seemed to put a little more back
into their labor when *el jefe* was around.

Gabriel joined him in the afternoon after walking
a mile from the bus stop. The young boy was strong
and focused and wielded a tool and drove the
machinery with a steady, practiced hand. Later, over
dinner, Quarry let Gabriel say the blessing while his
mother, Ruth Ann, and Daryl looked on. Then they
ate the simple meal, almost all of which had been
canned or made from previous harvests. Quarry also
listened to Gabriel expound on what he'd learned in
school that day.

He looked admiringly at the boy's mother. "He's
smart, Ruth Ann. Like a sponge."

Ruth Ann smiled appreciatively. She was rail thin
and always would be due to an intestinal disorder

that she didn't have the money to treat properly and in about ten years would probably kill her. "Don't get that from me," she said. "Cooking and cleaning, that's all what's in my head."

"You do that real good." This came from Daryl, who sat opposite Gabriel and had been busily shoving cornbread into his mouth before taking a huge gulp of lukewarm well water to wash it down.

"Where's Carlos?" asked Gabriel. "He didn't go off too, like Kurt, did he?"

Daryl shot his father an anxious look, but Quarry calmly finished sopping up some tomato gravy with his cornbread before answering. "He's just doing some things for me out of town. Be back soon."

After dinner, Quarry ventured to the attic where he sat amid the cobwebbed detritus of his family's history, mostly in the form of furniture, clothing, books, and papers. He was not up here for nostalgic purposes, however. He spread the plans out over an old side table that had belonged to his maternal great-grandmother, who'd ended up killing her husband via shotgun blast over—at least the family legend held—a lady with a pretty face, nice manners, and very dark skin.

Quarry studied the road, the building, access points, and potential problem areas detailed on the plans. Then his attention turned to a set of drawings he'd prepared of a more mechanical nature. He had earned a scholarship to college in mechanical engineering, but the war in Vietnam sent those plans awry when his father demanded he enlist to help fight the communist plague. When he'd gotten back home years later his father was dead, Atlee was his, and attending college just wasn't in the cards.

Yet Quarry could fix anything that had either a motor or moving parts. The guts of any machine, no matter how complicated, easily revealed themselves to his mind in startling simplicity. It had paid dividends at Atlee, for while other farmers had to send out for costly help when equipment broke down, Quarry just fixed it himself, mostly lying on his back, a big wrench in his muscled grip.

Thus he pored over the plans and drawings with an expert's eye, seeing where improvements could be made and disaster avoided. Afterward he ventured downstairs and found Daryl cleaning rifles in the small gunroom off the kitchen.

"Ain't no smell better than gun grease," Daryl said, looking up at his father as he walked in the room.

"So you say."

Daryl's sudden smile faded, perhaps because of the memory of a Patriot pistol being leveled against the base of his skull by the man now standing a few feet from him in a room filled with weapons of singular destruction.

Quarry closed and locked the door and then sat

down next to his son and unrolled the set of plans on the floor.

"I've already gone over this with Carlos, but I want you to understand it too, just in case."

"I know," his son said, as he wiped down the barrel of his favorite deer rifle.

Quarry rattled the papers at him. "Now this is important, Daryl, no room for screwing up. Pay attention."

After thirty minutes of back-and-forth, a satisfied Quarry rose and folded up the plans. As he patted them back into a long tube he kept them in he said, "Almost crashed the damn plane I was so broke up about Kurt."

"I know," Daryl replied, a tinge of fear in his voice, for he knew his father was an unpredictable man.

"Would've probably cried if it'd been you. Just wanted you to know that."

"You a good man, Daddy."

"No, I don't think I am," said Quarry as he left the room.

He went up to Gabriel's room and called through the door, "You want to go along with me to see Tippi? I got to stop on the way to visit Fred."

"Yes sir, I will." Gabriel put down his book, slipped on his tennis shoes, and spun his baseball cap backward on his head.

A bit later Quarry and Gabriel edged up in front of the Airstream in Quarry's old Dodge. On the seat between them was a box with a few bottles of Jim Beam and three cartons of unfiltered Camels. After setting the box on the wooden steps going up to the Airstream, Quarry and Gabriel lifted from the bed of the truck two crates containing some kitchen-preserved vegetables, ten ears of plump corn, and twenty apples.

Quarry rapped on the door of the old, dented trailer while the cat-quick Gabriel chased a lizard through the dust until it disappeared underneath the Airstream. The old, wrinkled man opened the door and helped Quarry and Gabriel carry in the provisions.

"Thank you," said the man in his native tongue as he eyed the crates.

"Got more than we need, Fred."

When the Indian had come here, he'd never told Quarry his name, he'd just shown up. After a couple of awkward months Quarry had started calling him Fred and the fellow had never objected. He didn't know what his Indian friends called him, but that was their business, Quarry felt.

The two other Indians were inside. One was asleep on a raggedy couch that had no legs and no springs, allowing the man to sink nearly to the floor. His loud snores indicated this did not bother him in the least. The other man was watching a comedy show on an old fifteen-inch television Quarry had given Fred a few years ago.

They cracked open the Beam, smoked, and talked while Gabriel played with an old mutt that had adopted Fred and his Airstream and sipped on a bottle of Coke Fred had given him.

When Quarry occasionally stumbled over a Koasati word, Gabriel would look up and supply it. Every time he did so, Fred would laugh and offer a sip of Beam to Gabriel in reward.

And each time Quarry would hold up his hand. "When he's a man he can drink, but I wouldn't advise it. Does more bad in the long run than good."

"But you drink, Mr. Sam," Gabriel pointed out. "A lot."

"Don't model yourself after me, son. Aim higher."

Later, they drove on to see Tippi. Quarry let Gabriel read from *Pride and Prejudice*.

"Kind of boring," the boy pronounced when he'd finished the long passage.

Quarry took the book from him and slipped it in his back pocket. "She don't think so."

Gabriel looked over at Tippi. "You never did tell me what happened to her, Mr. Sam."

"No, I never did."

25

Sean had talked to David Hilal again, catching him out in the parking lot as the man was heading home. Tuck's partner had not had much to add to what he'd already said. Yet he calmly answered each and every query as he leaned against his car and simultaneously read and typed messages on his BlackBerry.

When Sean brought up the issue of the buyout, however, his tone changed. He thrust the BlackBerry in his pocket, folded his arms across his chest, and scowled at Sean.

"What exactly was I supposed to buy him out with? I put all my money into this firm. I'm hocked to the limit. I couldn't even get a loan to buy a car right now."

"He said you made a lowball offer."

"We talked about something like that, but the key is, it was the other way around."

"Him buying you out?"

"That's right. For the lowball offer."

Okay, which one's telling the truth?

"Why would you think of bailing out before the

big contract award? Tuck says that would add millions to the value of the firm."

"It absolutely would. *If* we win it. But it's not a lock. We have proprietary technology that I think is the best out there. That's the reason our prime contractor teamed with us. But we're up against some big players with their own products that are very close in performance and reliability to ours. And the world of government contracting is not done on a level playing field. The big guys skirt the rules, throw the cash around. And because they usually have an inside track they also buy up the most sought-after talent and the little guys get stuck with the scraps. And I don't want to bail out, but I'm running out of money. And if we don't win the contract, the firm will be worth a lot less than the offer he made me. We might have the inside track right now, but like I told you before, the president of the United States' brother-in-law having an affair with Cassandra isn't helping matters. That gets out, we've got problems."

"He said there was nothing between him and Cassandra."

"Really? Then ask him where he stayed when he was down there. I'm sure he'll have some handy excuse."

"You said before you didn't think Tuck would kill his wife, but you don't sound like you love your partner all that much."

"I don't."

"You didn't mention that before."

"Didn't I?"

"I'm a great note-taker. So, no, you didn't."

"Fine. I'm not in the habit of trashing my partner to people I don't even know. But it's hard not to, to tell you the truth."

"Why?"

"Let's just say he's rubbed me the wrong way."

"Care to give an example?"

"Would you believe me if I told you?"

"I've got a very open mind."

Hilal looked off for a few moments before glancing back at Sean. "This is sort of embarrassing, actually."

"I'm very much into maintaining confidences."

Hilal popped a piece of gum in his mouth and started chewing and talking fast as though beating up on the gum and grinding his teeth were giving him the juice to confess everything. "Last year's Christmas party? We'd won a nice little contract. Nothing to write home about, but we splurged anyway to keep up morale. Booze, band, fancy buffet, and a private room at the Ritz-Carlton. We spent too much but that was all right."

"Okay. So what?"

"So Tuck gets shitfaced and makes a pass at my wife."

"A pass? How?"

"According to her, by grabbing her ass and trying to stick his tongue down her throat."

"Did you see it?"

"No, but I believe my wife."

Sean shifted his weight to his right foot and drilled Hilal with a skeptical look. "If you believed your wife, why the hell are you still partners with Tuck?"

Hilal looked down, obviously embarrassed. "I wanted to kick his ass and walk out the door. That's what I really wanted to do. But my wife wouldn't let me."

"*She* wouldn't let you?"

"We have four kids. My wife stays home. Like I said, everything we have is tied up in this business. I'm a minority partner. If I tried to pull out, Tuck could screw me, leave me without a penny. We couldn't survive that. We'd have lost everything. So we swallowed our pride. But I have never let my wife be in the same room with Tuck since then. And I never will. You can talk to her if you want. Call her right now. She'll tell you exactly what I just did."

"Was Pam at the Christmas party?"

Hilal looked surprised for a moment and then nodded. "Right, I see where you're going. Yeah, she was there. Dressed as Mrs. Claus if you can believe it. Bright red hair and skinny. I think some people were laughing *at* her not *with* her."

"You think she saw Tuck messing with your wife?"

"The room wasn't that big. I think a lot of people saw it, actually."

"But no visible reaction from Pam?"

"They didn't leave together, I can tell you that." Hilal paused. "Look, anything else? Because I've really got to get home."

Sean walked back to his car. The principal reasons he believed Hilal were twofold. First was "Cassandra" being the password on Tuck's computer. And second was Tuck's claim that he was having financial troubles and Hilal was trying to take advantage of that. After his meeting with Jane and Tuck, Sean had taken a much harder look at Tuck's financial records he'd found on the hard drive. The man had a stock and bond portfolio worth in excess of eight figures, and outstanding debts at less than a quarter of that amount, so his cry of poverty was total bullshit. Yet if they knew he had cracked Tuck's hard drive, they also had to know he would find that lie out. But sister and brother had still tried to snooker him. Sean put that aside and turned to the next obvious questions.

So why did you come back early, Tuck? And what were you doing for almost an hour between the airport and your house?

On the drive back to his office, he called Michelle.

She didn't answer. He left a message. He was worried about his partner. Yet he had spent much of his time worrying about her. On the surface she was the most rock-solid person he'd ever met. But he'd learned that rock had a few cracks if one poked at it deeply enough.

He drove home, packed an overnight bag, zipped to the airport, and paid an exorbitant walk-up fare to snag a flight to Jacksonville that was leaving in an hour.

He needed to talk to Cassandra Mallory. In person.

He got a phone call on his way to Washington Dulles Airport. It was his linguistics friend, Phil, from Georgetown University. "I've got someone who is familiar with the Yi language. If you want to send me a sample of what you're talking about I can let her look at it."

"I'll e-mail it to you," said Sean. When he got to Dulles he sent the sample. He walked to the security gate praying the letters on the arms would lead to something. But the more he thought about it he didn't see how that was possible. As Michelle had rightly pointed out, the sample wasn't even in Chinese.

He stared down at the picture of Cassandra Mallory that David Hilal had e-mailed him. She clearly had all the tools with which to tempt a man.

As the fifty-seat jet swept into a clear night sky,

Sean hoped this trip was not taking him in the opposite direction of where he needed to go to find Willa.

Every day that went by without the little girl being found meant it was far more likely they would discover her body instead of her.

26

Jane Cox looked out the window of the First Family's living room. Sixteen hundred Pennsylvania was in the middle of the capital city. And yet for those who called it home it might as well have been in a different solar system. There was no one on earth who could fully understand Jane's life other than the families who had inhabited this house, tying their fate to the office of the presidency. And even for some of these folks, times had indeed changed. Even as recent a president as Harry Truman could walk around town with only a single guard accompanying him. That was unthinkable now. And there had never been as much scrutiny over the smallest act, the fewest words, or the slightest gesture as there was now.

She could understand why some First Ladies had become addicted to drugs and alcohol or been clinically depressed. She stayed away from anything except the occasional glass of wine or a beer on the campaign trail when the photo op required it. Her only constant drug had been pot when she was in college and a snort of cocaine during a post-college jaunt to the Caribbean. This had thankfully gone largely unnoticed at the time and was never reported later when she had undertaken the long journey from liberated student to First Spouse.

She called Pam Dutton's sister and talked to John and Colleen, doing her best to reassure the children. She could sense their fear and wished she had more to tell them than that she was hoping and praying that Willa would soon be home. She next called her brother, who was still in the hospital for observation, though it was hoped he would be released soon. The two kids had visited him.

Jane had her dinner brought up to her by the White House staff and ate it alone. She had several invitations to dine out this evening and had declined them all. Most were from folks interested merely in pumping up their own status by breaking bread with the First Lady and snagging a cherished photo with which they could later bore their grandchildren. She would rather be by herself. Well, as alone as a home with over ninety full-time staff and too many security agents to count would allow.

She decided to take a stroll outside, accompanied, of course, by aides and the Secret Service. She sat for a while in the Children's Garden, a shady spot that was the brainchild of Lady Bird Johnson. Jane loved to look at the bronzed hand- and footprint pavers of presidential grandchildren lining the walkway. She hoped her own kids would get on the ball and start delivering some grandkids for her and Dan.

Later, she passed by the tulip beds in the Rose Garden where thousand of bulbs would bloom in the spring, giving dazzling color to the grounds. Next, she headed up to the solarium, which had been constructed from an attic room at the request of Grace Coolidge. It was the least formal room in the mansion and also, in Jane's opinion, had the best views. First Ladies had often led the charge on both enhancing the White House for future presidents and their families and also making it their own. Jane had done some of that in the last three years, though never approaching the level of work spearheaded by Jackie Kennedy.

She returned to her quarters and recalled the first day they had arrived here over three years ago. The former First Family had checked out at 10 a.m. and the Coxes had come in at 4 p.m. It was like a rental flipping. And yet when they had walked in the door, the clothes were in the closets, the pictures on the walls, the favorite snacks in the fridge, and her personal toiletries lined up on her sink. She still didn't know how they had managed it all in six hours.

Later, Jane sipped her coffee and thought about her discussion with Sean King. She could count on him. He had been a good friend, had saved her husband's political career, in fact. She knew King was peeved at her right now, but that would pass. She was more upset about her brother. For most of her life she had been taking care of him, largely because their mother had died when Jane turned eleven; Tuck was five years younger. Coddling, some might term it. She now had to face the fact that this protective instinct had done more harm than good. Yet she could hardly turn her back on him now.

Jane walked back over to the window, watching the pedestrians standing in front of the White House. *Her* house. At least for the next four years if the polls were to be believed. Yet the final decision would be rendered by over a hundred and thirty million Americans who would vote yea or nay on her husband's second term.

As she rested her cheek against the bulletproof glass, her thoughts came to rest, like an anchor at the bottom of the sea, on Willa. She was out there somewhere with people who had murdered her mother. They wanted something, only Jane didn't know what.

Jane Cox was girding herself for the possibility that Willa might not come back to their lives. To her life. That she was perhaps already dead. Jane had trained herself not to show emotion, certainly not publicly unless the political conditions on the ground required it. It wasn't that she lacked passion. But many political careers had been shipwrecked on the shoals of

erratic displays of anger or frivolity or else false
sincerity that to voters demonstrated an innate dis-
honesty. No one wanted immoral, erratic fingers
holding the nuclear codes, and the public also
frowned on the spouse of the holder of the nuclear
codes being a whack job too.

So for at least the last twenty years of her life, Jane
Cox had watched every word she said, calculated
every movement she made, diagrammed every physical, spiritual, and emotional action she ever contemplated. And the only price she had to pay for that
was to give up all hopes of actually remaining human.

The schedule she had been given tonight allowed
for a ten-minute window to call her husband, who
was at a rally and fund-raiser in Pennsylvania. She
made the call and talked the talk, congratulating him
on the latest poll numbers and his recent TV appearances where he had looked fittingly presidential.

"Everything okay with you, hon?" he said.

"Everything except Willa," she said back, in a
tone a little stronger than she probably intended.

Her husband's political skills had been deemed
first-rate, even by his opponents. Yet Dan Cox's
perception of his wife's issues and nuances had never
seemed to reach this sanctified level.

"Of course, of course," he said, as snatches of
conversations in the background filtered through to
her. "We're doing all we can. We just have to keep
our thoughts positive and our hopes high, Jane."

"I know."

"I love you," he said.

"I know," she said again. "Good luck tonight." She put the phone back down, her allotted minutes exhausted.

A half hour passed and Jane turned on CNN. She had a rule about not watching the political and news shows during an election year, but the exception to that rule was when her husband was appearing somewhere. The second banana's time onstage was over and the crowd of seventy-five thousand was just about to see the person they'd really come to hear.

President Daniel Cox strode onto the stage accompanied by an earsplitting song. Jane could remember when political appearances did not resemble rock concerts with warm-up acts, deafening music, and the crowd chanting some ridiculous slogan. It had once been more dignified and perhaps more real. No, there was no perhaps about it; it *had* used to be more genuine. Now it was all staged. Right on cue the fireworks went off as her husband stepped to the lectern and faced the twin and nearly invisible teleprompter screens. There used to be a time too, she knew, when politicians would actually wing it onstage, or simply glance down from time to time at their notes. She had read where politicians of the Revolutionary and Civil War eras could actually memorize speeches of their own making running several hundred pages long and deliver them flawlessly.

Jane knew there was not a political leader living today—including her husband—who could duplicate such a feat. However, a flub during Lincoln's time wasn't spread around the world in an instant either, like it was today. And yet as she watched her husband reading from his screens, thumping his fist against the lectern, while signs hidden from the cameras recording the event were raised and lowered instructing the crowd when to applaud, cheer, stamp their feet, and chant, a part of Jane longed for the old days. That was when she and Dan would arrive at an event alone, haul bumper stickers and lapel pins out of the trunk, give them out to the sparse crowd, and then watch as Dan simply stood in the center of the people and talked from his heart and his head, shook some hands, kissed some babies, and asked folks for their vote come election day.

Now, as president, it was like moving a small country whenever Wolfman went anywhere. It required nearly a thousand people, cargo planes, and enough communications equipment to start your own phone company and that would allow her husband to pick up his phone in any hotel room on earth and get direct U.S. phone service. Leaders of the free world could not be spontaneous. And unfortunately neither could their spouses.

She continued to watch him. Her husband was a handsome man and that never hurt in many careers, including politics. He knew how to work a crowd. He had that way, always did. He could connect with the people and find common ground with million-aires and mill workers, black or white, the serious and the silly. That's why he'd come this far. The people did love him. And they believed that he really cared about them. Which he did, Jane really believed that too. And no man ever became president without a commitment from "the other half."

She listened as he delivered his canned twenty-seven-minute stump speech. It was the economy tonight laced with support for union jobs and a plug for the steel and coal industries since he was in the Keystone state. She found herself saying the words of the speech along with him. Pausing as he did for one, two, three seconds before delivering the punch line to a joke crafted by some Ivy League speechwriter making far more than he should.

She undressed and slipped into bed. Even before she turned out the light, Jane felt the darkness closing in around her.

In the morning a White House maid would find the First Lady's pillows slightly wet from the tears shed.

27

Willa put down *Sense and Sensibility*. Not long after being brought here she'd tapped on each of the walls and detected something solid behind them. She had listened for footsteps and calculated by checking her watch that someone patrolled by every other hour. She made her own meals consisting of canned stews, eaten cold, or packaged MREs that she knew had to do with the military. They were not what she was used to but her stomach didn't care. She drank the bottled water, munched on crackers, tried to keep warm, and used the battery-powered lantern sparingly, turning it off while she rested and trying her best not to think of things coming for her in the dark.

She would listen for the man, the tall older man. She had learned to recognize his walk. She liked him better than the others who would come by with water, cans of food and clean clothes, and new batteries for her lantern. They never spoke, never made eye contact, and yet she was afraid of them.

Afraid their silence would be replaced with sudden anger.

She had tried to speak to them at first, but now she didn't. Instead, she tried to become invisible when they arrived. And she would let out a relieved breath when they locked the door behind them.

She looked at her watch. The footsteps had just come by. She had time now. Two hours free. She gripped the lantern and walked over to the door. She tapped on it lightly. Waited. Tapped. Waited.

"Hello?" she said. "Um, I think there's like a really big fire in here."

No answer.

She set the lantern down and from her pocket pulled out the pen that Quarry had given her. Or rather she pulled out the pen's *clasp*. It had the required ninety-degree-angled hook on the end. Next she took out a long piece of metal with a triangular-shaped bump on the end. She'd fashioned it from one of the canned stew tops she'd opened. She'd taken the circle of metal and painstakingly cut it in half using the heavy lantern to hold it against the table while employing the sharp edge of another can top to cut away at the metal. Then, like a rug, she'd rolled the remains of the top into a long cylinder and then hammered the end of it into the required shape.

She studied the lock, trying to mentally coax back

her lock-picking skills. Two years ago they had visited the First Family at a hundred-year-old coastal home in South Carolina that wealthy friends of the president had lent them for a two-week summer holiday. Colleen Dutton, who was then only five, had locked herself in the bathroom. The terrified girl had screamed and pounded on the old door and pulled on its antiquated lock, but to no avail. Then a Secret Service agent had come to the rescue, using a paper clip to pick the lock and setting Colleen free in under ten seconds.

Willa had held her inconsolable sister for hours after the episode. Later, she'd been worried that Colleen would accidentally lock herself in the bathroom when they got back home, so she'd asked the agent to teach her how to pick a lock. He had and had also shown her the difference between an ordinary lock and a dead bolt. Dead bolts were harder, requiring greater skill and two different tools, and that's what she was faced with here.

Hanging the lantern handle over the doorknob so her work area would be lit, Willa inserted the pen clasp, which served as her tension tool, into the bottom of the lock's opening. She turned it as if she were manipulating a key in a lock, applying enough pressure to keep the interior lock pins from falling back into place. She slid the pick tool into the upper part of the lock using her other hand. She was applying so much force that a bead of sweat appeared on her forehead despite the chill of the room. She pushed up with the pick, trying to rake the pins into their sheer alignment. Once her hand slipped and the tension tool came loose.

She reinserted it and tried again. She had practiced this many times at home, but found that she could never tell how long it would take her. She wasn't an expert and lacked the feel of the pins' touch against the pick. It could be minutes or hours. She prayed it was the former.

Willa froze as she heard footsteps coming toward her. She angled her wrist up and checked her watch. Only twenty minutes had passed. Was the man coming to see her? The old man who talked softly and yet she could sense the danger, the anger he possessed. No, it wasn't his tread. It was one of the other men. She pulled the pick and tension tool out and was starting to flee back to her cot when the footsteps receded. She waited a bit more, just to be sure.

The tools went back in and her concentration redoubled. Now she could feel the pins glancing off the pick. One by one she lifted them to the sheer line, all the while holding the tension tool so rigidly that her forearm and wrist started to ache.

The last pin fell into place and she pulled the pick out and turned the tension tool like a key. The dead bolt vanished into the door. She drew a deep breath and mouthed a prayer. Turning the lantern down to its lowest level, she listened intently and then swung the door open.

Willa waited a few moments and then slowly moved out into the darkness.

28

Sean sipped his coffee and watched the gate of the condo building through his camera's zoom lens. It was in the mid-eighties in Jacksonville and he'd taken off his jacket and thrown it on the passenger seat of his Avis rental and had the air cranked up. The parking lot of the condo building was in full view behind a fence of imposingly scrolled wrought iron.

A minute later he sat up and put the car in gear. His target had just walked out the sliding glass front doors and taken a moment to slide on her Maui Jims against the bright sun. He noted that she was loaded for bear in a pleated miniskirt, high heels, bare, tanned legs, and a tank-top blouse that showed off cleavage so deep a man could easily get lost.

She pointed her key fob, there was the ubiquitous chirp, and she climbed in her car. The combination of the low chassis of her Mercedes convertible and a sneaky breeze caused her skirt to lift enough to where the slim line of the white thong underneath was momentarily revealed along with her tanned upper thigh. She smacked a button on the console and the metal top mechanically hinged up and slid back into its receptacle.

Her car whipped through the automatic gates and sped off with the ocean gusts sending her hair straight back. The sight would've made a lovely car commercial for the Germans. Sean eased after her.

Her first two stops were dry cleaning pick up and a pharmacy run. Maybe birth control pills, thought Sean as he watched from the opposite curb.

He just had to smile though because the woman knew how to work it. Wherever she walked—and the lady definitely knew how to *walk*—men gawked. When she climbed in and out of her car, the woman seemed to do so in slow motion, displaying for an astonishingly long moment in time all the things that made men sweat at night and fantasize during the day. And when she slowed all the men seemed to slow with her. And then they would finally freeze in place until the tanned legs, perfect butt, and titillating cleavage disappeared in a Mercedes-Benz burst of power.

Her next destination, an exclusive residential neighborhood, was more promising. Sean watched her pull into the driveway of a magnificent and beautiful stucco and red tile house with palm trees out front. Using his zoom lens on the camera, Sean was able to see the person who answered the door. The gent was tall, distinguished, with thick graying hair and dressed in slacks and a polo shirt with a blue blazer.

Sean snapped several shots of them before they went into the house.

Sean noticed the mail truck working its way down the street. After it deposited the mail in the mailbox of the house, he waited until the truck had turned the corner before driving his car over to the box, flipping open the lid, and checking the mail there.

"Greg Dawson," he read off one envelope. He kept going through the stack. Another letter caught his eye. It was obviously a solicitation sent out to anyone on a database tied to a business. "Greg Dawson, Vice President, Science Matters, Ltd."

This was getting more and more interesting.

He put the mail back, drove down to the end of the street, and did a quick recon of the area. He saw an avenue of opportunity, a vacant tree-filled lot two doors down from Dawson's. He slipped out of his car and, camera in hand, walked through the vacant lot, jumped a small wall, skittered through the back-yard of the house next to Dawson's, and peered over a stucco wall separating the properties. The coast clear, he scaled the wall and dropped down at the rear of the lot and crouched behind a grouping of bushes.

The backyard was lushly and professionally land-scaped. He eyed the large pool, waterfall, and the pool house that matched the materials used on the main house. Dawson definitely had money. There was a table next to the pool. A pitcher of lemonade and two plates were laid out there. He focused his camera and waited. An Hispanic woman in a maid's uniform came out with a tray of food, laid it out, and then went back inside.

Dawson and Cassandra came out a few minutes later. Dawson held out the chair for Cassandra and they sat down to eat. Cassandra had a smile on her face as she looked around at the luxurious surroundings. Sean could easily discern the lady's thoughts. She could get used to this lifestyle real fast.

When Dawson pulled out an envelope from his jacket pocket and slid it across to Cassandra, Sean managed to get shots of this too. Dawson said something, but Sean couldn't hear over the sound of the waterfall. She opened the envelope and Sean saw the edges of cash as she slid some out. He got shots of this too.

A bit later Cassandra kicked off one of her stilettos, stretched a long leg out, and boldly planted her foot squarely in her lunch companion's crotch. The lady wasn't subtle, thought Sean. However, the man scowled at her and said something. Sean couldn't hear, but the lady looked severely put off as she hastily slipped her high heel back on.

He didn't know Dawson, but Sean applauded the guy's ability to so rebuff Cassandra, Queen of the Sluts.

After lunch, Cassandra drove back home. When she got there Sean dropped his tail and called David

Hilal. Without telling him what he'd just learned he asked about Science Matters, Ltd.

"They're one of our competitors on the contract."

"You know a Greg Dawson?"

"He's heading up the entire biodefense bid for Science. Cagey as hell and not above doing whatever it takes to nail a win. Why?"

"Just running a theory down. So you're counting on Cassandra's ties to DHS to win you the contract?"

"Well, we feel our proposal and technology is superior to Dawson's team, but having Cassandra really helps. She knows the project, the players, and the government side cold. Other things being equal, if it's a toss-up, the tie will probably go to us."

"So weren't lots of people trying to get her, like Science Matters? And they're a lot bigger than you, right?"

"Sure they are. And I know they probably offered her a lot of perks and probably more money, but Tuck was able to convince her to come with us."

Sean nodded thoughtfully. "Any idea how?"

"It's *just* an idea."

"Let me hear it."

"He might have offered her part of his equity stake in the company. I know she gets a salary because I pay the bills. But the equity part would be papered just between them."

"Even though you're a partner?"

"Like I told you, a *minority* partner. Which basically means I have to eat my gruel and ask for more, politely."

"But if Tuck and Cassandra are having an affair and it comes out?"

"It would not be good for us."

"Any reason why she might *want* the affair to come out?" asked Sean.

"I don't see why. If she does own a piece of the company it would just hurt her, right?"

"Not if she has a Plan B that pays her even more, Dave."

29

Two hours later Sean waited until a car drove through the gates of the condo building and he followed it in, the automatic gates closing behind him. He parked in a visitor's slot, grabbed the slender box off the front seat, and walked into the building's foyer.

The concierge, a wiry, balding man in a too-big blue blazer, looked up from his newspaper. "Can I help you?"

Sean patted the box. "Flower delivery for a Ms. Cassandra Mallory."

"Okay, you can leave 'em here."

"No can do. My sheet said personal delivery only. She has to sign for them."

"I can sign for them. We don't like delivery people using the elevators."

"Come on, give me a break. They barely pay me enough to cover my gas. I live on my tips. You're not going to tip me, right?"

"Those flowers ain't for me, so damn right I'm not."

"Look, I'm just a working stiff trying to make a living. I got a dozen long-stems in this box and another fifteen deliveries to make before eight tonight. I'm busting my butt for chump change."

"You look a little old to be schlepping flowers."

"I used to have my own mortgage finance business."

The man gave him a knowing look. "Oh."

"So can you just call up and tell her I'm here? If she doesn't want them, no sweat."

The man hesitated but then picked up the phone. "Ms. Mallory. It's Carl at concierge. Look, I got a flower delivery for you here."

He paused. "Uh, I don't know. Hang on a sec." He looked at Sean. "Who are they from?"

Sean riffled in his shirt pocket and consulted a blank piece of paper. "A Greg Dawson."

Carl repeated this into the phone. "Right, okay, you're the boss."

He hung up and looked at Sean. "Your lucky day. She's in Unit 756. Elevator's over there."

"Super. Hope she's a good tipper."

"You're a good looking guy, so if you're really lucky she might *tip* you something else."

Sean feigned puzzlement before saying, "What, are you saying she's a babe?"

"Let me put it this way, friend, when she saunters across the lobby I feel like I'm in a *Playboy* fantasy. Only reason I keep this crummy job."

Sean rode the glass elevator up, staring out at an incredible view of the coastline. Cassandra must've been waiting by the door because it opened only a second after he knocked. She was barefoot and wearing a terrycloth robe that stopped mid-thigh. Her hair was damp; she might have gone for a swim or taken a shower.

"Flowers?" she said.

"Right, from a Mr. Dawson."

"I have to say I'm surprised."

Sean gave her the once-over. "Ma'am, you strike me as someone who gets lots of flowers from gentlemen."

She flashed him a smile. "You're sweet."

"Just need you to sign here." He held out his pad and a pen. While she signed, he opened the box. Inside were twelve long-stem roses that he'd bought from a street vendor for four bucks.

She held one and smelled it. "They're beautiful."

"You have a vase to put them in? Good to get water on them right away."

She glanced up at him and her smile deepened. As she ran her gaze over his lean six-foot-two-inch frame and handsome face, she said in a throaty voice that made Sean feel suddenly unclean, "What's your name?"

"Sean."

"I haven't seen you around before, *Sean*."

"I haven't been around before. My loss, I guess."

"Why don't you bring the flowers in while I look for a vase?"

As she turned she managed to slide her breasts across his forearm. It was done so well that Sean could only conclude the lady had perfected the motion over the years. He followed her in and closed the door behind them, the lock automatically clicking into place.

The condo was a luxury one and Sean noted details of great expense everywhere. The lady also had good taste in art, furniture, and oriental rugs. She reached the kitchen, opened a cabinet, and bent over. The view this presented to Sean actually made him blush. A pair of tiny black panties had replaced the white thong, but the rest was all Cassandra.

Still bent over she turned, obviously to make sure he was watching. As her gaze followed his she feigned being startled. "Oh, I'm sorry."

He managed a grin. "I'm not. The female body is beautiful, why hide it?"

She smiled back. "I like your attitude."

She took so long retrieving the vase he could have identified her dead body by her butt cheeks alone. She finally straightened up and turned to him.

And stopped smiling.

She stared at his camera screen, at the shot of Greg Dawson handing her the envelope.

"What is this? Who the hell are you?"

Sean sat down on one of the barstools set next to the granite kitchen counter.

"Where did you get that picture?" she said accusingly.

"First go get some clothes on. Your striptease act is wearing kind of thin on me."

She scowled at him. "Why the hell shouldn't I just call the police?"

In answer he held up the camera again. "Because then this fab shot of you and Greggie boy will get sent to DHS. And unless you can explain to them why a man who runs the company that's *competing* with Tuck Dutton's firm is handing you an envelope at a nice cozy lunch at his house, Science Matters can kiss that fat contract goodbye. Am I right or am I right, *Cassandra*? Now go get some clothes on!"

She stalked off to change. When she came back she was covered up in a mauve-colored velour warm-up suit.

He nodded at her approvingly. "Much better. Now I can actually treat you like an adult." He sat down on the sofa in the living room that had impressive water views. She sat across from him and tucked her bare feet under her.

"So I take it the flowers *weren't* from Greg?" she said with attitude.

"Nope. His blowing you off at lunch was entirely

legit. Maybe he's used to chicks like you and knows better."

"So who exactly are you and what do you want?" she said. "Because the sooner you get out of here the better."

"One ground rule, you're not asking the questions, I am."

"Why—"

He held up the photo and she quickly closed her mouth.

"I know about you and Tuck Dutton."

She rolled her eyes. "Is that what this is about? Please."

"You were having an affair with him."

"Prove it."

"I actually don't have to. I can leave that to the FBI."

"FBI? What the hell are you talking about?"

"Tuck's wife was murdered and his oldest daughter kidnapped. You telling me you didn't know that?"

"Of course I knew about it. It's been in all the papers. His sister is the First Lady."

"You like screwing the First Brother-in-law?"

"Go to hell."

"That's something you should be worried about, actually."

"What is that supposed to mean exactly?" she said in a false bored tone.

"It means *exactly* that the oldest motivation in the book for a philandering husband to bump off his wife is so he can marry the mistress."

"It wasn't like that with me and Tuck."

"So what was it like? You can either tell me or the FBI. And the agent running the case isn't nearly as nice as I am."

"He was attracted to me."

"Yeah, that I know. But if you did the little bend and hold you just pulled with me, I can hardly blame the guy. Well, I can blame him, actually, because he's obviously a weak little bastard. So why'd you come to work for him when I'm sure you got better offers elsewhere from bigger companies?"

"You seem to know a lot about me."

"I've always been a curious guy. You were saying?"

"He said he'd be really good to me if we got the contract."

"So not just salary, a piece of the equity?"

"Something like that."

"I'm not interested in 'something like that.' I want facts."

"Twenty percent of the contract profit," she said hastily. "Over and above my salary and bonus."

"But then you did get a better offer, although it was after you signed with Tuck."

"I don't know what you mean," she said hesitantly.

"Sure you do. You have a fling with Tuck. Dawson has his ear to the ground and finds out, or maybe he put you up to it, who knows. But now he has the proof to take to DHS. Banging the president's brother-in-law. They find out, Dawson wins the contract and you get a backdoor payoff. Maybe part of it was in that envelope he gave you today." He held up the camera. "Only now I have the proof about you and Greggie to give to DHS and crater your dream. Interesting development, wouldn't you say? And why a cash payoff?"

"Greg said they can track any funds these days. Electronic, Swiss bank accounts, anything. The cash was sort of a down payment."

"Okay."

"Look, maybe we can cut some kind of deal."

"I'm not looking for cash in an envelope."

"Deals don't have to always be about money." She glanced at him anxiously. "I know you think I'm probably a slut, but I'm really not. We could have a lot of fun together. I mean a lot."

"Thanks, but I'm not really into women who show their ass to every delivery guy who knocks on their door. And not to be too blunt but when was the last time you were checked for an STD?"

She moved to slap him but he caught her by the wrist.

"You can't sleep your way out of this one, lady. This is not about some lousy government contract and screwing your way to the nice condo life on the water. Unless you cooperate with me you're looking at being a clear accessory on a murder-kidnapping charge. In Virginia, where it took place, that's a capital offense. And death by lethal injection may be painless but you still end up really dead."

The tears started to flow now from Cassandra. "I had nothing to do with any of that, I swear to God."

Sean pulled out a digital recorder and set it on the coffee table.

"Sit."

She sat.

"Here's the deal. Unless you tell me the absolute truth, and I know enough about it that if you try to screw with me even a little, this all gets turned over to the Feds ASAP, got it?"

She nodded, brushing tears from her eyes.

"Great." Sean turned on the device and said, "On the day before his wife was killed, Tuck was here with you. He stayed at your condo, is that correct?"

She nodded.

"I need to hear you."

"Yes, he was here."

"He'd spent the night before, hadn't he?"

"Yes."

"And you two were having an affair?"

"Yes."

"Did his wife know?"

"I don't know. Tuck didn't seem to think so."

"Tuck hired you because of your former job at DHS. He thought that would give him an inside track on winning a big contract from Homeland Security, correct?"

"Yes."

"And you're now double-crossing him with Greg Dawson and Science Matters?"

Cassandra hesitated. Sean reached for the recorder. "Okay, have it your way."

"Wait. Yes. I'm working with Greg Dawson behind Tuck's back. He was having us followed. He found out about the affair. He came to me and offered a better deal. I took it."

"Tuck Dutton was supposed to come back to Virginia on the day after his family was attacked. But he came back early. Do you know why?"

"We . . . we had a disagreement."

"About what?"

"I . . . I think he suspected something was going on."

"With Dawson and you?"

She looked surprised. "No. It was the opposite of that."

Sean looked puzzled. "The opposite?"

"He thought his *wife* was having an affair. I told him I thought he was being stupid. I said what were the odds that he *and* his wife would be screwing around at the same time? I guess that was sort of tactless, but men are such little boys when it comes to adultery. Okay, so you messed around. It's not that big of a deal. So get over it."

"But he didn't get over it."

"No. I actually thought he was going to hit me. He said he loved his wife. And here we're sitting naked on my bed after screwing each other's brains out. And I said something dumb like, 'Well, you have a funny way of showing it.' Then he yelled at me, grabbed his stuff, and left."

"Did he say why he thought his wife was having an affair?"

"He mentioned something about some phone calls he'd overheard. And he said one time that he followed Pam and she had coffee with some man he didn't know."

Sean sat back against the cushions. That was one angle he'd never considered. "Did he describe what the guy looked like?"

"No. He never did."

"There was about an hour unaccounted for between the time Tuck should've been home and when he actually got there. I'm talking around 9:30 to about 11:00 that night. Did he call you during that time?"

"No, I haven't heard a word from him since he bolted out of here."

Sean looked skeptically at her. "I need the absolute truth, Cassandra."

"I swear. Check my phone records. I went to bed and didn't talk to anybody."

Sean switched off the recorder. "If I need to talk to you again, I better be able to find you."

"Are you going to let this all come out?"

"No. At least not yet. But piece of advice. Tell Greggie to back off the contract."

"He's going to be really upset. He's already paid me a lot of money."

"That's your problem. Why don't you try the old bend and hold, since Greg just doesn't seem to be a foot-in-the-crotch kind of guy."

Sean was on a flight back to D.C. that night. He'd discovered a lot. The only trouble was he now had more questions than before.

30

Willa stayed close to the rock wall as she flitted along the corridor, her fingers scraping over the uneven surface. She listened for any sound, watching for any glow of light. She had her own lantern turned down so low that she could barely see. It was cold, and mists of her breath trailed the young girl down the dark path. She turned a corner and stopped.

Was that someone coming? She turned off the light and flattened herself against the rock. Five minutes later she started moving again. This time she kept the light off. Her hand grazed across wood and then hit the metal. She halted, turned the light on to its lowest level. It revealed the metal lock.

Just like the one on my door.

She found enough courage to lift her hand and tap lightly on the wood. No answer. She tapped again, a bit harder.

"Who is it?" a quavering voice said from the other side.

Willa looked around and then placed her face against the door and whispered, "Are you locked in?"

She heard footsteps and then the voice said, "Who are you?"

"My name is Willa. I was locked in too but got out. I think I can get you out too. What's your name?"

"Diane," she whispered back.

"Do you know why you're here?"

"No."

"Me either. Hold on."

Willa pulled out her pen clasp and rolled-up can top and went to work. It was more difficult than the first time because she had to keep the light turned down so low. While she concentrated on feeling for the lock pins to drop to the sheathing line, she was also listening for the sounds of someone coming.

The pins finally fell into place; Willa turned the tension tool and the door swung open. Diane Wohl looked down at her. "You're only a child."

"I'm nearly a teenager," Willa said firmly "And I managed to get out of my room. And get *you* out of yours. Come on."

As they headed off Diane looked around. "Where are we?"

"You really need to keep your voice down," whispered Willa. "Sound really carries in places like this."

"Places like what?" the woman said in a lower voice.

Willa touched the side of the wall. "I think we're in a tunnel or old mine."

Diane hissed, "Oh my God, if we're in an old mine it could come down on our heads at any second."

"I don't think so. The support beams look really sturdy. And the men who are keeping us here wouldn't have brought us to an unsafe place."

"Why not?"

"Because they might get hurt too."

"Do you know which way is out?"

"I'm just, you know, trying to feel some air movement."

"But if we keep going, we'll get lost. Maybe forever."

"No we won't." She shone the light on the dirt floor. "I cut up the paper labels off the canned food. I've been dropping pieces every ten feet or so. That way we'll know where we came from in case we have to turn back."

They kept going forward, around one turn and then another.

Willa checked her watch by lantern light. "We have about twenty minutes left before they come by again. But the other man might show up. He's unpredictable."

"The tall man with the white hair?"

"Yeah. He doesn't seem as bad as the others, but I'm still afraid of him."

"I'm terrified of them all."

"Where do you live?"

"In Georgia."

"I'm from Virginia. I hope my family's okay. The man said he contacted them and told them I was okay. Do you have a family?"

"No, I don't," Diane said quickly. "I mean, not of my own. But I asked him to contact my mother and tell her I was okay. But I don't know if I'm going to *stay* okay."

"Another good reason for us to get ourselves out of here," answered Willa.

"What was that?" Diane said sharply.

There had been a shout somewhere behind them.

"I think they found out we're not there," said Willa. At that instant she felt a bit of air current on her cheek. She grabbed Diane's hand. "This way."

They hurried down the passage.

"Look!" Willa said.

The corridor ended in a thick door.

Diane tried to turn the old door handle but it wouldn't budge.

Willa already had out her tools. While Diane held the light she inserted the instruments and worked quickly but methodically.

"How'd you learn to do this?"

"It comes in handy if your little sister keeps locking herself in the bathroom," said Willa as she pushed and prodded with her pick, praying for the pins to fall into their correct slots.

Diane looked down the passage. "They're coming. Oh my God, I think they're coming. Hurry. Hurry!"

"If I rush, it won't work, okay?" Willa said calmly.

"If you don't they'll catch us."

The last pin dropped, and Willa turned the tension tool and with Diane's help they pushed the stout wooden door open. The light bursting through caused them both to shield their eyes. They rushed out and looked around, squinting.

Then the pounding of footsteps hit them harder than the sunlight had.

"Come on," Diane yelled.

She grabbed Willa's hand and they ran toward the flat land straight ahead even as the little plane touched down.

Diane said, "Who do you think that is?"

Willa looked around, noting that the only way in or out looked to be by plane. "Not anyone we want to run into. This way, quick."

They changed direction and ducked behind a chunk of rock just as Daryl and Carlos erupted from the mineshaft and sprinted off in different directions. Willa and Diane crawled and clawed their way up the narrow, steep ridge, keeping as low as possible.

"Maybe we can get to the top and then go down the other side," gasped Willa.

Diane was breathing so hard she couldn't answer

back. She grabbed hold of Willa. "I just need to catch my breath. I've never been much into exercise."

A minute later they started their ascent again. They got to the top of the ridge, crossed it, and then looked over the edge on the other side.

"God help us," said Diane. It was steep and nearly sheer. "I can't make it down there."

"Well, I'm going to try," said Willa. "Do you think you can find a place to hide? If I get away I'll bring help."

Diane looked around. "I think I can." She looked over the edge again. "Willa, you'll get killed. You can't go."

"I *have* to try."

She gripped the edge of a boulder, aimed her foot at a narrow ledge, and took a step down. The ledge held though a few pebbles and dirt, disrupted by her maneuver, slid off the mountain and cascaded downward where they were caught by the swirling wind.

"Please be careful," said Diane.

"I'm trying," said Willa breathlessly. "It's really hard."

She lowered herself to another ledge and was just about to attempt another movement when the rock she was standing on gave way.

"Willa!" screamed Diane.

Willa grabbed at anything she could find to halt her fall, but nothing she touched held as dirt and rock pelted her.

231

"Help me!"

Diane was knocked to the side as the man raced past her, his long arm reaching out and snagging Willa by the wrist a second before she would have been lost.

Willa found herself being hauled up like a fish from the sea and then plopped down on a flat rock. She glanced up.

Sam Quarry did not look happy at all.

31

Michelle stared at her mother's body. The autopsy was complete and while there were some toxicology and other test results still pending, the conclusion was that Sally Maxwell had not died from natural causes. She had died from a blow to the head.

Michelle had spoken directly to the county medical examiner. Her brother being a sergeant on the police force had allowed access where otherwise there would have been none. The family of a homicide victim traditionally was only given words of official comfort and time alone with their dead, not facts. The reason for this was simple if disquieting: Family members often murdered each other.

The ME had been terse but unmistakable. "Your mother didn't fall down and hit her head. The wound was too deep. The smooth cement floor couldn't have done it, and there was no trace on the car handle or the stair railing. And those edges didn't match up with the wound shape in any case."

"What exactly was the wound shape?"

"I shouldn't be talking to you about this, you know," he said crossly.

"Please, it was my mom. Any help you can give me that doesn't break any rules you can't live without would be appreciated." This simple plea seemed to strike a chord with the man.

"It was an unusual shape. About ten centimeters long and a little over one centimeter wide. If I had to guess, it was metal. But it had an unusual line to it. Very odd footprint."

"So someone definitely killed her?"

The ME had looked down his progressive lenses at Michelle. "I've been doing this for thirty years and I have yet to see someone kill themselves with a blunt instrument strike to the head and then, after death, hide the weapon so well the police couldn't find it."

Her mother's body had been released by the ME's office and sent to the local funeral home. Michelle had come here to see her mother before the woman's remains were prepared for viewing. There was a sheet draped over her up to her neck, thankfully covering up the Y-incision the medical examiner had sawn into her.

None of Michelle's brothers had wanted to accompany her here. As police officers they all knew what a dead body looked like after an autopsy and particularly forty-eight hours after death. The phrase about "beauty being only skin deep" had never seemed more apt. No, her "tough" brothers would wait until after the preservation agent had been pumped into their mother's body, her hair done, her face caked with makeup, her clothes nicely arranged to obscure the assault of the postmortem, and her body placed in the three-thousand-dollar casket for all to see.

Michelle did not want to remember her mother this way, but she had to come here. She had to see the brutal effects that the work of someone had done on the woman who over three decades ago had given birth to her. She was tempted to angle her mother's head around, to look at the wound site for herself, but she resisted this impulse. It would be disrespectful, and if the ME couldn't figure out the weapon used there was little hope that Michelle could.

She imagined her mother's last moments. Had she seen her killer? Had she known him or her? Did she know the reason she'd been struck down? Had she felt any pain?

And the last and most crushing thought of all.

Had her father killed her mother?

She took her mom's hand and stroked it. She said things to the dead woman that she had never managed to say while Sally had been alive. It left Michelle feeling emptier than before. And lately her depressions had often run cavern-deep.

Five minutes later she was out in the fresh air, sucking in as much oxygen as she could. The drive home was lost in memories of her mother. When she pulled into the driveway of their house, Michelle just sat there for a bit trying to compose herself.

Her father had made dinner. Michelle sat down to eat with him. Her brothers had gone out together to do some bonding, she supposed, while also giving their kid sister time alone with the old man.

"Good soup," she said.

Frank spooned a bit of chicken and broth into his mouth. "Made it from scratch. I've been doing more and more of the cooking over the years." He added with a bit of resentment, "You wouldn't know that, of course."

She leaned back, broke off a bit of a roll, and chewed it slowly, thinking of how to respond to this. On one level there was no response. She *hadn't* been around. She *wouldn't* have known about that. On another level she wondered why he would be throwing a guilt trip on her right now.

"Mom kept busy too?"

"She had her friends. Your mother was always more social than me. I guess it was the job. Had to keep a certain distance. She never had that impediment."

And bitterness?

"Never knew when one of your buddies might break the law?" Even as she was saying the words, Michelle wished she had hauled them back into her mouth before they'd gained traction outside her head.

He took a long moment before answering. "Something like that."

"Anybody in particular? Friends, I mean?"

"Girlfriends," he said. "Rhonda, Nancy, Emily, Donna."

"So what'd they do?"

"Played cards. Shopped. Lots of golf. Lunch. Gossip. The things retired ladies do."

"You never joined them?"

"On occasion I did. But it was more a girl's thing."

"Who was she going to see that night?"

Again, he took another long moment to answer. If she were a gambler, Michelle would've wagered her father was about to tell her a lie.

"Donna, at least I think. Dinner, I believe she said. I can't be sure. Just said it in passing."

"Donna have a last name?"

This time there was no long moment. "Why?" he shot back.

"Why what?"

"Why do you want to know Donna's last name?"

"Well, has anyone called her and told her that the reason Mom didn't make it was because she was dead?"

"I don't care for your tone, little girl."

"Dad, I haven't been a *little girl* for over twenty years."

He put down his spoon. "I called her. Okay? It's not that big of a town anyway. She'd already heard."

"So it *was* Donna that Mom was going to see?"

For an instant he looked confused, unsure of himself. "What? Yes, I think it was."

Michelle felt a wrenching pain in her chest. She rose, made a mindless excuse, and left the house. Outside, she phoned the only person she had ever allowed herself to really trust.

Sean King had just landed at Washington Dulles.

"I need you," she said, after filling him in on what had happened.

Sean went in search of a flight to Nashville.

32

"You could've killed yourself," snapped Quarry as he sat across from Willa back in her "cell."

"I'm a prisoner here and prisoners have to try and escape," she said right back to him. "It's their job. Like *everybody* knows that."

Quarry drummed his long, thick fingers on the tabletop. He'd confiscated Willa's lock-picking tools and removed all the canned food too. He'd also had Daryl and Carlos install additional security on the door.

"Who's Diane?" Willa asked.

"A lady," Quarry said gruffly.

"That I already know. Why is she here?"

"None of your business."

He rose to leave.

"Thank you, by the way."

Quarry turned looking surprised. "For what?"

"You saved my life. But for you, I'd be at the bottom of that mountain."

"You're welcome. But don't try anything like that again."

"Can I see Diane again?"

"Maybe."

"When?"

"I don't know."

"Why don't you know? It's a pretty simple request."

"Why do you ask so many questions when I'm not answering any of them?" Quarry said, evidently both frustrated and intrigued by the girl's tenacity.

"Because I keep hoping that sometime you will start answering them," she said brightly.

"You're not like any little girl I ever met before. I take that back. You do remind me of somebody."

"Who?"

"Just somebody."

He locked the door behind him and slid the thick board into place on the outside of the room. Even if Willa somehow managed to pick the lock once more, she would not be able to swing open the door.

As he walked along he pulled the pieces of paper out of his pocket. These papers were the reason he had flown here today. He reached the door and knocked.

Diane's tremulous voice said, "Who is it?"

"I need to talk to you," he called through the door. "Are you decent? Cleaned up after your little trip outside?"

"Yes."

He unlocked the door and walked in.

Like Willa's they'd set the space up with a cot, small table, a lantern, portable toilet, water and soap for bathing, canned food and water, and some clothes. Diane had exchanged the dirty clothes she had been wearing when trying to escape with another pair of slacks and a white blouse.

Quarry closed the door behind him. "I just talked to Willa."

"Please don't hurt her for what she did."

"I'm not planning on hurting her." He added in a grim tone, "Unless you two pull something like that again. There's no way out of here even if you do get out of the mine."

"Why are you doing this?"

He sat down at the table and held up the pieces of paper. "This is why." He nodded to the only other chair in the room. "You want to sit down?"

"I want to go home."

"You need to look at this."

Gathering her courage, Wohl moved forward slightly. "If I do will you let me go?" Her voice was pleading, her eyes filling with tears. It was as though she desperately wanted to hear something from him that would allow for her eventual freedom.

"Well, I'm not going to keep you here much longer, that's for sure."

"Why did you bring me here? And Willa?"

"I needed you both," Quarry said simply. "None of what I need to do was gonna happen without you." He held up the papers. "I sent the blood I took from you in to a place that ran a bunch of tests on it. DNA tests. I could've just done a swab from inside your cheek but my reading on the subject made me believe working with the blood was just as good if not better. I didn't want any mistakes."

"DNA?"

"Yeah. Like fingerprints, only better. They use it all the time to get folks off Death Row that're innocent."

"I've committed no crimes."

"Never said you did." He looked at the pieces of paper, silently reading off the results again. "But you did give birth to a little girl twelve years ago. Gave birth but then you gave her up. Did you enjoy seeing her again today?"

The blood drained from Diane's face. "What are you talking about?"

"Willa is your daughter. Willa Dutton she's called now. She just celebrated her twelfth birthday. Her mom's name is Pam Dutton. Her adoptive mom, I mean. I had Mrs. Dutton's blood checked too just in case yours didn't match. But it did. And so did Willa's. You are, without no doubt at all, her ma."

"That's impossible," she said dully, her voice barely able to form the words.

"You got pregnant, had the baby, and then the Duttons adopted it." He waved the papers in the air. "DNA don't lie, lady."

"Why are you doing this?" she said, her voice low, but panicky.

"I got my reasons." He stood. "Would you like to see your daughter again?"

Wohl put a hand against the tabletop to steady herself. "What?" she gasped.

"I know you two just got acquainted, but I thought you might want to see her again now that you know."

She glanced at the papers. "I don't believe you."

He handed the pages across to her. "I had them put it in language folks like me could understand. The top batch test is Willa's. The one under that is yours. Read the result line."

She took the papers and read them slowly. "Ninety-nine point nine percent match for mother and child," she said dully.

She threw the papers down and screamed, "Who are you!"

"It's a long story and not one I'm willing to share with you. Do you want to see the girl or not?"

Wohl was already shaking her head, whipping it back and forth.

Quarry looked down at her with a curious mixture of sympathy and disgust. "You coulda kept the child. Guess I kind of understand why you didn't. But that doesn't mean I agree with it. Children are precious. Got to hang on to 'em. I learned that lesson the hard damn way."

Wohl straightened up. "I don't know who you are or what you want, but you have no right to judge me."

"If I were the judgmental type, maybe you'd already be dead."

This remark caused Wohl to drop to her knees, curl into a tight ball, and start sobbing.

Quarry bent down, picked up the DNA reports where she'd dropped them, and stood there watching her. "Last chance to see the girl," he finally said.

A minute passed. Finally, Wohl said, "Does . . . does she have to see me?"

"Ma'am, you two already met."

"But I didn't know she was my daughter," Wohl shot back. Then she added calmly, "I didn't know . . . I was her mother."

"Okay, I can see that."

Diane had a sudden thought. "Oh my God, does she know I'm her mother?"

"No. I saw no reason to tell her. 'Cause you're not the one who raised the girl."

"Do you know this Pam Dutton?"

"Never met her."

"But do you know if she's been good to Willa?"

"You telling me you didn't know the woman before you gave your daughter to her?"

"It wasn't that way. I really didn't have a choice."

"Everyone has a choice."

"So can I see her without her seeing me?"

"I got a way. If you're willing."

Wohl rose on unsteady legs. "I'd like to see her." Somehow this admission came out as a guilty confession.

"Give me a couple minutes."

Diane rushed forward and clutched at his arm. "You're not going to do anything that will hurt her?"

Quarry slowly removed the woman's fingers from his sleeve. "I'll be back shortly."

Five minutes later he returned and held the door open for her. She looked at it fearfully, as though if she walked through it she would never be coming back.

Sensing this Quarry said, "I give you my word, I'll take you to see the girl and then I'll bring you back here."

"Then what?"

"Then we'll just have to see. Can't promise you any more than that."

33

Quarry removed the board from metal hooks driven deep into the wall, opened the door, and motioned Wohl inside.

"Where is she?"

He pointed to his left. "Over there."

Wohl spun around and stared at a small lump under the blanket on a cot against one wall. Quarry lifted off the blanket. Underneath Willa lay there, sleeping.

Wohl crept closer. "What if she wakes up?"

"I gave her something to knock her out. Good hour or so. She looks like you," said Quarry quietly. "In the nose, the chin. You can't see her eyes, but they're the same color as yours."

Wohl involuntarily nodded. She could see the resemblance too. "Willa Dutton. That's a pretty name."

"You didn't name her?"

"No. I knew I was giving her up so I didn't . . . I mean I couldn't."

Wohl stroked the girl's dark hair. She looked back at Quarry. "You're not going to hurt her."

"She's not the one at fault here. Neither are you, really."

"But you said before—"

"There are degrees of guilt."

"So who . . ."

"Did you want to give her up?"

"I said I didn't have a choice."

"And like I told you before, folks always have a choice."

"Can I hold her?"

"Go on."

Wohl put her arms around Willa's shoulders. She touched her face, nestled her cheek against the girl's, and finally gave her a kiss on the forehead.

"What do you remember about the adoption?"

"Not much. I was only twenty."

"And the daddy?"

"None of your business."

"So you just gave her up?"

"Yes." She gazed at him. "I had no money. I was still in college. I couldn't care for her."

"So they took her off your hands. And your life turned out okay," said Quarry. "You finished college, got a good job. Married, but then got divorced. Never had any more children."

"How do you know all this about me?"

"I'm not a real smart man. But I work hard. And I needed to know about you. So I did."

"And what are you doing all this for?"

"None of *your* business."

Wohl turned back to Willa when the girl started moaning a little bit.

"Is she waking up?" she asked fearfully.

"Just dreaming in her sleep. But let's head on back."

After returning to her room Wohl said, "How much longer will I be kept here?"

"If I had an answer to that I'd give it to you, but I don't."

"And Willa?"

"The same."

"You said Pam was her adopted mother's name?"

"That's right."

"She must be terribly worried."

"I don't think so," said Quarry.

"Why not?"

"Because she's dead."

34

Sean was able to grab a flight to Nashville that night. Michelle picked him up from the airport. On the drive to her father's house he filled Michelle in on what he'd discovered about Tuck and Cassandra Mallory.

"She sounds like someone whose *ass* I would really love to kick," she snapped.

"Well, you sure wouldn't have any trouble finding it. The lady tends to put it right out there."

"So who was the man who was meeting with Pam? The one Tuck thought was having an affair with her?"

"I haven't had a chance to follow that up."

After they rode in silence for a few seconds he said, "You really think your father killed your mother?"

"I don't know what to think. I only know that someone killed her and he's acting like the prime suspect."

"Do the cops share your suspicions?"

"He's a former police chief and my brother Bobby is on the force here. They tend to cover their own."

"But if the evidence points in one direction, they'll have to act."

"I know that," she said tensely.

"Have you talked to this Donna person? The one your mom was supposed to be meeting for dinner?"

"Not yet. I was hoping you and I could do it together."

He gripped her shoulder. "I know this is hard, Michelle. But we'll get through it."

"I know you've got your hands full with the Dutton case. I mean the First Lady and all. I feel sort of guilty pulling you into this."

He smiled reassuringly. "I'm a great multitasker. You should know that by now."

"I still appreciate it."

"Have they canvassed the neighborhood? Anyone see anything?"

"There was a pool party going on next door. A sweet sixteen for the homeowner's granddaughter. Cars parked all the way up the street. Lot of noise. Music. But no eyewitnesses to anything."

"Maybe something will pop on that end," he said encouragingly.

The Maxwell house was full, so Michelle had gotten Sean a room at a local hotel. He dropped his bag in his room and they drove over to the house. Sean expressed his condolences to everyone and then Michelle led him out into the backyard, where they could talk.

"The funeral's tomorrow," she said.

"Your brothers seem to be wondering what I'm doing here."

"Let them wonder."

"Do they suspect their father?"

"Even if they did, they would never acknowledge it."

"And yet you have no trouble doing so."

"Whose side are you on?"

"Yours, always. How do you want to start digging?"

"I snitched my mother's address book. A Donna Rothwell is listed in there. She's the only Donna, so she must be the one. I know it's very late but I thought we could call her and meet with her."

"On what pretext?"

"My wanting to know who my mother's friends were? Stories she could tell me. Quaint memories that might just lead me to a murderer."

"And if that person turns out to be your father?"

"I don't make exceptions to that rule. If he's the one, so be it."

Donna Rothwell agreed to meet with them despite the late hour. She was in her early sixties, about five-five, with a compact, athletic build. She had meticulously styled hair and carefully applied makeup. She exuded considerable warmth and even vivaciousness. Her home was about four miles from the Maxwells'. It was large, richly furnished, and immaculate; a woman in full maid's uniform had answered the door.

The lady definitely had money, and from the many photos and mementos arrayed on shelves and tables, it was clear that she had traveled the world in high style.

She explained, "My late husband, Marty, was CEO of a large computer company and cashed out early. We lived a good life together."

"Your husband passed on?" Sean asked.

"Years ago. His heart."

"Never remarried?"

"Marty and I were college sweethearts. Doubt I'd get anything that good again, so why take a chance? But I date. Going steady right now, in fact. Sounds like high school, I know, but things come full circle if you live long enough."

"So you and my mom were close?"

"We did lots of things together. She was fun, your mom. I know this is all so horribly sad and depressing, but I want you to know that your mother knew how to have a good time."

"And my dad?"

Donna picked up her cocktail and sipped from it before answering. "He didn't get out as much. He liked to read, or so Sally told me. More reserved. He was a policeman, right? Seen the bad side of life for so many years. It probably does something to you, or at least that was my conclusion. Maybe causes you to be unable to have fun. I don't know. I'm just speculating here," she added quickly, probably noting the souring look on Michelle's face. "Your dad is a nice man. Very handsome. Lot of women around here thought your mom was very lucky."

"I'm sure. So Mom was coming to see you the night she died?"

Donna put down her cocktail. "Who told you that?"

"Does it matter?"

"I guess not."

"So was she?"

"We had talked about it, sure." She paused, seeming to gather her thoughts. "I actually think we were going to do something. Dinner, maybe a movie. We did that about once a week."

"It wasn't all that long ago. Can't you remember for sure?" Sean said politely. "I mean, the police will want to know for certain."

Donna picked her drink back up. "Police!"

"My mother's death is a homicide, Donna. The police are investigating."

"I thought she had a heart attack or hit her head or something."

"That's not how it happened."

"So what did happen?"

When neither of them said anything, Donna exclaimed, "Are you telling me she was murdered?"

"Why would you think that?" asked Michelle.

"Because if her heart didn't stop and she didn't hit her head and the police are investigating, what else is there?"

"What can you tell me about my mom's life here? Other people she knew? Things she did?"

Donna was staring off, her mouth moving but nothing coming out. Finally she said, "If there's a killer loose . . ."

"Nobody said that was the case. Now, getting back to my mom."

Donna gulped down the rest of her drink and said hurriedly, "She had a lot of friends. All female as far as I knew. We did things together. Had fun. That was it."

"Can I have their names?"

"Why?"

"Because I want to talk to them like I'm talking to you."

"Are you investigating this?" She eyed Michelle nervously. "Sally told me you used to be with the Secret Service. And that you're a private investigator now."

"That's true. But all I am right now is a daughter who's lost her mother. Can I have those names?"

Donna gave them to her along with addresses and contact information.

As they drove off, Michelle's phone rang. She answered, listened, and then clicked off. "Shit!"

"What is it?"

"That was my brother Bill. The cops just picked up my dad for questioning."

35

They drove with Bill Maxwell to the police station but despite Bobby's connection to the force they learned very little and ended up waiting in the lobby drinking bad vending machine coffee. Two hours before dawn Frank Maxwell, looking pale and worn, shuffled down the hall. He seemed surprised to see them.

Bill immediately put a hand around his father's shoulders. "You okay, Pop? I can't believe they pulled this crap."

"They were just doing their job, Billy. Just like you'd do."

"What did they want?" Michelle asked.

"The usual wheres, whats, whys," Frank said casually without looking directly at her.

"What did you tell them?" she said.

Now he gave her a hard stare. "The truth."

Michelle drew closer to her father. "Which was?"

Bill stepped between them and put a hand on his sister's shoulder. "Will you just back off? Mom's funeral is this afternoon, for God's sake."

"I know that," Michelle shot back, tugging his hand free. "What did you tell them, Dad?"

"That's between them and me. And my lawyer."

"Your lawyer?" gasped Bill.

"I'm being investigated. I need a lawyer."

"But you didn't do anything."

"Don't be stupid, Billy. Innocent men have gone to jail before, you and I both know that. I'm entitled to counsel like everybody else."

They drove home together, Frank and Bill Maxwell in the back. Neither of them said a word the whole way.

Later, as Sean was leaving the Maxwells' house to go to his hotel, he told Michelle, "Why don't you watch your dad and I'll take the list of friends and try to hit some before the funeral?"

"No, I'll go with you. We can do it afterwards."

"But your family—"

"He's got my four brothers. I doubt he'll even miss me. It might be a good thing since we're not exactly hitting it off."

"Okay, I'm going to grab a few hours' sleep."

"Me too," she said.

Back at his hotel Sean raided the minibar, slept for four hours, then made some phone calls. Tuck Dutton had been discharged from the hospital. He called Pam Dutton's sister in Bethesda. Tuck had come and gotten his two kids and gone to a rental house, she told him. Sean had Tuck's cell phone number so he tried that.

Someone picked up on the second ring.

It wasn't Tuck.

"Jane?"

"Hello, Sean."

"I heard Tuck moved to a rental with the kids."

"He did, I'm helping them all settle in."

"Where is the place?"

"In Virginia. It's a townhouse near the Vienna metro. The FBI uses it sometimes to put up visiting agents. The Secret Service is here as well, of course."

"How're Tuck and the kids?"

"Not great. Have you made any progress?"

"Yes, can you put Tuck on?"

"Can't you tell me?"

"I really need to talk to Tuck about this."

Sean heard a noise come out of the woman's throat that made it clear she did not appreciate this slight at all. Still, a moment later he heard Tuck's voice.

"What's up, Sean?"

"Is Jane standing next to you?"

"Yeah, why?'

"You're going to need some privacy when you hear what I have to say. Find it."

"But—"

"Find it!"

"Uh, hold on."

Sean heard him mumble something, and then other noises came over his phone that suggested Tuck was walking somewhere, and then a door closed. He finally came back on.

"Okay, what's this all about?"

"I was in Jacksonville."

"Why?" Tuck snapped.

"I needed a tan."

"Sean—"

"I know it all, Tuck. In fact, I know way more than you do."

"I told you that—"

"I spent all afternoon with Cassandra the Exhibitionist. That is, after Greg Dawson finished paying her off."

Tuck shouted, "Greg Dawson!"

"Knock down the decibels, Tuck, I'm losing my hearing fast enough as it is. So here's the scoop. Dawson found out about you and Cassandra and now the lady is working for him in screwing you out of your big government contract. I'm sure they've got pictures and everything of you two together in the sack to entertain DHS with."

"That asshole. And that bitch!"

"Yeah. By the way, this is a real good lesson in why fidelity is the way to go."

"You didn't tell Jane—"

Sean broke in. "That's not my job. In my book

you're a total shitbag for pulling this crap on your wife and the mother of your kids, but who cares what I think."

"She came on to me, Sean. I swear. She seduced me."

"Grow up, Tuck. Manipulators like Cassandra always come on to saps like you; that's what they do. And it's your job as a happily married man to tell her where to go. Hell, even I did when she flashed some ass at me, and I'm single! I could've jumped her bones without a guilty thought; luckily my good taste saved me. But I'm not a marriage counselor and that's not why I called."

"So why did you phone?" Tuck asked nervously.

"Cassandra said the two of you had a falling-out over the issue of Pam maybe having an affair. Is that true?"

"Well . . ."

"Either start telling me the truth or you can find Willa on your own."

"Yes. It's true."

"That would have been really nice to know before, Tuck," Sean said.

"I . . . I was confused about stuff, not to mention having my head knocked in."

"Cassandra said you overheard some conversations and you actually saw Pam with a guy."

"That's right. I couldn't believe she might be cheating on me."

"Yeah, can you believe the nerve of the woman? Okay, here's the next big question. I know your plane got in early. You said you never stopped, so where did you spend the extra hour or so you had between leaving the airport and arriving home?"

"How did you—"

Sean impatiently cut him off. "I'm an investigator, Tuck, that's what I do. We're wasting time and your kid is out there somewhere with some seriously violent folks. So where were you? And if you even think about lying to me I'm coming over there and, Secret Service protection or not, I'm gonna kick the shit out of you."

"I was outside my house," he said hastily.

"Outside *your* house?"

"Yeah. I was watching it. I thought if Pam believed I was still in Jacksonville, she and her 'friend' might get together. I wanted to catch them in the act. But nobody showed up, so I drove into the garage and went in the house."

"And if the guy did show, what exactly were you going to do?"

"Do? Um, I'm not sure. Kick his butt probably."

"And then what, confess to Pam your own infidelity and let her kick *your* ass?"

"Look, you asked and I told you. I don't need a sermon, okay?"

Something about this explanation was not adding up to Sean. "Your house is down a long driveway with woods on either side. Where were you watching from?"

"The driveway curves and there's a break in the treeline on the east side of the property. You have a clear line of vision to the front door as well as the garage side."

"It was night and it was dark."

"I had a pair of binoculars in my car."

"You just happened to?"

"Okay, so I bought them with that thought in mind."

"When you were watching your own house, did you notice anyone around who shouldn't have been there?"

"No. There was nobody."

"There was obviously somebody, Tuck. They weren't in the house while you were watching it or else you probably would have heard screaming. They had a surveillance zone set up before they made the hit, spotted you right away, and waited for you to go in before they slammed your house."

"But I would've seen them, Sean."

"No, you wouldn't. They obviously knew what they were doing. And you obviously didn't," he added.

"Shit," grumbled Tuck.

"What did you overhear on the phone calls? As detailed as you can."

"There were two calls. I just happened to pick up

the same time as Pam did on one of them. I heard a guy's voice. He said something like, 'I want to meet. And soon.' And Pam wanted to do it later. That's all I heard before I got nervous and hung up."

"And the other time?"

I was walking past the bedroom. She must've thought I had already left, but I forgot my briefcase and had come back from the garage. She was talking in a low voice but I heard her say that I was leaving town in two days and they could meet then."

"And what happened?"

"I only pretended to leave town. I changed my flight and followed her. She went to a coffee shop about a half hour away."

"And you saw the guy?"

"Yeah."

"Hair color, build, race, age?"

"Big guy. About your height. I know that because he stood when she walked in. He was white with short dark hair that had some gray. Maybe about fifty. Real professional-looking."

"So what did you do?"

"I sat in my car for about half an hour. Then Pam came out and I took off."

"Why didn't you wait around for the guy to come out and then confront him?"

"I told you, he was a big guy."

"Is that the only reason?"

Silence.

"Tuck, talk to me!"

"Okay, okay. He was dressed in a suit. I could see them looking at papers. They never did anything lovey-dovey. So, I suddenly started thinking . . ."

"What, that maybe he wasn't her lover boy? That maybe he was a lawyer and Pam was thinking about divorcing your ass?"

"Or that he was a PI like you that she'd hired to check up on me."

That was probably what Pam had wanted to meet with me about.

"Wait a minute, if you thought that, why did you come back from Florida early, the night Pam was killed? You said you wanted to catch them in the act, maybe kick the guy's ass. But now you just admitted you took off before because he was a big guy. And you also admitted that you started thinking he wasn't her lover but maybe a PI. Stop the bullshit. I want the truth."

"This is embarrassing, Sean."

"Tuck, do you want to get Willa back?"

"Of course I do!"

"Then forget your feelings of embarrassment and tell me the truth."

Tuck blurted out, "I thought if I caught the guy coming out of our house, I could intercept him and maybe buy him off."

"Why?"

"The same reason why Dawson obviously did

what he did. If Pam found out about the affair and went public the contract was down the crapper. I couldn't let that happen, Sean. I'd worked my tail off. It meant everything."

A big part of Sean wanted to reach across the ephemeral mist of cellular signals and flatten Tuck Dutton.

"Well, *obviously* it meant more to you than your marriage. And that story you and Jane fed me at the hospital? About your partner trying to force you to sell because you needed the money. That was all BS!"

"It wasn't exactly the truth, no."

"And Jane knew it wasn't the truth?"

"She was just trying to protect me, Sean. She always has. And I keep letting her down."

"Look, do you think Pam had anything written down that would lead us to this guy? Or maybe his business card if he was a lawyer or a PI?"

"Why? He's not connected to Willa and what happened to Pam. It must have to do with my fling with Cassandra."

"Tuck, will you pull your brains out of your crotch and stick them back in your head for just one damn second? This having to do with your fling with Cassandra is only *one* theory and a pretty implausible one at that. Think about it, okay? Why kill your wife and kidnap Willa over a government contract?

Dawson was already set to screw you over with Cassandra, so why would he do it? Are there any other competitors out there willing to risk the death penalty for that contract?"

"Well, no, not really. Government contracting is brutal, but not *that* brutal."

"Great, thanks for employing some logic. Now, another take is that this guy had something to do with Willa's disappearance and Pam's death and it's totally unrelated to your mess."

"But how could that be? Why would he call Pam and then meet with her if he was going to do something like that?"

"Ever heard of meeting under false pretenses to gain some inside intelligence? You folks in the government contracting arena seem to have made a science out of it."

Tuck said slowly, "Oh, yeah, I guess I see your point."

"Have you told the FBI any of this? About Cassandra and the guy you saw with Pam?"

"Of course not. Wait a minute, do I have to?"

"Don't ask me, I'm not your legal advisor. And when I get back to town you and I are going to straighten some things out with your sister."

"*Back* in town? Where are you?"

"In Tennessee."

"Why?"

"A funeral."

"Jesus, I just remembered. We're burying Pam on Friday. Jane is taking care of all the arrangements."

"I'm sure she is."

"Will you be back by then?"

"Yes, I will. But guess what, Tuck."

"What?"

"I'll be there for Pam. Not you! Oh, and while we're being so truthful here, tell me this, was Willa the adopted child?"

"What!" Tuck sounded shocked.

"The postmortem confirmed that Pam only had two C-sections and she couldn't deliver the normal way. You've got *three* kids, so which one was it? Willa?"

Tuck hung up the phone.

"Thanks for the answer," Sean said to himself.

36

Quarry slid his fat key ring out, found the right one, and opened the four-inch-thick door that had been built almost two centuries ago. Atlee was a jumble of dynamics; part southern baronial, part white trash, and part American history. This last part was demonstrated by the room he was now stepping into. It was in the bowels of the main house, dug so far down into the earth that one could never escape the sickly sweet smell of damp, hardened red clay. It was in this room that Quarry's ancestors had sent their most unruly slaves for lengthy stays so as not to incite the rest of the "unfree" population. Quarry had removed the leg and wrist irons from the walls, and also the wooden partitions of cells that had separated slaves from each other lest they gain any strength in numbers. That part of his family history he could live without.

People had died down here. Quarry knew this to be true from the excellent records kept by his slave-holding family. Men, women, and even children. Sometimes when he was down here at night he felt them, thought he heard their moans, the tailings of their final snatches of breath, their barely audible farewells.

He closed the door behind him and locked it. He noted, as he always did, the long and deep scratches on the thick hand-sawn oak; the fingernails of folks trying to gain their freedom. If one looked close enough, one could see the lingering dark traces of old blood on the wood. From the records he'd seen, Quarry also knew that not a single one of them had been successful in escaping from here.

The walls were now covered with painted plywood. He'd studded and framed the walls and then used a sturdy hammer and his own strong arms to nail in the half-inch plywood that came in eight-foot-long sections. It was heavy work, but the sweat had been welcome to him. He'd always embraced projects that made him tired at the end of the day.

And set forth on the painted plywood was work that represented entire years of Quarry's life. There were chalkboards he'd salvaged from torn-down schools and magic-marker boards he'd gotten cheap from a company going out of business. These surfaces were covered with writing, Quarry's precise, home-school-learned cursive. There were lines connecting to other notes, and still more lines intersecting with other collections of facts. Pushpins colored red, blue, and green were all over the place, each of them connected by string. It was like a mathematician's or a physicist's work of art. Sometimes he felt he was the John Nash of his little corner of Alabama. Except, he hoped, for the paranoid-schizophrenic part. One clear difference between him and the Nobel Prize-winning physicist was that there were no intricate formulas or numbers other than calendar dates on the walls. The bulk was simply words that still managed to tell a complex story.

It was here long night after long night that Quarry had pieced everything together. His mind had always worked in flows and movements, ever since he could remember. When he'd torn down his first engine, it was like he could see where the initial spark of energy ignited the fuel and then everything that followed as the internal combustion system worked its magic. The most complex schematics, or mechanical diagrams, while constituting unfathomable puzzles to most folks, had been as clear as water from the tap to him.

It'd been the same way with everything else; planes, guns, farm equipment so complicated and with so many moving parts that qualified mechanics would sometimes drink themselves into a stupor because they just couldn't figure something out from a million different possibilities. But Quarry had always been able to figure it out. He believed he'd inherited this gift from his tongue-talking mother, because his adulterous, racist father couldn't even figure out how to jump-start a car. Quarry was one of a fast-disappearing breed of Americans. He could actually build or fix something.

As he surveyed the greatest work of his life, it occurred to him that it represented a definite slice of time, place, and opportunity, a treasure map of sorts that had taken him to where he needed to go. Made him have to do what he had done. And would do in the future. The near future.

In front of the walls were old battered wooden filing cabinets filled with the investigative work that had allowed him to complete the gaps on the walls. He had traveled to many places, talked to lots of people, and taken hundreds of pages of notes that now rested in those cabinets, but the fruits of that investigation were displayed on the walls.

His gaze started at one end of this "mosaic," where it had all started, and then drifted along to the other end, where it had all come together. One end to the other, the dots finally connected. Some people would call this room a shrine to an obsessive mind. Quarry would not have disagreed with that. But for him it also represented the only route to the most elusive goals in the world: Not just truth but also justice. They were not necessarily mutually exclusive, but Quarry had found them immensely difficult to corral together. He had never failed at anything he'd ever really set his mind to. Yet his mind had often wandered over the possibility that he would eventually fail at *this*.

He moved around the far corner where there was a small space, and glanced behind a wooden partition at some heavy metal cylinders stacked there along with tubing, gauges, and other piping. There were also leftover rolls of lead sheathing on a wooden workbench. He patted one of the tanks, his wedding band clinking against its metal hide.

His ace in the hole.

He locked the door, walked up to the library, pulled on his gloves, slid the single piece of paper into his typewriter, and started hitting keys. As the inked words appeared in front of him on the page, there was no surprise or revelation in their substance. He had formed all that he was putting down a long time ago. Finished, he folded up the page, took a key out of his pocket, dropped it in a pre-addressed envelope along with the letter, sealed it, and drove off in his old truck. Two hundred miles later, now in the state of Kentucky, he deposited the letter in a mailbox.

He arrived back at Atlee in the morning. After having driven all night, he was not tired at all. It seemed as though with each step of his plan completed, his energy was renewed. He ate breakfast with Gabriel and Daryl, then helped Ruth Ann wash up the dishes in the kitchen. Six hours of working the fields next to his son left Quarry sweating. He figured his letter would get to its destination in the next day or so. He wondered about their reaction; the panic that would start to set in.

It made him smile.

After dinner he rode one of his horses to Fred's Airstream. Slipping down from his ride, he set himself down on the concrete-block furniture outside the trailer and handed out smokes, a bottle of Jim Beam, and cans of Red Bull that his Koasati friends liked. He listened to several stories Fred told about his youth spent in Oklahoma on a reservation there along with a man whom Fred had insisted was Geronimo's son.

"That was Cherokee up there, wasn't it?" Quarry said idly as he watched Fred's mutt lick its privates and then roll around in the dirt trying to shake off some fleas. "Thought Geronimo was Apache."

Fred looked at him, a mixture of mirth and seriousness on his flint-hard features. "You think people who look like you can tell the difference in people who look like me?"

The other Indians laughed at that and Quarry did too, shaking his head and grinning. "So why'd you end up coming back here? I never did know really."

Fred spread his short arms. "This is Koasati land. I came home."

Quarry wasn't about to tell him that this *wasn't* Koasati land, that this was good old American Quarry land. Yet he liked the man. Liked visiting him and bringing the man smokes, and Jim Beam and listening to the stories.

Quarry grinned and raised his beer. "To coming home."

"To coming home," they all said together.

A few minutes later they all went inside to get away from the mosquitoes and raise a few more toasts to nonsensical things. One of the Koasatis turned on the TV, adjusted the dials, and the picture cleared. The news was on. As Quarry sat and sipped his drink his gaze settled on the screen and he stopped listening to Fred's jawing.

The lead story was about the Willa Dutton kidnapping. Breaking news had just come in. A leak from somewhere had revealed evidence at the crime scene not previously disclosed to the public. Quarry stood as the news anchor said what this evidence was. Writings on the dead woman's arms. Letters that made no sense, but that the police were following up on.

Quarry jumped from the top step of the trailer to the dirt, scaring the old hound so badly it started whining and curled up in a protective ball. Fred arrived at the door in time to see Quarry astride his horse racing back to Atlee. Fred shook his head, mumbled something about crazy white people, and closed the trailer door.

Quarry found Daryl alone in the barn. The younger man watched in disbelief as his old man came at him like a blitzing linebacker. Quarry slammed him up against the wall and drove his forearm against his son's throat.

"You wrote something on her arms!" he roared.

"What?" gasped Daryl.

"You wrote something on her arms! What in the hell was it?"

"Give me some damn air and I'll tell you."

Quarry stepped back, but not before giving his son a hard shove that drove him back against the wall one more time. Breathing hard, Daryl told his father what he'd done.

"Why in the hell did you do that?"

"After the lady got killed I got scared. Thought we'd throw 'em off that way."

"What you did, boy, was stupid."

"I'm sorry, Daddy."

"You sure as hell are sorry."

"But the way I wrote it down no way they gonna figure it out."

"Tell me exactly how you wrote it."

Daryl grabbed an old seed catalogue from the workbench, tore off a page, and wrote the letters down on it, using a Bic pen.

Quarry took the paper, read through it.

"See, Daddy, it's gibberish to them, right? You know what it says, right?"

"Course I know what it says," he snapped. Quarry walked outside and stared at the sky, which was still light, though the lowering sun was coloring the clouds a flaming red like the underbelly of lit charcoals. He didn't notice that Daryl had followed and was now staring at him with a face that just begged for some sort of praise for thinking of this subterfuge. Thus he would never know it was the same pleading look Quarry had given his mother on her dying day.

Quarry struck a match and burned the paper to a black puff. He watched it drift away, propelled by a slight breeze until it crumbled to earth a few feet away.

"Is it okay, Daddy?" Daryl said nervously.

Quarry pointed to the black puff. "That's your second strike, boy. One more, it's all over, son or not."

He turned and walked off.

37

The Maxwell family, along with Sean King and a large crowd of mourners, watched as the preacher had his say. He read in a suitably devout tone from the scriptures, and then stepped aside to let folks come forward and touch the flower-draped coffin and have a private word with the deceased. Michelle's brothers walked up as a single group, followed by others. Later, as the crowd slowly trickled away, Frank Maxwell put his hands on his wife's coffin and bowed his head.

Michelle stood next to Sean and watched her father. He finally touched his eyes with one hand and, head still down, walked past them and on to his car. Michelle had started to reach out to grip his arm, but at the last second pulled back.

Sean said, "Are you going to go up?"

"Up where?"

"To the coffin? Last respects?"

Michelle stared up at the mahogany box holding her mom. In the background, cemetery workers stood ready to lower it into the ground. The sky was overcast. The rain would be coming soon and they were probably anxious to get on with their work. There were other funerals today; accommodating the dead was very much a full-time occupation, it seemed.

There were few things Michelle Maxwell was afraid of. But she was staring at one of them right now.

"Will you come with me?"

Sean took her arm and they walked together up to the front. She put her hand on top of the coffin, her fingers flicking at some of the flower petals.

"She never liked lilies," said Michelle.

"What?"

Michelle indicated the flowers on the coffin. "She preferred roses." As soon as she said the word, she jerked her hand back like she'd been stung.

"Are you okay?"

She stared down at her hand. There was nothing there. She hadn't been stung or bitten or anything. And lilies didn't have thorns.

She looked up at him.

"Michelle, are you okay?" he said again.

"I . . . I don't know." She added more firmly, "Let's get out of here."

Back at the house there were mounds of food, friends stopping by; quiet, somber talk mixed with the occasional joke and twitter of laughter. In the middle of it all Frank Maxwell sat on the couch and stared off. Anyone who approached him to offer condolences was soon on his way when the man failed to even acknowledge their presence.

Sean watched Michelle, who was watching her father. When a group of people came in, Frank Maxwell finally did stir. The scowl on his face made Michelle and Sean turn to see what he was looking at. Six people had come in the door, four men and two women. They were carrying platters of food and were chatting among themselves. Michelle recognized a few of them from the funeral service. When she turned back to her father, she started.

He was gone.

She and Sean exchanged glances. Sean motioned toward the back hall where the master bedroom was located. Then he tapped his chest and nodded at the new group of folks. Michelle blinked her understanding at him and headed for the bedroom.

She tapped on the door.

"What!"

Her father sounded angry.

"It's me, Dad."

"I'm just taking a minute," he said. His tone was calmer but she could still sense the underlying fury.

"Can I come in?"

A thirty-second silence passed.

She tapped again. "Dad?" she finally said.

"All right. Jesus, come in."

She opened the door and then closed it behind

her. Her father was sitting on the edge of the bed holding something. She sat next to him and glanced down.

It was their wedding photo. They'd done it right. A big church service with her mom looking radiant in flowing white and her crewcut dad in tie and tails. Only twenty-one, he'd just returned from Vietnam. He was tall, tan, and handsome with a confident smile. Sally Maxwell, not yet twenty, was beautiful. There was much of her mother's good looks in Michelle, though growing up she had never focused on that. She had been closer to her father, the classic tomboy who wants to impress big, strong, tough Daddy.

She took the photo from him and placed it back on the night-stand. "Do you need anything?"

"I'm peopled out, Michelle. I can't go back out there."

"Then you don't have to. I'll take care of it. Maybe you should get some sleep."

"Yeah, right," he said dismissively.

"Has your lawyer contacted you?"

He glanced up sharply. "What?"

"You said you had a lawyer. I was just wondering if you'd talked to him yet."

He just shook his head and looked back down.

She waited another minute but he didn't say anything. She finally rose to leave after giving him a hug.

As she reached the door he did say something. It caused her to freeze with her hand on the doorknob.

"You think I killed her, don't you?"

She slowly turned back around. He was holding the wedding photo again, though he wasn't looking at the happy young couple captured for all time there. He was staring straight at her.

"You think I killed *her*." He held up the photo as though the evidence to support that accusation was all right there.

"I never said that."

"You didn't have to *say* it," he snapped.

"Dad—"

He cut her off. "Just get the hell out of here. Now!"

She fled the room.

38

Everyone had gone, the food was put away and the tears had been cried. The Maxwell brothers were clustered in the backyard talking quietly over their beers. Frank Maxwell was still in the bedroom.

Sean and Michelle sat in the living room as outside the dusk slowly evolved to night.

"So he accused you of thinking he was a murderer?"

Michelle nodded slowly, obviously still trying to wrap her arms around this notion. "I guess I can't blame him," she said. "And once a cop always a cop. He knows the lay of the land. He'd be a suspect under the usual parameters."

"That's true. When a wife dies violently, it's usually the husband."

"I don't think they loved each other."

Sean put down his can of soda and stared at her. "Why?"

"They never really had anything in common, other than the five kids. Dad was always working. Mom was always at home. When he retired they barely knew each other. Remember when they went on that trip to Hawaii to celebrate their anniversary? They ended up coming back early. I talked to Bill about that later. He said Dad told him they'd run out of things to talk about after one day. And they didn't even have anything they liked to do together. They'd just grown apart."

"They ever consider divorce?"

"I don't know. They never mentioned it to me."

"But you weren't that close to your mother, were you?"

"Closer to my dad, but even that got strained over the years."

"Why?"

"I'm not in the mood to get psychoanalyzed right now."

"Okay, I was just asking a question."

"Who were those people that came in right before Dad shot to the bedroom?"

"You didn't know any of them?" said Sean.

"I don't know any of my parents' friends."

"I made the rounds. Mostly they were friends of your mom's. Played golf, cards, shopped together. Did a little charity thing."

"Nothing out of the ordinary? It seemed like my dad didn't want to even see them."

"Nothing that stuck out. They seemed genuinely sorry about your mom's death."

They turned when they heard the door open. Frank Maxwell was past them and outside before they even rose off the couch.

Michelle made it to the front door in time to see her dad climb in his car and drive off a lot faster than he should have.

"What the hell was that about?" asked Sean, who'd joined her at the door.

Michelle just shook her head. She glanced at the hall leading to the bedroom. "Come on."

The first thing that Michelle noticed when she walked into the room was that the wedding photo was not where it should have been.

Sean happened to glance in a corner. He reached over and picked it up. "Why would he have put this in the trash can?"

"I'm getting a really bad feeling about something."

Sean looked down at the photo. "Your mom's dead. On the day of her funeral he chucks their wedding photo in the trash. What would make him do that?"

"Do you think Pam Dutton ever threw her wedding photo in the trash?"

"Because Tuck was screwing around on her? You think your mom . . ." He obviously couldn't finish the thought in her presence.

"I'm just . . . I don't know."

"You sure you want to go down that road?"

"I want to get to the truth. Any way I can."

"There are usually some telltale signs." He added, "Other than wedding pictures in trash cans."

Michelle was already opening the drawers of the bureau while Sean checked through the closet. A few minutes later Michelle held up some pretty revealing lingerie with the price tags still attached while Sean had pulled from the closet three new-looking outfits and a pair of spiky boots.

They eyed each other, but left the obvious thought unspoken.

They put the clothes back and Michelle led him to the small den across from the dining room. There was a desk in one corner. She started going through the drawers. She pulled out the checkbook and handed it to Sean. "My mom handled the bills."

While Sean sorted through the check register, Michelle methodically examined the credit card statements.

A few minutes later she looked up. "There's hundreds of dollars' worth of recent charges for men's clothing from four different online retailers. I didn't see any stuff from those stores in the bedroom."

He held up the check register. "There's an entry here for a local golf tournament fee. Did your dad play golf?"

"No, but Mom did. So that's not out of whack."

Sean held up a piece of paper he'd pulled from the desk. "This is part of the entry form for the golf tournament. It's fifty bucks per person, but the check was for a hundred."

"So two people."

"Michelle, the form says it's a *couples* tournament."

Michelle snatched the paper from him and glanced down it before laying it aside.

Sean looked uneasily at her. "Don't you think your father could have easily found all this out? I mean, we did in about ten minutes."

"My mom didn't seem to work very hard to cover it up. Maybe she didn't care. Maybe he didn't."

"Your dad doesn't strike me as the type to meekly accept being cheated on."

"You don't really know my father, Sean." She looked down at her hands. "And maybe I don't either."

"What's going on here?"

They both looked up. Bill Maxwell was staring at them. He glanced around at the checkbook and credit card statements.

"What're you doing, Mik?"

"Going through some of the bills. I know Mom took care of that and I didn't want Dad to get messed up in something."

She shoved the items back in the drawer and rose. "Dad left."

"Where'd he go?"

"I don't know. And he didn't ask my permission."

She glanced at the beer can in his hand. "Is that

what you guys plan to do all the time now? Drink beer and gab?"

"Geez, Mik, we just buried our mother. Cut us some slack."

"I'm sure she didn't mean it that way, Bill."

Michelle snapped, "Yes I did."

She grabbed her keys and headed for the door. Sean gave Bill an apologetic look and hurried after her.

Sean caught up to Michelle as she was climbing in her SUV.

"Where are we going?"

"To see Donna Rothwell again."

"Why?"

"If my mom was having an affair, she probably knows who it was with."

39

Shirley Meyers stared down at the letter, not really knowing what to make of it. She'd collected the mail earlier but hadn't opened any of it. Now, as she was preparing to leave for work, she had taken a few moments to go through the small stack.

There was no return address on the letter she was holding. When she looked at the postmark, squinting a bit to see it, she shook her head in confusion. She didn't know anyone in Kentucky. She turned the envelope over. It wasn't from a business; it wasn't a solicitation. It was just a plain white envelope. And there was a small bulge inside it. Something besides paper.

She opened the letter, using her pinkie to break the seal. There was one piece of paper inside and a small key. After looking at the key that had some numbers engraved on it, she unfolded the letter. It was typed and it wasn't addressed to her. Shirley covered her mouth when she saw the name of the person the letter was actually for. She read through the words and then quickly put it back in the envelope along with the key. For a long moment she just stood there. Things like this were not supposed to happen to people like her.

But she couldn't just stand here. She pulled on her coat and left her little house. She rode the bus into the city. She checked her watch. Shirley prided herself on punctuality. She was never late for work. Yet part of her didn't want to go to work today, not with the letter in her pocket. She continued to fret as she walked to the entrance, went through security, and gained admittance to the building, nodding at people she knew as she passed by them.

She entered the kitchen, took off her coat, and hung it up. She washed her hands and turned to her job of food prep. She kept sneaking glances at her watch as other people came and went. She tried not to look at them, only nodding when they said hello. She didn't know what to do. Every thought that flitted through her head was worse than the one before. Could they put her in jail? But she hadn't done anything other than open her own mail. But would people believe her? Another terrifying possibility assailed her. What if they thought she had stolen it from here? But wait, they couldn't, she told herself. Her address was on the envelope, not this one.

At one point she looked so upset that her supervisor finally asked her what was wrong. She at first tried to resist telling him the truth, but the fact was, if she didn't tell somebody she was just going to collapse.

She slid the letter out of her pocket and showed it to the man. He read through it, looked at the key, and then glanced sharply at her.

"Damn," he said.

"It's addressed to her," Shirley said.

"All mail coming here has to be checked out first, you know that," the man said in a scolding tone.

"But it didn't come here, now did it?" Shirley shot back. "It came to *my* house. No law against opening my own mail," she added defiantly.

"How'd they know to send it to you?"

"How do I know? I can't stop someone from mailing me something."

The man thought of something. "There wasn't any white powder in it, was there?"

"You think I'd be here if that was the case? I'm not stupid, Steve. It was just the letter. And that key."

"But you might have messed up fingerprints and stuff like that."

"How was I to know? I didn't know what it was until I opened it."

Steve rubbed his chin. "It *is* addressed to her."

"The letter was, but not the envelope. But I can't take it to her. I'm not allowed. I mean, you know that, right?"

"I know. I know," he said impatiently.

"So what do I do?"

He hesitated and then said, "The police?"

"You read what the letter said. You want her to die?"

"Damn! Why did I have to get involved in this?" Steve complained, but lowered his voice when more kitchen staff walked in. He looked like he wanted to go and attack the White House wine cellar to fortify his sagging spirits. If he did, his choices would be limited. The place had only carried American-made wine since the Ford administration.

"We have to do something," she hissed. "If somebody finds out I got this letter and then didn't do anything about it . . . I won't have her blood on my hands. I won't! And now you know too. You got to do something."

"Just calm down." Steve thought for a few moments. "Look, let me make a call." He thrust the letter back in her hands.

Five minutes later a woman dressed in a black suit walked into the kitchen and asked Shirley to follow her. They passed into a part of the massive house Shirley had never been to before. As she looked around at all the people rushing this way and that, and then the stoic men and women standing at attention outside doorways, and still others in military uniforms or else nice suits carrying thick binders and looking harried, she felt her mouth drying up. These were folks you saw on the TV all the time.

Important people. She just wanted to run back to the kitchen and finish making her fruit and cheese platter.

When they arrived at the woman's office she wheeled on Shirley and said sternly, "This is highly irregular."

"I didn't know what to do. Did Steve tell you about it?" Shirley added nervously.

"Yes. Where's the letter?"

Shirley slipped the envelope from her pocket and handed it to the woman. "Read it for yourself, ma'am. What else could I do?" she said.

The woman put the key on her desk, unfolded the letter, and read through it, her eyes widening as she did so. She quickly put the two items back in the envelope. "I want you to go back to work and forget you ever saw this."

"Yes, ma'am. Are you gonna give it to her?"

The woman had already lifted up her phone. "That's not your concern."

After Shirley left the room, the woman punched in a number and spoke quickly. Minutes later a man, even more stern-looking than her, arrived and took the envelope.

He walked hurriedly up a staircase, crossed a broad foyer, headed down another hall, and finally arrived at a door. He knocked quietly. A woman opened the door, took the letter, and closed the door without exchanging a word with her visitor.

A minute later the letter was placed on the woman's desk, the door was closed, and the lady sat alone staring down at the plain white envelope.

Jane Cox took out the letter and read through it. The writer had been concise. If Jane wanted Willa Dutton back alive and well, the next letter that would be sent could not be shown to anyone else. If the police got hold of it, the writer said that he would know. And the contents of that letter, the writer claimed, would destroy everything if the public became aware of the contents. And it would cost Willa Dutton her life.

She read through one critical part several times. It said, *I do not want to kill the girl, but if I have to, I will. The next letter you will be sent will reveal a lot. In some ways, it will reveal everything. If the public finds out, all will be lost for you. I know that you know what I mean. If you follow the instructions, Willa will come back to you alive and well. If you don't Willa dies and everything else will be over. That is the only way it can be.*

The writer informed her that the next letter would be sent to a P.O. box in D.C. that was identified for her in the letter. That was what the key was for. To open the mailbox.

Jane sat back in her chair. There was a creeping dread working its way through her body that was nearly incapacitating. She picked up her phone and then put it back down.

No, she would not make that call. Not yet. She locked the letter away in her desk and slipped the key in her jacket pocket.

She was hosting a reception in ten minutes for a delegation of female governors and other women in politics who were in town for a caucus on healthcare reform. She was to give brief remarks, all carefully typed out and waiting for her at the lectern set up in the East Room. It was the sort of thing she had done hundreds of times before, and almost always flawlessly. She'd had lots of practice. The White House typically entertained thousands of such visitors a week.

Now she knew it would take all her willpower merely to walk to the lectern, open the book, and read the words someone else had written for her. As she walked down the hall five minutes later surrounded by her staff and security, her mind was not on healthcare reform. Nor was it on the contents of the letter.

After she pressed him mercilessly, her brother had finally told her what Sean had asked him over the phone.

Was Willa the adopted one?

She stumbled a bit as she thought this, and a Secret Service agent immediately took her arm.

"Ma'am, are you okay?"

"Fine. I'm fine. Thank you."

She marched on, going into full-scale First Lady mode.

But one terrible thought pierced this usually rock-solid armor like it was paper.

Is the past finally catching up?

40

Quarry drove. Gabriel was in the middle, and Daryl on the other side of him. The truck rocked, pitched, and rolled until it reached the firmness of asphalt. They'd spent pretty much all day in the fields and were bone-tired. But this visit was not an option. They'd headed out right after dinner.

Gabriel looked out the window and said, "Mr. Sam, I think you were right about old Kurt. He moved on. Not hide nor hair of him."

Daryl glanced at his father but said nothing.

Quarry said nothing either, just kept one hand on the wheel and stared dead ahead, the smoke curling off the end of his Winston. They pulled into the parking lot of the nursing home. As they climbed out Quarry snatched a cassette recorder off the dashboard, crushed his smoke out on the pavement, and they all headed in.

As they moved down the hall, Quarry said, "Been a long time since you visited your sister, Daryl."

Daryl made a face. "Don't like seeing her like that. Don't want to remember her that way, Daddy."

"She didn't have any choice about it."

"I know that."

"She might look different on the outside, but your sister is still in there."

He pushed open the door and they walked inside.

The nurses had turned Tippi on her right side, so Quarry slid chairs over that way. He slipped the Jane Austen book out of his pocket and handed it to Daryl.

"I ain't no good at reading," Daryl said. "Especially that old stuff, Daddy."

"Give it a whirl. I'm not handing out prizes for performance."

Daryl sighed, took the book, sat down, and started reading. His delivery was halting and slow, but he was doing his best. When he made it through four pages, Quarry thanked him and then handed the book to Gabriel.

The little boy was clearly the superior reader and he whipped through an entire chapter, getting into the personalities of the characters and changing his voice to accommodate them. When he was done Quarry said, "Didn't sound like you were too bored that time, little man."

Gabriel looked sheepish. "I read the book back at Atlee. Figured if you and Miss Tippi liked it so much I needed to give it another go."

"And your verdict?" Quarry asked, a smile playing across his lips.

"Better than I thought it would be. But I still can't say it's my favorite."

"Good enough."

Quarry set the cassette recorder on the nightstand next to the bed and turned it on. He picked up Tippi's hand and held it tightly as the voice of Cameron Quarry, Sam's dead wife and Tippi's mother, engulfed the room. She was talking directly to her daughter, expressing words of love and encouragement and hope and all the things she was feeling in her heart.

Her voice grew weak toward the end because these had been Cameron Quarry's dying words. At her insistence Sam had recorded his wife at the end of her life, as she lay in bed at Atlee slowly passing on.

The last words were, "I love you, Tippi, darling. Momma loves you with all my heart. I can't wait to hold you again, baby girl. When we're both healthy and fine in the arms of Jesus."

Quarry mouthed these last words his wife had spoken, ending exactly when she did. He cut the recorder off. As soon as the name Jesus had passed across her lips Cameron Quarry had taken her last breath and just died. For a God-loving woman, Quarry felt, it was a dignified way to head on. He'd closed her eyes and put her hands across her chest, much like he'd done with his own mother.

Daryl and Gabriel had tears in their eyes. They

both brushed them away while steadfastly not looking at each other.

"Momma was the best damn woman that ever lived," Daryl finally said in a hushed voice while Quarry nodded in agreement.

Quarry touched Tippi's cheek. "And this one here is right up there with her."

"Amen to that," said Gabriel. "Is she ever going to get better, Mr. Sam?"

"No, son. She's not."

"You want to say a prayer for her?" Gabriel put his hands together and started to kneel.

"You can if you want, Gabriel. But I don't go down that road anymore."

"Momma says you don't believe in God. Why's that?"

"Because he stopped believing in me, son."

He stood and put the small recorder in his jacket pocket. "When you're done I'll be outside in the truck smoking."

Quarry sat in his junk of a truck, the window down, an unlit smoke dangling from between his parched lips. The Alabama heat was in all its glory at nearly nine o'clock at night, and Quarry flicked a bead of sweat off his nose as a mosquito buzzed at his right ear.

The skeeter wasn't bothering him too much. He was watching a meteor flame across the sky, the Big Dipper serving as a celestial backdrop to the show.

After it was over his gaze dropped to the low cinderblock building that was his daughter's home now. No husband, no kids, no grandkids for Tippi. Just a dead brain, a beaten body, and a feeding tube.

"You messed up there, God. Shouldn't done that. I know the 'work in mysterious ways' crap. I know the 'everything has a purpose' BS. But you got it wrong. You're not infallible. You shoulda let my baby girl alone. I'll never forgive you for that, and I don't give a damn if you never forgive me for what I got to do." He spoke in a lurching, halting voice before he fell silent. He wanted the tears to come, if for no other reason than to relieve the pressure on his brain. On his soul. But they wouldn't bleed through his eyes. His soul apparently was scorched earth, no water left to give.

When the two came out and climbed in the truck, Quarry tossed his unlit cigarette out the window and they drove back to Atlee in silence.

Quarry went immediately to his library, sat behind his desk, fortified himself with a slug of 86-proof Old Grand Dad, lit the fire, thrust the poker into it, rolled up his sleeve, and held it against his bare arm, making a second mark perpendicular to and at the right end of the long burn already there. Ten seconds later the poker fell to the carpet, burning another hole in it, and Quarry collapsed back in his chair.

Breathing heavily, his eyes staring up at the sooty ceiling that had caught the flameouts and driftbacks of centuries of his ancestors, Quarry started talking. Most of it made little sense except to Quarry; he found it crystal clear. He started out telling folks that he was sorry. He named names and his voice rose and sank at odd intervals. He took another pull of Grand Dad, holding the bottle to his lips for the longest time.

More came from his mouth, his entire heart and soul poured forth. Planted on the ceiling up there were Cameron and Tippi, in each other's arms. He could see each so vividly he wanted to rise to them, hold them both. Let them soar off together to a better place than the sorry one he was in right now.

He sometimes wondered what the hell he was doing. One little uneducated man against the world. Outrageous, unbelievable, foolish. It was all those things. Sure. But he couldn't stop now. It wasn't just that he'd come too far to quit. It was that he had nowhere else to go.

When he closed his eyes and then reopened them his wife and daughter were gone. The fire already crackled low; he'd built it up just enough to get the burn on the poker. He looked down at his arm again, at the intersecting lines. Hercules had had his labors. Ishmael the albatross of the whale. Jesus the burden of the cross and the lives of all resting on his weary shoulders.

This was Sam Quarry's cross to bear. It certainly

was. Not just the square miles of Quarry land reduced to almost nothing. Or the ramshackle house that would never again see better days. Not just the dead wife, the ruined daughter. The dim son and the distant other daughter. Neither was it just the history of the Quarry family that was so wrongheaded in many respects as to be a shameful badge for any decent-minded descendant.

It was that Sam Quarry was no longer the man he once was. He was unrecognizable to himself. And not because of the burns on his arm. But because of the hellish scorch marks on his inner self. He'd lied to Gabriel. Maybe he'd lied to himself too. He didn't *not* believe in God. He *feared* him. With all his heart and soul. Because what he'd done on this earth meant that he would not be reunited with his beloved wife or with his beautiful, resurrected daughter, when the time came. His price for justice was eternal separation. It was why he listened to his wife's last words over and over. It was why he visited Tippi as often as he did. Because when it was over, it was really going to be done.

He looked back at the ceiling and said so softly it could barely be heard above the tired pop of the fire, "Eternity is damn well forever."

Outside the closed door Gabriel skittered away. He'd come down to get another book to read, and heard far more than he'd wanted to. Far more than the little boy, smart as he was, could possibly understand.

He'd always looked up to Mr. Sam. Never knew a man who treated him any better than the current head of the Quarry clan did. And yet even with that, Gabriel ran all the way back to his room, locked the door, and slipped under the bedcovers.

And he never did fall asleep that night. It seemed the wails of Sam Quarry from down below were able to leach into every square inch of Atlee. There seemed to be nowhere that was safe or free from them.

41

Donna Rothwell didn't think Sally Maxwell was having an affair with anyone, she told them. They were sitting in the woman's vast living room.

"I think it's a smear on your mother's memory to even propose such a thing," she said in a strident voice, hurling a dark look at Michelle.

"But someone did kill her," Sean pointed out.

"People get murdered all the time. A burglary? A robbery?"

"Nothing was taken."

She waved a hand dismissively. "So they got scared and ran."

"The last time we talked you were terrified at the thought of a murderer running loose around here, and now you seem to have accepted it pretty readily," noted Michelle in a voice filled with skepticism.

"This is a nice area, but crime happens everywhere. Sure, I'm scared, but that doesn't mean I'm not realistic. I've got a good security system. I have two maids who live here with me. And I've got Doug."

"Doug?"

"My steady. But I think you're being very unfair to your mother by accusing her of something like that. Especially when she can't defend herself."

Sean put a hand on Michelle's arm because he could sense she was about to come out of her chair at the woman, and it would hardly be a fair fight. At that moment a man wandered into the room holding a small bag of pretzels.

He was about six feet tall and very fit-looking. He had a TV anchor's mane of silvery hair and a deep tan. A handsome man of sixty-odd.

"My *steady* I mentioned to you before, Doug Reagan," said Donna proudly. "A very successful founder of a global IT company. He sold it four years ago and now lives the good life. With me."

"Well, that's the American dream," said Michelle with a trace of disgust.

Doug shook their hands. "Really sorry about Sally," he said. "She was a fine woman. A good friend to Donna."

"Thanks," said Michelle.

Doug looked at Donna and took her hand. "We're going to miss her smiling face, aren't we?"

Donna clutched a tissue in her hand and nodded. "But Michelle thinks Sally might have been having an affair."

"What?" Doug looked at them. "That's absurd."

"Are you in a position to know for sure?" asked Sean.

The man opened his mouth and then closed it. "What? I . . ." He glanced at his *steady*. "Donna would know better than I would. I knew Sally but not like Donna did. But still, it's a small community here. Someone would have known, wouldn't they?"

Michelle said, "That's what we're trying to find out. But we need folks to be *truthful*."

"I am telling you the truth," snapped Donna. "Your mother was not having an affair with any man that I know of. And like Doug said, it's a small community."

"My mom bought a golf tournament couples package. My dad doesn't play golf."

"Oh for goodness sakes. She played with Doug," said Donna.

Michelle and Sean looked at Doug, who had a pretzel up to his mouth. "Donna, you asked me to, remember? Because she didn't have anyone to play with."

"That's right, I did."

"Why didn't he play with you?" asked Michelle. "You're a golfer too."

Donna said, "Because even though it was for charity it was a competitive tournament and my handicap was too high to get in. Your mom was an excellent golfer and so is Doug."

"About all I do anymore," he said, smiling. "Hit the little ball in the little cup." He added quickly, "And spend time with Donna."

"My steady," said Donna.

"Sounds like what everyone should aspire to in retirement," said Michelle, while she scowled at Donna.

"Look, if you came here to insult us," Donna began before Sean cut her off by saying, "This is understandably a very tense time for everyone. We appreciate your comments. I think we need to go now."

Before Michelle could protest, Sean took her by the arm and propelled her out the door.

It took them a moment to realize that Doug had followed them out.

"I am truly sorry about your mother. I liked Sally a lot. Everyone did."

"Well, one person didn't," snapped Michelle.

"What, oh, yes, of course." They stood there awkwardly on the front porch with towering support columns done in the Corinthian style on either side of them. For Michelle they felt like elaborate bars on a jazzed-up cage.

"Is there something you wanted to tell us?" asked Sean.

"This is very awkward," said Doug.

"Yes, it is," agreed Michelle. Sean gave her a look.

"I didn't really know your father, but Sally talked to Donna and me about him sometimes."

"Is this where you tell me they weren't happy and my mother was thinking of leaving him?"

"No, no, not at all. I think your mother was, well, moderately happy with your father. I . . . well . . ."

"Just say it, *Doug*."

"I don't think your father was very happy with Sally. They seemed to have grown apart. At least that's how she phrased it."

Michelle's face fell.

Doug studied her. "Did you think that too?"

"It really doesn't matter what I think. It just matters who killed my mom."

"Well, she didn't tell us about anyone bothering her, or stalking her. She led a very normal life. Friends, golf, gardening. There are no psychopaths that I know of running around here."

"That's the thing about psychopaths, Doug, with the really crazy ones, you never see them coming until they've stuck a knife in your heart," she said.

He mumbled a hasty goodbye, and then Doug the steady almost ran back into the house. They heard the lock click into place.

As they were walking to the SUV Michelle said, "Do you think it was just a robbery that went down wrong?"

"It might be."

They climbed in the SUV. "You feel like some food?" she said. "I know a place."

Ten minutes later they were seated in a small restaurant and had ordered.

Sean said, "Okay, the cops worked the garage area and found no trace. The garage overhead door was down and the exit door from the garage onto the side yard was locked. But the killer could have secured it on the way out. It was just a simple button lock."

"So anybody could have gone in, waited for her, killed her, and left that way. The ground was dry, no footprints."

"And there was a privacy fence on the garage side. More concealment."

She said, "ME reported the window of death was between eight and nine. You think someone would have seen something. Or maybe heard Mom crying out when she was attacked?"

Sean looked thoughtful. "But the noise from the pool party would have drowned out anything like that." He added, "I take it they've all been interviewed? The folks at the party?"

"I guess so." She studied him. "Why, what are you thinking?"

"I'm thinking if I wanted to kill someone I'd get myself invited to that party, slip out, do the deed, and slip back in."

"I thought of that too, but you would have had to

know that my mom was going to be going out, that she'd be in the garage at that time."

"Not necessarily. They might have entered through the garage side door and were planning to go into the house when your mom came out and saved them the trouble."

"That's still risky, Sean. My dad was home. He's a former cop and keeps a gun in the house too. Like Donna said, it's a small community. Folks would know that."

Sean sat back, lost in thought. Their food came and they ate mostly in silence.

"Can I ask you a favor?" she said as they were leaving.

"One can always ask," he said, smiling.

Her next words drove the smile away.

"When I was a little girl, we lived about two hours south of here in a little rural slice of Tennessee. I want to go back there. I *need* to go back there right now."

42

They pulled off the main road and the SUV's tires bit down hard on the crushed gravel. Sean was driving and had followed Michelle's precise directions.

"When was the last time you were here?" he said.

She was staring straight ahead. A curve of moon provided the only illumination other than the truck's headlights. "When I was a kid."

He looked surprised. "If that's the case, how did you remember how to get here? Did you look it up?"

"No. I . . . I just knew. I don't know how."

He looked over at her, a frown creasing his face. A curious mixture of emotions swept across her features. He could see heightened expectations. And he could also see fear. The latter was not something he normally associated with the lady.

They pulled down a dark street, revealing a neighborhood that had been brand-new about sixty years ago. The houses were falling in, the front porches far off plumb, and the yards a tangled mass of weeds and diseased trees and bushes.

"Seen better days," she said.

"Looks that way," he replied quietly. "Which one is it?"

She pointed up ahead. "That one. The old farmhouse, only one like it on this street. The rest of the neighborhood was carved from that property."

Sean pulled the SUV to a stop in front. "Doesn't look like anyone lives here now," he said.

She made no move to get out.

"What now?" he finally asked her.

"I don't know."

"You want to get out, go up for a look? We came all this way."

She hesitated. "I guess so."

They walked up the worn path. The house was set well off the street. There was an old tire attached to a rotting coil of rope that was tied to the one remaining limb of a dying oak. An old wheelless truck sitting on cinderblocks was parked in the side yard. The screen door was lying on the sagging front porch.

As they passed one spot, Michelle stopped and stared at the remains of some bushes. They'd been cut down to the point where only bare sticks were left. There was an entire line of them.

"It was a hedge," Michelle said. "Forgot what kind. We woke up one morning and it was gone. My dad had planted it for one of their anniversaries. After they got whacked down, it never grew back. I think whoever did it poured some plant killer or something on it."

"Ever find out who did it?"

She just shook her head and continued walking to the house. They stepped over the screen door and Michelle tried the doorknob. It turned easily. Sean put a hand over hers. "You sure you want to do this?"

"We came all this way. And I doubt I'll ever come back."

He removed his hand and they walked in. The place was empty and filthy.

Sean had grabbed a flashlight from the SUV and now swung it around, revealing ragged blankets, food wrappers, empty beer bottles, and more than a dozen used condoms.

"Not exactly one for the memory books," she murmured, taking all of this in.

"Walks down memory lane usually aren't. It's hardly ever as good as you remember."

She eyed the stairs.

He followed her gaze. "Which bedroom was yours?"

"Second on the right."

"Want to head up?"

"Maybe later."

They walked around the main floor, taking in more trash and rot, and Sean noticed that Michelle didn't really register on anything. She pushed open the back door and stepped outside. More trash, the carcass of the truck in the side yard, and a leaning one-bay garage with its overhead door gone, revealing a mound of junk inside.

It was all pathetic and depressing and Sean could barely stand being here. He didn't quite know how Michelle was able to keep from running away screaming.

"So what are we doing here?" he asked.

She sat down on the back porch. He stood beside her.

"Did you ever go back to the place where you grew up?"

"Once," he said.

"And?"

"No grand revelations. Other than everything being a lot smaller than I remember, which makes perfect sense because I'm a lot bigger now. So I just saw the house and kept on driving."

"I'd like to do that. See the house and keep on driving."

"Let's go then." He reached in his pocket, pulled out the keys to the SUV, and flipped them to her. "You can do the honors."

They walked back through the house; she paused at the stairs.

"Michelle, you don't have to beat yourself up about this."

She started up the stairs.

"You sure about this?" he said.

"No," she said, but kept on going.

They reached the wide landing and stopped. There were four doors, two on each side.

"So the second one there was yours?" He pointed to the right.

She nodded.

Sean moved to open the door but she stopped him.

"Don't."

He pulled back, looked at her. "Maybe we should leave."

She nodded, but as he stepped down the hall, she abruptly turned back, gripped the knob on the second door, and opened it.

And screamed as the man stood there staring at her.

Then he pushed past Michelle and raced by Sean, clattering down the stairs and out the busted screen door.

Michelle was shaking so badly that Sean gave up all thoughts of going after the guy. He raced to Michelle and held her. When she finally settled down he drew away. They stared at each other, no doubt the same question on each other's mind.

Sean articulated it first. In a stunned tone he exclaimed, "What in the hell was your father doing here?"

43

Air Force One thudded down at Andrews Air Force Base, the 747's quartet of engines sending their power backward as the pilots engaged the reverse thrusters. The president sat in the nose of the plane in his suite that housed two daybeds, a bath, and a tied-down-tight elliptical machine. Shortly after that Marine One flew along in the standard multichopper deployment. It was close to midnight when the skids of the chopper carrying the president touched down on the White House lawn.

Dan Cox sprang down the chopper steps looking full of energy, ready to start the day instead of ending it. The man was like that on the political trail. He consistently left much younger aides gasping for air and sucking down troughs of coffee as they state-hopped across the country. The thrill of the competition seemed to fill him with enough adrenalin that he could soldier on endlessly. And there was a high associated with being the president of the United States that couldn't be duplicated by any other occupation. It was like being a rock legend, A-list movie star, sports icon, and the closest thing to a god on earth all rolled into one.

Tonight, as always, the president moved along in a bubble that the Secret Service referred to as "the package," consisting of the president, high-level staff, personal security detail, and a few fortunate members of the media pool. As he approached the mansion, staff and reporters were nimbly herded off with only one senior staff member and the security detail remaining with the man.

All doors opened for the leader of the free world and he strode into the White House like he owned it. Which unofficially he did. Though financed by the American taxpayers, it was really his house, his chopper, his jumbo jet. No one got to come for a visit or go for a ride if he didn't say it was okay.

The senior staff member returned to her office and the president continued on to the First Family's living quarters, leaving the Secret Service detail behind. He was in the true bubble here; as safe at 1600 Pennsylvania Avenue at it was possible to be. If the Secret Service had its way, he would never leave the building, until either he was termed out or the voters gave the job to somebody else. But he was the president, the man of the people. Thus he had to actually mingle with the citizens while ulcers grew silently in the bellies of his guards.

Dan Cox threw off his jacket, pressed a button on a small box resting on a table and a White House steward appeared. Cox gave his order and a minute later he was handed a gin and tonic on the rocks with two slices of lime. That was a nice perk of the job. The president could get pretty much anything he wanted, at any time. After the steward departed, Cox flopped down next to his wife, who sat on the couch reading a magazine and trying her best to appear relaxed.

"See the latest poll numbers?" he asked gleefully.

She nodded. "But there's still a long way to go. And the polls tend to tighten."

"I know it's early yet, but let's be honest, the other side has no traction."

"Don't be overconfident," she scolded.

He held up his cut crystal glass. "Interested?"

"No thanks."

He munched some unsalted almonds. "When have you ever known me to either be overconfident or lose an election?"

She gave him a kiss on the cheek. "First time for everything."

"They still want three debates. I'm thinking two."

"You should only do one."

"Why only one? Graham's not that good of a debater."

"You're being far too kind, Danny. Graham is not only a poor debater; he's mediocre on all levels. It'll only take the American people *one* time to realize how hopeless he is. So why waste your time? And

you don't need to give him three bites at the apple
to change anyone's mind, or be raised up to your
level. And let's face it, honey, you are human. And
humans make mistakes. So why put that much pressure on yourself? He has everything to gain from that
strategy and you have everything to lose. The opposition knows their best chance is four years from now
when you're termed out. They're counting on the
fact that they'll be able to find a young buck with a
brain, some real ideas, and a core constituency that
they can expand on by then to *really* challenge for
the White House. Graham is just a stopgap."

He smiled and held up his drink in the manner of
a tribute. "I don't know why I even have a campaign
strategy team. I can just come and ask the missus."

"You survive enough battles, the lessons tend to
sink in."

"You know *I'll* be termed out, but you could
run," he said playfully. "Keep a Cox in the White
House another eight years."

"The White House is a nice place, but I really
don't want to live here."

He seemed to remember something. He put his
drink down, wrapped an arm around her, and said,
"Any news on Willa?"

"None."

"The whole damn FBI on the case and nothing?
I'll get on the horn to Munson first thing in the
morning. That is totally unacceptable."

"It seems so strange that someone would kidnap Willa."

He held her more tightly. "Jane, smart as you are, I know you've already thought about this. The reason they took Willa could have to do with us. They'll try to hurt us and perhaps this country by using that precious little girl."

She gripped his arm. "What if they ask for something? Something in return for letting her go?"

Dan Cox let go of his wife, stood, and paced in front of her. He was still a very attractive man. As she watched him walk up and down, she took in the thick shoulders, the perfect hair, the solid chin, the nuggets of cheekbones, and the sparkle of eyes. Physically, he was an amalgam of JFK and Reagan with an intimidating heft of burly Theodore Roosevelt thrown in.

She had fallen in love with him on seeing the man for the first time on a college campus on a beautiful early fall day. He'd been a junior and she an incoming freshman. It was a day that now seemed a million years ago. And in many important ways, it was. That life had been over for a long time. She could hardly call it part of her history anymore, for so much of immense importance had come in the intervening years.

"It depends on exactly what they want, Jane. The nuclear codes? I can't do that. One of the founding documents? I can't do that either. In fact, in all candor, the president of the United States cannot give in to blackmail of any kind. The precedent that would set would be untenable for any future administration. It would emasculate the office."

"So you're saying that we'll never see Willa again?"

He sat down next to her, rested a hand on her knee. "What I'm saying is that we will do everything in our power to get that little girl back safe and sound. We just have to keep thinking positive thoughts. We have the might of the United States behind us. That's no small thing."

"Will you be at the funeral tomorrow?"

He nodded. "Of course. I have an early rally in Michigan, but I'll be back in plenty of time. Air Force waits for no one. And at moments like this family needs to stick together. And not to sound too crass about it, but it'll let the country know that the Coxes put family first in periods of crisis. And that's the truth."

She put her magazine down. "I can see you're still in full campaign mode. It's late but I'm not really sleepy. Would you like to watch a movie in the theater? Warner Brothers just sent one of their latest over. I don't even think it's in theaters yet."

He finished his drink, stood, and held out his hand.

"No movie. I missed you, love of my life."

He gave her the same heart-stopping smile he'd flashed at the college freshman over twenty-five years ago. She rose obediently and followed him into the bedroom. He closed the door behind them. He took off his tie and shoes and unzipped his pants. She slipped off her dress and undid her bra straps. She lay back on the bed, he on top of her. What followed was a private, intimate moment, an extraordinarily rare event for the First Couple. Sometimes, Jane thought, as he heaved and thrust above her and she moaned in his ear, that making love to her husband was the only privacy they ever had anymore.

When he was done he fell away from her, gave his wife a final kiss, and went to sleep. Air Force One was out the gate early the next morning and even the tireless Dan Cox needed a few hours of rest before hitting the road again.

The first time they'd made love in this very bed Jane had started to giggle. The newly sworn-in president had not been amused, interpreting her glee as aimed at something lacking in his lovemaking skills. However, when she'd told him why she was laughing, he'd joined in with her.

What she'd told him was, "I can't believe I'm getting screwed by the president of the United States."

Now Jane lay there for a half hour before rising, showering, dressing, and surprising the Secret Service agents by going back downstairs. She opened the door to her office, closed it behind her, unlocked her desk, and took out the letter and the key.

When would she get it? What would it say? What would she do then?

She looked at her watch. It was late, but she *was* the First Lady.

She made the call, woke him up.

Sean King said groggily, "Jane?"

"I'm sorry for the lateness of the hour. You're coming to the funeral of course." It was not even close to being a question.

"Ironically, I just attended one."

"What?"

"Long story. Yeah, I'm planning on being there."

"Tuck told me that you'd called."

"Did he also tell you what we talked about?"

"That was a mistake, Sean. I'm sorry. We should have been truthful with you from the very beginning."

"Yes, you should have."

"I was concerned about the . . . the . . ."

"Your brother screwing around on his wife?" he said helpfully.

"That it would reflect badly on the president's re-election campaign."

"Well, we can't have that, can we?"

"Please don't be cynical. I don't need that right now."

"Your concern was well justified. But it took me down a detour I didn't need to go down. A waste of time we couldn't really afford."

"So you think it has nothing to do with Willa's disappearance?"

"Can I tell you that for sure? No. But my professional instinct is telling me that it doesn't."

"So what now?"

"Talk to me about Willa."

"What about her?"

"Pam only had two children, both by C-section."

Ice seemed to congeal in Jane's bloodstream. "Pam had *three* children as you very well know."

"Okay, but she didn't give *birth* to all three. The postmortem confirmed that. I told Tuck about this. I thought he would have told you."

Tuck of course *had* told her, but she had no intention of revealing this to Sean. "So what exactly are you saying?"

"That one of the kids was not Pam's. Was it Tuck's by another woman? And was the child Willa?"

"I can't answer that."

"Can't or won't?"

"Why is this at all relevant?"

Sean sat up in his hotel room bed. "Are you serious? It's *relevant* because if Willa isn't Pam's daughter, then her real mom and/or dad could be behind her kidnapping."

"Willa is twelve years old. Why would someone wait all this time?"

"I thought that too, but the fact is I don't have the answer to that. And I'm convinced that I *need* the answer to that question if we're going to solve this thing and find Willa. So can you help me out?"

"I don't know anything about it."

"Well, if she is Pam's daughter, then the lady had to be pregnant with her all those years ago. Was she?"

"I . . . She . . . Now I remember, they weren't living in the U.S. back then. They were in Italy. Tuck's business. And now that I think about it, they returned shortly after Willa was born."

Sean leaned back against the headboard. "Well, that was convenient. So you don't know for sure if she was pregnant? Never saw any pictures? Mom and newborn in the hospital? No baby showers? Didn't visit them over there?"

"You're being cynical again," she said coldly.

"No, I'm actually being politely probing."

"Okay, I admit that I can't tell you for sure if Willa is Pam's daughter. I always believed that she was. Let me put it this way, I had no reason *not* to believe that she was."

"Well, if you are withholding something from me I will get to the truth at some point and the results may not be to your liking."

"Is that a threat?"

"Threatening any member of the First Family is a felony, as you well know. And I'm one of the good guys. See you at the funeral, *Mrs. Cox*."

He hung up the phone.

Jane locked the letter and key back in her desk and nearly ran to the living quarters. As she undressed and climbed back into bed, she listened to the soft snores of her husband. He never had trouble going to sleep. Even after working the phones until the wee hours of the morning, he would finally put the receiver down after haggling over some mind-numbingly important national business, brush his teeth, and be asleep within five minutes. She, on the other hand, took hours to do so, if she ever managed at all.

As she lay on her side and stared over at the wall she imagined she could see Willa's face there, the child beckoning to her. Pleading.

Help me, Aunt Jane. Save me. I need you.

44

"What's the matter, Gabriel? You look like you're not feeling too good."

Quarry eyed the little boy across the heft of the kitchen table.

"Haven't been sleeping too good the last couple of nights, Mr. Sam," he said miserably.

"Kids are always supposed to sleep good. You got something on your mind?"

Gabriel couldn't look at him when he said, "Nothing important. I'll be okay."

"You got school today?" Quarry asked, as he studied the boy closely. "'Cause if you do, you're gonna miss the bus."

"Nope. Teacher day. I thought I'd help Ma, do some field work, and then get some reading done."

"I need to talk to your ma after I go into town."

"What about?"

"Personal business."

Gabriel's face fell. "I didn't do anything wrong, did I?"

Quarry smiled. "You think the whole world

revolves around you? Naw, just business stuff. You get a chance to clean out the toolbench in the barn some, that'd be real good. Get rid of anything that's rusted up bad. And I got another stamp for you."

Gabriel did his best to smile. "Thank you, Mr. Sam. Got me a good collection going. I checked on one you gave me on the computer at school. On eBay."

"What the hell is that?"

"You buy and sell stuff on there. Like a bunch of stores on the Internet."

Quarry looked mildly interested. "Go on."

"Anyway, this one stamp you gave me is worth forty dollars!"

"Damn. You gonna sell it?"

Gabriel looked shocked. "Mr. Sam, I'm not selling anything you give me."

"Piece of advice for free, little man. That stamp collection is gonna help fund your college education. Why you think I been giving 'em to you? And the old coins too?"

Gabriel looked puzzled. "I guess I never thought about that."

"See, your brain's not as big as you think it is, now is it?"

"Guess not." They ate some more and the boy said, "You been flying up to the mine a lot."

He grinned. "Trying to find me some diamonds."

"Diamonds in the mine?" Gabriel said sharply. "Thought all those mines were in Africa."

"Might have us some right here in Alabama."

"I was thinking maybe I'd go with you."

"Son, you been all over that mine with me. It's still just dirt in a big hole."

"I mean on the plane. We always went in the truck."

"We always went in the truck 'cause you don't like to fly. Hell, you told me every time you watch me take off you want to crawl inside the earth and never come out."

Gabriel smiled weakly. "I'm trying to get over that. I want to see more of this world than just Alabama, so I've got to get on planes, right?"

Quarry smiled at the boy's spot-on logic. "That's pretty right, yeah."

"Let me know then. I'll be getting on with the chores."

"You do that."

Gabriel put his dishes in the sink and scooted out of the kitchen.

As he headed to the barn, Gabriel was thinking hard. Thinking about what he'd heard Mr. Sam talk about when he was drunk in the library last night. He'd heard the name Willow or something like that, maybe like the weeping willow, he figured. And he'd heard Mr. Sam say the word "coal," or at least it sounded like it, which had made Gabriel think of the mine too.

He wouldn't ask Mr. Sam directly because he didn't want him to know that Gabriel had been eavesdropping, even though he'd just come down for another book to read. Mr. Sam sure had been sad about something, Gabriel told himself while he was cleaning out the toolbench in the barn. And the other day he'd watched as Mr. Sam had rolled up his sleeve to help with washing the dishes. There were burn marks on his forearm. Gabriel wondered about that too.

And he'd heard Daryl and Carlos talk about things in the gunroom at night while they'd been cleaning their rifles. But none of it made much sense. Once they'd been talking about Kurt. When Gabriel had come in the room, they'd shut up real fast and then showed him how to break down and reassemble a pistol in under fifty seconds. And why go up to the mine every day? And why had Carlos and sometimes Daryl stayed up there overnight? Was there something going on up there? Gabriel didn't think it was about diamonds.

And more than once he'd gotten out of bed in time to see Mr. Sam head down to the basement with a fat ring of keys. Gabriel had followed him all the way one time, his heart beating so hard he thought for sure Mr. Sam would hear it. He'd watched as the man had opened up a door down a long passageway that smelled foul. His ma had told him once that that was where the Quarrys used to keep their bad slaves. He hadn't believed her at first and had asked Mr. Sam about it. But Mr. Sam had confirmed his mother's statement.

"Your family had slaves, Mr. Sam?" he'd asked him once when they were walking the fields.

"Most folks 'round here did back in the old days. Atlee was a cotton plantation then. Had to have people to work it. A lot of people."

"But so why didn't they just pay 'em? Not keep 'em as slaves just 'cause they could."

"I guess it comes down to greed. You don't pay folks, you make more money. That and thinking one race wasn't as good as another."

Gabriel had stuck his hands in his trouser pockets and said, "Now that's a damn shame."

"Too many people think they can do anything, hurt anybody, and get away with it."

But that didn't explain why Mr. Sam went down into the stink of the basement where they used to keep the bad slaves. Strange things going on at Atlee for sure. But it was Gabriel's home; he and his ma had no other, so it really wasn't any of his business. He was just going to keep going on his way. But he was still curious. Real curious. It was just his way.

45

Quarry stopped the pickup truck in front of Fred's Airstream and tapped the horn. Fred came out, a store-bought cigarette dangling from one hand and a paper bag in the other. He had on an old sweat-stained straw hat, corduroy jacket, faded jeans, and boots withered by sun and rain. His white hair hung to his shoulders and looked shiny and clean.

Quarry leaned out the window. "You remember to bring some ID with you?"

Fred climbed in the truck, took out his wallet, really two flaps of leather hooked together with rubber bands, and slipped out an ID card. "White man's way of keeping tabs on us *real* Americans."

Quarry grinned. "I got news for you, buckaroo. Old Uncle Sam ain't just watching folks like you. He's watching *all* of us. Real Americans like you and the ones just renting space here like me."

From the paper bag Fred drew out a bottle of beer.

"Damn, can't you wait until we're done before you suck that down?" said Quarry. "I don't want to ever see what your sorry liver looks like," he added.

"My mother lived to ninety-eight," Fred replied as he took a long drink and put the bottle back in the bag.

"Yeah? Well I can pretty much guarantee *you* won't. And you've got no health insurance. Neither do I. They say the hospital has to treat everybody, but they don't say *when* they do. Been over the county hospital mor'n once lying on the waiting room floor with the fever and the chills and the heaves so bad I think I'm gonna die. Two days go by and then some kid in a white coat finally comes out and asks you to stick out your tongue and wants to know where it hurts while you're lying on the floor with your stomach coming out your ass. By then you've pretty much lived through it, but some damn drugs would've been nice too."

"I never go to hospital." Fred said this in Indian. And then he started talking fast in his native tongue.

Quarry interrupted him. "Fred, I don't have Gabriel here, so when you start going full Muskogean on me, I'm lost, man."

Fred repeated it all in English.

"There you go. When in America, speak the English. Just don't try to go to the damn hospital without an insurance card. I don't care what language you're talking, you're screwed."

The truck bumped along. Fred pointed to a

buildting in the distance. It was the little house that Quarry had built.

"You do good job on that. I watch you sometimes while you do it."

"Thank you."

"But who did you build it for?"

"Someone special."

"Who?"

"Me. My vacation home."

They drove on.

Quarry pulled out a bulky envelope from his jacket and passed it across to Fred. When Fred opened it, his hands shook slightly. Stunned, he looked up at Quarry, who was eying him from under bushy eyebrows.

"One thousand dollars in there."

"What is it for?" Fred asked, as he hacked up some phlegm and spit it out the window.

"For coming back home," he said, grinning. "And for something else too."

"What?"

"That's why you needed your ID."

"And why do I need my ID? You never said."

"You're gonna be a witness to something. Something important."

"This is too much money to be a witness," Fred said.

"You don't want the cash?"

"I did not say that," the man replied, the heavy wrinkles on his face deepening as he spoke.

Quarry playfully jabbed him in the arm with his elbow. "Good. 'Cause I ain't no *Indian* giver."

Thirty minutes later they reached the small town. Fred was still looking down at the envelope packed with twenties. "You didn't steal this, did you?"

"Never stole nothing in my life." He looked at Fred. "Not counting people. Now I stole me some people, you know." A long moment passed and then Quarry laughed and so did Fred.

"Cashed in some old bonds my daddy had," explained Quarry.

He pulled in front of the local bank, a one-story brick building with a glass front door.

"Let's go."

Quarry headed to the door and Fred followed.

"I've never been in a bank," said Fred.

"How come?"

"I've never had any money."

"Me neither. But I still go to the bank."

"Why?"

"Hell, Fred, 'cause that's where all the money is."

Quarry snagged a banker he knew and explained what he wanted. He pulled out the document. "Brought my *real* American friend here to help witness it."

The stout, bespectacled banker looked at the scruffy Fred and attempted a smile. "I'm sure that's fine, Sam."

"I'm sure it's fine too," said Fred. He patted his jacket where the envelope full of money was, and he and Quarry exchanged a quick grin.

The banker took them into his office. Another witness was called in along with the bank's notary public. Quarry signed his will in front of Fred, this other witness, and the notary. Then Fred and the other witness signed. After that, the notary did her official thing. When it was all completed, the banker made a copy of the will. Afterward, Quarry folded up the original and put it in his jacket.

"Make sure you keep it in a safe place," warned the banker. "Because a copy won't be good enough for probate. How about a safe-deposit box here?"

"Don't you worry about that," said Quarry. "Anybody tries to break into my house gets their head blown off."

"I'm sure," said the banker a little nervously.

"I'm sure too," said Quarry.

Fred and Quarry stopped at a bar for a drink before heading back.

"So *now* it is okay to drink, Sam?" asked Fred, tipping the mug of beer to his mouth.

Quarry pitched back a few fingers of bourbon. "It's after noon, right? All I'm telling you, Fred, is to have some reasonable standards."

They drove back to Atlee. Quarry dropped Fred off at the Airstream.

As the old man slowly made his way up the

cinderblock steps, he turned back to Quarry who sat in the old truck. "Thank you for the money."

"Thank you for witnessing my will."

"Do you expect to die soon?"

Quarry grinned. "If I knew that I'd probably be off in Hawaii or something going for a swim in the ocean and eating me that calamari. Not riding around in a rusted-out truck in nowhere Alabama talking to the likes of you, Fred."

"By the way, my name isn't Fred."

"I know that. 'Cause that's the name I gave you. What is it, then? Your real name? I didn't see your ID that good or how you signed the will."

"Eugene."

"Is that an Indian name?"

"No, but it is what my mother named me."

"How come?"

"Because she was white."

"And she really lived to ninety-eight?"

"No. She was dead at fifty. Too much booze. She drank even more than me."

"Can I still call you Fred?"

"Yes. I like it better than Eugene."

"Tell me the truth, Fred. How much longer *you* got to live?"

"About a year, if I'm lucky."

"I'm sorry."

"So am I. How did you know?"

"Seen a lot of death in my day. The chest hack

you got. And your hands are too cold and your skin under the brown is too pale."

"You're a smart man."

"You know we all got to go one day. But now you can enjoy what time you got left a thousand times better than you would've a few hours ago." He pointed a finger at his friend. "And don't leave nothing for me, Fred. I won't be needing it."

Quarry drove off in a swirl of dust.

When he got back to Atlee the first plump drops of rain from an approaching front were starting to fall. He walked in and went straight to the kitchen because that's where he heard her. Ruth Ann was scrubbing some big cook pots clean when Quarry's boots hit the kitchen floor. She turned and smiled.

"Gabriel was looking for you."

"Told him I was going into town with Fred."

"Whatcha go into town for?" Ruth Ann asked as she worked.

Quarry sat down and took the document out of his jacket and unfolded it. "What I wanted to talk to you about." He held up the paper. "This here is my last will and testament. I got it signed today. Now it's all official."

Ruth Ann put down the pot she was scrubbing and wiped her hands on a dish towel.

Her brow creased. "Your will? You ain't sick, are you?"

"No, at least not that I know. But only a fool

waits until they're sick to make a will. Come on over here and take a look at it."

Ruth Ann took a hesitant step forward and then quickly crossed the room and sat down. She took the paper from him, slipped a pair of drugstore glasses from her shirt pocket, and put them on.

"I don't read all that good," she said, a little embarrassed. "Get Gabriel to do it for me mostly."

He stabbed a finger at one part of the paper. "It's mostly lawyer talk, but right there is all you got to pay attention to, Ruth Ann."

She read where he indicated, her lips moving slowly as she read the few words. Then she looked up at him, the paper trembling in her hands.

"Mr. Sam. This ain't right."

"What's not right about it?"

"You leaving all this to me and Gabriel?"

"That's right. My property. I can give it to whoever I damn well want to, 'scuse my French."

"But you got family. You got Mr. Daryl, and Miss Tippi. And your other daughter too."

"I trust you to take care of Daryl, if he's still around. And Tippi. And Suzie, well, I doubt she'd want anything from me seeing as how she hasn't even called me in over four years. And you and Gabriel are my family too. So I want to provide for you. This is my way of doing that."

"You sure 'bout this?"

"Sure I'm sure."

She reached across the table and took his hand. "You a good man, Mr. Sam. You probably outlive all of us. But I thank you for all you done for me and Gabriel. And I take care of everybody, Mr. Sam. Everybody real good. Just like you would."

"Ruth Ann, you can do anything with the property you want. Including selling it if you need the money."

She looked appalled by the suggestion. "I ain't never gonna sell this place, Mr. Sam. This here's our home."

There was a noise at the doorway and they looked over to see Gabriel standing there.

"Hey, Gabriel," said Quarry. "Me and your ma just talking about some things."

"What things, Mr. Sam?" Gabriel looked at his mother and noted the tears sliding down her thin, flat cheeks. "Is everything okay?" he said slowly.

"Come on over here, you," his mother said, beckoning to him. He ran to her and she hugged him. Quarry patted Gabriel on the head, folded up his will, put it back in his pocket, and left the room.

He had another letter to write.

And he had to go see Tippi.

And then he was going to the mine.

It was getting close to the end now.

46

For the second time in as many days, Sean and Michelle listened to a preacher talk about the dearly departed. It was a rainy, blustery afternoon and black umbrellas were braced against the elements as Pam Dutton was laid to rest in a cemetery five miles from where she'd died. The children were in the front row under the canopy with their father. Tuck's head was bandaged and the man looked like he had downed a few cocktails and a handful of pills. His sister, the First Lady, sat next to him, her arm protectively around his shoulders. Colleen Dutton was perched in Jane's lap. John was snuggled against his father. Next to Jane was her husband, who was dressed in black and looking solemnly presidential.

A wall of "A-team" Secret Service surrounded the burial site. The surrounding streets had been cleared and shut down, with every manhole cover in the roads the motorcade had taken welded shut. The cemetery was closed to everyone other than the bereaved family and invited friends. A regiment of journalists and TV crews waited just outside the gates hoping to catch a glimpse of the president and grieving First Lady when they left the graveyard.

Michelle nudged Sean and inclined her head to the left. Agent Waters of the FBI was in attendance. And his gaze was dead on Sean and Michelle.

"He doesn't look too happy," she said.

"I bet he's never been happy in his entire life."

They'd caught an early morning flight back from Tennessee. On the plane back they'd talked about what had happened the night before.

When they'd gotten back to Frank Maxwell's house, the man hadn't returned. Michelle had tried calling him on his cell phone but there was no answer. They were just about to call in the cops when he had come through the garage door.

"Dad?"

He had pushed right past her, gone to his bedroom, and closed the door. When Michelle had tried the door, it was locked.

"Dad?" she'd called through the door. "Dad!" She started beating on it, until a hand grabbed her. It was Sean.

"Just let him be for now."

"But—"

"There's something going on here that we don't understand, so let's not push it for now."

Sean had slept on the couch and Michelle in one of the spare bedrooms. Her brothers were staying at Bobby's house nearby.

When they woke the next morning to catch their flight, Frank Maxwell was already dressed and gone. This time Michelle didn't even try to call his cell.

"He won't answer it," she said over a cup of coffee at the airport.

"What do you think he was doing at the farmhouse?"

"Maybe the same reason I was there."

"Meaning what exactly?"

"Meaning I don't know exactly," she said miserably.

"Do you want to stay here? I can pop up for the funeral."

"No, I don't think there's anything I can do down here right now. And going to another funeral won't be nearly as depressing as staying here and watching my family finish disintegrating."

The service for Pam Dutton was over now and people were filtering away, though Sean did notice that many folks did their best to finagle a handshake with the president. And to his credit he accommodated them as best he could.

"Can't chance ticking off a potential voter," Michelle said sarcastically.

Jane walked out with her brother and the kids. Several agents flanked them, but the bulk stayed with the president. As he watched this scene, Sean well knew that *that* one life trumped all others. The First

Lady was a vitally important protectee in the world of the Service, but her ranking was so far below the president's that if a choice had to be made as to whom to save, it would not be a difficult decision.

Michelle apparently read his thoughts because she said, "Did you ever wonder what'd you do?"

He turned to her. "What'd I do about what?"

"If you had to choose between the First Couple? Which one to save?"

"Michelle, you know if there's one rule the Service bangs into your brain it's *that* one. The president's the one life you can not let end."

"But let's say he's committing a crime. Or what if the guy goes nuts and is attacking the First Lady. He's getting ready to kill her. What would you do? Take him out or let her die?"

"Why are we having this conversation? Isn't the fact that we're at a funeral depressing enough?"

"Just wondering."

"Good, you wonder. I'll stay out of it."

"It's just a hypothetical."

"I have enough trouble dealing with reality."

"Are we going to see the First Lady?"

"After my last phone call with her, I'm not sure. I'm not even sure if we're on the same side as her anymore."

"What do you mean by that?"

Sean let out a long sigh. "I'm just talking and not

making much sense." He looked over at the man coming toward them. "This day just keeps getting better and better."

Michelle glanced over in time to see Agent Waters striding toward them.

"I thought I asked you two not to leave town," he said sharply.

"No, I think you said you wanted us to be available for further questioning," Michelle said back. "Well, here we are. All *available* and everything."

"Where have you been?" he demanded.

"Tennessee."

"What's in Tennessee?" he said angrily. "Some lead you're not sharing?"

"No. We were at another funeral."

"Whose?"

"My mother's."

Waters eyed her closely, perhaps trying to gauge if Michelle was pulling his chain or not. He apparently came away satisfied because he said, "I'm sorry. Was it unexpected?"

"Murder usually is," Michelle said before walking on toward the row of parked cars.

Waters shot a glance at Sean. "Is she on the level?"

"Afraid so."

"Damn."

"Did you need us for anything?"

"No. I mean not right now."

"Good. See you around."

He caught up to Michelle and they were about to climb in her SUV when they heard someone behind them. And the person was out of breath.

Tuck Dutton looked like he'd just run a mile. His face was flushed and his chest was heaving.

"Tuck, what the hell is it?" Sean asked, grabbing hold of his arm. "Come on, man, you just got out of the hospital. You shouldn't be running sprints."

Tuck sucked in a breath, put a steadying hand against the SUV, and nodded toward the presidential limo. Jane Cox was just climbing in it, along with her husband, while agents hovered around them.

"The guy I saw with Pam," he said breathlessly.

"What about him?" Michelle asked.

"He's here."

"What? Where?" Sean snapped, looking around.

"Right over there."

Tuck pointed toward the limo.

"Which one?"

"The big guy right at the president's elbow."

Sean looked at the man, back at Tuck, and then at Michelle.

"Aaron Betack?" said Sean right as the rain picked up.

47

A reception was held for the people attending the funeral. Not at the White House, but at Blair House, right across the street. It was actually four houses connected together and at about seventy thousand square feet was larger than the White House. Normally the residence was used by visiting foreign heads of state and other high-ranking VIPs. Harry Truman and his family had even stayed there in the 1950s when the White House had been stripped down to its support beams and totally rebuilt. But today it would be a place for people to gather and remember Pam Dutton, have a few drinks and nibble on some food prepared by the world-class White House kitchen chefs.

Sean and Michelle passed through the metal detector, walked under the long awning, were wanded at the front door, and then entered the house. They had both been here before on high-level dignitary protection during their years at the Service. However, this was the first time they had seen the place in a nonworking capacity. They accepted drinks from a waiter and hugged a corner, watching and waiting. The president arrived with Jane, and then Tuck and the kids followed them in.

"There he is," said Michelle.

Sean nodded as Aaron Betack entered the room and scoped it out grid by grid as every agent who had ever worked for the Service instinctively did, retired or not. It was simply a habit you never forgot. Or else couldn't break.

"How do you want to do this?" she asked.

"He can't exactly fire us for grilling him."

"But should we tip our hand that we know about his seeing Pam?"

"That's the big question. Let's circle around it with him and see if the answer falls out of his mouth."

They waited until Betack had broken away from another group and walked into an adjoining room.

"Hey, Aaron," said Sean as he and Michelle came in behind him.

Betack nodded at them but said nothing.

Sean eyed the glass in the other man's hand. "Not working today?"

"Just paying my respects."

"Sad day," said Michelle.

Betack clinked the ice cubes in his glass and nodded, biting down on a cracker. "Shitty day all around, actually."

"More than the funeral, you mean?" said Sean.

"Nothing on the girl. First Lady's not happy."

"But FBI's still working leads. We just saw Waters. He didn't strike me as a guy who gives up easily."

Betack drew closer. "Best detective in the world needs to have a lead of some kind."

"Can't argue with that."

"So no more communications from the kidnappers?" asked Michelle.

"Not since the bowl and spoon."

"Odd," commented Sean.

"Everything about this sucker is odd," Betack said strangely.

"But it was also really well planned. If Michelle and I hadn't shown up at the house unexpectedly, we'd know even less. So you think they'd be in regular communication."

Betack shrugged. "It is what it is."

"Anything on the letters on Pam's arms?"

"Not that I know of."

Sean glanced at Michelle and said, "I remember the first time I met Pam. She was really great. Terrific mom. Did you know her at all?"

Sean said this casually but he gazed intently at the other man.

"Never had the pleasure," Betack said matter-of-factly. "When I said I was coming to pay my respects, it was for the First Lady."

Sean glanced toward the doorway where Jane Cox

passed by, followed by several of her assistants. "She is special."

"So you two got anything going on this case?"

Michelle spoke up first. "If we did we'd already have let Waters know."

"Important thing is to get Willa back, screw the credit," Sean added.

"Nice philosophy," commented Betack, swallowing the rest of his drink. "And rare in this town."

"But that includes everybody stepping up to the plate and telling everything they know," Michelle said pointedly, her gaze dead on Betack.

The man noticed this and shot a glance at Sean and then back at her. "You implying something?"

Sean lowered his voice. "Tuck Dutton saw you meeting with his wife when he was supposed to be out of town."

"He's wrong."

"He described you pretty accurately. And he fingered you at the funeral as the guy."

"I look like a lot of guys. And why would I be meeting with Pam Dutton?"

"I was hoping you could tell us that."

"I can't, because it never happened."

Sean stared at him for a long moment and then said, "Okay, Tuck was wrong."

"That's right. He was wrong. Excuse me." He stalked off.

Michelle turned to Sean. "How long you figure before he contacts whoever he was working with?"

"Not that long."

"So we just wait?"

Sean gazed around the room and then stopped as Tuck walked by. "I'm actually tired of waiting."

48

Willa finished the last of her books, replaced it on the stack, sat back on her cot, and stared at the door. When she was reading, she forgot where she was. When she had turned the last page, she realized once more exactly *what* she was.

A prisoner.

She was never going to see her family again. She could just tell.

She stiffened as the footsteps approached. It was the big man. The old man. She recognized his tread. The door opened a few seconds later and there he was. He shut the door behind him and walked toward her.

"You doing okay, Willa?" He sat down at the table and rested his hands in his lap.

"I finished all the books."

He opened the knapsack he carried and pulled out another stack of books and set them on the table. "There you go."

She eyed the books. "So I'm going to be here for a long time then?"

"No. Not that much longer."

"So I'll be back with my family then?"

He looked away. "Did you like the lady you met here?"

Willa kept her gaze right on him. "She's scared. *I'm* scared too."

"I guess we're all scared in a way."

"Why should you be afraid? I can't hurt you."

"Hope you enjoy the books."

"Is there one where the kid dies at the end? That way I can like prepare myself!"

He stood. "You're not sounding like yourself, Willa."

She stood too. Although she was over two feet shorter than the man, she seemed his equal. "You don't know me. You might have found out things about me, but you don't know me. Or my family. Did you hurt them? Did you?" she demanded.

Quarry's gaze flitted around the room, looking everywhere except at her.

"I'll let you get some sleep. Seems like you need it."

"Just leave me alone," she said in a loud, firm voice. "I don't want to see you anymore."

Quarry had his hand on the door. "Do you want to see the lady again?"

"Why?"

"It'll give you somebody to talk to, Willa. Other than me. I understand why you don't like me. If I were you, I wouldn't either. I don't like having to do what I'm doing. If you knew the whole truth, maybe you'd understand better. Maybe you wouldn't."

"I'll see her," Willa said grudgingly, turning her back on him.

"Good enough," said Quarry quietly.

Her next words froze him.

"Does this have to do with your daughter? The one who can't read anymore?"

He turned slowly back around, his gaze now burning into her. "Why do you say that?" His voice was hard, fierce.

She stared back at him. "Because I'm somebody's daughter *too*."

Yes you are, thought Quarry. *You just don't know whose*. He closed and locked the door behind him.

Minutes passed and then the door opened again. The lady was standing there, Quarry behind her.

"I'll be back in an hour," he said.

He shut the door and Diane Wohl moved cautiously forward and sat down at the table. Willa joined her and turned the lantern light up higher.

"How are you doing?" Willa said gently.

"I'm so scared it's hard for me to breathe sometimes."

"Me too."

"You don't act scared. I'm the adult but you're obviously a lot braver than I am."

"Did he talk to you at all? The man?"

353

"Not really. Just told me to come with him. To see you."

"Did you want to?"

"Of course, honey. I mean . . . I mean it gets so lonely in that room."

She eyed the books. Willa followed her gaze. "You want some books to read?"

"I've never been much of a reader, I'm afraid."

Willa picked up several and slid them across to her. "Now would be a good time to start."

Diane fingered the cover of one. "He's a very strange kidnapper."

"Yes he is," Willa agreed. "But we still need to be afraid of him."

"Trust me, that won't be a problem."

"We almost got away," said Willa defiantly. "We were like so close."

"Because of you. I was probably the reason we didn't get away. I'm not very heroic."

"I just wanted to get back to my family."

Diane reached out a hand and gripped the girl's arm. "Willa, you are very brave, and you just have to keep being brave."

A sob jumped from her throat. "I'm only twelve. I'm just a kid."

"I know, sweetie, I know."

Diane slid her chair around the table and put her arms protectively around Willa.

The girl started shaking and Diane held her tight

against her chest. She whispered to her, that things really would be okay. That her family was no doubt fine and that she was definitely going to see them again. Diane knew Willa would never see her mother again, because the man had told her she was dead. But still she had to say it to the stricken little girl.

My little girl.

Outside the door Quarry leaned against the wall of the mine and rubbed an old coin between his fingers. It was a Lady Liberty he was planning on giving to Gabriel. Not for eBay. For college. But Quarry wasn't really focused on the coin. He was listening to Willa cry her heart out. The wails from the little girl swooped up and down the shafts of the mine, as had decades ago the moans of battered miners, and generations before them the shrieks of Union soldiers dying of diseases that riddled their bodies.

Yet he couldn't imagine any more painful, heart-wrenching sound than what he was hearing now. He slipped the coin back in his pocket.

He'd gotten his affairs in order. People he cared about were provided for. After that, it was out of his hands.

People would condemn him, of course, but so be it. He had endured far worse than the negative opinions of others.

Still, he would be glad when this was over.

It *had* to be over soon.

None of them could take much more of it.

Sam Quarry knew that he couldn't.

Late that night he took the truck to see Tippi. This time he went alone. He read to her. He played the tape of mother talking to daughter.

He looked around the ten-by-twelve-foot confines of Tippi's world for all these years. He'd memorized every piece of equipment needed to keep her alive here, and had pelted the staff here with questions about each one of them. They had no idea why he was being so inquisitive, but that didn't matter. He knew why.

When he finally gazed down at his daughter's withered face, her atrophied limbs, her skeleton of a torso, he felt his own big frame start to droop as though gravity had decided to exert more force on him. Perhaps as punishment.

Quarry had no problem with punishment, so long as it was dealt out fairly, evenly. Only it never was.

He left the room and ventured to the nurses' station. He had to make some arrangements. It was time for Tippi to finally leave this place.

It was time to bring his little girl home.

49

"Look, King, we have orders to keep them all here," said the agent to Sean and Michelle.

They were at the entrance to Blair House. The decision had been made to allow Tuck and his kids to remain at the residence where they would have the full protection of the Secret Service, at least temporarily.

"All I'm asking you to do is to let Tuck Dutton know that we're out here. If he wants to see us, there's really nothing you can do about it, is there? He's not a criminal. He's not in protective custody. He's here voluntarily. And if wants to leave, you have to let him leave."

Michelle added, "We'll keep a close eye on him."

"Right, and it's my ass on the line to the president if anything happens to his brother-in-law."

"I'd actually be more afraid of the First Lady," advised Sean.

"I'm not going to get Dutton. Now I suggest that—"

"Sean?"

They all looked up at the front door. Tuck was standing there holding Colleen in one arm and a cup of coffee in the other.

"Mr. Dutton, please get away from the door," warned the agent.

Tuck put Colleen down and told her to go join her brother. Then he set down the coffee cup and came outside.

"Mr. Dutton!" The agent took a step toward him as two other agents moved forward from their outside posts.

Tuck held up his hand. "I know, I know. You're here to protect me. But why don't you go protect my kids? I'll be fine."

"Mr. Dutton," the agent began again.

"Look, buddy. I'm only here because my sister said it was okay. Great, I appreciate it. But the fact is this is America and I can leave here with my kids any damn time I want, and there's not a damn thing you can do about it. So go hang out with my kids or go smoke a cigarette while I talk to these folks. Okay?"

"I'll have to let the First Lady know about this," the agent snapped.

"You do that. And she might be the First Lady to you, but to me she's just the older sister whose panties I used to let my friends see for a buck a peek."

The agent's face flushed. He glanced angrily at

Sean and Michelle, then turned on his heel and went inside the house.

"Tuck, that's a side of you I've never seen," said Sean as they walked down the street across from the White House.

Tuck flicked a cigarette out of a pack, cupped his hands, and lit up. He exhaled a small cloud of smoke. "It gets to you, you know? I don't know how Jane and Dan do it. Talk about a freaking fishbowl. It's actually more like living your life under the damn Hubble Telescope."

"Every flaw revealed," said Michelle, as her gaze swept, like radar, grid by grid, in front, to the side, and also behind them. They might be in one of the safest spots on earth, but, as she well knew, that could change in a single explosive moment.

"How are the kids?"

"Scared, nervous, anxious, depressed. They know Pam's gone, of course. And that's devastating enough. But not knowing what's happened to Willa. It's just too much. It's killing all of us. I haven't slept a wink since they took me off the drugs in the hospital. I don't even know how I'm functioning."

Michelle eyed the cigarette. "They've only got one parent left now, Tuck. Do yourself and them a favor and cut out the cancer sticks."

Tuck dropped the smoke on the pavement and crushed it with the heel of his shoe. "What did you guys want with me?"

"One thing."

Tuck put up his hands. "Look, if this is that crap about Willa being adopted."

"No, it's actually about the guy you saw Pam with."

"Did you talk to him? Who is he?"

"He's a Secret Service agent. A pretty high-ranking one," said Michelle.

"His name is Aaron Betack. And he basically says you were wrong in identifying him as the guy you saw with Pam."

"Then he's full of shit. I was staring at him through a clear glass window. No more than ten feet. It was him! I'd swear on a stack of Bibles."

"We believe you, Tuck," said Michelle.

"And there might be an easier way than the Bible thing," added Sean.

"What do you mean?"

Sean pointed across the street. "He's over there right now. We saw him go in. That's why we're here."

"Betack?"

"Yep," said Sean.

"So what do you want me to do?"

"We want you to call your sister and ask to see her with us. When we get in there we want her to call Betack in and we'll confront him with what we know. Then if he wants to lie to her face, let him."

Tuck suddenly didn't seem so sure of himself. "I'm sure she's pretty busy right now."

first family

Michelle took hold of his arm. "Tuck, you just buried your wife. Your oldest child has been kidnapped. I don't think you should be worried right now about your sister being *busy*."

Sean eyed him intently. "What's it going to be?"

Tuck pulled out his cell phone. "Five minutes?"

"Works for us," answered Sean.

50

Sean King, who'd worked presidential protection detail when he was in the Secret Service, had been allowed in the top security clearance-required White House Situation Room when guarding the president. Yet he had never seen the private quarters of the First Family. That omission had now been corrected. After riding the elevator up and being let out of the small cage by a genuine elevator operator, he and Michelle looked around at the room they were in. It had luxurious furnishings, heavy moldings, and beautiful flower displays. Then his attention returned to the woman who was sitting on the couch across from him, a cup of hot tea in hand. A warming fire crackled in the fireplace. Across the street, protestors could be heard chanting about something in Lafayette Park.

Jane obviously heard this too. "You'd think they would have held off, with everything that's happened."

"It's done by permit," said Michelle. "They have to take their shot when they get it."

"Of course."

She looks tired, Sean thought. And it obviously wasn't just the campaign. The tiny lines on the First Lady's face were more pronounced, the pouches under the eyes thicker, the hair not as meticulous as usual. She also seemed to have lost weight. The clothes she wore hung more loosely.

Michelle's gaze was on Tuck. Jane Cox's brother sat next to his sister, shooting nervous glances around the room. He held a mixed drink that had been brought to him by one of the White House attendants. He gripped it so tightly his fingers were white. The guy probably wanted to light up, but the White House was a no-smoking zone, much to the chagrin of many stressed-out folks who labored there.

"How are John and Colleen doing?" Jane asked.

"Not great."

"We can have them stay here, Tuck."

"It wouldn't matter, sis. It's not the place."

"I know."

Tuck looked around the spacious room. "And this house doesn't really seem geared for kids."

"You'd be surprised," said Jane. "Remember Dan Jr. had a birthday party in the State Dining Room when he turned sixteen. And lots of small children have lived here. Teddy Roosevelt's family. JFK's."

"It's okay, sis, really."

She glanced at Sean. "Thank you for making it to the funeral."

"I told you we'd be there."

"We left things in an awkward way the last time we talked."

"I thought I was pretty clear, actually."

Her mouth set into a frown. "I'm trying to handle this as professionally as possible, Sean."

He sat forward as Michelle and Tuck watched him nervously.

"And *we're* trying to find Willa. I don't really care whether we accomplish that *professionally* or not so long as we get her back. I hope you don't have a problem with that." He glanced at Tuck. "Either of you."

"I just want my daughter back," Tuck said quickly.

"Of course," said Jane. "That's what we all want."

"Good, I'm glad we have that settled." He gave Tuck an encouraging nod.

Tuck opened his mouth. "So . . . is Dan around?"

Sean rolled his eyes and sat back while Michelle just stared at Tuck like he was the biggest loser she'd personally ever seen.

"Working in his office. Then he's flying to the West Coast late tonight. I'm to join him there tomorrow, but my plans are up in the air right now, as you can imagine. I doubt that I'll go now."

She eyed Sean. "Have you got anything to tell me?"

"No, but I think your brother does. That's why we're here, in fact."

She glanced at Tuck. "What is it?"

Tuck swallowed the rest of his drink so quickly, he nearly choked. When he recovered he still didn't say anything.

An exasperated Michelle said, "Tuck saw Agent Betack meeting with Pam about a month before she was killed. Agent Betack denies that happened. We wanted you to have him come in here and settle the issue once and for all. We know he's at the White House. We followed him here, in fact."

Tuck's gaze was glued to his shoes as his sister first looked at Michelle and then over at Sean.

"That won't be necessary."

"Why not?" asked Sean.

"Because Agent Betack *did* meet with Pam."

"How do you know that?"

"Because I asked him to."

For a very awkward minute, the only sound was the crackle of the fire and the faraway chants of the protestors.

Surprisingly, it was Tuck Dutton who broke this silence.

"What the hell is going on, sis?"

She put down her tea. The look she gave each of them, coming to finally rest on Tuck, was one of the oddest Sean had ever seen. It was a combination of dominance and desperation. And he wasn't quite sure how she pulled it off, but she did.

"Don't be stupid, Tuck."

The tone, Sean thought, was just a tad ugly for a sibling who'd just buried his wife.

"How am I being stupid by asking that question?"

"Pam suspected you were having an affair. She came to me for advice. As usual, I tried to smooth things over for you."

"You *knew* I was having an affair?"

"After I asked Agent Betack to look into it, yes. He had you followed and reported back to me that you were indeed *screwing* around." She looked at Sean and Michelle. "Not the first time, of course. My brother seems to have an inability to keep it in his pants unless he's around his wife. It's not just my brother. I think it afflicts all married men. As soon as they take the vow one of their chromosomes informs them that it's time to cheat."

Tuck looked like a very large man had just punched him flush in the face. "I can't believe you would—" he began.

"Just shut up, Tuck. We're way past that now."

Okay, thought Sean, *this is a side I've never seen of the woman and I don't like it.*

"So Betack was talking to Pam about what he'd found?" asked Michelle.

"Not exactly, no."

"So, what exactly then?" asked Sean.

"I had Agent Betack inform Pam that Tuck was *not* cheating on her."

Even Tuck looked slightly disgusted by this information, although the lie had obviously covered up his infidelity. Perhaps he was thinking of his dead wife out there in the muddy ground all by herself.

"So you had him lie to her, in other words?" said Michelle.

"My husband's re-election is a foregone conclusion barring any unforeseen calamity, including personal."

"So if Tuck's affair came out you were afraid it would tank your husband's chances? *That's* why you had Betack lie to Pam?" said Sean, who did not try to conceal his rising anger.

"But you're not your brother's keeper and neither is the president," Michelle pointed out. "Tuck's a big boy. There might be a scandal, but it wouldn't involve the First Family."

"Sometimes it's hard to determine where the First Family starts and stops," shot back Jane. "And in any case, I was determined not to find out that the public's opinion of my husband would be adversely affected by such a revelation. If nothing else it would give traction to an opposition that so far has found none."

There was *another* reason, but the First Lady chose not to elaborate for reasons that were obvious to her.

"Well, I don't think Pam believed Betack," said Sean.

"Why?"

"Because the night she was killed, we were going over to see Pam at her request. She didn't know Tuck would be arriving home that night. She said she had a matter she wanted us to look into. I'll give you three guesses at what that might be."

"I could tell at the party at Camp David that she was still concerned about it," admitted Jane.

Tuck looked at Sean. "And when I suddenly showed up at the house that night, she did look sort of freaked out."

Sean nodded. "She might have even wanted to call me to cancel, but she only had my office number, not my cell. And we were already on our way when Tuck showed up."

"So now you know all," said Jane.

"No, not all."

They all turned to see Agent Aaron Betack standing there.

"What?" asked Sean.

Betack advanced into the room.

"I don't recall asking you to come here, Agent Betack," said a surprised Jane.

"You didn't, ma'am. I . . . I took it upon myself." The veteran agent looked very pale.

"I'm not sure I understand how you can do that," she said bluntly.

Betack gazed around uneasily at the others. "There

was a letter delivered to one of the women who works in the kitchen here. Shirley Meyers."

Jane rose. "You will leave right now, Agent Betack. This instant."

Sean rose too. "What the hell is going on?"

"You will leave now!" snapped Jane.

"Aaron, what letter?" asked Michelle.

Before Betack could answer, Jane snatched up the phone. "One call, Betack. Either you leave now or your career is over."

"Maybe it already is," said Betack. "But what's a career compared to a little girl's life? Have you even thought about that?"

"How dare you speak to me that way!"

Tuck stood. "I dare. If it's got something to do with whether my daughter lives or dies, I sure as hell do dare."

Jane looked at him, and then at the others, one by one. Her confidence seemed to fall away under their gazes. She looked to Sean like a cornered animal desperately seeking a way out.

Sean said, "Jane, if you received a letter that has something to do with Willa, we need to know. The FBI needs to know."

"That is impossible."

Tuck grabbed her arm. "The hell it is."

Betack instinctively rushed forward to protect the First Lady. But Michelle had already snagged Tuck's arm and forcibly removed his grip. She pushed him down on the couch.

"Just chill, Tuck. You're not helping matters. She's still the First Lady."

"I don't give a shit what she is. She could be the president and I wouldn't give a damn. If she knows something that'll help get Willa back, I need to know what the hell it is."

Jane was looking steadily at Betack. "How do you know anything about this?"

"Nothing happens in this building without the Secret Service knowing, Mrs. Cox."

"Was the letter from the kidnappers?" asked Sean.

Jane finally looked away from Betack. "It might be. It's impossible for me to tell. For anyone to tell."

"Was it checked for prints?" asked Michelle.

"Since it wasn't sent here and passed through multiple hands before landing in mine, I think the answer to that is no," she said coldly.

"Where is it?" asked Sean.

"I destroyed it."

Sean looked uneasily at Betack. "Jane, this is a federal investigation. If you're found to have knowingly withheld and then destroyed evidence. . . ."

"Now *that* could tank the election for your husband," added Michelle.

"But why would you withhold it?" Sean wanted to know.

Jane did not make eye contact with him. "It was a shock to receive it the way that I did. I was trying to evaluate things before I determined what to do with it."

Okay, now she's on full spin, thought Sean.

"I think the *authorities* need to evaluate it," said Betack. "Please, Mrs. Cox, you need to understand fully what you're doing here. You need to tell them what was in the letter."

"Fine, I'll tell *you*. The letter said that I would be getting another letter sent to a post office box. They also sent me the address for that box and the key for it."

Sean, Michelle, and Betack exchanged glances.

Jane noticed this because she added, "And it said if anyone who remotely looked like a police officer or a federal agent went anywhere near the box, we would never get Willa back."

"Is that why you kept the letter to yourself?" asked Tuck.

"Of course. Do you seriously think I want anything to happen to Willa? I love her like she's one of my own children."

How she said this struck Sean as a little odd. "When did it say the other letter would be coming?"

"It didn't. But that I should check regularly. As of today there was nothing there."

Betack said, "We *have* to tell the FBI about this."

Sean and Michelle nodded in agreement but Jane shook her head. "If you do then we will never see Willa again."

"Jane, the Feds are really good at this."

"Yes, they've been superb so far. Figured everything out, haven't they? I can't imagine why they'd screw it up now."

"That's hardly fair," began Michelle.

Jane Cox raised her voice. "What do you know about fair?"

"When you get the letter, you have to let us see what it says."

She glanced over at Sean. "I *have* to?"

"You retained us to investigate this case, Jane. So far, you've lied to us, withheld vital information, and caused us to waste time we didn't have. Yeah, you need to let us and the FBI see the letter when it comes. Or else we can just pack it in right now and be done with it."

Tuck spoke up. "Jane, for God's sake, this is Willa we're talking about. You have to let them help."

"I'll think about it."

Tuck looked dumbstruck by this, but Sean said, "Fine, you *think about it* and let us know." He rose and motioned Tuck and Mchelle to join him in leaving.

"Tuck, why don't you stay here with the children?" said Jane.

He didn't even look at her. "No thanks."

Tuck stalked out of the room. Michelle and Sean followed him.

Betack had turned to join them when Jane said, "I'll never forget this betrayal, Agent Betack. Never."

Betack wet his lips, but whatever he was about to say back he seemed to think better of. He turned and left.

As they were leaving the White House, Sean pulled Betack aside. "Aaron, one thing."

"You need any freelance investigators? I see an involuntary career change coming in my future."

"I do need you to do a little sleuthing."

"Meaning what?"

"The letter the First Lady got."

"She said she destroyed it."

"Considering that just about everything that's come out of the lady's mouth has been a lie, chances are even money that she didn't."

"And you want *me* to find it?"

"I'd try. But I think someone might notice me snooping around here. I understand the security's pretty good."

"Do you realize what you're asking me to do?"

"Yeah. I'm asking you to help save a little girl's life."

"Where the hell do you get off hitting me with a guilt trip like that?"

"Would you do it if I didn't hit you with it?"

Betack looked off for a moment. When he stared back at Sean he said, "I'll see what I can do."

After they dropped off Tuck back at Blair House, Sean's phone buzzed. He answered, listened, smiled, and clicked off. "I can feel the tide turning a little."

"Why? Who was that?" asked Michelle.

"My language department friend. They might have something to tell us about the marks on Pam's arms."

51

"We'd exhausted just about everything we could think of," said Phil Jenkins, Sean's professor friend at Georgetown University. "Of course it wasn't the Chinese Yi as you initially suspected. Wrong alphabet. But college professors love a challenge like this, so I called in other faculty from some of our interdisciplinary studies. At least it beat grading fifty exams."

"I bet," said Michelle as she perched on the edge of Jenkins's desk in his cluttered office. She would have opted for a chair but the two in the room were piled with five-pound books.

"And you found what?" asked Sean impatiently.

"Ever heard of Muskogean?"

"Isn't that a town in Wisconsin, or maybe Oklahoma?"

"That's Muskogee. No, it's Indian. Native American Indian. Without getting too technical, it's a family of languages, actually."

"So the markings we gave you are Muskogean?" asked Michelle.

"The language is actually Koasati, or more typically known as Coushatta. But it is of Muskogean origin."

"So what does it say?" asked Sean. "What we gave you."

Jenkins looked down at a sheet of paper with scribbles all over it. "It was a bit difficult to figure out because none of the accent marks or other pronunciation points were included. For instance, there should have been a colon between *Chaffa* and *kan*. And, of course, the letters weren't separated into words. That made it far more difficult."

"Sounds like they didn't want to make our job easy," commented Sean.

"And they didn't," remarked Jenkins. "So what it says, as best we can figure, is this. *Chaffakan* means one. *Hatka* means white and *Tayyi* means woman."

"One white woman?" said Sean.

"One *dead* white woman," amended Michelle.

Jenkins glanced up sharply at her. "Dead?"

"It's a long story, Phil," said Sean. "What can you tell us about this Koasati stuff?"

"I consulted with a professor here who specializes in Native American languages. He's the one who really cracked this. The Koasati tribe was part of the Creek Confederacy in what is now Alabama. However, when the Europeans started immigrating there, and because they were also under attack from rival tribes, the Koasati and the Alibamu tribes moved to

Louisiana and then on to Texas. There are apparently no members of the tribes still living in Alabama. The bulk of the people who still use the language, and they only number in the hundreds, reside in Allen Parish, which is a little north of Elton, Louisiana. Although there are apparently a few speakers living in Livingston, Texas."

Michelle and Sean stared at each other.

She said, "Texas and Louisiana. Pretty big places to search."

"But if it's narrowed down to towns, and to a few hundred people?" said Sean.

"But why put the words on Pam's arms to begin with? Sure, they made it hard, but not impossible," she commented.

Jenkins broke in. "These words were on a woman's arms? And you said something about dead?"

"Not just dead, *murdered*," said Michelle.

"Oh dear Lord," said Jenkins and he dropped the page on his desk.

"It's okay, Phil, I doubt these folks are going to come back for another language demonstration. Thanks for the assist."

As they walked from his office, Sean was shaking his head. "Why does this seem like a diversionary tactic?"

"And a knuckleheaded one at that, because they didn't have to do it at all."

"Agreed."

"So what now?"

"We need to talk to Waters. Tell him what we know."

"That jerk? Why?"

"Because we promised. And we need to find Willa just as fast as we can. So we're going to need the Feds' muscle behind us."

"Yeah, well, don't be surprised if that muscle comes down on us instead."

52

Sean called Waters and they arranged to meet at a bar a few blocks away from the FBI's Hoover Building.

"Didn't expect to get a call from you," Waters said as they sat at a table in the back.

"I told you if we had anything to report we'd be in touch."

"So report."

"The markings on Pam Dutton's arms are a Native American language known as Koasati."

Waters sat up straighter. "Do you know what it says?"

"'One white woman,'" answered Michelle. "Something we obviously already knew."

"That makes no sense," said Waters.

"It was probably a clumsy attempt at a red herring because they'd messed up."

"Messed up how?"

Sean said, "Guy panicked, killed the lady when he didn't want to, and painted her arms to throw us off. I don't think anybody was supposed to die that night.

Tuck would've been the most obvious threat and even then they just knocked him out when they could've easily just pumped a round into him."

"Okay, so tell me about this Koasati stuff."

Sean relayed what they'd learned from Phil Jenkins about the Indian tribe.

"Well, maybe that narrows it down some," Waters said doubtfully. "But some Indian tribe having a beef with the president to such an extent they grab his niece? Pretty far-fetched."

"Second point," said Sean. "Pam Dutton only gave birth to two kids. We think Willa's adopted."

"That one I know. ME gave us the heads-up after you two brought it to her attention."

"We've talked to Tuck and he won't say a word about it. Just says we're nuts. The First Lady claims ignorance. Says the Duttons were living in Italy when Willa was born. Or supposedly born."

"Maybe Willa's not the adopted one," said Waters.

"The other two look a lot like their parents," Michelle pointed out.

"But the ME said only two, so, regardless of which kid it is, Tuck is lying," said Sean. "You may have to lean on him to get to the truth."

"Leaning on the president's brother-in-law isn't that easy," noted Waters nervously.

"There must be some records somewhere that

would definitively state that Willa is adopted. Either here or in Italy. The FBI can surely find that out."

"You think if she was adopted it had something to do with her kidnapping?"

"How could it not?"

"But back up a minute," said Michelle. "So what if Willa is adopted? Why would Tuck not want to admit that? It's not like adoption is illegal."

"It might make a difference if the mother's identity is an issue somehow," said Sean slowly.

"Or maybe the *father's*," pointed out Michelle.

The three stewed on that for a few silent moments.

Waters finally spoke up. "And the First Lady didn't know anything about this? Her own brother?"

"So she claims," answered Sean.

Waters gave him a sharp glance. "But you don't believe her?"

"I didn't say that."

"So you *do* believe her?"

"I didn't say that either." Sean sat back and stared at the FBI agent. "So anything on your end?"

Water's face went slack. "I'm sorry, I didn't know this was a two-way conversation."

"If we work together the odds of getting Willa Dutton back alive might go up a little bit."

Waters still didn't seem convinced.

"Look, I told you, I don't care who gets the credit or the glory. We just want the girl back."

"You can't possibly have a problem with that deal," said Michelle.

Waters finished his beer and eyed her curiously. "Was your mother really murdered?"

"Yes."

"Any leads?"

"The chief suspect is my dad."

"Jesus!"

"No, his name's Frank."

"Shouldn't you be focused on that?"

"I'm a woman."

"Meaning what?"

"Meaning, unlike men, I can handle more than one thing at a time."

Sean tapped his arm. "So what's it gonna be, Chuck?"

Waters motioned to the waiter for another round, then said, "We found a hair on Pam Dutton that didn't belong to her or anyone else in her family."

"I thought the trace DNA didn't produce a criminal database hit," said Michelle.

"It didn't. So we ran a different test on the hair. An isotopic exam looking for geographic clues."

Sean and Michelle exchanged glances.

"What'd you find?" asked Sean.

"That the person whose hair it was has eaten a diet high in animal fats for years but also one with plenty of vegetables."

"What can you deduce from that?" asked Michelle.

"Not a lot, although the typical American diet doesn't include a lot of veggies anymore."

"Were the fats or vegetables processed?" asked Michelle.

"Don't think so, no. But the sodium levels were high too."

Sean looked at Waters. "Maybe a farm? They slaughter and eat their own meat? Cure it with salt, maybe. Harvest crops. Preserve and can them, again with salt."

"Maybe," said Waters. "They also found something else in the exam." He hesitated.

"Don't keep us in suspense," joked Sean.

"The water the person drank. That's reflected in the hair isotope too. The lab narrowed it down to a three-state area."

"Which three?"

"Georgia, Alabama, and Mississippi."

"That dovetails with the mail triangulation," noted Michelle.

"Three across," said Sean softly, staring at his drink. "Three states right in a row."

"Apparently both the rain and drinking water down there has some pretty distinctive markers," said Waters. "And it's been mapped pretty comprehensively over the years. That's why the lab feels very confident about the findings."

"Could they tell if it was well or city water?"

"Well," said Waters. "No commercial chlorine or other purifiers like that."

"So that means rural?"

"Possibly, although there're certainly some sub-divisions on well water down there. I used to live in one of them before I got assigned here."

"And with diets high in unprocessed animal fat and veggies?" exclaimed Sean.

"Okay, quite possibly rural. But with all that, it's still a big area to focus on."

"But those states don't square with the Koasati piece," said Michelle. "Texas or Louisiana."

"But the Koasati *are* from Alabama originally," pointed out Sean.

"Originally, yeah, but not now."

"Can you still run down the Koasati angle?" he asked Waters.

Waters nodded. "I'll have agents down there get started immediately on it." He studied them both. "So is that all you know?"

Sean finished his drink and rose. "It's all we know that's worth sharing."

They left Waters to his second beer and walked back to the SUV. Along the way Michelle's phone buzzed. She looked at the screen.

"Who is it?" asked Sean.

"My caller ID says a Tammy Fitzgerald."

"Who's she?"

"Somebody I don't know."

She put the phone away and said, "You didn't mention the letter the First Lady received to our little FBI chum."

"That's right, I didn't."

"But why not?"

"Because I'm willing to let her come to her senses before I throw her to the Feds on an obstruction charge. That'll probably screw the election for the president too. And he's done a good job."

"Are you kidding me? Who the hell cares what it does politically to the First Couple? What if it costs Willa her life? Isn't that what you care about, getting Willa back? Or was that a load of shit you were shoveling Waters back there?"

Sean stopped walking and turned on her. "Michelle, I'm doing the best I can here, okay? It's complicated. It's damn complicated."

"It's only complicated if you make it so. I like to keep things simple. Find Willa, any way I can."

He was about to say something when he stopped and stared over her shoulder.

Michelle finally turned to see what he was looking at.

There were two men across the street dressed in Army cammies walking along.

"Damn."

Michelle turned back to look at Sean. "Damn what?"

"You said you thought the guy you saw with the MP5 was wearing military-level body armor?"

"That's right."

"Yeah, that's right," said Sean.

53

Gabriel was trying his best not to even breathe. He held the big set of keys steady in his hand and was trying to locate every sound throughout the many nooks and crannies of Atlee before taking each step. Part of the little boy wondered why he was doing what he was. The other part of him well knew why: curiosity. Sam Quarry had often told Gabriel that curiosity was a good thing, meant you were really alive, wondering what made the world tick. He didn't think Mr. Sam would think it was so good right now, because Gabriel was just this minute slipping down to the basement in the middle of the night to see something Mr. Sam probably didn't want him or anybody else to see.

He passed by the old furnace that in the dark resembled nothing but an iron monster ready, willing, and more than able to swallow little boys. Then he saw the old safe with the spin dial that had the numbers and slashes nearly worn off, and the bronze handle that one had to crank down on to open the door. Gabriel had never tried to get into the safe, but he'd often thought about it. What adventure-seeking child wouldn't?

He skittered down the corridor, trying not to breathe in all the musty damp. You couldn't spend much time at a place like Atlee and not experience some type of mold allergies; it just came with the territory. Yet he gamely hurried on.

He reached the thick door and looked down at the fist of keys. He examined the lock and then tried to figure which key might fit it. He was able to eliminate about three-quarters of the potential ones using this method and then finished off the task by simply inserting one remaining key after another in the old lock. The third one he tried did the trick.

It made a big click as the lock tumblers slid neatly into place. Gabriel froze, thinking he might have heard a heavy step on the stairs coming down here. But after a minute of holding his breath and praying that it wasn't Mr. Sam woken out of a dead sleep by him sneaking around the house, he put the wad of keys in his pocket and tugged on the door.

It opened on well-oiled hinges. Mr. Sam, he well knew, was good about keeping things in fine working order. One reason he had come down here, perhaps the overriding reason, was to see where the slaves had been kept for doing crazy things like try to escape to freedom, as if anyone finding themselves bound by chains, white or black, would not try to do that very thing.

When he closed the door behind him and flicked on the small flashlight he carried with him, the first thing he saw was the row of battered file cabinets. Then his beam hit the wall above. That's when his jaw slackened, when he took in the boards full of writing, pushpins, connective string, photos of people and places and index cards. He drew closer, his youthful brow crinkled in both confusion and wonderment. As he spun around and his light hit off the other walls revealing still more of this, something tugged deep in Gabriel's chest.

Fear.

And yet curiosity eventually won out and he moved forward and focused on what appeared to be the first board in the sequence, at least judging from the dates written on each section of wall. Names, places, events, times, details of seeming insignificance were given life here. And as Gabriel followed the tale around a space where over a hundred and fifty years ago, people with the same color skin as him were left to die, the fear slowly began to return.

Gabriel had a wonderful memory, which was one of the reasons he was such a stellar student. He absorbed as much as he could, but even his mind began to overfill with all the bytes of information on these walls. The little boy had to marvel at the brain that Sam Quarry must possess. He had always known that the man was smart, tough, and as self-reliant as anyone he'd ever met. There didn't seem to be much that Quarry couldn't figure out. But still, what he was seeing now took his respect, no, his awe, to a whole different level.

But then there was still the fear. And it was metastasizing right now.

So concentrated was Gabriel on the story revealed on the walls that he never heard the door open, never caught the sound of the footsteps coming up behind him.

When the hand gripped his shoulder his legs buckled and it was all he could do not to scream out.

"Gabriel!"

He whipped around to see his mother standing there wrapped in her old bathrobe.

"What you doing down here?"

"Momma?"

She shook him. "What you doing down here?" she said again, her voice both angry and frightened. "Been looking all over for you. Thought something happened to you. Scared me to death, boy."

"I'm sorry, Momma."

"What you doing here?" she said one more time. "You tell me, right now!"

He pointed his light at the walls. "Look."

Ruth Ann's gaze slowly drifted over the space, but unlike her son there was no curiosity behind it. She turned back to him. "You ain't supposed to be down here. How'd you get in here?"

He pulled the key ring out and she snatched it from his hand.

"Momma, look. Please." He pointed frantically at the covered walls.

"I ain't looking at nothing 'cept getting your butt back to bed."

"Look at that picture of that girl. I saw her on the TV at school."

She slapped his face. The shock that registered on Gabriel's face evidenced that this was something that had not occurred before.

"Let me tell you something," she said. "Mr. Sam done give us his home. All his land and this house when he die. All we got is 'cause of him. So don't you say nothing against that man or I'll slap you again only harder."

"But Momma—"

She raised her hand and he drew back from her.

"Let me tell you something else. I know Sam Quarry a good long time, from when you weren't much bigger than my fist. He took us in when he ain't got no reason to. He a good man. If he doing something down here, that's his business." She pointed around the room. "Whatever this all is, then he got himself a damn good reason for doing it. Now let's go, boy."

She grabbed his arm and hustled him out of the room, locking the door behind them. As they rushed up the stairs, Gabriel looked back once at the room below before nearly sprinting back to his bedroom, propelled by a smack on the backside by his still obviously upset mother.

54

David Baldacci

Jane Cox had not entrusted the task of checking the post office box to her staff. It was too important. The dilemma was, as First Lady, it was nearly impossible to go anywhere without an enormous entourage. By law, the president and First Lady could not travel unaccompanied.

She came downstairs from the First Family's quarters. She had a rare two hours where she had nothing to do, so she'd informed her chief of staff that she wanted to go for a ride. She had done this every day since receiving the letter. She had put her foot down, though. No motorcade. One limo and one tail car. She had insisted on this.

It wasn't Cadillac One or what the Service referred to as "the Beast," the ten-thousand-pound nearly nuclear-attack-proof ride that was reserved for the president or the First Couple when they traveled together by car. In truth, she hated riding in the Beast. The windows were phonebook thick and you couldn't hear a single sound from outside. It felt suffocating, like you were underwater or on another planet.

Three agents rode with her in the limo, six others in the tail SUV. The agents were not pleased with this arrangement, but they took some comfort from the fact that no one could know the First Lady was even inside the vehicle. Many limos left the White House at all hours, and the First Lady's public schedule listed no trips today. Still, they kept a constant vigil as they tracked through the streets of D.C.

At her instruction, the car stopped across the street from a nondescript Mail Boxes Etc. shop in the city's southwest quadrant. From this vantage point Jane could see directly through the store window to the line of post office boxes against one wall. She wrapped a scarf around her head, put a hat on over this and tugged it down low. Sunglasses covered her eyes. She put up the collar of her overcoat.

"Ma'am, please," said her security detail chief. "We haven't cleared the shop."

"You haven't cleared the shop anytime since I started coming here," she said imperturbably. "And exactly nothing has happened."

"But if something does, ma'am . . ." His voice trailed off, the strain in his eyes clear. If something did go wrong, his career was over. The rest of the detail looked just as anxious. None of them wanted to blow their careers up over this.

"I told you before, I will accept all responsibility."

"But it could be a trap."

"I will accept all responsibility."

"But it's our job to protect you."

"And it's my job to make decisions about my family. You can watch from the car, but you are not to leave the vehicle for any reason."

"Ma'am, rest assured, I *will* leave this vehicle if I see you threatened in any way."

"Fine. I can live with that."

As soon as she left the car, the lead agent said, "Shit." Under his breath he added another word that rhymed perfectly with "twitch."

All faces in the two cars, including four using high-powered optics, were glued to the glass watching the First Lady cross the street and enter the shop. Unknown to Jane Cox, there were three Secret Service agents already in the shop, all dressed casually and ostensibly customers, plus two more in the rear guarding that entry. The Service was well used to dealing with high-spirited, demanding, and independent-minded First Family members.

Jane went directly to the mailbox, used her key to open it, and found nothing there. She was back in the car in under a minute.

"Drive," she said, as she sank back against the leather.

"Ma'am," said the detail leader. "Is there anything we can help you with here?"

"No one can help me," she said defiantly, but her voice broke slightly.

The ride back to the White House was made in silence.

The moment the First Lady had left the White House Aaron Betack had gone into action. Under the pretense of doing a routine bug sweep of the corridor where the First Lady's office was situated, he entered her suite and asked the staff members there to step outside while the check was conducted.

It only took him a minute to go into the First Lady's inner office, pick the lock of her desk drawer, find the letter, make a copy of it, and return the original to the desk. He glanced at the contents of the paper before thrusting it in his suit pocket.

It was the first time in his government career that he'd ever done anything like that. He had in fact just committed a criminal act for which he would pull several hard years in a federal prison if he were ever caught.

Somehow, it seemed worth every minute of such a sentence.

55

Sean and Michelle had spent most of the evening and much of the next day learning that collectively there were dozens of military facilities located in Georgia, Mississippi, and Alabama with hundreds of thousands of military personnel assigned to them. Too many, in fact, for that to be of much use in their investigation. They were sitting in their office when Sean had an idea. He called Chuck Waters and left a message. A few minutes later the FBI agent called back.

"The isotope exam you did on the hair sample?" Sean began.

"What about it?"

"Did it show anything else?"

"Like what?"

"I know that it can tell what your diet has been like for years, but can it also show any anomalies in that chain?"

"Anomalies?"

"Like a break in the chain, where it shows a different type of diet, at least for a period of time?"

"Hold on."

Sean heard some paper rustling and a chair squeaking.

"I don't see anything like that," Waters said.

"Nothing out of the ordinary?"

More paper rustled. "Well, I'm no scientist, but you know how we were discussing that the perp was probably rural because of the unprocessed meats and vegetables and the well water?"

"Yeah."

"Well, there was elevated levels of salt, which makes sense if these folks are preserving stuff, right?"

"Right. We already discussed that."

"Well, in addition to the elevated levels of that, there was higher than normal amounts of sodium."

"But, Chuck, sodium *is* salt. That would be from canning vegetables and curing meat. We covered that."

"Hey, Einstein, I know that. But they've developed new technologies that can let them distinguish between certain *types* of sodium found with the isotope exam. What the tests show is elevated levels of a specialized sodium product that is commercially produced but not readily available to the public."

"Would that be because they supply a certain government entity? Like the military? Like sodium in MREs?"

"If you knew about the meals-ready-to-eat angle why are you wasting my time?" Waters said angrily.

"I *suspected*. I didn't know for certain until you

just told me now. And since *you* obviously knew already, it would've been nice if you had volunteered the info before now."

"I'm running an investigation here, King, not a consulting service."

"There are commercially available MREs. For like the survivalists. You sure it's not that sort of sodium?"

"The sodium level in the military MREs are higher than the commercially available stuff. But so it was military, so what? That only narrows it down to millions of people."

"Maybe, maybe not."

"What do you mean by that?"

"If the perps are military, can't you run the hair sample for a DNA match through the Pentagon's enlistment records? They require DNA samples from everybody now."

"I tried to, but their damn system crashed. Fighting two wars has apparently strapped their budget for computer maintenance. Won't be back up for a couple weeks."

"Great." Sean clicked off and looked at Michelle.

"So where do MREs get us?" she said.

"Now we know the odds are very high that the perp *was* military. It's at least good to confirm that. But we still have the little issue of tracking him down. It doesn't sound like we'll be getting a DNA match anytime soon."

"He couldn't still be in the military, could he?"

"And went on some R and R to conduct a little kidnapping? And got back to base with his face all scratched up and a bullet bruise on his chest?"

"So discharged?"

"Presumably. Either honorably or dishonorably. But that still doesn't help us. Because there are literally millions of former members of the military."

Michelle was staring at Sean's chest.

He looked down. "Coffee spill?" he said.

"He was wearing body armor. Sure, you can leave the military with some government stuff, but body armor?"

"You can get that on the street."

"Maybe, or you can just take it with you."

"Pretty tough to hide that when you're discharged."

"What if you left without being discharged?"

"AWOL?"

"Cuts down on the millions we'd have to check. Know anybody who can look into that for us?" she asked.

Sean picked up his phone. "Yeah, I do. A two-star I met when I was in the Service. I might be able to shake him down with an offer of Redskins tickets."

"You have Skins tickets?"

"No, but for a worthy cause I can get them."

56

This is highly irregular, Mr. Quarry," said the physician on duty.

"Not to me it's not," Quarry said back. "I'm here to get my daughter and take her home. Nothing more normal than that."

"But she's on life support. She can't breathe on her own." The man said this as to a child.

Quarry pulled out the papers. "I've been through this crap with the folks back in the office. I got full medical power of attorney and all that stuff. Basically I can take her anywhere I want to and there's not a damn thing you can do about it, mister."

The doctor read over the documents Quarry handed him. "She'll die if we take her off the machines."

"No she won't. I got that all covered too."

"What do you mean, *all covered*?" the doctor said skeptically.

"Every piece of equipment you got in her room keeping her breathing, I got too."

"How could that possibly be? It's all very expensive. And complicated."

"Medical supply warehouse had a fire about a year ago. They had lots of stuff that wasn't even damaged that they let go cheap because of health regulations. Ventilator with a trach tube. Vital signs monitor. Feeding tube. Oxygen tanks and a converter. IV meds dispenser unit. I checked it all out and it works just fine. In fact, I'll bet you a hundred bucks the stuff works better than the shit you got here. It's all pretty old. I should know, I been coming here many a year, and I don't think you folks have changed any of it."

The doctor gave a forced chuckle. "Now really, Mr. Quarry."

Quarry cut him off. "Now you just get her all ready to go. I'll get them to pull the ambulance up front."

"Ambulance?"

"Yeah. What? You expect me to take her home in my pickup truck? Use your damn head, man. I hired me an ambulance, a special one with life support equipment. It's waiting outside." He snatched the papers back. "Now you just make sure she's ready to go." He walked off.

"But how will you possibly take care of her?"

Quarry wheeled back around. "I know the routine better than you do. I know how to feed her, medicate her, clean her, exercise her limbs, and turn her to keep the bedsores away, the whole shebang. You think I just come here and look at the damn floor? By the way, you ever read to her?"

The man looked perplexed. "Read to her? No."

"Well I do. Have all these years. Probably the thing that really kept her alive." He pointed at the doctor. "Just get her ready, 'cause my little girl's finally getting outta here."

Quarry signed a mountain of papers absolving the nursing home of any liability and, at last, Tippi left her prison while the sun was still shining. Quarry squinted against the glare and watched as they loaded his daughter into the back of the ambulance. He climbed in his old truck, gave the nursing home the finger, and led the ambulance down the road to Atlee.

When they arrived home everything was ready. Carlos and Daryl helped the ambulance attendants carry in the gurney. Ruth Ann, tears running down her cheeks, and Gabriel, watched the procession. The adult daughter was returned to the same room she'd occupied as a young girl. Everything that had been in the room when she was young was now in it once more. Quarry and his wife had kept it all, ever since Tippi had headed out in life for what had turned out to be a too brief time. College, a stint at a marketing firm in Atlanta; and then sucking on a breathing tube at a nursing home when she was still in her twenties.

His beautiful girl had come home, though.

The ambulance left after a critical care nurse who had come along made certain that the equipment Quarry had was adequate and was connected up the right way. After that, Quarry closed the door behind all of them, sat next to Tippi, and took her hand in his.

"You're home, little girl. Daddy brought you home, Tippi."

He held up her hand and pointed with it to various items in the room.

"There's that blue ribbon you got for writing that poem. And over there's your prom dress that your ma made for you. And you looked so beautiful in it, Tippi. Didn't want to let you out of the house with that dress on. No sir. Didn't want to let the boys see you like that. So pretty." He pointed her hand at a photo on a small bookcase.

The picture was of the entire family. Mom, Dad, and the three kids when they were still just children. Daryl wasn't thickset yet, just cute with some baby fat. Suzie was in the middle with her usual defiant look. And then there was Tippi wearing a hat she'd made from a newspaper and a strip of leather, cocked sideways on her head, her golden hair draped around her shoulders. She had this wondrous smile on her face and this mischievous look in her eyes. Nothing much could make Quarry weep anymore. Yet every time he stared at that image of Tippi, with her life all ahead of her, in that funny hat, with those eyes burning to take the world head-on, not knowing, not even suspecting for one moment the despair, the devastating loss that they would all have to endure, the tears rose to the man's eyes like chill bumps on a fall evening.

He gently put her hand back down next to her side and rose to look out the window. His girl was home. And he would rejoice in that while he could. And then he would type his next letter.

He turned back to Tippi, listening to the mechanical rise and fall of the machine that was keeping her lungs pumping, and her heart beating. Then he glanced over at the photo and managed, by closing and then reopening his eyes, to transfer the Tippi in the photo to the one in the bed. In this imaginary world, his daughter was merely resting. And at least in his mind, she would wake up, get up, hug her daddy, and get on with life.

Quarry sank into a chair, closed his eyes again, and stayed in this other world for a little bit longer.

57

Michelle's phone rang again. They had been waiting two days now to hear back from Sean's Army buddy, but apparently getting records on AWOLs in three states was not an easy matter.

"Who is it?" Sean asked as he leaned back in his desk chair.

"Same number who called me before but I didn't know who it was."

"Might as well answer it. We're just sitting in neutral here anyway."

Michelle shrugged and punched the button. "Hello?"

"Michelle Maxwell?"

"Yes, who's this?"

"I'm Nancy Drummond. You left me a message about your mother. I was a friend of hers."

"But the area code on your phone number isn't Nashville. And the caller ID said Tammy Fitzgerald."

"Oh, I'm sorry, I didn't think about that. I'm using my daughter's cell phone. Fitzgerald is her married name. She lives in Memphis but she's staying with us for a while. It's cheaper to use the cell for long-distance calls. I only have a hard line."

"Oh, right, sure. Why didn't you leave a message?"

"I get flustered with cell phones and voice mail." She added bluntly, "I'm old."

"That's okay. Sometimes I get flustered by them too."

"I was out of town when your mother died. I'm so sorry about her."

"Thank you. I appreciate that." Michelle sat down at her desk while Sean doodled on a legal pad. "I was calling you because, well, I guess you heard my mom's death wasn't by natural causes."

"I heard that someone had killed her."

"Who told you that?"

"Donna Rothwell."

"Right. Look, Mrs. Drummond."

"Please call me Nancy."

"Okay, Nancy, I was calling because I wanted to know if you had any idea about who could have wanted to hurt my mom." Michelle expected the woman to issue a resounding "no" in a shocked, breathless tone, but she didn't.

"When I said I was sorry your mother was dead, I meant that Michelle. I liked her. But I can't in all honesty say I was surprised."

Michelle sat straight up in her chair and motioned

at Sean, who stopped doodling. Michelle hit a button on her cell, turning it to speakerphone mode.

"You say you're not surprised that someone killed my mother?"

Sean put down his pen and walked over to Michelle's desk and sat on the edge.

"Why would you say that?"

Nancy Drummond's mellifluous voice swooped into the room. "How well did you know your mother?"

"I guess not all that well, actually."

"This is difficult to say, your being her daughter and all."

"Mrs.—Nancy, don't pull any punches. I just want to find who did this."

"I didn't know your father very well. He and your mom didn't go out much together. But Sally enjoyed the social circle we had down here. *Very much.*"

Michelle noted the emphasis on the last words. "How *much* is very much?"

"I don't like to talk out of school."

"Listen, if my mom was messing around on my dad, that's very important to know, Nancy. Do you know who she was seeing?"

"It was more than one, actually."

Michelle slumped back in her chair. "How *many* more than one?"

"Three, at least that I knew of. Two moved away, the last about a month ago."

"Where'd they move to?"

"One to Seattle, the other overseas."

"And who was the third?"

"You didn't hear this from me because it's not common knowledge. Your mother was very discreet, I'll give her that. And I don't know if they were, well, you know, intimate. Maybe they were just spending time with each other. Maybe they were just lonely."

"Who?" Michelle said calmly, although she wanted to fire a round into the phone to make the woman answer without any more qualifiers.

"Doug Reagan."

"Doug Reagan? As in Donna Rothwell's steady, Doug Reagan?"

"That's the one. Do you know him?"

"Not really, but I think I will now. How long were they having an affair?"

"Well, I thought they were still having it, up until your mother died, I mean."

"Wait a minute, how do you know all this?"

"Your mother confided in me. We were very good friends."

"So no one else knows that you know?"

"I don't know if she told anyone else. But I've never talked about it to another soul until right now. A confidence is a confidence. But now that she's gone, well, I thought you had a right to know."

To know that my mother was a slut. Thanks.

"Are you there, dear?"

Michelle snapped back. "Yeah, I'm here. Would you be willing to tell the police what you just told me?"

"Do I have to?"

Sean put a hand on Michelle's arm and shook his head.

"Maybe not," Michelle said quickly. "At least not right now." She paused. "Uh, did my dad know about . . . the things my mom was doing?"

"As I said, I didn't know your father that well, but he always struck me as a man that if he *did* know he would've done something about it."

"Yeah, he strikes me that way too. Thanks, Nancy. Just sit tight and don't tell anyone about this, okay?"

"All right, dear. If you say so."

"I really appreciate you being so candid."

"I have four grown daughters of my own, two of them divorced. I know things happen. Life is never perfect. I want you to know that when your mother told me what she was doing I strongly suggested that she stop seeing these other men. To go back to your father and try and work things out. Like I said, I didn't know him all that well, but I could tell he was a good man. He didn't deserve what was happening."

"Nancy, you're a jewel."

"No, I'm just a mother who's seen it all."

Michelle clicked off and gazed over at Sean. "No wonder I'm so screwed up, right?"

"I think you're remarkably sane, actually."

"Why didn't you want her to talk to the police?"

"I don't know. Just call it a hunch."

"So what do we do now?"

"Until we hear back from my two-star, we don't have a lot to do. How about a quick trip to Nashville to run this down?"

They quickly found that the next direct flight to Nashville wouldn't leave until the next day, unless they wanted to connect through Chicago and then Denver and take most of a day, much of it sitting in airport lounges or else on tarmacs.

"Gotta love air travel," said Sean, clicking off his phone after listening to the flight options. "Fly north or west to head south."

"Screw 'em. Feel like a drive?" Michelle said.

"With you, anytime."

They bought some sandwiches and two giant cups of coffee and set out at eight that night. On the way down Michelle had phoned her brother Bill and learned that all her male siblings had returned to their respective towns except for Bobby, of course, who lived there.

"Got some good news," Bill had told his sister.

"What's that?"

"Dad isn't a suspect anymore. At least not a serious one."

"Why?"

"ME said the blow came from a lefty and Dad hits from the other side."

"They didn't know that before?"

"The wheels of justice move slow, sis, but it's still good news."

"How come you all left Dad?"

"We didn't, actually. He left us."

"Meaning what exactly?"

"Meaning he told us to get the hell out of town because he was sick of us being around. I wish he would've been more direct, you know." Michelle could almost feel her oldest brother smiling through the phone.

"You really think you should leave him alone?"

"Bobby's there. And Dad's a big boy. He can take care of himself."

"That's not what's bothering me."

Before Bill could ask what was bothering his sister she'd already ended the call.

Sean said, "So good news he's been cleared, but bad news because your dad knows the killer's out there and he may take matters into his own hands."

"My brother's are great cops but clueless sons. They could never even contemplate my dad doing something like that. Or my mom cheating on him."

"But you can?"

She glanced at him and then looked away. "Yeah, I can."

Michelle drove with her usual total disregard of all speed limits and, after stopping only twice for bathroom breaks, they arrived at her father's house at a little after five o'clock a.m., beating the arrival time of the nonstop morning flight by a good four hours.

Michelle glanced in the garage and shook her head. The Camry wasn't parked there. She used her key to get into the house. A quick search showed it was empty.

"Does your dad have a gun safe somewhere?"

"Just a pistol box, I think. Probably in the bedroom closet."

Sean checked. He found the box but there was no gun in it.

They sat on the unmade bed and looked at each other.

"Should we call Bobby?" Sean asked.

"Take too long to explain it to him. Maybe we should go see Doug Reagan. Ask him why he forgot to mention he was banging my mom."

"You have an address for the man?"

"Easy enough to find. Like everybody keeps saying, this town just isn't that big. Or we can always check with his hot *steady*, Donna."

"Well, first how about we shower and change our

413

clothes? I haven't pulled an all-nighter in a car in a long time. In fact, the last time was with you."

"Expanding your horizons. It seems to be my lot in life."

Michelle showered first in the guest room bathroom. When she was done she opened the bedroom door and called down the hall.

"You're up, King."

He walked in as she was finishing wrapping herself in a towel. He held up a fresh cup of coffee. "Interested?"

"Always."

She sat on the bed drinking the coffee while he went into the bathroom.

She raised her voice. "What about the party next door? Maybe we should get a guest list and start hitting that too."

"Or we can get it from your brother," he called back. "I have to believe that was one of the first things the police did."

She moved closer to the door as the shower came on. "I'd rather we did it ourselves."

"What?"

"Do it ourselves," she said in a loud voice.

"Okay, your wish is my command."

"That'll be the day." But the comment still drew from her a smile.

She went into her father's bedroom and looked around. The photo of her mother was gone. She checked the trash can. It wasn't in there either. She looked under the bed for some reason. There it was. She pulled it out. The glass was cracked. She stared down at it. A bit of sharp glass had ripped across her parents' faces.

Is this what a nearly fifty-year marriage came down to? The next thought was equally devastating.

And where exactly is my life going?

She carried the picture back into the guest bedroom, slumped on the bed, and started trembling.

"Damn it!"

She cursed again, stood and walked to the bathroom. She started shivering again and hesitated. She swallowed hard, opened the door, and passed through. She was still trembling, sobs bumping up and down her throat.

Sean saw her through the shower door. "Michelle?" He looked at her questioningly, keeping his gaze on her eyes that looked ready to dissolve into tears. "What are you doing?"

"I don't know. I don't know what the hell I'm doing, Sean!"

He grabbed a towel and wrapped it around himself before stepping out of the shower. He led her out of the bathroom and over to the bed. They sat on the edge, her head cradled against his chest.

"I really think I'm losing it," she said.

"You've been through a lot. It's only natural to feel overwhelmed."

"My parents have been together forever. Had five kids. Four brothers and me the mutt. The bring-up-the-rear mutt."

"I don't think anyone feels that way about you. I certainly don't."

She turned to face him. "How exactly *do* you feel about me?"

"Michelle, I—"

She picked up the cracked photo. "Nearly fifty years of marriage and five kids and this is what you get? This?"

"Michelle, we don't know what's really going on here yet."

"I feel like I've wasted so much of my life."

"An Olympian, Secret Service agent, and now my partner?" He attempted a smile. "I think a lot of people would like to switch places with you. Especially about being my partner."

She didn't smile. She didn't cry. She leaned over and kissed him gently on the lips.

She breathed into his ear. "I don't want to waste any more time, Sean. Not another second."

She kissed him again and he kissed her back. She leaned into him.

And then Sean pulled back.

Their gazes locked. "You don't want me?" she said.

"Not like this. Not this way, no. And neither do—"

She slapped him and turned away.

"Michelle—"

"Leave me alone!"

She started to run, but then it was like a hard wall of something both hot and cold slammed into her, inflaming her organs, icing her skin. Her knees buckled and she was on the floor, sobbing, curled into a ball so tight that she seemed to have shrunken down to a child. Her fingers clawed the floor, found the fractured picture where it had fallen. She held it against her chest.

A moment later Michelle was lifted off the floor and her head fell against Sean's chest. He spoke to her, urgently, but she didn't answer.

Sean laid Michelle on the bed, took the photo from her, and covered her with the sheet and sat next to her. He put his hand out and she instinctively gripped it. As the minutes went by and the sun came up, her sobs started to subside. Finally, her grip around his hand loosened and fell away as she slept. He tucked her hand up under the sheet.

Sean lay next to her, a finger sliding against her wet hair. He watched her until, exhausted, his own eyes closed and he fell asleep.

58

Quarry marched across the dirt in front of his little house, Carlos behind him. The big man stopped and pointed to the berm.

Quarry said, "The camera feed goes right to where you'll be. The TV monitor is all set up. I checked it out, works fine. It's an exterior shot only, though. No way to hide it inside the house."

"Understood."

They had been over this several times already, but Carlos had learned that the one thing that Sam Quarry lived by was repetition. Like the pilot he was, the man's firm belief was that going over it and over it was the only way to extract out as much potential error as was possible.

"The camera sight line is dead-on," Quarry added. "But I'll check it right up to the last minute."

"Chances of it being discovered and taken out of operation?"

"Slim at best given the time parameters, but if it does you've got to resort to the backup." Quarry slipped a pair of heavy binoculars from his knapsack and handed them to Carlos. "An old-fashioned decent pair of optics and two good eyes. I've got a sightline for you that won't reveal your position. You just slide the lever I showed you in the bunker open, like a gun turret."

Carlos nodded in understanding. "And the other thing?" he said, eying the house, the treeline, and the critical ground in between.

Quarry smiled. "That's the beauty of the whole damn thing, Carlos. It's all activated when you hit the one button." He grinned like a schoolboy who'd just won the science fair. "Took me a while to build, little tricky, works off a split feed, but I got there. And once you push it, Carlos, there ain't no going back, my friend."

"And how do I contact you at the mine?"

"First, you'll contact me whether things go right or go to hell. And you'll do it with this." Quarry handed him a boxy device. "Like a SAT phone," he explained. "The call will get to me, even up at the mine. I've already tested it. But the slit in the hole you'll be in has to be open so it can communicate with the satellite. But it'll only take you a few seconds to make the call. No long-winded messages, just yea or nay."

Carlos held the phone. "Where did you get this?"

"Built it out of spare parts."

"But the signal from the satellite?"

"Piggybacked on an existing platform. Went to

the library and got some info off the computer that showed me how to do it. Easier than you might think if your mind works that way. Hell, Carlos, all this stuff I did here is easy compared to what we had to jury-rig in 'Nam. So this way saved me a lot of money. Money I ain't got."

Carlos looked at him in unconcealed awe. "Is there nothing you can't do?"

"There's lots of things I can't do. Most of them important. I'm just a working man. Don't know squat about shit."

"So when is all this going to go down?"

"I'll let you know, but it'll be soon."

Carlos once more looked over at the knoll. Quarry watched him closely.

"You'll be hidden, but exposed at the same time," Quarry said. "Close quarters."

"I know this," answered Carlos, whose gaze shifted to a buzzard making lazy ovals in the sky.

"It's only an issue if they make it one. Otherwise you walk away."

Carlos nodded, but kept his gaze on the bird.

"You want me to switch with you I got no problem with that, Carlos. But I'll ask this one time only."

The wiry man shook his head. "I told you I would do this and I *will* do this."

Carlos left and Quarry unlocked the door to the

little house and walked in. Everything was ready, except for one missing piece. But that would come.

An hour later Quarry lifted into the sky in his Cessna. The low-level winds were rough and his little plane crab-walked across the sky, but it didn't bother him. He'd flown through a lot worse. A little turbulence would never kill him. A lot of other things could, though. And probably would.

He had a lot to think about, and he did his best thinking while flying along. At a few thousand feet up, his mind seemed to clear even as the air thinned. In the back of the plane was a box filled with cables and wires. In that box, and in a second box up at the mine, he would draw out his doomsday scenario. He would only use it if he had to, and he hoped he didn't.

As he flew, Quarry's thoughts went back to the last time Tippi had ever spoken. He and his wife had rushed to Atlanta when they'd been told how desperately ill their daughter was. Quarry had never wanted his little girl to move to the big city, but children grow up and you have to let them.

When the doctor at the hospital told them what had happened, neither of them could believe it. Not their Tippi. There must have been some mistake. But there had been no mistake. She had already sunk into a coma because of the blood loss. However, the physical evidence was conclusive, they'd been told.

Cameron had left the room to get some coffee and Quarry had been leaning up against the wall, his jeans dirty, his shirt stained with sweat from the long ride over from Alabama in summer heat with no air conditioning. He'd come right from the fields after his wife had raced across the tilled dirt screaming about the phone call she'd gotten. The compressed, artificial air in the big hospital had been foul, suffocating for a man used to wide-open spaces.

The police had also come in and Quarry had had to deal with them. He'd become so enraged at their line of questioning that Cameron had been forced to make him leave the room, the only person on earth, other than Tippi, who had that sort of influence over him. The cops had finished and gone on their way. From their sour looks as they trudged past him down the hall, Quarry held out little hope of getting any justice that way.

And so he'd been alone in her room, just him and his little girl. The machines had been clunking, and the pumps pumping; the monitor making its little screeches that felt like the boom of artillery to Quarry. Even screaming shots of anti-aircraft fire aimed at his Phantom in the skies over Vietnam had never scared him as badly as the whine of that damn machine while it dutifully recorded his baby's desperately poor condition.

It was extremely doubtful she would ever recover,

the doctors had warned them. One unsympathetic white coat with the bedside manner of a hyena had been especially pessimistic. "Too much blood loss. Brain damage. Part of her mind had already died." He added, "If it makes you feel any better, she's not experiencing any pain. And it's not really your daughter there anymore. She's already gone, actually."

This had not only *not* made Quarry feel better, he'd knocked the doctor's front teeth out and nearly been banned from the hospital because of it.

And then while he'd been standing there Tippi had opened her eyes and looked at him. Just like that. He remembered every moment of it precisely, vividly, as he flew along the thermals in his Cessna.

He'd been so shocked that at first he didn't know what to do. He'd blinked, thinking his vision was just messed up, or he was merely seeing what he wanted to see rather than what was actually there.

"Daddy?"

He was next to her in an instant, holding her hand, his face bare inches from hers.

"Tippi? Baby. Daddy's right here. Right here."

Her head started swaying from side to side and the monitor was screeching like it never had before. He was terrified he would lose her again to the shadows, to the part of her mind that was no longer there.

He squeezed her hand, gently held her chin in place, stopping the swaying so her eyes focused only on him. "Tippi. I'm right here. Your momma'll be right back. Don't you go away now. Tippi! Don't you go away!"

Her eyes had closed, panicking him. He looked around to maybe call somebody. Get some help to hold his daughter with them.

"Daddy?"

He jerked back. "I'm here, baby." Despite trying to hold them back, the tears came hard and fierce down his lined face, a face that had aged more in the last day than in the last ten years.

"I love you."

"I love you too, baby." He put one hand against his chest trying to stop his heart from ripping through. "Tippi, you got to tell me what happened. You got to tell me who did this to you."

Her eyes started to lose focus again and then closed. He searched frantically through his mind for anything to keep her attention.

"It is a truth universally acknowledged, that a single man in possession of a good fortune, must be in want of a wife," he said.

It was the first line from *Pride and Prejudice*.

They'd read the book back and forth to each other over the years.

Tippi opened her eyes, smiled, and a gush of air came out of Quarry, because he was convinced that God had just given him his little girl back, despite what the white coats had said.

"Tell me who did this to you, Tippi. Tell me, baby," he said as firmly as he could.

She mouthed only four words but it was enough. He understood them.

"Thank you, baby. God, I love you so much."

He looked up at the ceiling. "Thank you, sweet Jesus."

The door to the room had opened. Quarry turned. It was Cameron with two coffees. He nearly leapt the width of the room and grabbed her so violently that she spilled both cups. He dragged her to the side of the bed.

"Our little girl's awake, Cam, she's back."

Cameron Quarry's eyes had gotten so big and her smile so wide that Quarry hadn't known how her face had contained them. When she looked down at the bed, though, the eyes grew small and the smile had vanished.

Quarry had looked down too. Tippi's eyes were closed. Her smile was gone. She would never wake up again. He would never hear her voice again.

It was because of the smile he'd gotten, the last one from his daughter he would ever receive, that Quarry had read Austen's work to her all these years. It was a tribute to the author for what she had given him, he felt. A few precious last moments with his daughter.

The quartet of words Tippi had said that day were forever seared in Quarry's mind, but he did not act on them then, because they did not clearly point to one person. And, more maddening, even though the doctor had been called and Quarry had told him about Tippi awakening, it was clear that the physician didn't believe him.

"If she did wake up," said the doctor, "it was only an anomaly."

It was all Quarry could do not to break his teeth too.

No, he didn't act on those words, and he wasn't exactly sure why. But after Cameron died, he didn't have anything holding him back. And that's when he'd begun his long journey to the truth. To the point where now justice might be closer for him and Tippi than it ever had been.

As he flew along he thought that there was only one thing more terrible than dying alone, and that was dying unfinished.

He would not die unfinished.

59

"I'm sorry."

Michelle was sitting fully dressed on the edge of the bed in the guest room. Sean was just waking up, the towel still around his middle, the pillow wet from his damp hair.

He turned to look at her, working a kink out of his shoulder. "There's nothing to be sorry about. You've been through hell and back. Anybody would've broken down."

"You wouldn't have."

He sat up and stuck the pillow behind him. "You might be surprised." He looked out the window. It was growing dark. He glanced at Michelle in surprise. "What time is it?"

"Nearly seven in the evening."

"I've been asleep all this time? Why didn't you wake me?"

"I haven't been awake that long myself." She looked down. "Sean, did I say anything? I mean, while I was sort of out of it?"

He rubbed her arm. "Michelle, you can't be

perfect all the time. You bottle stuff up until you blow. You've got to stop doing that."

She rose and looked out the window. "And speaking of which, we've *blown* a whole day." She whirled around. "What if something came in on Willa?"

She obviously didn't want to dwell on what had happened here.

Sensing this, Sean reached over to the nightstand for his phone. He scrolled through messages and e-mails. "Nothing. We're in a holding pattern until some of the leads we ran down click. Unless you can think of something else."

She sat back on the bed and shook her head. "It doesn't help matters that Tuck and Jane Cox have been basically lying to us from day one."

"No, that didn't help. But we're here now and maybe we can get something done on your mom's case. Like tracking down Doug Regan."

"Okay."

The house phone rang. It was her brother Bobby.

"What are you doing there?" he said.

"We got in this morning. Just . . . just coming to check on Dad."

"So how is he?"

"He's not here." Michelle suddenly froze. Was her Dad here? Would he be thinking that she and Sean were in bed together, in their home, after her mom just died? "Wait a minute, Bobby." She put down the phone and hurried out of the room. She came back a minute later and picked up the receiver.

"No, he's not here. His car's gone. Why?"

"I'm over at the country club."

"Okay. You a member?"

"Not a full member. Cops don't make that much money. I play a few rounds every now and then."

"Little dark to be playing a few rounds."

"There's a lady here I've been talking to."

"What lady?"

"Lady who was walking her dog the night Mom was killed. She doesn't live in the neighborhood so the police never questioned her."

"Did she see something? If so, why didn't she go to the police?"

"Scared, I think."

"What made her change her mind?"

"Friend of hers. A Nancy Drummond told her to come forward. So she called me."

"I talked to Nancy."

"That's what she said. That's why I called in fact."

"What, you mean you were tracking *me* down?"

"Yeah."

"Bobby, why didn't you just call me on my cell?"

"I did, like six times over the last few hours. Left four messages."

Michelle glanced over at the nightstand where her cell phone also sat. She picked it up and saw the list of recent calls. "I must've turned it to silent mode by accident. Sorry about that."

"I thought Dad might know where you were, but this kills two birds."

"What do you mean?"

"What I mean is this lady will only talk to me if you're here. Apparently you made quite an impression with her friend, Nancy. Nancy told her she can trust you."

"But you're the police, Bobby, she should talk to you."

"She's stubborn. And a grandmother of twelve. I don't think I can break her. But I'll take the simple route. She tells you while I'm here too. And then we nail the bastard who did this to Mom."

"She's at the club now?"

"Right now."

Michelle's empty stomach rumbled. "Do they serve dinner there?"

"It's on me."

"We'll be there in twenty minutes."

60

With Daryl's help Quarry strung the cables up and down the mineshafts at strategic points, finishing off at the entrance.

As they worked away Daryl said, "You looking pretty happy."

"Tippi's back home so why wouldn't I be?"

"She's not really home, Daddy, she's—"

Daryl didn't finish because his father's forearm was across his windpipe.

Daryl could feel the hot, stinging breath of his old man. "Now why don't you think real long and hard about what you were about to say, boy. And then why don't you keep your damn mouth shut!"

Quarry pushed his son away. Daryl bounced off the hard rock. But instead of going meekly away he lunged at his father and drove him up against the wall. Quarry wedged an arm under his son's thick neck and, using the wall of rock for leverage, forced him off. The two struggled over the uneven ground, each trying to get the upper hand as their breaths shot out of their mouths and the sweat stained their armpits despite the chill.

Daryl stumbled backward but then regained his balance. He charged forward again, wrapping his arms around his father's middle and lifting him off the ground and slamming him up against the rock.

All the air went out of Quarry's lungs, and his front teeth popped through his bottom lip with the impact. But when Daryl dropped him he found the strength to launch a knee into his son's gut, and then follow that with a powerful roundhouse to the face, putting his whole body into it. Daryl fell back on his butt, his cheek ripped, his mouth bleeding.

Quarry almost toppled over with the force of his blow. He half spun around and squatted in the dirt, hacking and spitting up blood. "You couldn't kick my ass even if I was in a damn wheelchair sucking on oatmeal through a straw," he yelled.

Daryl eyed the stick of dynamite bound to a long cable lying on the floor of the mine. "You gonna blow me up too, old man?"

"Blow us all up if I have to, dammit!"

"I ain't spending my whole life doing what you tell me to do."

"You ain't got no life but for me. The Army come looking for your ass and who saved it? Me! And then you screwed up with the woman. And you kept screwing up. Shoulda shot you back then."

"Why didn't you then, old man? Why!" shouted Daryl as he balled his fists and tears slid down his face to mix with the blood there.

"Killed Kurt."

"And you ain't had no right to do that! I was the one what killed that woman. Not Kurt."

"I shoulda shot you instead," Quarry said again, spitting up bits of his torn lip.

"So why didn't you, Daddy! Why didn't you kill me?"

Quarry wasn't looking at him now. He put a hand up against the wall to steady himself, his breaths coming in short gasps.

"'Cause I need you, that's why," he said in a quieter voice. He bent down and offered Daryl a hand up. His son didn't take it.

"I need you, Daryl. I need you, boy." Quarry stayed bent over, his feet stumbling across the floor of the mine. Quarry looked over at his son and imagined him as a young, adoring boy with big blue eyes and a lopsided grin. *Tell me what needs doing, Daddy*.

When his eyes cleared, all he saw was a large, thickset, angry man struggling slowly to his feet.

"I need you, boy," Quarry said again, offering his hand again. "Please."

Daryl pushed past him. "Let's just get this done," he said, wiping the blood off his face with one of his filthy hands. "Sooner the better. Then I'm outta here."

Quarry unlocked the door and stepped into the room. The light from the lantern on the table was turned down low so he couldn't see her. But he felt her presence.

"I didn't want to give her up," Diane Wohl said as she emerged from the shadows.

Quarry came into the wash of light.

"You're bleeding," she said.

"Ain't nothing," said Quarry as he sat down at the table and ran a hand through his thick, sweaty hair. He was still wheezing a bit from his struggle with his son.

Damn smokes.

Diane sat down across from him. "I didn't want to give her up."

Quarry drew a long breath and sat back, studying her from under a tangled mass of eyebrows.

"Okay."

"You scare the hell out of me. Everything about you terrifies me."

"You scare me too," he said.

Diane looked stunned. "How could I possibly scare you?"

"There's lots of ways to be scared. Physical. In your head. Both."

"So which way do I scare you?"

Quarry put his hands together and leaned forward, his big head dangling over the table center, as blood from his punctured lip plopped on the wood. "You make me afraid that this old world will never be good again. For none of us."

She sat back, stung by his words. "I'm a good person! I've never hurt anyone."

"You hurt that girl, even if she don't know it."

"I gave her up so she'd have a better life."

"Bullshit. You gave her up so you wouldn't have to deal with it."

She reached across the table and slapped him, then drew back, a look of terror on her features. She eyed her hand as though it belonged to someone else.

"At least you got some spirit," said Quarry, who had been unfazed by the blow.

"So I've ruined the whole world?"

"No, you let other folks do it. People like you let other assholes walk all over 'em. Even when they're wrong. Even when you *know* they're wrong. That makes you as bad, as evil as them. People like you don't stand up to nothing where you got to fight for what's right. You just crawl into the dirt. You just take it. The shit they hand out. Take it with a smile and say thank you where can I get me some more shit please?"

A tear from Diane's right eye hit the table where it mixed with Quarry's blood. "You don't know me."

"I know you. I know you and people just like you."

She brushed at her eyes. "So what are you going to do? Kill me?"

"I don't know. I don't know what I'm gonna do with you." He slowly rose, his back killing him from where he'd hit the rock. "You wanta see Willa again? Might be for the last time. Things coming to a head now."

Diane's eyes were blurred with tears. "No, I can't." She wagged her head from side to side, her fingers coiled tight and shaking.

"Crawling in the dirt again, lady? Trying to hide? You say you're scared of me? You just slapped me. Showed some backbone. You can stand up to folks if you want to. The people who think they're strong, who look like they got everything? The rich and the powerful? They ain't got shit. One time you stand up to them, they just run away, 'cause they ain't really strong, or tough. They just got stuff. They just got puffed-up pride based on nuthin'." He slammed his big fist down on the table so hard it knocked the lantern over and the light went out. From out of the sudden darkness he said, "I asked you if you wanted to see your daughter? What's it gonna be?"

"Yes."

61

The country club was quiet and though the evening wasn't chilly a fire crackled in the large stone-faced fireplace in the main restaurant. Sean and Michelle sat on one side of the table while Bobby and June Battle, a wisp of a woman in her early eighties, with snowy hair cut severely short, sat on the other side of them.

They had just ordered their food.

Michelle fired the first shot. "I'm glad you talked to Nancy Drummond. Because we really need your help."

Instead of answering, June methodically swallowed a number of pills she had placed on the table, using a big glass of water to wash them down.

Perhaps sensing Michelle's growing impatience, Sean slipped a hand under the table and squeezed her thigh and slightly shook his head.

June finished off the last pill and looked up at them. "I hate medicine, but it's apparently the only thing keeping me alive, so there you go."

"So you were walking your dog down the street

where the Maxwells live on the night Sally Maxwell was killed?" said Sean encouragingly.

"Didn't know she was killed then," said June matter-of-factly. "Just walking Cedric. He's my dog. Pekinese. Little dog. Used to have a big dog, but can't handle big anymore. But he's a good dog. Cedric was my older brother. Dead now. I liked him better than my other siblings so I named my dog after him."

Michelle loudly cleared her throat and Sean's grip on her leg increased in pressure.

Bobby said, "So I told my sister here that you'd talk to her only."

"Don't like police." She patted Bobby's hand. "Don't get me wrong. I know we need police and all. But what I meant was that when the police are around, something bad happened."

"Like my mother being murdered?" said Michelle, looking dead at June.

The little woman finally settled her gaze on her. "I'm sorry about your loss, child. I've lost two of my children and one grandchild, but to illness, not crime."

"You saw something that night?" said Sean.

"A man."

Sean and Michelle both hunched forward at the same time, as though connected by rope.

"Can you describe him?" asked Michelle.

438

"It was dark, and my eyes aren't as good as they used to be, but I can tell you he was tall and he wasn't fat or anything. He didn't have a coat on, just pants and a sweater."

"Old, young?"

"Older. I think he had gray hair but I couldn't be sure. I remember it was a warm night and I was surprised he even had a sweater on."

"And in fact a *pool* party was going on next door," said Sean.

"Don't know about that but there were lots of cars parked up and down the road."

"What time was this?"

"Always start my walk at eight o'clock. Always get to that point at about eight-twenty unless Cedric poops and I have to pick it up, but he didn't. Poop I mean."

"So eight-twenty," said Sean.

He, Michelle, and Bobby exchanged glances.

"The ME puts time of death at between eight and nine," Bobby reminded them.

"Which puts our guy there right in the sweet spot," Michelle commented.

"Sweet spot?" said June, looking quizzically at her.

"Window of opportunity," explained Sean. "So the guy was there. What was he doing?"

"Walking, walking away from me. I'm not sure he even saw me. The street was pretty dark. I bring a flashlight with me but I hadn't turned it on because the moon was out and Cedric and I walk very slowly. We both have arthritis."

"So he was walking away from you. Did you see anything else? Like where he came from?" prompted Michelle.

"Well, it appeared to me that he came out from between two houses. The one with all the cars parked out front and the one next to it on the right."

"My parents' house," said Michelle.

"I guess so, only I didn't know them."

"What else?" asked Sean.

"Well, that was the strange thing," began June.

"Strange?" said Bobby.

"Yes. I was on the other side of the street from him, but I could still see it."

"See what?" Michelle asked, her voice shaking slightly.

"Oh, that's right, I didn't say. It was the flashes."

"The flashes?" said Sean and Michelle together.

"Yes. The man was walking up the street, but he was stopping at each of the parked cars. Then he would raise his hand and a little flash would appear."

"Was he next to each car when he did this, in front, in back?" asked Michelle.

"In back, and he bent over a little bit each time. Like I said, he was tall."

Michelle looked at Sean. "He was photographing the license plates of the cars."

"The flash was from the camera," added Sean while Bobby nodded.

"And he did this at each car?" asked Michelle.

June nodded. "Looked to be that way."

"Why would our perp be taking pictures?" wondered Bobby.

June's face brightened. "Perp? I've heard the word before. I watch *Law & Order* religiously. I loved Jerry Orbach, God rest his soul. And that Sam Waterston. He played Lincoln, you know."

"Did you see anything else?" asked Michelle. "Like where the guy went?"

"Oh, yes. He finished with the cars and then he walked back toward me, but on the other side of the street. He looked around, probably to make sure no one was watching. I doubt he saw me and Cedric. There're some large bushes where we were and I was standing sort of behind them, because Cedric was peeing and he gets embarrassed if people see him using the facilities. Then he turned up the driveway and went inside the house."

Michelle looked bewildered. "House? Which house?"

"The house next to the one where the cars were parked. He went right in the front door."

Michelle, Bobby, and Sean all looked at one another.

The tall older man taking pictures had to be Frank Maxwell.

62

After they finished dinner they needed to take June Battle to the police station to make a formal statement.

"You two take her," said Michelle.

"What?" Sean looked at her in surprise.

"I just need a little time alone, Sean," she said. "I'll meet you back at my dad's house."

"Michelle, I don't like splitting up with you."

"I can take care of Mrs. Battle," said Bobby. "No sweat."

"Sean, just go. I'll see you back at Dad's."

"You sure?"

She nodded. "Real sure."

As the three left Sean glanced back at her, but Michelle wasn't looking at him.

She sat at the table for ten minutes before slowly rising, opening up her jacket, and looking down at the Sig on her belt holster.

He had to know that his wife was lying dead inside the garage. And he was outside taking photos of car plates? What a callous bastard. What had he been doing? Looking to frame somebody for the murder he'd committed? He could easily have hit her mother from the left instead of the right to throw off the cops. Her father was a strong man. Either way Sally Maxwell would've been dead.

And he was out there somewhere. Her father was out there, and he had a gun.

She got up and walked with a purpose toward the exit. On the way she passed the trophy case for the golf club. She barely glanced at it but one glance was all it took. Her head snapped back around and she hurried over to the glass case. It was full of shiny hardware, plaques, photos, and other awards paraphernalia. Two items interested her deeply and she didn't even play golf.

She bent low and drew close.

The first one was a photo of three women, with the one in the middle holding up a huge trophy. Donna Rothwell was smiling broadly. Michelle glanced down at the inscription on the bottom of the plaque.

"Donna Rothwell, Club Amateur Champion," she read. It was for this year. They had her scores posted for the tournament on a laminated card next to the photo. Michelle didn't know that much about golf, but even she knew those scores were impressive.

The second photo was one of Rothwell hitting a tee shot. The lady looked like she knew what she was doing.

As she was standing there a bearded man in khaki pants and a golf shirt walked by.

"Checking out our local golf legends?" he asked with a smile.

Michelle pointed at the two photos. "These in particular."

The man looked to where she was indicating. "Oh, Donna Rothwell, right. One of the best natural swings I've ever seen."

"So she's good?"

"Good? She's the best female golfer over the age of fifty in the entire county, maybe the state. There are even some pretty good thirty- and forty-year-olds she can consistently beat. She was an athlete in college. Tennis, golf, track, she could do it all. She's still in remarkable shape."

"So her handicap is low?"

"Nearly nonexistent, relatively speaking. Why?"

"So she'd have no trouble qualifying for a tournament here, I mean based on her handicap?"

The man laughed. "Trouble qualifying? Hell, Donna's won just about every tournament she's entered as far back as I can remember."

"Did you know Sally Maxwell?"

The man nodded. "Beautiful woman. Damn shame what happened. You know, you sort of look like her."

"She was a good golfer?"

"Oh, sure. Nice game. Better putter than on the fairways, though."

"But not in Donna's league?"

"Not even close." He smiled. "Why all the questions? You interested in taking on Donna, scoping out the competition? You're a lot younger than she is, but she'll still give you a challenge, I bet."

"I might be taking her on, but it won't be on a golf course." Michelle walked off, leaving the man to stare puzzled after her.

She walked out into the parking lot and headed to her SUV.

She whipped her head around because she thought she heard something. She used her thumb to pop off the leather support on her holster. Michelle gripped the butt of her gun and tensed to pull it. But she reached her truck safely and climbed in.

A half hour later she got to the house. She drove past, parked down a side street, and climbed out. Donna Rothwell's big house was set back from the street. There was a gate out front and a windy drive up to a front motor court. As she walked along the street, she found a gap between the hedges. The house was dark, at least in front. It was large enough to where any lights in the back rooms would not be visible from where she was.

Michelle checked her watch. It was nearly ten o'clock.

Why had Rothwell lied about such a seemingly trivial point? She'd told her and Sean that Sally Maxwell had played with Doug Reagan in a local amateur charity tournament because Rothwell's handicap was too high and she couldn't qualify. But apparently she was a far better golfer than Michelle's mother had been. It was a stupid lie. She could only assume that Rothwell must've been counting on the fact that Michelle, not being a local, would never find out it wasn't true.

But why lie in the first place? So what if her mother had played with Doug?

Michelle stopped. A footfall, some breathing other than her own; the slap of skin against metal. Gun metal. This was stupid. She wasn't going to break into Donna Rothwell's place, giving the woman an excellent reason to have her arrested. And she wasn't going to stay out here waiting for someone to get the drop on her.

She got back to the SUV and called Sean, relaying what she'd learned about Rothwell.

"Bobby and I will meet you at your dad's place," he said. "Get there and stay put."

She reached the house and parked in front. She glanced in the garage window. Her dad wasn't home. She used her spare key to let herself in.

As soon as she closed the door behind her she sensed it. She pulled her gun, but a second too late. The blow hit her on the arm. The Sig clattered to

the floor, discharging as it hit and the round ricocheted off the stone tile. Michelle grabbed her
injured arm and rolled as something heavy fell close
to her.

Then she felt something smash next to her head.
She leapt up and kicked out with her leg, but caught
nothing but air. Someone screamed and another blow
hit Michelle painfully on the leg. She cursed, ran
toward the living room, and threw herself backward
over the couch. She at least knew the layout of the
house.

When the person came at her again, she was ready.
She ducked the blow, came up, and delivered a snap
kick to the attacker's gut, followed by a jab to the
head. She heard a loud grunt as though the air had
been driven right out of the attacker's lungs. Someone hit the floor. Michelle leapt forward to take
advantage of this when whatever weapon the person
had been holding flew up and caught Michelle on
the chin. It was metal. She tasted blood. She moved
to her left and tripped over the coffee table, falling
hard. Her arm and leg killing her and now her chin
throbbing, she sat up.

Michelle felt the presence right on top of her,
smelled something hot.

Shit, it's my gun. They've got my gun.

She dove behind the coffee table, braced for the
shot.

It rang out, but she felt nothing. There was a

scream, high-pitched and terrified. Something clattered to the floor and someone fell next to her.

The lights came on.

She sat up, blinking rapidly.

When she saw him, she gasped. Doug Reagan was lying by the door with a gunshot wound in his chest.

And next to her was Donna Rothwell on her knees, holding her bloody hand and sobbing in pain. Michelle's pistol was next to the woman. Michelle quickly grabbed it.

Then she froze again.

He was standing by the front door, next to where Reagan was, his gun out, a wisp of smoke floating off the muzzle.

Frank Maxwell came forward and put out a hand to help up his daughter. "You okay, baby?" he said anxiously.

63

"I took the photos of the license plates because I knew there was a party going on next door. I got the list of the people at the party and then compared it to the owners of the cars on the street that night."

Frank Maxwell put down his cup of coffee and sat back.

It was the next morning and they were at police headquarters. Donna Rothwell had been arrested for the murder of Sally Maxwell and the attempted murder of Michelle Maxwell. She had been taken to the hospital to have her hand wound treated from where Frank Maxwell had shot her. Doug Reagan was in the hospital in stable condition with a hole in his chest from when Michelle's gun had dropped and accidentally discharged. He was expected to fully recover, if only to be charged along with Donna.

Bobby Maxwell said, "How'd you get the car records?"

"I have a buddy at motor vehicles."

"You found Mom dead in the garage and you just

went out and started taking pictures?" Michelle said incredulously.

Frank Maxwell's gaze swiveled to his youngest child. "She'd just been killed. No pulse, pupils unresponsive. There was nothing I could do to bring her back. The body was still warm. I knew the murderer was still in the area. I wasn't in the shower. I was in the living room. I heard a sound in the garage and then a door slam."

"You didn't tell the cops that," Bobby pointed out. "Hell, Pop, you didn't tell *me* that."

"I had my reasons. Anyway, I could've just called the cops and then sat crying next to her body, but I know how critical it is to get an early jump on a homicide, and I didn't plan on wasting a second of it. I ran to the garage side door and opened it. I didn't see or hear anyone. I ran up and down the street but saw nothing. I also didn't hear a car start up so I figured that the perp was either on foot or hadn't driven off yet. I heard the sounds coming from the pool party next door. I debated whether to go there, tell them what had happened, and see if anyone was there who didn't belong there, but I opted for a different approach.

"I knew I didn't have much time. I ran to the house and grabbed my camera. I snapped the pictures of the car plates. After that I went back into the house and phoned the cops. It took all of maybe two minutes. Then I ran back out to see if I saw anyone, but I didn't. Then I went back to the garage to be with Sally." He said this last part softly, his head down.

"You're sure you didn't see anyone?" asked Sean, who was sitting across from Frank.

"If I had I would've done something about it. As it turns out, when my friend ran the plates the car parked at the very end of the street was Doug Reagan's. I didn't believe that he'd been invited to a teenager's birthday party. I confirmed that with the invitation list. It was the only vehicle unaccounted for. The other's were people either at the party or who lived on my street."

"Nifty piece of detective work," noted Sean. "But why didn't you tell the police?"

"Yeah, Pop," added Bobby. "Why?"

Michelle was staring at her father with a mixture of anger and sympathy. The latter finally won out. "He obviously wanted to work the angle to make sure he was right. So he wouldn't waste everyone's time," said Michelle.

Frank looked at his daughter. Michelle thought she could see a glimpse of gratitude on his features.

"So you believed Reagan was involved. How about Rothwell?" she asked.

He said, "I never liked her. There was just something off about her. Call it cop's instinct. After Sally was killed I started doing a little digging on the pair. Turns out that in Ohio about twenty years ago two people very closely resembling Rothwell and Reagan, but using different names, were charged with using a power of attorney to embezzle millions from a retired CEO. Then the old man was found dead in his bathtub one morning after his children started getting suspicious. The pair skipped town and were never heard from again. I don't think that was the only time they did it. I found a couple of other similar instances that I believe they were involved in, but no one could ever build a case. People like that, that's how they make their living. A dog doesn't change its spots."

"So her story of her husband being a retired CEO who she lived the good life with was bullshit?" said Michelle.

"It's easy to make up a past, particularly these days," added Sean. "She comes here as a wealthy widow who has traveled the world and sets up shop. Who can prove otherwise?"

"So her 'recent' steady Doug Reagan has actually been working with her for decades? Preying on old, rich people," said Bobby.

"I believe so, yes," answered his father. "But I had no real proof."

"But why target Mom?" asked Michelle. "It's not like you two are rolling in dough."

Frank Maxwell looked uncomfortable. He stared down again, his hands clenching the Styrofoam cup tightly. "I don't think they were targeting us. I think

. . . I believe your mother *enjoyed* Doug Reagan's company." He paused. "And he enjoyed hers." He fell silent and no one in the room apparently wanted to interrupt that quiet.

He continued. "He'd been everywhere, done everything, knew everybody, at least so he said. Stuff Sally had never been exposed to. He was handsome and wealthy and moved in certain circles. He was charming. He had a way about him. I was just a cop. I couldn't compete with that. Hell, I could understand why she'd be intrigued." He shrugged, but Michelle could tell that her father couldn't really understand his wife's infatuation at all.

"And Rothwell found out about it?" said Sean.

"Donna Rothwell is not the sort of person you ever want to cross," said Frank tersely. "I didn't know her all that well, but I knew her *kind* real well. I notice things other people don't. Just the cop's eye again. I'd seen how she looked sometimes when she wasn't the center of attention, or when lover boy was paying some woman more attention than he was her. She was obsessive, she was controlling. And she couldn't admit to anyone, much less herself, that she wasn't in control. And that made her dangerous. Even on the golf course she was competitive beyond all reason. Would get pissed off if she was losing."

Michelle said, "That must be why she made up that lie about letting Reagan play in the golf tournament

453

with Mom. She didn't want to admit that it was done without her permission."

"Or being so adamant that your mother was not seeing another man," said Sean.

Michelle added, "So she planned to kill Mom because she was fooling around with Reagan. She made a dinner date with her, obviously knew about the pool party next door and all the noise. She slipped into the garage and waited until Mom came out . . ." Michelle's voice trailed off for a moment. "What did she use? To kill her?" she asked Bobby, who had a cluster of tears in his eyes.

He drew a deep breath. "Golf club. A newfangled putter. That accounted for the weird shape of the head wound. The police found it in her car trunk. Still had trace on it. She went after you last night with a club too. Except it was a driver."

Michelle rubbed her arm and leg where the bruises were large and purple. "Lady has a natural swing," she said wryly. "But why come after me?"

Her father answered. "Reagan was at the country club last night. I know because I was too. I was following him. He saw you by the trophy case. He overheard you talking to the man about Donna. He must've put two and two together. Did you notice in the picture in the trophy case?"

"That Donna was a lefty? Yeah, I did."

"So then he slipped away, made a phone call, certainly to Rothwell, and hightailed it off."

"To your house?"

Frank said, "I wasn't sure about that because I stopped following him and started following you. But it ended up there because they were planning to ambush you."

"Why?"

"Why? Because you were getting closer to the truth."

"No, I mean why did you start following *me*?"

"Because I was worried about you. Because there was no way in hell I was going to let that scum hurt you. Guess I failed at that."

She reached out and touched his arm. "Dad, you saved my life. But for you I'd be at the morgue right now."

These words had a remarkable effect on her father. He put his face in his hands and started to cry. His children rose and knelt next to him, holding him.

Sean rose too, but he didn't join them. He left the room, closing the door quietly behind him.

64

Quarry sat in the library at Atlee counting his remaining cash. Two years ago he'd done something he never thought he would. He had sold some of his family's heirlooms to an antiques dealer to help finance what he was doing. He hadn't gotten anywhere near what they were worth, but he wasn't in a position to be choosy. He put the cash away, pulled out his typewriter, slipped on gloves, wound the sheet of paper in, and commenced the last letter he would ever compose on this machine. Like the others he had thought through each word.

The communication after this one would not be through letters. It would be far more direct. He finished and called Carlos in. The wiry little man was staying at the house while Daryl pulled guard duty at the mine. He had a task for Carlos to perform. And after his fight with Daryl he'd decided to keep his son closer to home.

Carlos wore gloves too, as instructed by Quarry. He was going to take one of the pickup trucks and drive north and then out of state to mail this last letter. The man didn't ask any questions; he already knew what was expected. Quarry gave him money for the trip along with the sealed envelope.

After Carlos left, Quarry locked the door to the library, stoked up the fire, lifted the poker, plunged it into the flames, got it hot, rolled up his sleeve, and added the third line to the mark on his arm. This was a slash perpendicular to the long burn, but on the left side of it. As the skin sizzled and puckered under the touch of the red-hot metal, Quarry sank back in his old desk chair. He didn't bite his lip since it was all bandaged up and swollen from his fight with Daryl. He cracked open a bottle of Beam, winced as the alcohol burned his cuts, and watched the rise and fall of the flames in the fireplace.

He only had one more line to burn into his skin. Just one more.

He left the library and staggered up the steps to Tippi's room. He opened the door and stared into the dark space. She was in the bed. *Hell, where else would she be?* Quarry said to himself.

Ruth Ann had quickly learned Tippi's needs and had settled into a routine helping Quarry take care of her. He contemplated going in and reading to her, but he was tired, and his mouth hurt.

"You want me to read to her, Mr. Sam?"

Quarry slowly turned around to see Gabriel standing there on the landing, his small hand on the thick wooden railing that a man who'd owned hundreds of slaves had put there a couple centuries ago. Quarry figured that wood was just about rotted out now, as was the man who'd built it, or rather had the sweat and labor of his slaves to do it for him. To see that small dark-skinned hand on top of that old chunk of rotted wood was comforting to Quarry somehow.

"I'd appreciate it," he said, his damaged lip moving slowly.

"Ma said you fell and hit your mouth."

"Getting too old for farming."

"You want me to read any particular part?"

"Chapter five."

Gabriel stared at him curiously. "Why that one?"

"Don't know other than the number five just popped into my head."

"Mr. Sam, you think Miss Tippi might want us to read her some other books too?"

Quarry turned away from him to stare at his fallen daughter. "No, son, I think the one book'll be just fine."

"Then I'll get to it."

Gabriel walked past him and clicked on the overhead light. The sudden blast of illumination was painful to Quarry and he turned away.

I've definitely become a creature of the night, he thought.

He didn't notice Gabriel staring at him until the little boy said, "Mr. Sam, you doing okay? Anything you want to talk about?"

Quarry focused on him as Gabriel sat there next to Tippi, the precious Austen novel cradled in his hands.

"Lots I want to talk about, Gabriel, but nothing you'd find interesting."

"Might surprise you."

"Might," Quarry agreed.

"That was real nice what you did. Leaving this place to Ma."

"And to *you*, Gabriel. And to you."

"Thank you."

"You go on and read now. Chapter five."

Gabriel turned to this task and Quarry listened for a while and then he walked downstairs, his boots clunking hard on the floorboards. He sat on the front porch for a bit admiring a night that had a crispness too rare down south.

A minute later he was driving his old truck. He bounced and heaved over uneven dirt roads. Finally he got there, pulled to a stop, and climbed out. His stride ate up the distance, but he halted before he got to the little house he'd built. He squatted on his haunches about ten yards from it.

Two hundred and twenty-five square feet of perfection, stuck out here in the middle of nowhere. His legs weary, he finally sat on his butt in the dirt and continued to stare at the house. He flicked a smoke out of his pack, slipped it between his lips, but did not light it. It just dangled there like a piece of straw. Somewhere along the treeline an owl hooted. In the sky he could see the wink of an airplane as it skated by. No one up there could see him here in Alabama. The plane would never land here, probably heading on to Florida or maybe Atlanta. Never stop here. Not much here worth stopping for, he knew. Still, he lifted his hand up and did a slow wave to the passengers even though he doubted any of them were looking out their windows.

He got up and strode over to the spot where Carlos would be. He looked back at the house, did a rough eye trajectory, probably for the thousandth time. It hadn't changed, not once. Not a millimeter. The camera was up there, the live feed to Carlos. The remote that would trigger it all. The SAT phone to Quarry at the mine. The dynamite. Willa. Her real mother. Daryl. Kurt already lying dead in a shaft in the south end. His Patriot buried in ignominy.

Ruth Ann.

Gabriel.

And finally Tippi.

See, that was the hardest part of all. Tippi.

He left the knoll and walked with a purpose in the direction of the house. This time he kept going, though, and walked up to the porch. He didn't unlock the door. He just sat on the planked porch, his back against a support post; his gaze dead on the door.

That was the hardest part.

He breathed in a bit of chilly air and then spit it out. It was as though his lungs didn't like the crispness of it, the purity. He coughed. He was getting the hack like Fred.

For a few seconds Quarry did the unimaginable, at least for him. He actually thought about stopping. The letter was already gone, but he didn't have to follow it up. He could fly up to the mine tomorrow, get Wohl and Willa, and leave them somewhere safe, where they would be found. He could just stay here with Tippi.

He got back in his truck and drove hard to Atlee. He hustled to his library, locked the door, ignored the Beam, and took a drink of Old Grand Dad. He sat at his desk, stared at the empty fireplace, felt the swollen skin on his forearm. He abruptly lashed out and swept everything off his desk; it all crashed down on the floor.

"What the hell am I doing!" he cried out. He stood there, bent over, breathing fast; his nerves had no elasticity left. He rushed out, plunged down the stairs, pulling the set of keys from his pocket. He hit the basement, ran down the passageway, unlocked the door, and went in the room. He flicked on the light and stared at the walls. His walls. His life. His road map to justice. He stared at all the old names, places, events, the intersecting lines of string that represented years of sweat, of tenacity, of an overpowering drive to figure it all out.

His breathing grew regular and his nerves reclaimed their rigidity. He lit a cigarette, released the smoke out slowly. His gaze settled on a photo of Tippi over at the far end of the walls, the place where it had all began.

The walls had won out. He was in this until the end. He clicked off the light, banishing the walls to darkness, but they had already fulfilled their purpose. He locked the door and headed upstairs.

Gabriel had finished reading to Tippi and gone to bed. Quarry checked on him as he passed by his bedroom. He opened the door a crack and listened to the soft breaths of the boy, saw the rise and fall of the blanket covering him.

A good boy. Probably grow into a fine man. And lead a life that would take him far away from this place. Good thing. He didn't belong here. Gabriel didn't belong here to the same degree that Sam Quarry did.

Everyone had to choose his road. Gabriel still had his decision to make. Quarry had already picked his route. There was no exit off his highway. He was heading a million miles an hour straight down it.

As he walked upstairs to bed he checked his watch. Carlos would be dropping the letter off in a couple more hours. Figure a day or two to reach its destination, three tops. He'd allowed for that in his instructions.

Then it would happen. Then he could have his

say. And they would listen. He was sure of that. He would make it clear. And then the decision would be up to them. He had a pretty good idea of what that decision would be. But people were strange. Sometimes you could just never figure them out. As he reached his bedroom at the top of the house, he realized that he was a testament to not being able to figure folks out.

He didn't turn on the light. He just chucked his boots and socks, undid his belt, unzipped his pants and let them drop to the floor. He moved over to the couch and started to pick up his bottle of liquid painkiller. Then he glanced over at the bed.

What the hell? He lay down on it, put aside the bottle, and started to dream of better days.

Yet that's just what it would remain for him. Only a dream.

65

Michelle and Sean watched as Frank Maxwell laid the cluster of flowers on his wife's fresh grave, bowed his head, and mumbled a few words. Then he just stood there, looking off, at what neither of them knew.

Sean whispered to her, "Do you think he's going to be okay?"

"I don't know. I don't even know if *I'm* going to be okay."

"How're your leg and arm?"

"Fine. And that's not the part of me I'm talking about."

"I know," he said quietly.

She turned to him. "Do you have these kinds of family problems?"

"Every family has issues. Why?"

"Just wondering."

They fell silent as Frank walked toward them.

Michelle put a hand on his arm. "You okay?"

He shrugged but then nodded. As they walked back to Michelle's SUV he said, "I probably shouldn't have left Sally to go and investigate. I probably should have stayed with her."

"If you had, we might not have caught Rothwell and Reagan," Sean pointed out.

When they got back to the house, Michelle made some coffee while Sean prepared sandwiches for lunch. They both looked up when the voice on the small countertop TV in the kitchen came on.

A moment later they were both looking at Willa's image on the screen. The news story was not enlightening. It said all the usual things. FBI still investigating. The First Couple anxious. The country wondering where the little girl was. They knew all that. But the mere sight of the little girl seemed to mesmerize them both, lifting them to a more heightened sense of urgency.

Sean stepped outside to make some phone calls. When he returned Michelle looked at him questioningly.

"Checking in with the First Lady and Chuck Waters."

"Anything new?"

"Nothing. I left another message for my two-star buddy."

"How's Waters coming on tracking down the Koasati angle?"

"They've had people all over that town in Louisiana. Nothing so far. Everybody checks out."

They fell silent. It was clear that now that the

mystery of Sally Maxwell's death had been solved, the priority was finding Willa. Alive. But they needed a break. Just one break.

Later, as they sat eating in the kitchen, Frank wiped his mouth with his napkin and cleared his throat.

"I was surprised you went back there," he said.

"Back where?" she countered.

"You know."

"I was pretty stunned to see you there too."

"We were never happy there, you know. Me and your mom."

"Apparently not."

"Do you remember much of it?" he asked cautiously. "You were so little. Not much more than a toddler."

"Dad, I wasn't a toddler. I was six. But, no, I don't remember much about it."

"But you remembered how to get there?"

Michelle lied and said, "That's what we call GPS."

Sean fiddled with a potato chip on his plate while he tried to look everywhere except at father and daughter. "I'll be right back," he said and got up and left before either of them could say anything.

"He's a good man," Frank said.

Michelle nodded. "Probably better than I deserve."

"So you two are like a couple?" He gazed over at his daughter.

She fiddled with the handle of her coffee cup. "More business partners," she said.

Frank glanced out the window. "I worked a lot back then. Left your mother alone too much. It was hard. I see that now. My career as a cop was my life. Your brothers have balanced things a lot better than I ever did."

"I never felt ignored, Dad. And none of the boys did either as far as I can tell. They worshipped you and Mom."

"But did you?"

The look in his eyes was so pleading, she felt the breath harden in her throat. "Did I what?" But she already knew.

"Worship us? Me and your mom?"

"I love you both very much. I always have."

"Right, okay." He went back to his lunch, methodically chewing his sandwich and drinking his coffee, the veins in his strong hands pronounced. But he never looked at her again. And Michelle could not bring herself to amend what she'd already said.

As she and Sean were cleaning up after the meal someone knocked at the front door. She went to answer it and came back a minute later holding a large cardboard box.

Sean put the last cup in the dishwasher, closed it, and turned to her. "What's that? For your dad?"

"No, for you."

"Me!"

She set it down on the table and read the return address. "General Tom Holloway? Department of Defense?"

"My two-star buddy. Looks like he came through with the AWOL records."

"But how did they get here?"

"I e-mailed him on the drive down to Tennessee and left this address just in case he had something and we were still down here. Open it up, quick."

Michelle used a pair of scissors to slit open the box. Inside were separate plastic binders, about three dozen of them. She pulled a few out. They were copies of official Army investigation reports.

"I know he's your friend and all, but why would the Army provide a civilian with this stuff? And do so with such speed?"

Sean took one of the binders and started sifting through it.

"Sean? I asked you a question."

He glanced up. "Well, aside from the football tickets I might've let slip that the White House was behind our investigation and that any cooperation they could lend would be personally pleasing to both the president and the First Lady. Knowing the Army, I'm sure they checked that out and found it was true. First rule in the military, never do anything to piss off the commander in chief."

"I'm impressed."

"That's apparently what I live for."

"So we go through these?"

"Page by page. Line by line. And hope to God it's the break we need."

A door slammed. Michelle rose and looked out the window in time to see her father climb in his car and drive off.

"Where do you think he's going?" asked Sean.

Michelle sat back down. "How should I know? I'm not the man's keeper."

"The *man* saved your life."

"And I thanked him for that, didn't I?"

"Before I go any further, am I getting close to the point where you usually tell me to go to hell?"

"Perilously close."

"I thought so." He turned back to the binder.

"I do love my father. And I loved my mother."

"I'm sure. And I know these things get complicated."

"I think my family wrote the book on complicated."

"Your brothers seem pretty normal."

"I guess I got all the issues."

"Why did you want to go back to the farmhouse?"

"I told you, I don't know."

"I've never known you to take an idle trip."

"First time for everything."

"Is that how you want to leave it with your dad?"

She gave him a look. "Exactly *how* am I leaving it?"

"Up in the air."

"Sean, my mother was murdered after apparently cheating on my dad. The woman who killed her almost killed me. My father saved my life, but there are issues there too, okay? In fact, for a while there I thought he'd been the one who killed her. So excuse me for being a little conflicted right now."

"I'm sorry, Michelle, you're right."

She laid down the binder she was holding and put her face in her hands. "No, maybe you're right. But I don't know how to deal with this, I really don't."

"Maybe you start with just talking to the guy. One-on-one, nobody else around."

"That sounds absolutely terrifying."

"I know it does. And you don't have to do it."

"But I probably do have to do it if I ever want to get past this." She stood. "Can you take over going through these? I'm going to try and find my dad."

"Any idea where he might've gone?"

"I think so."

66

Jane Cox rode in the limo coming back from Mail Boxes Etc. Unbeknownst to her, the FBI had run a trace on the post office box she'd been visiting every day. They had come up empty. Phony name, paid in cash for six months, and no paper trail. They'd given the store manager hell for not following the rules.

"This is how 9/11s start, you clueless moron," Agent Chuck Waters had snapped at the middle-aged man behind the counter. "You let a terrorist cell get a mailbox here with no background info, you're helping the enemies of this country attack us. Is that what the hell you want to be remembered for? Aiding and abetting Osama bin Laden?"

The man had been so distressed by this tongue-lashing that his eyes had actually started to tear up. But Waters had never seen this. He was already gone.

Jane reached the White House and climbed slowly out of the car. She had not been seen much in public as of late, which was a good thing, actually, because she looked older and haggard. The HD cameras deployed now would not have been too flattering. Even the president had noticed it.

"You okay, hon?" he'd asked during a brief stop-over on the campaign trail where he would give an address to a group of veterans followed by a belated visit from the women's college basketball national championship team. She had gone straight from the limo up to their private quarters to find him sitting there going over some briefing papers.

"I'm fine, Danny. I wish people would stop asking me that. I'll start to think there's something actually wrong."

"The FBI has briefed me about these visits to the post office box."

"And not the Secret Service?" she'd said quickly. "The spies among us?"

He sighed. "They're just doing their job, Jane. We're national property now. National treasure, at least you are," he'd added with a quick smile that usually did the trick in boosting her spirits.

Usually, but not today. "You're the treasure, Danny. I'm just the baggage."

"Jane, that's not—"

"I don't really have time to waste on this and neither do you. The kidnappers communicated with me through a letter. It gave me the post office box and a key to that box. They said I would receive a letter at some point and to check that box every day. I have. And so far, no letter."

"But why work through you at all. Why not Tuck?"

"Yes, why not Tuck? I don't know, Danny, because I apparently cannot think like a kidnapper."

"Sure, sure, I didn't mean that. So maybe we were right. They're going to ask me to do something in order to get Willa back. It can't be money because your brother has more of that than I do. Hell, we can barely cover our personal grocery bills at this place. It must be tied to the presidency."

"And then it becomes problematic, like you said. Emasculate the office, I believe were your words."

"Jane, I will do all that I can do, but there are limits."

"I thought the power of the Oval Office was unlimited. I guess I was wrong about that."

"We will do all we can to get her back."

"And if all we can *do* isn't enough?" she said angrily.

He stared at her, a slightly hopeless look in his eyes.

The most powerful man in the world, she thought. *Emasculated.*

Her anger cooled as suddenly as it had risen. "Just hold me, Danny. Just hold me."

He rushed to do this, pressing her tightly against him.

"You're shivering. Are you coming down with something? You've lost weight too."

She stepped away from him. "Look, you need to go. You have your speech in the East Room."

He automatically checked his watch. "They'll call up when it's time."

He went to hold her again, but she moved away, sat down, and stared off.

"Jane, I am the president of the United States. I am not without influence. I can probably help."

"You'd think so, wouldn't you?"

The phone rang. He picked it up. "Yes, I know, I'll be down in a minute."

He bent down and kissed his wife on the cheek. "I'll come back up and check on you later."

"After the women's basketball team."

"Just what I've always wanted to be around," he quipped. "A bunch of leggy women far taller than I am."

"I've got some events too."

"I'm going to have Cindy cancel them. You need to rest."

"But—"

"Just rest."

As he started to walk away she said, "Danny, I will need you at some point. Will you be there for me?"

He knelt beside her, wrapped an arm around her shoulders. "I will always be there for you, just like you have with me. Get some rest. I'll have them send up some coffee and something to eat. I don't like how thin you're getting. We need some more meat on those curves." He gave her a kiss and left.

I have always been there for you, Danny. Always.

67

Michelle put the SUV in park and climbed out. Her shoes touched hardened dirt and she looked up at the old house with the dying tree, the rotting tire swing, the skeleton truck up on blocks in the back.

She glanced across the street. At the house where an old lady named Hazel Rose had once lived. Her house had been meticulous, the yard the same. Now the structure was beyond saving; a bare few inches from giving one last heave and falling down for good. Yet someone was living there. Toys were strewn across the front yard. She could see laundry flapping in the breeze on the line in the side yard. It was still a depressing scene. Her past was eroding away before her eyes, like sludge off a mountaintop.

Hazel Rose had always been kind to Michelle. Even when the little girl stopped going over there for the tea parties she gave for neighborhood kids. Why that memory had slipped into her mind just now, Michelle didn't know. She turned back to the house, knowing what she had to do, even if she didn't want to do it.

Michelle's hunch had been right. Her father's car was parked in front of hers. The front door to the farmhouse was open. She walked past his car and then by the stunted remains of the rose hedge.

That's what it was, she now recalled. A rose hedge. Why had *that* popped into her head? And then she remembered the lilies on her mother's coffin and telling Sean that her mom preferred roses. And she had felt a pain in her hand, like a thorn had pricked her. But there was no thorn, because there were no roses. Just like now. No roses.

She walked on, wondering what she would say to him.

She didn't have long to think.

"I'm up here," his voice called out to her. She gazed up, using her hand to shield her eyes against the sun. He was standing at an open window on the second floor.

She stepped over the fallen screen door and walked inside a house she had called home for a brief time when she was a child. In a way she felt like she was traveling back in time. With each step she was growing younger, less confident, and less competent. All her years of living, her experiences in college, in the Secret Service, as Sean's partner, were dissolving away. She was six years old again, dragging a battered plastic baseball bat around, looking for someone to play with.

She eyed the old stairs. She had slid down them on

flattened cardboard when she was a kid. Something her mother didn't really like, but she remembered her father laughing and catching her as she hurtled down.

"My youngest son," he sometimes called her because she had been such a fearless tomboy.

She headed up. Her father met her on the landing.

"I thought you might come here," he said.

"Why?"

"Unfinished business, maybe."

She opened the door to her old room, walked over to the window, and sat on the edge of the sill, her back to the filthy glass panes.

Her father leaned up against the wall and put his hands in his pockets, idly stabbing the scuffed wooden floor with his shoe. "Do you remember much about this place?" he asked, his gaze fixed on his shoe.

"I remembered the rose hedge when I was walking up to the house. You planted that for an anniversary, didn't you?"

"No, your mother's birthday."

"And somebody chopped it all down one night."

"Yes, they did."

Michelle turned to look out the window. "Never found out who."

"I miss her. I really miss her."

She turned back to find her father watching her. "I know. I've never seen you cry like you did the other morning."

"I was crying because I almost lost you, baby."

This answer surprised Michelle and then she wondered why it had.

"I know that Mom loved you, Dad. Even if she . . . if she didn't always show it exactly the right way."

"Let's go outside, getting sort of stuffy in here."

They walked along the perimeter of the backyard. "Your mother and I were high school sweethearts. She waited for me while I was in Vietnam. We got married. Then the kids started coming."

"Four boys. All in four years. Talk about your rabbits."

"And then my little girl came along."

She smiled and poked him in the arm. "Can we say accident?"

"No, Michelle, it was no accident. We planned for you."

She looked at him quizzically. "I guess I never really asked either of you about it, but I always assumed I was sort of a surprise. Was it because you were trying for a girl?"

Frank stopped walking. "We were trying for . . . something."

"Something to hold you together?" she said slowly.

He started to walk again but she didn't. He stopped, looked back.

"Did you ever consider divorce, Dad?"

"It was not something our generation did lightly."

"Divorce is not always the wrong answer. If you weren't happy."

Frank held up a hand. "Your mother wasn't happy. I, uh, I was trying to work at it. Although I'd be the first to admit that I spent too much time on the job and away from her. She raised the kids and she did a great job. But she did it without a lot of support from me."

"Cop's life."

"No, just *this* cop's life."

"You knew about Doug Reagan, obviously?"

"I saw some of the signs that she was attracted to him."

Michelle couldn't believe she was about to ask this, but she had to. "Would it have bothered you if you knew they had slept together?"

"I was still her husband. Of course it would have hurt me, deeply."

"Would you have put a stop to it?"

"I probably would've beaten Reagan within an inch of his life."

"And Mom?"

"I hurt your mother in other ways over the years. And it wasn't her fault."

"By not being around for her?"

"In some ways, that's worse than cheating."

"You think so?"

"What's a quick fling in the sack compared to decades of indifference?"

"Dad, you weren't gone all the time."

"You weren't alive when the boys were little. Trust me, your mother was a single parent for all intents and purposes. You can never get that time, that trust back. At least I never did."

"Did you cry for her too?"

He held out his hand for her to take. She did.

"You cry, sweetie. You always cry."

"I don't want to stay here."

"Let's go."

Michelle had nearly made it to her SUV when it happened. Without any warning at all, her feet pointed toward the house and she started to run.

"Michelle!" her father screamed.

She was already inside the old building and racing up the stairs. Feet pounded after her. She took the steps two at a time, her breaths coming in gasps, as though she had run miles instead of yards.

She reached the top. The door to her bedroom was closed. But that was not her destination. She raced to the door at the end of the hall and kicked it open.

"Michelle, no!" her father roared from behind her.

She stared into the room. Her hand went to her gun. She flicked off the cover strap. The Sig was out, pointed straight ahead.

"Michelle!" Feet pounded closer.

"Get away from my mom!" she screamed.

In Michelle's mind her mother looked back at her, terrified. She was on her knees, her dress half torn off. Michelle could see her mother's bra, the indentation of her heavy cleavage, and this exposure terrified her.

"Baby!" Sally Maxwell yelled out to her. "Go back downstairs." Her mother was young, young and alive. Long white hair had been replaced with soft dark strands. She was beautiful. Flawless, except for the torn dress, the terrified expression, the man in Army fatigues standing over her.

"Get away from her. Stop hurting her!" Michelle screamed in a voice she had only used for arresting someone.

"Baby, please, it's all right," said her mother. "Go back down stairs."

Michelle's finger slipped to the trigger. "Stop it. Stop it!"

The man turned and looked at her. He would have probably smiled, like he had all the other nights. Except she was pointing his own gun at him, the one she'd pulled from the holster he'd carelessly tossed on the chair. You didn't smile when a gun was pointed at you. Even by a six-year-old child.

He made a move toward her.

Just as she had that night, Michelle now fired a

single shot. It passed through the air and slammed into the wall opposite.

A big hand clamped down on her pistol, took it from her. She let it go. It was so heavy, she couldn't hold it anymore. She looked into the room. Saw her mother screaming. Screaming at what Michelle had done. At the dead man on the floor.

A hand was on her shoulder. Michelle turned to look.

"Dad?" she said in an odd voice.

"It's all right, baby," her father said. "I'm here."

Michelle pointed into the room. "I did that."

"I know. Protecting your mom, that's all."

She gripped his shoulder. "We have to take him away, but don't leave me in the car, Dad. Not this time. I can see his face. You have to remember to cover up his face."

"Michelle!"

"You have to cover his face. If I see his face—" Her breaths were coming in short swells. She was barely able to draw one breath before she needed another.

Her father put the gun down and squeezed her tight, until her breathing slowed. Until Michelle looked into that room and saw what was really there.

Nothing.

"I shot him, Dad. I killed a man."

He drew back a bit, studied her. She looked back

at him, her eyes clear, focused. "You did nothing wrong. You were just a kid. Just a scared little child. Protecting your mother."

"But she—he came before. He was *with* her, Dad."

"If you want to blame anyone, you blame me. It was my fault. Only my fault." Tears were staining his cheeks and Michelle felt her own tears start to fall.

"I'll never do that. I'll never blame you for that."

He gripped her hand and steered her down the stairs.

"We need to leave here, Michelle. We need to leave here and not come back. This is the past, and we can't relive it anymore. We have to keep going, Michelle, it's the only way life works. Otherwise, it'll just destroy us both."

Outside, he held the SUV door open for her and she climbed in. Before he closed it, he said, "Are you sure you're okay?"

She drew a deep breath and then nodded. "I don't know exactly what happened in there."

"I think you know all you ever need to know. Now it's time to forget."

She glanced over his shoulder. "You cut down the rose hedge, didn't you?"

He followed her gaze and then looked back at Michelle. "Your mother loved those roses. I never should have taken those from her."

"You probably had good reason."

"Fathers aren't perfect, Michelle. And I never had a good enough reason to do a lot of things."

She stared up at the old house. "I'm never coming back here."

"No reason for you to."

Her eyes drifted back down to him. "We need to do things differently, Dad. *I* need to do things differently."

He squeezed her hand and closed the SUV door.

As he walked back to his car, Michelle stole one more glance up at the house, her gaze counting the windows until it got to *that* room.

"I'm sorry, Mom. I'm so sorry that you're gone. I never wanted to have any regrets, and now it's all I seem to have." The tears poured out so hard, she just rested her forehead on the steering wheel and sobbed, her chest rising and striking the wheel with the regularity of a clapper against a bell.

She looked up ahead in time to see her father wipe his face free of his own tears and climb in his car.

Right before she fired up the SUV, Michelle said, "Goodbye, Mom. I . . . don't care what you did. I'll always love you."

68

As he was going through the binders, Sean's cell phone rang. It was Aaron Betack.

"You didn't hear any of this from me," the Secret Service agent said.

"You found the letter?"

"It was a good call on your part, Sean. Yeah, it was in her desk. Found it a while back, actually. Sorry it took me so long to tell you. Anybody found out I did this, my career is over. I'll probably go to jail."

"Nobody will find out from me, I can guarantee you that."

"I haven't even told the FBI. Don't really see how I could without explaining how I got it."

"I can see that. Was it typewritten like the first one?"

"Yep."

"What did it say?"

"Not all that much. The writer was pretty economical, but there was enough in those words."

"Like what?"

"Some things we already know. That she had to keep checking the post office box. She's been going there every day. Waters has run a trace on the box. Dead end. The plan is when the letter does come that the FBI will take it from her."

"Forcibly take it from the First Lady?"

"I know. I sort of envision a standoff between the FBI and the Service. Not pretty. But the truth is it'll get worked out behind the scenes. Wolfman isn't going to let the election get blown up over this, niece or not."

"What else did the letter say?"

"That was the most troubling part."

"Troubling how?" Sean said warily.

"I'm not sure this whole thing is related to the Duttons. I think it might have something to do with the First Lady."

"You mean the kidnappers want something from the president?"

"No. The letter said that the next communication she got would reveal all. And that if she let anyone else read it, that it would all be over for her and everyone she cared about. That there would be no way out then for her. Her only chance to survive would be to keep the letter away from everyone else."

"It actually said that?"

"Not word for word, but that's the clear intent. Sean, you obviously knew her way back when. I've only been around her during this term. What could the person be referring to? Something in Mrs. Cox's past?"

Sean thought back to the first time he'd met Jane Cox, while awkwardly carrying her newly minted U.S. senator and drunken husband into their modest house. Yet nothing had come of that.

"Sean?"

"Yeah, I was just thinking. I'm coming up with zip, Aaron."

He heard the other man sigh. "If I just risked my career for nothing."

"I don't think you did. What that letter said changes things, Aaron. I just don't know how."

"Well, if this does involve the First Lady and the shit hits the fan, right in the middle of a campaign, I don't want to be within a thousand miles of that fallout."

"We might not have a choice."

"Anything on your end?"

"Just trying to follow up some leads along with Waters."

"How's Maxwell? Heard her mother died."

"She's doing okay. Best as can be expected."

"For what it's worth I thought you both got raw deals at the Service."

"Thanks."

Aaron clicked off and Sean went back to his binders after spending a few minutes fruitlessly racking his brain about anything in Jane Cox's past that could explain the current situation.

A few minutes later the door opened and Michelle walked in.

"Did you find your dad?" he asked, rising from the table.

"Yeah, he was where I'd thought he'd be."

"At the farmhouse?"

She gazed darkly at him.

"I'm a detective," he said gamely. "It's what I do."

"Sometimes I wish you didn't do it so well, particularly when it concerns me."

He studied her. "Have you been crying?"

"Tears are sometimes good. I've been finding that out lately."

"Did you hash things out?"

"Pretty much, yeah."

"Did he come back with you?"

"No, he went over to see Bobby."

She looked at the piles of binders. "Sorry I walked out on you. Any revelations?"

"Not yet. I've hit it hard for the past four hours, but got zip. However, judging from the number of investigations, apparently desertions are becoming a real problem for the Army. I did hear from Betack." He filled her in on the conversation.

Michelle made a pot of fresh coffee and poured out cups for her and Sean. They both sat down at the kitchen table. "That would explain why she's been so high-strung. And why she's been playing things so close to the vest."

"You mean obstructing justice?"

"That too."

She reached out her hand. "Give me a binder and let's find that kid."

Two hours later they were still there.

"Six more to go," said Sean as he stretched out and then handed another binder to her.

They read slowly, looking for any clue that might allow them to lift their butts from these chairs and plunge into action once more. Their intensity levels were as high as if they were taking a college final exam. There was no room for mistakes. If there was a clue buried in all this, they knew it was probably going to be a subtle one and they could not afford to miss it.

"How about some dinner?" Sean finally said. "I'm buying. And we can keep reading."

They drove to a local restaurant.

"So you really think things are okay with your dad?"

She nodded. "I think so. I mean, we both have to work at it. I haven't been the most loving, attentive daughter in the world."

"Or sister," he pointed out.

"Thanks for reminding me."

As they ate she eyed him nervously. "Sean, about what happened back at my father's house."

"What about it?"

"It won't happen again."

"But if it did happen again, I'd be there for you, okay? There are few guarantees in life, but there's one of them."

"I'd do the same for you. I hope you know that."

"That's why we're partners, right? So any little hiccups that come along, we'll deal with them. Okay? Together."

"Okay."

He slid a binder across to her. "Now let's get back to work."

Before she opened the binder she leaned across and gave him a kiss on the cheek.

"And that was for what?" he asked.

"For dealing with the hiccups so damn well. And for not taking advantage of a lady when you could have."

69

"Can I see the daylight?"

Quarry had flown his plane up to the mines and was now watching Willa as they sat in her room.

"Why do you want to see the daylight?"

"Because I haven't seen it in a while, that's why. I miss it. I'm a sun person."

"You can't get away. There's no one to yell to for help."

"So there's no reason not to let me see it, then," she answered reasonably.

"What'd you and the lady talk about the other day?"

"Just things. I like her."

"You've never seen her before, have you?"

"Why would I have?" Willa asked, her large eyes squarely on Quarry.

"I guess seeing the daylight will be okay. Come on."

"Now?"

"Why not now?"

She followed him out. As they walked down the long passage she said, "Can Diane come too?"

"I guess so."

They retrieved Diane and the two ladies followed the tall Quarry toward the exit. Willa's eyes darted left and right, taking in all details, while Diane simply trudged along, her gaze only on Quarry's back. Behind them Daryl walked along, his face still bruised from his fight with his father. His mood seemed to match his injuries.

One thing Willa picked up on was the cables running along some of the passageways that she did not remember seeing before. She didn't know what they were for, but intuitively concluded that their presence did not portend anything good.

Quarry unlocked the door and they all stepped outside, blinking to adjust to the light.

"Right nice day," said Quarry as he led the little group outside.

And it was. The sky was a light blue and cloudless. The breeze from the west was warming but gentle. They sat on a large rock and gazed around. Willa looked interested, Diane Wohl indifferent, and Daryl just scowled off into the distance.

"Where'd you learn to fly?" said Willa, pointing at the little Cessna parked on the grassy strip.

"Vietnam. Nothing like a war to teach you how to fly real good. 'Cause you don't fly real good in a war, the problem ain't that you don't arrive on time, it's that you don't arrive at all."

"I've been on a plane," said Willa. "We went to

Europe last summer. Me and my family. And I've flown to California. Have you been on a plane?" she asked Diane.

She said nervously, "Yeah, I travel a lot for work. But not planes like that one," she added, pointing at Quarry's ride. "Big ones."

"What sort of work do you do?" asked Willa.

"Look, Willa, I'm not exactly in the mood to chitchat, okay?" she said, eying Quarry warily.

"Okay," the girl said, apparently unperturbed by this. "Can I walk down there?" she asked Quarry, pointing to the grassy strip.

Quarry gave Daryl a look and then nodded at Diane.

"Sure, let's go."

They made their way down the short slope, Quarry holding on to Willa's hand. When they got to level ground he let go and they walked side by side.

"Is that your mountain?" she asked, pointing behind her.

"More of a hill than a mountain, but yeah, I guess it is mine. Or at least it was my granddaddy's and it got passed down to me."

"You sure you told my family that I'm okay?"

"Sure I'm sure, why?"

"Diane said she didn't think you had contacted her mother to let her know she was all okay."

"Is that right?" Quarry looked back up Diane, who sat on a rock looking as miserable as she no doubt felt.

Willa said quickly, "Don't be angry at her, we were just talking." She hesitated. "Did you call her mother?"

Quarry didn't answer. He just walked on. Willa had to hurry along to keep up with his strides.

"How's your daughter?"

Quarry stopped walking. "Why all the questions, girl?" he said darkly.

"Why not?"

"That's just another damn question. Answer mine."

"I don't have anything else to do," Willa said simply. "I'm alone almost all the time. I've read all the books you brought. Diane doesn't say much when we're together. She just mostly cries and hugs me. I miss my family and this is the first time I've seen the sun since I tried to get away. I'm just basically trying to hold everything together. Would you rather I like screamed and ranted and bawled my eyes out? Because I can if you want."

Quarry started walking again and so did she. "I got two daughters, actually. Lot older than you. All grown up."

"I meant the daughter who doesn't read anymore. How is she doing?"

"Not too well."

"Can I ask some more questions? Or will you get mad?"

Quarry stopped, snagged a rock off the ground, and tossed it about twenty feet. "Sure, it's okay."

"Is she really sick?"

"You know what a coma is?"

"Yes."

"Well, that's what she's in. Has been for over thirteen years. Longer than you've been alive."

"I'm sorry."

"I'm sorry too."

"What happened to her?"

"Somebody hurt her."

"Why would they do that?"

"Good question. Turns out some people don't care who they hurt."

"Did they ever catch the person?"

"No."

"What's your daughter's name?"

"Tippi."

"Can you tell me *your* name?"

"Sam."

"I know you can't tell me your last name, Sam."

"It's Quarry. Sam Quarry."

Willa looked stricken.

"What's the matter?" he asked.

"You just told me your whole name," she said shakily.

"So? You asked."

"But if you told me your whole name, I could tell the police, but only if you plan on letting us go. So that means you're not going to let us go." She said this last part in a hushed voice.

"Why don't you think about that again? There's another answer. You're smart, go for it."

Willa stared up at him with a strange look on her face. Finally she said, "I guess it could be that you don't care if I tell the police your name."

"Hell, I expect lots of folks will know my name soon enough."

"Why's that?"

"Just will. You know, speaking of names, there's a little black boy that lives with me called Gabriel. Almost as old as you. And he's about as smart as you too. He's a real good boy. Nice as they come."

"Can I meet him?" she said quickly.

"Not right now, no. See, he doesn't know anything about this and I intend to keep it that way. But what I want you to do is make sure that folks know him and his ma, Ruth Ann, didn't know nothing about this. Not a thing. Will you do that for me, Willa?"

"Okay, sure."

"Thanks. Because it's important."

"Is he your son?" Willa was now looking back at Daryl.

"What makes you say that?"

"You have the same eyes."

Quarry stared up at Daryl. "Yeah, he's my boy."

"Did you two get in a fight? I heard stuff in the mine. And his face is all messed up. And your mouth too."

Quarry touched his injured lip. "Sometimes people don't see eye to eye 'bout things. But I still love him. Just like I love Tippi."

"You're a very unusual kidnapper, Mr. Quarry," she said bluntly.

"Just call me Mr. Sam, same as Gabriel does."

"Will it be too much longer? All this?"

Quarry drew a deep breath and let the air rustle around inside his lungs before expelling it. "Not too much longer, no."

"I think you're sorry you had to do this."

"In one way yes, in another way no. But this is the only way I had."

"Do we have to go back in yet, Mr. Sam?"

"Not yet. Soon. But not yet."

They sat on the ground and enjoyed the warmth of the sun.

When they went back inside later, Quarry let Diane and Willa spend some time together in Diane's room.

"Why are you being nice to that guy?" Diane said as soon as Quarry had locked the door and walked off.

"There's something strange about him."

"Of course there is, he's a psycho."

"No, I don't think he is. But as far as being nice to him, I'm trying to stay on Mr. Sam's good side."

"Assuming he has one. God, I could use a cigarette."

"Cigarettes can kill you."

"I'd rather die by my own hand." She pointed at the door. "Instead of his," she yelled.

"Now you're scaring me." Willa drew back a little.

Diane calmed and sat at the table. "I'm sorry, Willa. I'm sorry. We're all under a lot of stress. You miss your family, I miss mine."

"You told me before you didn't have a family of your own. How come?"

Diane looked at her in a strange way. "I wanted to get married and have children, but it just didn't work out."

"You're still young."

"Thirty-two."

"You have plenty of time. You can still have a family."

"Who says I want one now?" Diane said bitterly.

Willa fell silent as she watched Diane rub her hands nervously together and stare down at the tabletop.

"We're never getting out of here, you know that, don't you?" said Diane.

"I think we will, if things go according to Mr. Sam's plan."

Diane leapt up. "Stop calling him that! It makes him sound like he's somebody's doting grandfather and not some crazy freak."

"Okay," Willa said fearfully. "Okay. I'll stop."

Diane sank back down in the chair. "You miss your mom?" she said in a low voice.

Willa nodded. "I miss everybody. Even my little brother."

"Did he tell you that everybody was okay in your family?"

"Yes. He—" Willa broke off and looked sharply at her. "Why do you ask that? Did he tell you something differently?"

Diane looked surprised. "No, I mean, we didn't talk about it. Him and me ... I don't know anything."

Willa stood, her gaze searching the woman's face, easily boring through the thin veneer of lies.

"He told you something," she said accusingly.

"No, he didn't."

"Is my family okay? Are they?"

"Willa, I don't know. I ... he ... Look, we can't trust anything he says."

"So he *did* tell you something. What did he tell you?"

"Willa, I can't."

"Tell me! Tell me!" She raced at Diane and started slapping at her. "Tell me! Tell me!"

Footsteps could be heard outside of the room. A

key turned in the lock. The door was thrown open. Quarry ran over to them, lifted Willa up. She turned on him, slapping at his face.

"Tell me that my family is okay. Tell me!" she yelled at Quarry.

Quarry glared once at Diane, who shrank against the wall. "Willa—stop," he said.

But she slapped him on his injured mouth. She kept punching, hitting, slapping. She was uncontrollable.

"Daryl," roared Quarry.

His son hustled in, carrying a syringe. He uncapped it and popped the needle into Willa's arm. Two seconds later she was slumped in Quarry's arms. He handed her off to his son.

"Take her back to her room."

When he was alone with Diane, Quarry turned on her. "What the hell did you tell her?"

"Nothing. I swear it. She asked about her family."

"You told her you were her mother?"

"No, I would never do that."

"Then what the hell happened?"

"Look, you killed her mom."

"No I didn't."

"Well, you told me she was dead. Is she or isn't she?"

Quarry looked toward the door and then back at her. "It was an accident."

"I'm sure," she said sarcastically.

"You told her she was dead?" he said, his anger rising.

"No, but she's a smart kid. I told her you couldn't be trusted. She put two and two together. And if you do let us go she's going to find out for sure at some point."

Quarry scowled at her from under thick tufts of eyebrow. "You shouldn't have told her that."

"Yeah, well, you shouldn't have killed her mother, by accident or otherwise. And you shouldn't have kidnapped us in the first place. And right now I don't really care if you kill me. You can just go to hell, *Mr. Sam*."

"I'm already in hell, lady. Been there for years."

He slammed the door behind him.

70

Jane Cox drew a quick breath as she peered inside the post office box. Every time she had opened it before the container had been empty. But today there was a white envelope inside. She glanced around, held her purse close to the box, and slid the envelope inside it.

She had just climbed inside the limo when there was a rap on the glass. Jane looked at her security detail leader. "Let's go."

Instead of going, the door to the limo opened and FBI agent Chuck Waters was standing there. "I need the letter, Mrs. Cox."

"Excuse me, who are you?"

Waters held up his badge. "FBI. I need the letter," he said again.

"What letter?"

"The letter you just took out of that box in there." He pointed over his shoulder to the Mail Boxes Etc. store.

"I don't know what you're talking about. Now please leave me alone." She looked over at her detail chief. "Drew, tell him to leave."

Drew Fuller, a veteran Secret Service agent, looked back at her nervously. "Mrs. Cox, the FBI has had you under surveillance from day one on this."

"What!" she exclaimed. From the resigned look in Fuller's eyes, he had realized that a reassignment in his future to a far less desirable outpost was probably coming fast.

Waters said, "I have a warrant here." He held up the piece of paper. "To search your purse and your person."

"You can't do that. I'm not a criminal."

"If you have evidence critical to a kidnapping investigation and you are knowingly withholding it, then you are a criminal, ma'am."

"I can't believe your gall!"

"I'm just trying to get your niece back. I assume you want that too."

"How dare you!"

Waters looked at Fuller. "We can do this easy or hard. It's up to her."

Fuller said, "Mrs. Cox, the Service has been aware of the FBI's actions and the official position is that we have no right to stop them on this. It's a federal investigation. The White House lawyers also are in agreement with this."

"So it seems that everyone is in agreement. That everyone has been going behind my back to plot against me. Does that include my husband?"

"I can't speak to that," Fuller said hastily.

"Well, I can. And I will when I get back to the White House."

"That's certainly your prerogative, Mrs. Cox."

"No, that will be my mission!"

Waters said, "The letter, Mrs. Cox? This is all very time-sensitive."

She slowly opened her purse and put her hand inside.

"Ma'am, if you don't mind, I'll get it myself."

She gave him a look that he would probably remember for the rest of his life. "Let me see the warrant first."

He handed her the paper, which she read through slowly, then held open her purse. "I have lipstick in there too, if you're so inclined."

He stared down into the contents of her purse. "The letter will be fine, ma'am."

He slid the letter out and she snapped her purse shut, nearly pinching his fingers. "I'll have your badge for this," she snapped. Jane glared at Fuller. "*Now* can we go?"

He immediately turned to the driver. "Hit it."

Back at 1600 Pennsylvania, Jane went swiftly up to her family quarters. She took off her coat, slipped off her shoes, went into her bedroom, and locked the door. She opened her purse and slid her hand behind the barely visible tear in the lining. She pulled the letter out. It was addressed to her at the post office box. All typed. She opened it. There was only a single page inside, also typed.

She had known she was being watched by the FBI. When she opened the box and saw the letter in there, she had held her purse close to the mailbox and slid the letter behind the torn lining of her large purse, while appearing to merely place it *in* her purse. The letter she'd allowed Waters to take was one of her creation that she had typed on a typewriter she'd found in storage at the White House. She had placed the fake letter in her purse before she'd left to check the mailbox. What man would think to look behind the lining of a purse when another letter was sitting in there next to her cosmetics? She'd even thrown a prescription bottle in there for some menopause issues she was having to rattle the man further, so he wouldn't dare linger in her purse.

The envelope she'd received through the White House kitchen staff had been white, so she assumed any follow-up one would be as well. She knew that the watchers could only see a snippet of the envelope as it went from the box to her purse.

She also knew that she would be confronted once the envelope did arrive. She had sources at the White House. Like the Secret Service, there was nothing that went on there that she did not know about. Thus the FBI and the warrant were not surprises to her. Well, she'd fooled the vaunted agency.

This sense of triumph was short-lived, however.

With trembling hands she unfolded the letter and started to read. It gave her a date and time to place a call to a phone number that was included in the letter. The number was untraceable, she was told. More importantly, it said that if anyone else was on the phone call, where the truth of all this would be revealed, then it would not only cost her Willa, but it would also destroy all their lives, *irreversibly*.

She noted that last word. "Irreversibly." It was oddly placed, oddly used. Was there hidden meaning there? There was really no way for her to tell.

She wrote the phone number down on another slip of paper, rushed into the bathroom, crumpled up the letter, and flushed it down the toilet. For one paralyzing moment she envisioned federal law enforcement agents hiding somewhere in the White House intercepting her toilet water and reconstructing the letter. But that was impossible. That was the stuff of Orwell's *1984*. Yet in some ways, by living at the White House, she had already seen Orwell's masterpiece of "fascism perfected" in a way most Americans could never imagine.

She flushed the toilet once more for good measure and then trudged slowly out of the bathroom. She made a call and canceled all of her appointments for the day. In over three years at the White House serving as First Lady she had never missed an event, no matter how small or relatively trivial. Ever since Willa had disappeared she had struck them off with regularity. And she had no regrets. They had had her pound of flesh. She had served her country well. The fact that her husband was running hard to earn four more years of it now made her sick to her stomach.

Suddenly chilled, she ran a hot bath and took off her clothes. Before climbing into the tub she stared at her naked self in the full-length mirror. She *had* lost weight. It was something she had been meaning to do, but not in this manner. She didn't look better with the pounds gone. She looked weaker, older even. It was not a pretty sight, she concluded. The skin was slack, bones stuck out where a woman wouldn't want them to. She turned the light off and slid into the hot water.

As she lay there she had to figure out a way to do something that no other American, perhaps other than her husband, would ever have to worry about. Jane Cox had to come up with a way to make a simple phone call that was entirely private, with no one else around. She couldn't do it from here. If the FBI had a warrant to search her bag, they probably had a warrant to monitor calls here, at least the ones that she made. And for all Jane knew, every phone call coming in or out of this building was monitored by someone, perhaps the NSA. They seemed to listen in on anyone they wanted to.

And if Jane couldn't make the call from here, there was really nowhere else where she was not with someone. On a plane or chopper, in a limo, eating meals, working at the office, attending a tea, cutting a ribbon for a new children's hospital, christening a ship, visiting wounded soldiers at Walter Reed.

It was the price to be paid for winning the White House. She would think of a way, however. It would come to her. She had fooled the FBI with the letter. She'd used gloves, so there would be no prints. She'd used vague language saying that the sum of ten million dollars would be required and that the kidnappers would contact her by letter again. It had bought her some time at least, but not that much actually. The time to call the provided number was for tomorrow evening. No, not much time at all.

She closed her eyes. The word "irreversibly" kept coming back to her. And then her eyes opened as she recalled the words immediately preceding that inexplicable one.

She mouthed them while lying in the hot water in the darkness. "*Your* lives will be irreversibly destroyed."

Not just my life, but your *lives*.

She knew, unfortunately, just what those words referred to.

71

Jane had figured it out. She was on her way to Georgetown, to eat at her favorite French restaurant just off M Street on Wisconsin. She was going with her brother, Tuck, and two other friends. And the usual Secret Service detail. The advance team had already gone over every inch of the restaurant. Then an overlap squad had been deployed to babysit the space until the First Lady and her guests arrived to make sure no terrorist, nutcase, or local bomber could take up residence in the interim and wait for his target to arrive.

The plan to eat here had been hastily arranged, because the First Lady had decided to go at the last minute. Because of that the Secret Service had had to really scramble to do their job, but they were used to it. Particularly lately, with Jane Cox, who had been all over the map schedule-wise since her niece had been taken.

The meal was served, the wine was drunk, and every so often Jane would snatch a look at her watch. Tuck was oblivious to this. He was too focused on his own problems to notice much else. Jane had chosen the other two guests solely based on their inability to observe anything that was outside the realm of power politics. After the perfunctory discussion regarding what had happened to Tuck's family, they chatted on aimlessly about this senator and that congresswoman, about the state of the election, and the latest polls. Jane just nodded through it all and gave them enough feedback to encourage them to keep going.

And she kept checking her watch.

She had not selected this establishment solely on its excellent menu and wine list. There was another reason.

At five minutes to eleven she signaled her detail chief over at a corner table. He spoke into his wrist radio. A female agent raced to the ladies' room. She checked to make sure it was clear, gave the all-okay signal, then stood in front of the door barring entry by other female patrons no matter how much in distress their bladders or bowels might be.

The First Lady entered the ladies' room at two minutes to eleven and went directly to the back and stared at it.

This was why she had come here. It was the only restaurant that she knew of that still had a working pay phone in the ladies' room.

She had a prepaid phone card. She wanted no credit card record of this call. She dialed the number from memory.

It rang once. Twice. Then someone answered. She braced herself.

"Hello?" the man's voice said.

"It's Jane Cox," she said as clearly as she could.

Sam Quarry sat in his library at Atlee, a fire roaring in the fireplace. He would get the damn poker good and hot tonight. He was using a cloned cell phone that Daryl had bought off a guy he knew that specialized in that line of business, meaning illegal and untraceable.

He swallowed a sip of his favorite local moonshine. In front of him were photos of Tippi and his wife. The scene was all set. It had been years in the planning. Now it was finally here.

"I know it is," he said slowly. "You're right on time."

"What do you want?" she said sharply. "If you've hurt Willa—"

He cut her off. "I know you probably got a zillion people all around wondering where you got to, so let me do the talking and we can get this done."

"All right."

"Your niece is fine. I've got her mother with me too."

Jane said sharply, "Her mother is dead. *You* killed her."

"I meant her *real* mother. You knew her as Diane

Wright. She goes by Diane Wohl now. She got married, moved, and started over. Didn't know if you knew that. Or if you even cared."

Jane stood there in the ladies' room holding the phone feeling like she had been shot directly in the head. She put her hand out against the tiled wall to steady herself.

"I don't know what—"

He cut her off again. "I'm going to tell you what you're going to have to do if you want to see Willa again in any way other than a corpse."

"How do I even know you have her?"

"Just listen up then."

Quarry pulled out a recorder and turned it on, holding it next to the phone. When he'd visited both Willa and Diane he'd had the recorder with him and had secretly taped them.

"Willa first," he said. Willa's voice came across clearly as she was talking to Quarry about why he had kidnapped her.

"Now Diane. I thought you might want to listen in about our conversation of her giving up her daughter."

Diane's voice came on, and then Quarry's recorded words where he explained the results of the DNA tests.

He clicked the device off and picked up the phone. "Satisfied?"

"Why are you doing this?" Jane said dully.

"Justice."

"Justice? Who was harmed by Willa being adopted? We were doing her a favor. The woman didn't want her. I knew someone who did."

"I don't really give a damn about Diane Wohl or making your brother and his wife happy by getting them a little girl to call their own. I needed her and Willa so I could get your attention."

"Why?" she said in a raised voice.

"Mrs. Cox?" It was the female agent from outside. "Are you okay?"

"Just talking to someone," she said quickly. "On the phone," she hastily added.

She turned back to the phone in time to hear Quarry say, "The name Tippi ring any bells, or did you just throw that one right out of your old memory?"

"Tippi?"

"Tippi Quarry. Atlanta," he added in a louder voice, his gaze directly on his daughter's photo.

One second, two seconds, three seconds. "Oh my God!"

"Oh my God is right, lady."

"Listen, please—"

"No, *you* listen. I know everything. I got dates, names, places, the whole ball of wax. Now I'm going to give you an airport to fly to. After you arrive there I've got very precise map coordinate points that'll take you where you've got to go. You just give it to your federal flyboys; they'll know what to make of it. It's mostly numbers so get some paper and write it down. Now. No room for mistakes."

Jane fumbled in her purse for pen and paper.

"All right," she said in a trembling voice.

He gave her the airport location and the additional coordinates.

"You want me to come to this place?"

"Hell no! I want you *both* to come."

"Both? When?"

Quarry looked at his watch. "Nine hours from now. Exactly. Not a minute before or a minute after if you want that little girl still breathing."

Jane glanced at her watch. "That's impossible. He's in town tonight, but he's flying to New York tomorrow morning to give a speech to the United Nations."

"I don't care if he's got an appointment with God. If you ain't there exactly nine hours from now, then the next time you see Willa, she won't be able to see you back. And those DNA tests I had run will be all over the media along with everything else. I got proof of it all. Spent years of my life doing nothing else. You threw us in the shit, lady, and went on with your life. Well, it's payback time now. It's Tippi's time. It's *my* damn time!"

"Please, please if you can just give us—"

"Here are your instructions for when you get there. And you better follow them to the letter,

515

'cause if you don't, or you sic the FBI on this thing, I'll know. I'll know right away. And then Willa dies. And all the truth comes out. And no second term for old Danny boy. Guaranteed!"

Tears were streaming down Jane's face.

And tears were flowing down Quarry's cheeks too, as he gazed at the two most important women in his life; both gone from him now forever. Because of the woman he was talking to right now. Because of her. And him.

"Are you listening?" he said quietly.

"Yes," she gasped.

He gave her the instructions.

She mumbled, "And if we do this, Willa goes free? And you won't . . . you won't tell?"

"I give you my word."

"That's all? How can I trust you? I don't even know who you are."

"You do know me."

"I . . . do?" she said haltingly.

"Hell yes you do. I'm your worst nightmare. And you wanta know why?" Jane didn't answer. He said, "Because you two were my worst nightmare."

"Are you her father?" Jane said in a hollow tone.

"The clock starts now," said Quarry. "So you better get a move on. It's not like you and the man can just hop in a cab. Ain't all that power just something special right now? Move as fast as a dead cow." He clicked off, threw the phone across the room, and sat back exhausted. Then he grabbed the poker, seared the end in the fire, rolled up his sleeve, and burned the last line into his arm. The mark was now complete. The pain was awful. It didn't get easier with each burn, it got worse. And yet he didn't make a sound, didn't grimace, didn't cry. He just stared at the picture of Tippi while he was doing it.

And felt nothing. Just like his little girl felt. Nothing. Because of them.

Then he quickly left the room and the fire behind. There was a lot to do before they came. The adrenalin was really flowing.

Back in Georgetown, Jane dropped the phone and raced out of the ladies' room.

The clock was indeed ticking.

72

Sean and Michelle had packed up the SUV and were saying goodbye to her father and brother.

She hugged them and said, "I'll call soon, Dad. And I'll come and stay with you. We can—"

"Get to know each other again?"

"Yeah."

As they were walking to the door Frank said, "Oh, I almost forgot. A package came for Sean earlier today. I have it in the living room."

He left and came back a minute later with a small cardboard box. When Sean saw who it was from, he exclaimed, "My two-star bud came through again. More AWOL binders."

"AWOL binders?" said Bobby.

"A case we're working," explained Michelle.

They headed out to the SUV. "I'll go through the binders, Sean, while you drive. That'll save time, which we don't have a lot of."

"Thanks, Michelle," he said earnestly. "That's very nice."

"Nice has nothing to do with it. You get carsick

when you read. I don't want you puking in my truck."

Bobby smiled. "Now that's my little sister."

They drove off and headed through town toward the highway. Michelle opened the box and took out the first binder.

"It's a good thing your brother lives here. He can keep your dad company."

"I plan on keeping him company too. If this has shown me anything, you can take nothing for granted. Here today, gone tomorrow."

"I'll stop for some coffee before we hit the interstate," said Sean. "It seems like we always start these trips late at night."

"Make mine a double."

Sean got the coffee and they headed north.

Michelle went through five more binders and then stretched her arms.

"You want me to take over? I can hold the puke in," he said.

"No, I'll keep going. But if we don't find something here, then what?"

"Just pray you do find something in that stack because there is no *then what*."

Sean checked the clock on the dashboard and then pulled out his phone and pecked in a number.

"Who you calling?"

"Chuck Waters. Want to get an update. Maybe he's got a lead he'll share."

"Right. And I'm going to try out for *Dancing with the Stars*."

The FBI agent picked up on the second ring. Sean and he talked for a few minutes and then Sean clicked off.

"Anything new?" asked Michelle.

"Jane got the letter in the post office box, and Waters confiscated it."

"What did it say?"

"Something about a ten-million-dollar ransom. Only Waters thinks she pulled a fast one and fed them a fake letter."

"Why does he think that?"

"Things in this letter didn't match the one that was sent with the bowl and spoon. Different type-writers, for instance. And he said there was something funky about the postmark."

"Why would she pull a switch?"

"She's got a vested interest in this case, Michelle. From what Betack found with the second letter, this thing is personal to Jane Cox. She didn't want anyone else to read this last letter."

"You don't think Willa is her kid, do you? Maybe she was fooling around on the president before he was the president? Got pregnant and handed it off to her brother and his wife?"

"I might think that except about twelve years or so ago I saw Jane Cox and she wasn't pregnant."

"*About* twelve or so years ago?"

"I mean I saw her off and on during that period of time. She couldn't be Willa's mom unless they're lying about the girl's age."

Michelle shook her head and continued reading. A half hour later she yelled out, "Turn the car around!"

Sean nearly ran the truck into a Jersey wall. "What is it?"

"Turn the car around."

"Why?"

"We need to head south."

Sean put on his turn signal and started to edge to the right lane. "Why south?"

She scanned the pages of the binder she was holding, speaking rapidly. "Three AWOLs from the same address in Alabama, but they all had different last names. Kurt Stevens, Carlos Rivera, and Daryl Quarry. They were supposed to report to their base and be shipped out to Iraq, only they never showed up. MPs went to check it out. Place called Atlee, like an old plantation. Father Sam Quarry, Vietnam vet, owns it. MPs couldn't find any trace of them."

"Okay, they're Army deserters and it's one of the states on the isotopic probable list, but that's not conclusive, Michelle."

"They interviewed Sam Quarry, a Ruth Ann Macon, and her son, Gabriel. And a guy named Eugene."

"Again, so what, Michelle?"

"Gotta love the Army's attention to detail. The report says that Eugene identified himself to the MPs as a member of the *Koasati* Indian tribe."

Sean squealed across all lanes, horns blaring at him, and took the next exit. Two minutes later they were on a slingshot path to Alabama.

73

There is probably no more formal, preplanned space for sale in the world than the Oval Office. Who was allowed into the room, from the prime minister of a relatively unimportant country, to a large campaign donor, could take days if not weeks of wrangling behind the scenes. Simply an invitation to the Oval Office for folks not routinely engaged in business with the man must be fought for with equal parts ferocity and delicacy. Once you gained entry to the hallowed space, the treatment you received—a hand-shake, a pat on the back, a signed photo as opposed to merely the picture—was all in the details. And in the negotiations. The Oval Office was not an environment that encouraged spontaneity. The Secret Service in particular frowned on anything approaching unplanned movements.

It was late, but Dan Cox was knocking out a few of these obligatory requests before he left in the morning for his UN address. He had been briefed on who these people were; mostly elite campaign sup-porters who'd opened their checkbooks and, more importantly, induced lots of their rich friends to do the same.

They came in one by one, and the president went into automatic greeting mode. Shake hand, nod, smile, pat back, say a few words, and accept the groveling thanks in return. For some particularly heavy hitters, deftly pointed out by his team of aides who hovered everywhere like the guardian vultures they were, the president would pick up some national treasure off his desk and talk to them about it. A lucky few even received a small memento. And these happy folks left believing that they had registered a personal connection with the man. That some brilliant thing they had said had precipitated the world leader giving them a signed presidential golf ball, or box of presidential cuff links, or pens that had the seal on it, all of which the White House kept by the ton for just such occasions.

This carefully planned process was ripped savagely apart when the door to the Oval Office was flung open, no mean task since it was quite a heavy door.

Dan Cox looked up to see his wife standing there—no, rather, teetering there in her high heels, stylish dress, her coat trailing behind her, her eyes wild and unfocused, her normally perfect hair in disarray. Right next to her were two anxious-looking Secret Service agents. The conflicted looks on their faces were clear. Despite the unofficial policy allowing the First Lady to enter the Oval Office mostly when she wanted to, on this occasion they obviously hadn't known whether to let her in or tackle the woman.

"Jane?" the astonished president said as he dropped a golf ball he was about to hand to a real estate developer from Ohio who had raised a truckload of money for Cox's campaign.

"Dan!" she exclaimed breathlessly. And she was indeed out of breath since she'd run all the way from where the limo had dropped her off and the White House has a pretty large footprint.

"My God, what is it? Are you ill?"

She took a step forward. So did the agents, as they delicately moved in front of her. They might have thought she actually had become ill, or had been doused with some poisonous substance and they were duty-bound not to let it infect the leader of the free world.

"We need to talk. Now!"

"I'm just finishing up here." He glanced at the man who had retrieved the golf ball from the floor. Smiling, Cox said, "Been a long day for everybody." He took back the ball. "Let me just sign that for you . . ." Usually terrific with names, the interrupted president had just had a very human brain fart.

Jay, his "body man," sprang forward to remedy this. "As we discussed, Mr. President, Wally Garrett here has raised more money for your re-election campaign in the Cincinnati area than anyone else, sir."

"Well, Wally, I really appreciate—"

What the president *really appreciated* would never be known because Jane had shot forward, grabbed the golf ball from her husband's hand, and flung it across the room, where it struck a portrait of Thomas Jefferson, one of Dan Cox's personal heroes, leaving old Tom with a gouge where his left eye had been.

The Secret Service agents rushed forward, but Dan held up his hand, stopping them in their tracks. He nodded at his aides and Garrett was rushed from the room without his coveted golf ball. However, no politician who had achieved the position Dan Cox had, ever left anything to happenstance or let a donor go away unhappy. The Ohio man would receive a signed photo of the president, and VIP tickets to an upcoming event, with the understanding that what he'd just seen would never be made public.

Dan Cox reached out to his wife. "Jane, what the hell is—"

"Not here, upstairs. I don't trust this room."

She glared at the agents and aides, turned and rushed from the room as fast as she had entered it. The aides and agents looked from her to the president as soon as the thick door had slammed behind her. No one dared to speak. There was no thought that any of them had about what they had just seen that they would ever voluntarily verbalize in front of their boss.

Cox stood there for a few moments. Any politician who'd reached the level that he had, had truly seen it all. And handled it all. Yet even for the veteran Dan Cox, this was a new situation.

"I guess I better go see what she wants," he finally said. The sea of bodies parted and the president headed out.

Larry Foster, his protection detail chief who had been called while this had been going on, appeared and said, "Mr. President, do you want us to accompany you . . .?" The strain was evident in the veteran agent's face as he struggled to finish his thought in the most judicious way possible. "All the way, sir?"

Meaning beyond the door to their private quarters, which was typically taboo for the security detail to cross, unless asked.

Cox seemed to consider this for a moment before saying, "Uh, no that won't be necessary, Larry." As he walked out, he added over his shoulder, "But stay close. Um, just in case *Jane* needs anything."

"Absolutely, Mr. President. We can be in there in seconds."

Cox headed upstairs to confront his wife. The Secret Service team followed and stood a few feet beyond the portal to their private quarters, listening for anything that would indicate the president was in jeopardy in any way. No doubt each of them was wondering the same thing. They were duty-bound to protect the president from all danger. They had been trained to sacrifice their own lives so that single life could continue.

Yet what they had not been exactly prepared for was a situation that might be materializing a few feet away right now. What if the danger the president was in was coming from *his wife*?

Could they use deadly force if necessary? Could they even kill her to save him? That was not really spelled out in the Secret Service manual, but each agent was thinking the answer to that was probably "yes."

This had happened once before if presidential lore was to be believed. Warren G. Harding had been president and he and his mistress had been found out by Mrs. Harding. They had taken refuge in a closet in the White House and the angry First Lady had attempted to chop down the door, allegedly with a fireman's ax. The Secret Service had to delicately relieve her of the weapon and Harding had survived. However, he had succumbed later in a San Francisco hotel room under mysterious circumstances while still president. Some thought the missus had finally gotten her revenge through a poisoned dish served to her husband. That had never been proved because Mrs. Harding had not allowed an autopsy, and had ordered her husband's body quickly embalmed. It was a fine example of a cheated-on wife's sheer will topping the desires of an entire nation.

Fire axes were no longer kept in the White House. And while there was a small kitchen in the private quarters, the First Lady never really did any of the cooking anymore. Or if she did, it was far from certain that any president who knew how Harding had died would actually eat it.

Larry Foster racked his brain, trying to remember if there were any letter openers in the personal quarters that could be used as a weapon. A heavy lamp that could crack a presidential skull? A poker from the fireplace that could end that supreme life on his watch? Foster thought he could feel the ulcer actually forming in his belly as he stood in the hall contemplating the end of his career. Though it was far from warm inside the White House, sweat stains appeared under Foster's armpits and trickles of the stuff rose on his forehead. He and his team inched closer as their collective heart rates spiked.

Each of the agents could envision the next day's headlines in six–inch-high letters:

SECRET SERVICE KILLS FIRST LADY TO SAVE PRESIDENT.

There were half a dozen heavily armed agents poised in the hallway to take action if necessary. And all six of their asses clenched with nearly this very same thought at nearly the very same time.

Twenty anxious minutes later Larry Foster's phone rang. It was the man.

"Yes sir?" he said quickly.

He listened intently, his features finally dissolving into confusion. But he was the president so Foster only had one thing to say.

"Right away, sir."

He clicked off and looked at his second in command. "Bruce, call Andrews and get a bird ready."

"You mean AF-One?"

"Any plane the president rides on is Air Force One."

"But I mean—"

"I know what you meant," snapped Foster. "No, we're not taking the 747. See if one of the support planes is available. The 757 maybe, no insignias."

"Wolfman is taking an unmarked 757 to New York?" Bruce said, looking astonished.

Foster said grimly, "We're heading somewhere, but I don't think it's New York."

"But we haven't sent an advance team anywhere else."

"We're going stealth, like we do to Iraq and Afghanistan."

"But we still advance-team it. It takes a week of logistics minimum for the man to make a trip."

"Tell me something I don't know, Bruce. Thing is, we don't have a week. We've got a few hours and I don't even know where the hell we're going. So call Andrews and get me a ride. And I'm going to get on the horn to the director and see how the hell I'm supposed to handle this. Because let me tell you, I've seen a lot over the years, but this is new territory for me."

74

Quarry checked the machinery and oxygen levels that were keeping Tippi alive. It was all working fine off the fully charged generator. It was still dark outside; the sun would not be up for hours yet.

As he touched his daughter's face, he thought about his phone call with Jane Cox. He had never talked to a First Lady before; folks like him never had that opportunity. He had read about her for years, of course, followed her husband's career. He had expected more from her on the phone, educated, refined, but battle-tested person that she was. But she had disappointed him. She'd sounded human on the phone. Meaning scared. So safe in her high tower all this time; never saw the shit going on down below. Well, she had seen it now. And she would see it even closer soon enough.

He took a long breath. This was really it. At any point up to this Quarry could have called it off. And he almost had until the walls in the basement had brought him back. He pulled *Pride and Prejudice* from his pocket. By the light of his daddy's old flashlight he read the last chapter of the novel. And this really would be the last chapter he would ever read to her.

He closed the book and laid it gently on her chest. Quarry took one of her hands and squeezed. He had done this for years, always hoping that she would squeeze back, but she never had. He had long since given up the thought that he ever would feel Tippi's fingers curl around his own; they didn't this time either. He put her hand back down, slid it under the covers.

He slipped the small tape recorder out of his pocket, set it on the bed and turned it on. For the next several minutes he and his daughter listened to Cameron Quarry saying her last words on earth. As always, Quarry spoke the last line along with his dead wife.

"I love you, Tippi, darling. Momma loves you with all my heart. I can't wait to hold you again, baby girl. When we're both healthy and fine in the arms of Jesus."

He switched the recorder off and pocketed it.

The memories washed over him, coming in long, undulating waves. It could've turned out so differently. It should've turned out so differently.

"Your momma will be real happy to see you, Tippi. I wish I could be there too."

He leaned down and kissed his daughter for the final time. He left the door open, and then turned and looked back in the room. Even in the dark he could make out Tippi's form under the illumination of the machines that had been the only thing keeping her from the grave all these years.

They had tried to get the Quarrys to pull the plug many times.

Persistent vegetative state. No brain activity. Brain dead in fact, they had told the couple, throwing in big medical jargon that Quarry felt certain was meant to both intimidate and confuse. After listening to them wax eloquent over the ultimate fate of his daughter, Quarry had asked each of them one simple question. "If she was your child would you let her die?"

The blank faces and still tongues he had gotten were all the answer he needed.

A part of him was unwilling to leave his child now, but he really had no choice. He stepped off the porch and looked toward the treeline. In the little bunker that Quarry had dug out and reinforced with wood sat Carlos, remote in hand, with one cable line hooked into a port on the device, and the other end embedded in the wall of the little house. The bunker was covered with dirt and grass, and underneath all that was lead sheathing that would block X-rays and other electronic imaging. Knowing that the Feds would be bringing specialized equipment, Quarry had fashioned the lead covering from old X-ray blankets he'd gotten from a dentist's office.

No one looking at it from even a few feet away

would be able to determine that a man was in there watching, and the lead covers would block most anything the Feds would have with them. The other cable line Quarry had run down the tree and then underground and into the bunker where it was hooked into the small TV monitor that Carlos was now no doubt staring at right now. It gave him the live feed from the camera in the tree. Carlos was supposed to stay in the bunker for as long as he needed for things to clear out. The bunker was ventilated and he had plenty of food and water. The plan was for him to escape to Mexico and from there to keep heading south. Quarry hoped he made it.

Quarry stood in a spot where he knew Carlos could see him on the TV. He gave a thumbs-up and then a salute. And then he left and drove home.

Quarry had written a letter that he left in the room in the basement. It wasn't addressed to Ruth Ann or Gabriel, but it was about them. He wanted the people who would be coming to know the truth. This was his doing and nobody else's. He also left his will.

He crept upstairs and looked in on Ruth Ann, who was sleeping soundly. He next went to Gabriel's room and watched the little boy sleeping peacefully. Then he pulled a silver dollar from his pocket and placed it on the table next to the bed.

Under his breath he said, "You go to college, Gabriel. You get on with your life and you forget you ever knew me. But if you do think of me from time to time, I hope you'll remember I wasn't all bad. Just dealt a hand in life I didn't know what to do with. But did the best I could."

He walked through the house to his library. The fire was out now, doused with a bucket of water. He flexed his arm where the burns were, where the completed mark was. He clicked the light on, stared at the walls of books for a bit, and then turned off the light and closed the door for the final time.

A half hour later he parked his truck next to his Cessna. Twenty minutes later he was lifting off from the ground. As he soared over the land he looked down to where the little house was. He didn't wave, didn't nod, didn't indicate he knew it was there at all. Now he had to be focused. What was past was past. He had only to look ahead now.

Daryl had illuminated the runway for him using lit torches spread ten feet apart. He landed with a hard jolt because of the winds, taxied down, turned around, got out, and chocked the wheels.

If things went according to plan he and Daryl would fly out of here and land in Texas. It all shouldn't take more than a few hours. From there they had set up a way to sneak across the border into Mexico. It was easier to go south across the border than it was to go north over it. Once there Quarry would use a stolen cell phone to call the FBI and give them the exact location of the mine so that

Willa and Wohl could be rescued. They would be perfectly fine there until then, with plenty of food and water.

It was a good plan, but only if it worked.

He grabbed his knapsack and trudged toward the mine entrance.

Well, he would have his answer in a very few hours.

75

When Sean and Michelle pulled into the packed dirt road leading to Atlee the sun was very near to starting its ascent up the eastern seaboard.

"Creepy," said Michelle as they drove down the lonely, winding road. "You left a message for Waters?"

"Yeah, but no telling when he might get back to us. And this might be a wild-goose chase anyway."

"My gut's telling me otherwise."

"Mine too," he admitted.

"How do you want to play this out?"

"Get the lay of the land. See what we can accomplish. Pray for a miracle, find Willa."

Michelle pointed up ahead. "That looks like it might be Atlee." The place had appeared as they rounded a curve. Big southern longleaf pines lined both sides of the drive heading to the old antebellum mansion. It made the darkness even more opaque.

"I don't see any cars out front," said Michelle, as she slipped her pistol out.

"Lots of places around here to park I would imagine."

The ringing phone startled them both.

It was Aaron Betack. Sean listened for a couple of minutes and then clicked off and looked at his partner.

"The shit has hit the fan at the White House. Apparently Jane Cox came back from dinner and stormed into the Oval Office. She and the president went up to their private quarters, had a discussion, and the next thing you know the First Couple are taking a flight, in an unmarked jet, to an undisclosed location."

"What the hell is going on?"

"Someone made contact with her while she was out at dinner, obviously."

"But why an unmarked jet?"

"They apparently don't want anyone to know about this. Certainly not the public."

"The Service must be freaking out because they've had no chance to advance-team this."

"Exactly. They're cobbling stuff together as best they can, but when you don't know where you're going?"

"You didn't tell him what we found out."

"He has his hands full, and this may pan out to be nothing. But if we find anything that connects to the president, we'll let him know ASAP."

"Cut the lights and the engine!" Michelle hissed.

The SUV went dark and quiet. "What's up?"

"Someone just came out of the house." She pointed up ahead. "Let's do the rest on foot."

They slipped out of the truck and crept toward the dark house.

Michelle held up a hand. She'd obviously seen something that he hadn't. Her night vision was beyond human, he'd found.

"Where?" Sean whispered in Michelle's ear.

"There, on the front porch."

He stared in that direction and saw some small shape apparently sitting on the steps. Michelle hissed in his ear. "I think that might be Gabriel, the little boy the MPs interviewed. He was nearly nine then, the report said. That would put him at ten or eleven now."

As they waited to see if anyone else joined Gabriel, the darkness around them started to lift with increased speed. From somewhere a rooster crowed.

"Haven't heard that in a while," confessed Sean.

"We need to do something," she said. "We're losing our cover and he might spot the SUV."

"You, left, I'll go right."

They split up. A minute later their creep up to the house ended with them on either side of the shape that the coming light indeed showed to be a little boy.

A little boy who was crying. He was crying so hard, in fact, that he never even noticed Michelle step up beside him. When she touched his shoulder, though, he nearly jumped off the porch. Sean was on the other side of him, and managed to snag his arm before he had a chance to run for it.

"Who are you?" sputtered Gabriel, looking at them both with wild, tearstained eyes.

"Are you Gabriel?" asked Michelle, putting a hand on the boy's other arm.

"How do you know my name?" he said fearfully.

"We're not going to hurt you," Sean said. "We're just here looking for someone. A little girl named Willa?"

"Are you the police?"

"Why would you think we're the police?" asked Michelle, her grip tightening slightly on Gabriel's thin arm.

Gabriel snuffled and then hunched over, studying his bare feet. "I don't know."

"Do you know where Willa is?"

"I don't know anybody named Willa."

"That wasn't what we asked you," said Sean. "We asked you if you knew where she was."

"No, I don't, okay? I don't."

"But you know about her?" said Michelle.

Gabriel looked up at her, his lids droopy, his features miserable. "I didn't do anything wrong. Neither did my ma."

"No one said you did. Where is your mother?" asked Michelle.

"Sleeping."

"Anybody else in the house?"

"I think Mr. Sam's gone."

"Sam Quarry?" said Sean.

"You know him?"

"I've heard about him. Why do you think he's gone?"

"Truck's not here," the boy answered simply.

"Why were you crying when we came up?"

"Just . . . just because, that's all."

"There must be a reason," Michelle said gently.

"You always have a reason why you cry?" Gabriel said defiantly.

"Yes."

"Well, I don't. Just cry sometimes."

"So Sam's gone, your mother's sleeping. Anybody else inside?"

Gabriel started to say something but then stopped.

Sean said, "It's really important that we know who's here."

"So are you the police or what?"

Michelle snaked out her PI creds and showed them to him. "We're working with the FBI and the Secret Service on Willa Dutton's kidnapping. You got a Koasati Indian around here who goes by the name Eugene?"

"No, but there is one. His name's Fred."

"Is he in the house?"

"No, he lives in an old trailer on the property, just over that way," he said, pointing to the west.

"So who else is inside?"

"Tippi was, but she's not there now."

"Who's Tippi?"

"Mr. Sam's daughter. He brought her home from the nursing home not too long ago."

"What's wrong with her?"

"She got sick a long time ago. Hooked her up to machines to breathe and all. Was in the nursing home for years. Mr. Sam and me would go and read to her. Jane Austen. *Pride and Prejudice*. You read it?"

Michelle said, "Why'd he bring her home?"

"Don't know. He just did."

"But now she's not here?"

"She's not in her bedroom. I checked."

"Was that why you were crying? Because you thought something had happened to her?"

Gabriel looked up at Michelle. "Ma'am, Mr. Sam is a good man. He took me and my ma in when we didn't have nowhere else to go. He helps people, lots of people. He wouldn't do nothing to Miss Tippi. He's done everything for her."

"But you were still crying. There must be a reason why."

"Why should I tell you?"

"Because we want to help," she said.

"That's what you say, but I don't know if that's what you really mean."

"You're a smart young man," said Sean.

"Mr. Sam said don't trust nobody till they give you a good reason why you should."

"What you doing here?" snapped a voice.

They turned to see Ruth Ann standing there in her old bathrobe. They didn't focus on the robe, though. Their attention was occupied by the single-barrel shotgun she was pointing at them.

76

They had settled on a Boeing 757 that the secretary of state used to fly before she'd been upgraded to a wide-body 767–300. The plane had been kept at Andrews Air Force Base along with the rest of the presidential fleet. All government markings had been previously removed and it was now primarily used to shuttle agents, aides, and the press, as well as necessary equipment.

The secretary of state had a private office and bedroom on the plane and that configuration had not changed. It was in the office where the president and Mrs. Cox were sitting when they went wheels up from Andrews a few hours after Jane Cox had burst into the Oval Office and planted a golf ball in Thomas Jefferson's left eye socket. The rest of the plane housed a hastily assembled skeleton crew of Secret Service agents who were more bewildered than anything else by what was happening.

The president sat looking at his wife, who was hunched in her seat staring at the floor. When they reached their cruising altitude, the president undid his seat belt and looked around the quarters.

"Nice office. Not as big as mine on AF-One, but nice."

"I'm sorry, Dan. I'm sorry you didn't get to ride in your usual big toy." Her arms were folded across her chest and she was looking at him with alternating expressions of fear and hopelessness.

"Is that what you think all this is? Toys?"

"I actually don't know what I think right now. No, actually I do. I think we've finally reached rock bottom."

He took off his shoes, rubbed his feet, and paced around the cabin.

"I don't even really remember it."

"I'm sure you don't. But I do."

"I've changed."

"Okay."

"I have, Jane. And you damn well know it."

"Okay, you've changed. That does not help the present situation."

He sighed and sat down next to her, massaging her shoulders. "I know it doesn't. I know this has been hell for you."

She slowly looked at him. "He took Willa because of this."

"So you told me. No, so you *screamed* at me."

"You said you couldn't compromise the office of the president in order to get her back."

"That's right, Jane. I can't. Even if this mess weren't my responsibility I couldn't."

"Our responsibility."

"Jane—"

She took his hand in hers. "Ours," she said softly.

"I don't know why you ever stayed with me, really."

"I love you. Sometimes I don't know why, but I do. I attached my star to yours, Dan. We shot to the sky together."

"And we may fall back to earth just as fast."

"We may."

"This election is mine to lose. Haven't had one of those in this country in a while." She said nothing. He glanced at her. "Do you think he'll keep his word? If we do what he asked?"

"I don't know. I don't know the man. All I know is that he sounded like someone who had it all figured out. Not just us, but what he wants."

"The Secret Service is very upset at all this."

Jane looked like she wanted to laugh. "I'm very upset too. And regardless of how this turns out, they'll still have a job. I can't say the same about *you*."

"About *us*," he reminded her.

"You know, a little self-control, that's all it would've taken."

"It was like a disease. You know it was. In all honesty I have to say I'm stunned actually that nothing has ever come up before now."

"Stunned? Really? When I was behind you all the time picking up the pieces? And you're stunned?"

"I didn't mean it that way."

"What other way could you possibly have meant it?"

"Now is not the time to be divided, Jane. We have to stand together on this. If we're going to survive."

"I guess we'll have all of our golden years in which to fight."

"If that's what you want," he said coldly.

"What I want is not to be on this plane going to where we're going."

"How did he sound on the phone?"

"Determined. Full of anger and hatred. Can you blame him?"

"You think he was being straight? I mean, it seems like such a small thing to do in return for, you know . . ."

"Would you rather he killed Willa?" she said darkly.

"That wasn't my point! Don't put words in my mouth."

A knock at the door interrupted this bickering.

It was Larry Foster, the protection detail chief. "Sir, the flight crew has our ETA into Huntsville in about one hour and thirty minutes. It's fortunate that they just opened a new runway that'll support an aircraft in this class."

"Fine, right."

"And then we are to go on to another location."

"You were given the coordinates."

"Yes sir. We have them."

"Well, is there a problem?"

"Sir, can I speak frankly?"

Cox glanced at his wife and then turned back to Foster. "Go ahead," he said tersely.

"This whole thing is a problem. We have no idea where we're going, or what we'll be confronted with. I'm understaffed on this and don't have even one-quarter of our regular support and equipment. My strong recommendation is that we turn around and head back to D.C."

"That's impossible."

"Sir, I'm very strongly recommending that we don't go through with this."

"I'm the president. I just wanted to go for an unscheduled trip. It's not that big of a deal."

Foster cleared his throat. His clenched hands evidenced the anger that he was feeling but trying hard not to show. "The other issue is we don't have a motorcade, sir. And the destination in question is about eighty miles southeast of the airport in Huntsville."

"We have to get there"—Cox checked his watch—"in exactly four hours and seven minutes."

"I had a C-130 fly ahead of us with two choppers on it. It'll take a little bit of time to get the choppers out and be ready to go."

"You have the timetable. And we cannot miss that deadline."

"Sir, if you could just fill me in on what's going on? I know the director has spoken with you and he supports my position, but—"

Cox pointed a finger at him. "The *director* serves at my pleasure. I can replace him tomorrow. And I will if I get any more flack from him. I want you to just do what you're told. I am the commander in chief. If you won't do it, then I'll get the damn Army to take over. *They* won't question my authority."

Foster stood very straight. "Mr. President, by federal law we provide your principal protection." He glanced at Jane. "*Both* your protection. What is going on right now is completely unprecedented and potentially very dangerous. We've had no opportunity to check out where we're going. No recon, no threat assessment, no—"

"Look, Larry," Cox said in a calmer tone. "I know this is all screwed up. I don't want to be doing this either." He motioned in the direction of his wife. "She doesn't want to be here either. But here we are."

"Does this have to do with your niece?" Larry was asking this of Jane Cox. "If so, I think at the very least the FBI should be informed of what we're doing."

"We can't do that."

"But—"

Cox put a hand on the man's shoulder. "I trust you to protect us, Larry. You'll have time to check things out, as much time as I can give you. I'm not foolhardy. I'm not going to walk into something that will get me killed, much less my wife. It'll be okay."

Foster said slowly, "All right, sir, but if things look out of whack, I'm pulling the plug. I can exercise that authority, sir. I have it by federal statute."

"Let's just hope it doesn't come to that."

After Foster left Jane said, "What if *Larry* won't let you do what you need to do?"

"That's not going to happen, Jane."

"Why not?"

"I'm still the president. And besides, I've led a charmed life. And my luck has not run out. Not yet."

Jane looked away. "Don't be too sure," she said.

He glared at her. "Whose side are you on, anyway?"

"I've been thinking about that all night now. And I haven't reached a decision yet."

She left the cabin.

The president sat behind the desk and prayed that he could hold on just one more time.

77

Are you Ruth Ann?" asked Michelle, her eyes now on the woman and not the weapon.

"How you know my name?"

"Momma, they're with the government. They're here about Mr. Sam."

"You be quiet 'bout Mr. Sam, boy."

"Ruth Ann," said Sean, "we don't want anyone to get hurt, but we think this Mr. Sam has kidnapped a little girl named Willa Dutton."

"No he ain't!" Her finger tightened on the trigger.

"Momma, I saw the name down in the room. And her picture. We saw it on the TV."

"Hush up, Gabriel. I ain't telling you again."

"A little girl's life is at stake," said Michelle. "A little girl not much older than Gabriel."

"Mr. Sam ain't hurting nobody. He ain't like that."

"Miss Tippi's gone, Momma," said Gabriel.

Ruth Ann's jaw went slack. "What!"

"She's not in her room. Mr. Sam took her."

"Took her where?"

"Don't know."

"Ruth Ann, if you let us just look through the house, and we find nothing wrong, we'll leave," said Sean. "All we want to do is find Willa and take her back to her family."

"That the little girl what her momma got killed?" said Ruth Ann, her grip on the shotgun loosening a bit.

"That's the one."

"What Mr. Sam got to do with that? You tell me!"

"He may have nothing to do with it. And if he doesn't, then nothing happens to him. It's that simple. And if you don't believe he's involved then you shouldn't have a problem with us looking around," said Michelle.

"Please, Momma, let 'em."

"Why you so all fired on them doing this, Gabriel?"

"'Cause it's the right thing to do. Mr. Sam, he'd say the same thing if he were here."

Ruth Ann stared at her son for a long moment, then lowered the shotgun and stepped back.

Sean and Michelle hurried into the foyer of Atlee and stared around.

"Like stepping back into the past," muttered Sean.

Michelle had her attention on the woman who trailed them. "Ruth Ann, I'd like you to put that gun down and step away from it. Now." Michelle had her hand on the butt of her pistol.

"Do it, Momma!" Gabriel had tears in his eyes.

Ruth Ann did as she was told and Michelle snagged the gun and emptied out the ammo.

"Gabriel," said Sean. "What's this room you're talking about?"

They trooped down the stairs to the massive door.

"I don't have the keys. Mr. Sam has 'em."

"Step back," said Michelle firmly. They did and she took aim and placed two shots on either side of the lock. Then she holstered her gun, leapt across the space of the hall and leveled a crushing kick right where the lock connected with the doorjamb. It crashed open as Gabriel stared wide-eyed at the woman. Then he glanced over at Sean, who shrugged and smiled.

"She's always been kind of a show-off," he said.

They rushed into the room and Gabriel punched the light switch. When Sean and Michelle saw what was on the walls, their mouths gaped. Photos, index cards, written notes on chalkboards, pushpins, string connecting this part and that part.

Sean said, "Gabriel and Ruth Ann, do you know what any of this means?"

"No sir," said Ruth Ann.

"Who would have done all this?" he asked.

"Mr. Sam," said Gabriel. He added, "I came down here one night when he wasn't around. That's when I saw the picture of that girl, right there."

He pointed to a section of wall. A moment later Sean and Michelle were staring at a photo of Willa.

When Sean's gaze swung around the walls he froze on one spot. "Ruth Ann, Gabriel, you need to wait outside."

"What?" said Gabriel. "Why?"

"Outside, right now!"

He hustled them through the doorway and then closed it, returning to stare at the picture of the woman.

"Sean, what is it?"

"You remember me telling you how I met Jane Cox?"

"Yeah, you brought her drunken senator husband home after you found him in a car with some tramp."

Sean pointed at the picture. "That's the tramp."

It was a picture of a younger Diane Wohl.

Michelle eyeballed the photo. "*She* was with Cox?"

Sean nodded. "The name next to the photo says Diane Wohl, but that's not the name she used back then. I mean her first name I think was Diane, but I don't remember Wohl."

"She might have changed it, or gotten married." She gazed at another spot where a string from Wohl's name intersected with another index card.

"Diane *Wright*? That ring any bells?" she read off the card.

"That's it. That was her name!"

He pointed to a recent newspaper article pinned next to the photo. It reported the disappearance and presumed kidnapping of Diane Wohl from Georgia.

"He's got Diane Wright too," said Sean. He pointed to the walls. "This all tells a story, Michelle. Quarry has put all this together."

She pointed to the far left side of the room. "And I think it starts there."

At the very beginning of this wall there was written a calendar date from nearly fourteen years ago.

Michelle read the four words written next to the date. "He raped me, Daddy."

Beside it was the name Tippi Quarry and next to that was a photo of Tippi in her hospital bed hooked up to life support. She turned to look at Sean. Her expression of panic was matched by his.

"Sean, I'm starting to get sick to my stomach."

"Just keep going, Michelle. We have to keep going."

They started following the story around the walls in the basement at Atlee.

When they had finished one entire wall Michelle said quietly, "He raped her. Then they got her to have a back-alley abortion. The First Lady was involved."

"She nearly bled out and ended up in a coma," added Sean in a hollow voice.

"But if Cox raped her why didn't she report it to the police?" asked Sean.

"Maybe someone convinced her not to. Like Jane Cox. She's good at controlling people."

"But how does Willa tie into this?"

They went to the wall where Willa's picture was. It was unnerving to see the missing little girl smiling at them in this room with its tale of misery spelled out so sharply in chalk and index cards.

As they followed this line of Quarry's investigative work, Michelle said, "How long ago did that incident with Cox happen, Sean?"

He calculated in his head. "About thirteen years ago."

She said, "Willa just turned twelve. Plus nine months for the pregnancy. Sean, Willa's the president's daughter. You happened on them *after* they'd had sex, not before. And the lady got pregnant."

"I guess this time around they decided adoption by Jane's brother beat a back-alley abortion and another coma."

"But you're sure he didn't force himself on Diane Wright?"

"It appeared to be consensual."

"If Dan Cox sexually assaulted Tippi Quarry and then she fell into a coma after a botched abortion, Sam Quarry is exacting his revenge."

Sean looked puzzled. "By kidnapping Willa? And killing her mother? How does that make sense?"

"By giving him leverage."

"Leverage with what?"

"I don't know," she admitted. "But it may have something to do with where the president and his wife are heading right now." Michelle stared at the walls. "How do you think he figured it all out? This would've taken years."

"He must've really loved his daughter. He never gave up."

"But he's also a killer. And he has Willa. And we've got to get her back."

"Do you still have your camera in the SUV?"

Michelle rushed outside and was back in a couple of minutes with her Nikon. She took shots of all the walls, zooming in on all the writing and photos. Meanwhile, Sean searched through the cabinets and took out armfuls of files that he intended to take with him. Then he saw the letter that Quarry had left on the table along with his last will. He picked them up and read through them before putting the papers away in his pocket.

He and Michelle were breaking just about every crime scene preservation rule there was. But this wasn't your average crime scene and he had decided to adopt some new rules. He wasn't sure how this was all going to play out, but he felt fairly certain how he wanted it to conclude.

"All done," said Michelle as she finished snapping the last shots.

Sean handed her some of the files to carry out. "Michelle, why would he bring Tippi home from the nursing home and then take her somewhere else?"

"I don't know. It doesn't make sense."

Sean went farther into the room while Michelle was talking. He turned a corner, peered around an old partition, and cried out, "What the hell is that?"

She joined him as he rushed over to some metal cylinders stacked in the back of the room. He set down the files he was carrying and turned several cylinders over. Some contained oxygen, some didn't.

"What is it?" Michelle asked.

Instead of answering, Sean ran back to the door and threw it open. He brought Gabriel and Ruth Ann in and over to the cylinders.

They both looked blankly at them and shook their heads when he asked if he knew why Quarry had these. Then Sean eyed the other equipment lying around on a workbench next to the cylinders. The remains of a gutted video camera, some old remotes, cable wire, and rolls of metal sheathing.

"What is all that for?" he asked.

Gabriel shook his head. "Don't know, but I do know that Mr. Sam can build anything he wants. Fix anything mechanical. Electronics. Real good carpenter."

"He just got a head for that," agreed Ruth Ann. "Ain't nuthin' the man can't fix or build."

"Any idea where he might have gone? You said a truck was missing?"

"Yeah, but he's got a plane too," said Gabriel.

"What kind of plane?" Michelle said quickly.

"Little single-engine Cessna."

"Why would he need a plane?"

"He a pilot in Vietnam," answered Ruth Ann. "And he go up to the old mine sometimes. Fly to get there."

"What old mine?"

Gabriel explained about the coal mine. He finished by saying, "It was an old Confederate prison one time, Mr. Sam told me."

"A prison," Sean said, looking at Michelle anxiously. "You think he might have gone up there?"

"If the plane is gone, that's where he went. Only place he goes in it."

"You think he took Tippi up there?"

"Don't think so. All the equipment and what-not she needs, don't think it would fit on the plane. It's pretty small."

"So where do you think she is?"

Gabriel thought about this. "Mr. Sam built a little one-room house a ways from here on land his family owned. Nothing there, really. No electricity or anything so I don't think Miss Tippi would be there. 'Cause she would need the electricity for the machines."

"Why'd he build a place like that, then?" asked Michelle.

Gabriel shrugged. "Don't know. He built it himself. Took him a long time."

Sean looked nervously at Michelle before turning to Gabriel. "Do you think you can show us how to get to the mine?"

"I know it if I go with you."

"Gabriel!" exclaimed his mother.

"I don't know the directions to tell 'em, Momma. But if I go I know the way."

She looked anxiously at Sean. "He's been real good to us, Mr. Sam has. If he done anything bad it be for a good reason, you can count on that."

"He left us his house and property," volunteered Gabriel.

"And he give Fred a thousand dollars cash. Fred told me," added Ruth Ann.

"You think he believed he wouldn't be around much longer?" said Sean.

"Who knows how long they be around?" countered Ruth Ann. "Drop dead tomorrow, any of us. Lord's will."

"Who else is up there at the mine, you think?" asked Sean.

Gabriel answered, "Maybe Daryl, his son. Maybe Carlos."

"How about a guy named Kurt Stevens?"

"Mr. Sam said Kurt left town, headed on," said Gabriel.

"They keep any guns up at the mine?" asked Michelle.

"Mr. Sam likes his guns. Daryl too. Shoot the wings off a bee, both of 'em."

"Wonderful," said Sean. "Gabriel, can you drive with us to where he keeps his plane? And if it's not there will you go with us to the mine?"

Gabriel looked at his mother as she put a protective hand on his shoulder. "Momma, I think I have to do this."

"Why, boy? Why? This ain't your concern."

"Mr. Sam isn't a bad man. You said that yourself. I've known him most all my life. If I can go up there and help him make things okay, then that's what I want to do. That's what I want to do."

A tear trickled down Ruth Ann's face.

"We'll take good care of him, Ruth Ann," said Sean. "We'll bring him back to you. I promise."

Ruth Ann turned her red eyes on Sean. "You better damn sure bring him back to me, mister. 'Cause that boy's all I got."

78

The two choppers lifted off the ground and flew southeast. In one were the president and his wife with a company of Secret Service agents and as much equipment as they could cobble together at the last minute. The second bird carried still more agents, the two best bomb-sniffing dogs the Feds had, more equipment, and Chuck Waters, who'd been tipped off to what was happening by Larry Foster and, unknown to the First Couple, had come along for the ride. Next to him was Aaron Betack, who had joined the party too, also unknown to the First Lady. The skies were growing lighter by the minute, the low-level winds were calm, and the rising sun was rapidly burning off the morning chill.

Betack's phone rang.

"Yeah?"

"Aaron, it's Sean King. We need to talk."

"I'm sort of busy."

"I'm in Alabama."

"What? We are too."

"We as in who?"

Betack looked at Waters and then said into the phone, "Like I told you before, Wolfman and Lynx are on the move," he said, referring to Dan and Jane Cox's Secret Service code names. "What are you doing in Alabama?"

"If I had to guess, I'd say pretty much on the same trail you are. Where exactly are you headed?"

"We don't know, Sean. I told you that before."

"I know, but I thought that status would've changed by now. You're with the president and you don't know where you're going?"

"Everything's screwed up. We're flying blind here, stomping on every rule and protocol in the Secret Service manual. Larry Foster is the detail chief and he's about to have a coronary. But after that confrontation in the Oval Office the next thing we know we're in Alabama taking a chopper to a set of map coordinates."

"Aaron, that's nuts. You could be walking right into a trap."

"Tell me something I don't know. You think the Service is happy about this? But he's the president, man."

"You're telling me the director of the Secret Service is letting this happen? Or the president's senior advisors? How about the vice president?"

"You know it's all a balancing act. He's the commander in chief and we're his serfs. But we've worked our butts off behind the scenes, called in support from the FBI and the military, and we think we have a decent protection bubble set up even given the crummy circumstances."

Waters looked over and motioned for Betack to give him the phone.

"King? This is Chuck Waters."

"Hey, Chuck, I left you a message."

"What the hell are you doing?"

"If I told you, Chuck, you wouldn't believe me. Aaron filled me in on what's going on there. You guys could be heading into an ambush."

"Yeah, but what the president doesn't know is that we've got two choppers full of HRT riding ahead of us. By the time we land, and before the president steps one foot off his bird, they'll have scoped the area and set up a perimeter that not even an ant could get through. Then if we still don't like what we see, we're out of here, president or not."

"But what if they shoot you out of the sky?"

"We got that covered too. Each of the choppers is equipped with the latest air-to-air and ground-to-air countermeasures. Plus we got military birds all over the place riding shotgun over us. And a battalion of Apache gunships is moving outward grid-by-grid from the ground zero coordinates we were given, looking for any threat. And, man, you see an Apache heading your way you either surrender, shit your pants, or both."

"Okay, but we found something that you need

to know about. Maybe an Achilles' heel." Sean explained about the metal cylinders.

"Where'd you find them?"

"I'll explain later. I hope you got something to counter it."

"I'll see what I can do. Where are you now?"

"Headed to an abandoned mine with a little boy named Gabriel."

"Gabriel? And why a mine?"

"Because I think there might be a little girl there."

"Willa?"

"Hoping and praying, Chuck. Let's keep in touch. And good luck."

79

Sam Quarry stared down so intently at the improvised SAT phone in his hand it was like he was cradling a poisonous snake. It wasn't nearly time for Carlos to be calling him but a part of him wanted the call to have already come. He wanted this over.

He checked with Daryl to make sure everything was ready and then headed to Willa's room. When he entered, she and Diane were huddled around the table. He'd decided that on this day, this last day, the two women should be together. They looked up when he walked in and closed the door behind him.

He leaned against a wall and lit up a cigarette.

"What's going on?" Willa said in a trembling voice. She had never been the same since she'd discovered it was possible something had happened to her family.

"It's just about over," said Quarry. "At least I'm hoping it is."

"Hoping?" said Diane, her face weary and her voice equally tired.

"Yeah, hoping," said Quarry. "And praying."

"And what if your hopes don't turn out?" asked Willa.

"Yeah, tell us. *Mr. Sam*," said Diane coldly. "What then?"

He ignored her and looked at Willa. "I brought my daughter home. The sick one."

"Why'd you do that?"

He shrugged. "It was time. Said my goodbyes and all. It's all good."

"Your goodbyes?" asked Willa in a fearful voice.

"See, whichever way this turns out, things are over for me. All done. Ain't gonna see anybody anymore."

"Are you going to kill yourself?" said Diane, with a hopeful edge to her voice.

Quarry's lips eased into a smile. "Can't kill a man who's already dead."

Diane merely looked away, but Willa said, "Who'll take care of your daughter if you can't?"

Diane looked back over with a curious expression. It was obvious that she had not even considered this issue.

Quarry shrugged. "It'll be okay for her."

"But—"

He moved to the door. "You two just sit tight."

He left.

Diane drew close. "It's not going to be okay, Willa."

Willa just stared at the door.

"Willa, do you hear me?"

Apparently Willa didn't hear her. She just kept staring at the door.

The plane hadn't been there so Michelle was driving hard. Gabriel was next to her feeding directions and Sean was in the backseat looking at the sky and checking for a chopper carrying a president and a First Lady who had much to answer for.

"Turn there, left," said Gabriel.

Michelle cut a hard left that flung Sean across the backseat.

"If we die before we get there, it will really be counterproductive," he said sharply as he struggled to sit back up and slipped on his safety harness.

"How much further, Gabriel?" said Michelle.

"Another hour," he said. "Mr. Sam can make it there a lot faster in the plane. I've never been on a plane before, have you?"

Michelle was studying the road ahead. Every time they came to a straightway she would floor it, but as they moved up into hilly ground the straight roads were rapidly disappearing. "Yeah, I've been on a plane." She jerked her head in Sean's direction. "He's been on Air Force One with the president."

Gabriel turned to stare in awe at Sean. "You met the president?"

Sean nodded. "But remember, he puts his pants

on the same way you and I do. Only when he has his on he can push a button and blow up the world."

Michelle turned around and gave him a "what the hell?" look before saying, "If you want to go on a plane ride one day, Gabriel, we can arrange it."

"That'd be cool. You go right at the next road."

"What road?" said Sean as another jarring bump nearly unseated him. "You mean this obstacle course we've been on for the last ten miles?"

As she made the turn and the road grew steeper, Michelle engaged her four-wheel drive and they bumped along.

"Tell us about the mine, Gabriel," said Michelle.

"Like what?"

"One entrance in or more?"

"Just the one I know about. Got a grassy runway Mr. Sam put in. I came up here in the truck with him sometimes and we'd mow the grass flat."

"Keep going," Michelle said encouragingly. "The more we know the better we'll be prepared."

He explained about the shafts and the rooms Quarry had built inside.

"Why did he do all that?" asked Sean

"He said if the world was coming to an end that we'd all go up there and stay. He has food, water, lanterns, stuff like that."

"And guns," said Michelle.

"And guns," agreed Gabriel. "Probably lots of them."

Sean pulled out his own nine millimeter along with two extra mags he always carried.

Two pistols, a few extra mags, a little boy, two potential hostages, and going into a dark mine where the other side was armed to the teeth, knew every crevice, and you didn't. He caught Michelle's gaze in the rearview mirror.

She was obviously thinking the same thing he was because she mouthed, "I know."

Sean's eyes went to the side window. The terrain here was growing ever steeper. Even as the warming sun came up, it seemed dark and cold. He thought back to the room at Atlee. To a story on a wall that had probably taken Sam Quarry years to construct. Then he thought back to that night in Georgia, walking down that street, seeing the young lady on top of the future president, falling out of the car with her panties dangling around her ankles. The man had a beautiful, intelligent wife at home waiting for him. He'd just been elected to the U.S. Senate. And he was getting balled by some twenty-year-old chick in a car?

And then his mind turned to another woman. Tippi Quarry.

He raped me, Daddy.

A bloody abortion.

A coma for all these years.

Persistent vegetative state, Quarry had written on the wall, underlining each word three times.

571

Sean had no children. But if he had and something like that had happened to his daughter, what would he do? How far would he go? What sort of a story on a wall would he construct? How many people could he kill?

He slid the gun back in his belt holster.

They would find Sam Quarry up at the mine. He was sure of that. They would find Willa and this Diane woman too. Whether alive or not he was uncertain.

But as to the question of what he and Michelle should do about it all?

He really didn't know.

80

An hour before the two choppers carrying the president and his security detail landed, a pair of large helicopters with two dozen Hostage Rescue Team members and lots of equipment hit the dirt about a hundred yards from Quarry's little house. The men rolled off and then fanned out, guns ready. Equipment was hauled off the chopper and then deployed. They did a recon of the immediate area but came up with zero.

In the lead-lined bunker, Carlos, who had heard the chopper come in, hunkered down below the grade line, but his gaze never left the TV monitor set up in front of him. He did make the sign of the cross and mumble a short prayer.

Half the HRT squad set up a temporary perimeter while the other half pulled some more equipment from the second chopper.

Principal among these were two mobile robots, weighing about a hundred pounds apiece. They set them on the ground, fired them up, and one HRT member, using what looked like a very sophisticated joystick, sent the first robot into action. It rolled around and around the perimeter of the house, growing closer to it with each pass and finally entering the house and making a sweep inside. If there were any mines, IEDs, or other explosives here, the robot's onboard infrared sensors would detect them before detonation occurred. Then the HRT explosives specialists could dispose of them safely.

No explosives were detected, so they sent out the second robot. This was even more cutting-edge than the first. The HRT squad had named this machine the Gamma Hound. Its role was to detect radiological, biological, or chemical substances over whatever ground it passed. The HRT squad member used a practiced hand at the joystick to send Gamma Hound on its rounds, even rolling it up on the porch and into the house. Gamma Hound never once "barked." The place was clean.

Only then did the HRT squad approach the house and then go inside. What they found in there stunned even the most veteran members of the group.

The leader got on his two-way and reported, "We got a nonresponsive Caucasian female between thirty and forty in a hospital bed hooked up to what appears to be an elaborate life support system juiced by a battery generator. We've checked the place for weapons and other threats and found none. Other than her the place is clean."

The squad leader waiting outside listened to this

report and then exclaimed, "What in the hell did you just say?"

His man repeated it. The HRT leader in turn radioed this information back to the president's chopper.

One of his men looked at him and said, "What do we do now?"

"We go over that house with a fine-toothed comb. And we lock this whole area. I don't want one living thing, other than the coma lady in there, within a thousand yards of this place."

"Who is she?"

"I have no idea, and I don't need to know. All I know is the president is coming and nothing is going to harm him on my watch. Now move out!"

Another careful search was made of the area. HRT men tramped on and around the bunker where Carlos sat huddled. They didn't find the camera in the tree because Quarry, ever the detail man, had cut a hole in the oak, placed the camera inside, and patched up the hole with bark glued on so that only the camera lens was showing. And as high up as it was, and covered from the ground by dense foliage, except for the sightline Quarry had cut in it, it might as well have been invisible.

Some of the HRT went back inside the house and used a crowbar to pry up one of Quarry's fine floorboards. Underneath was a standard sheet of one-inch plywood. An HRT member pounded on it with

his fist. "Solid as a rock. Must be the cement foundation underneath."

"Make sure," said the squad leader.

A drill was brought in and they drilled through
the plywood until the drill bit hit something hard
and would go no farther.

"Solid."

"Okay, good enough."

They put the floorboard back. And then did the
same probe with each of the four walls. Solid again.

The area secured, no threats found, and the perimeter established, the HRT squad patiently waited
for the president of the United States to land. Once
he got here they had no idea what he intended to
do. All they knew was if a threat did show up, they
would destroy it with enough firepower to take out
an Army battalion.

They'd parked the SUV and gotten out. They had
no choice because the road had ended at a wall of
fallen boulders.

"That wasn't here before," said Gabriel. "Used to
be able to drive up to the door."

"That probably wasn't going to be an option for
us anyway," said Sean.

With Gabriel leading, they headed toward the
mine. They had to scramble over more rock and

slippery dirt. Sean tumbled down one section before righting himself.

"Showing my age," he said with an embarrassed look.

"Hey, when's the last time you took a weapons refresher course?" asked Michelle.

"If we run into something that needs to be hit, I'll hit it. I'm just counting on you to hit it *first*."

"Gee, I'll try to keep that in mind."

They kept moving forward.

Gabriel said, "I don't have a key to the door to the mine."

"That won't be a problem," said Michelle. "Just get us to it."

A few minutes later they cleared the rock and could see the grass runway.

"Is that his plane?" Sean asked, pointing at the little Cessna.

"That's it."

He suddenly pointed to the right. "And that's Mr. Sam," he whispered.

They all looked in that direction.

Sam Quarry had come out of the mine carrying what looked to be a small black box. From their hiding spot Michelle took aim with her pistol, but from this distance there was no guarantee of a killing round with the sidearm. She glanced at Sean and shook her head.

"He's older than I would have thought," whispered Sean as he studied the tall, white-haired man.

"Strong as a bull," said Gabriel. "I seen him knock a man down even bigger than him and half his age 'cause the fella cursed at my momma. He fights real good."

"I hope I don't have to find out *how* good," said Sean dryly.

"But we came up here to make sure everybody's okay. That girl and Mr. Sam, right?"

Sean and Michelle exchanged another glance.

"Right. But look, Gabriel, that's up to him. If he starts something, then we have to respond, okay?"

"I'll talk to him. It'll be okay. He won't hurt anybody. I know Mr. Sam."

Michelle eyed Sean. Neither of them looked nearly as confident as Gabriel about how this would turn out.

81

The two choppers landed softly.

The president looked out the window and his face flushed. "What the hell is going on here? Who are they?" He was pointing to the HRT squad.

Before anyone could answer, Chuck Waters tapped on the glass. One agent opened the chopper door and put down the staircase.

"Who are they?" the president demanded again.

Waters said, "HRT, sir. They came ahead to secure the area."

"That was not authorized by me."

"No sir, it was okayed by the director of the FBI."

Cox didn't look happy about this, but the FBI director was the one man who did *not* serve at his pleasure but rather was appointed to a fixed term and remained there regardless of whether there was a change in the White House.

As they watched, the two bomb-sniffing dogs from the other chopper were led by their handlers toward the building. Even though the robot had already made a sweep of the area, when the president's safety was at issue, redundancy was standard procedure. The dogs patrolled the perimeter and then went inside. A few minutes later they came out, with one of the handlers signaling the all-clear.

Back at the chopper Waters continued, "He was advised of the situation by the Secret Service director and concluded that this was the best course of action if you insisted on coming here, sir."

"How very thoughtful. Let's hope that my niece isn't dead because of his little *conclusion*."

"So that *is* why we're here?" asked Larry Foster. "Because the kidnappers made some demand?"

Everyone looked over at Jane Cox.

Waters said, "We know the letter that I took from you, Mrs. Cox, was not the real thing. Did the actual letter tell you to come here?"

"No, it gave a phone number to call. I did. On that call I was told to come here with the president, if I wanted to get my niece back alive."

"Did the caller tell you what you had to do once you got here?"

"Go inside a house and see a woman in a bed," she said.

"Well, the HRT found a lady in a bed in that building. She's hooked up to life support systems. Who is she?"

"I don't know," Jane said firmly. "I'm just here to get my niece back."

Waters said skeptically, "You don't know her? You're sure?"

"How am I supposed to know? I haven't even seen who she is!" snapped Jane.

Foster looked confused. "All right, but what exactly are you supposed to do in there? From what the HRT said, the woman is unconscious."

Jane and the president looked at each other. She said, "All I can tell you is that I was told that the president and I were to go inside the house and see the woman. That was it."

The president said, "And we were to go in alone. At least that's what Jane was told," he added hastily.

Waters and Foster exchanged a worried look. Foster said, "Mr. President, I don't like this at all. The only reason for someone to bring you here is to do you harm. Nothing else makes sense. That building might as well have an X painted on the roof. We need to take this chopper back to Huntsville and go home. Right now."

"And then my niece dies!" exclaimed the president. "You really just expect me to fly away and let that happen?"

"Sir, I understand what you must be going through. But you don't have a choice. And neither do I. You are the president of the United States. Your safety cannot be compromised. As far as my duty is concerned no life takes precedence over yours. Not your niece." He glanced at Jane. "Not even your wife's. That's the law. That is my job, and I intend to carry that mission out."

"I don't give a damn about the law. Or your mission, Foster. We're talking about a little girl's life. I will not go back."

"Sir, please don't make me do this the hard way. I told you I had the authority to force you to go back and I am prepared to exercise that authority right now."

"Didn't your people check this place out? Haven't those HRT fellows checked everything out? What danger is there? Is the woman in there going to jump up and kill me?"

"She's on a neck-trach ventilator," answered Foster.

"Then she's no threat to me. You brought the bomb dogs. They found nothing. There's an army of heavily armed men out there. You told me we have aircraft and choppers all over the sky. Only a tank, plane, or mobile or fixed missile launcher could hit that house from long-distance, and I really don't think there are any of those in the great state of Alabama that don't belong to us. We're all alone out here. What could hurt me? What?"

"Sir, if I knew where the danger was, it would cease to be dangerous. It's the unknown that I'm concerned about."

"Unknown!" snapped the president. "Let me tell

you about the *known*, then, Larry. If I turn around and fly back home and let my niece die when I could have saved her and the word gets out, I will lose this election, pure and simple. Do you understand that, my friend?"

Foster, Waters, and the other agents in the chopper all exchanged glances, obviously not quite believing what they had just heard.

"Okay," Foster began slowly. "You'll lose the election."

"That didn't come out in quite the way the president intended," Jane said quickly after noting the men's stunned looks even if her husband hadn't. "The president is very upset about all this, as am I. He is terribly worried about our niece, as am I. But he has worked long and hard for this country. We do not intend to allow some criminal psychopath or terrorist cell to either harm our niece or change the history of this country by denying my husband a second term. My niece's life is of course paramount, but there is a lot at stake here. A lot, gentlemen. Let's not kid ourselves."

"I'm sorry, Mrs. Cox," said Foster, shaking his head. "Even with all that I'm not going to let either of you go in that building." He spoke into his headset to the pilot. "Jim, let's prepare to go back—"

Foster did not finish what he was going to say because at that moment Dan Cox grabbed the pistol off the agent sitting next to him, smacked off the safety, and leveled the gun's muzzle against his own temple.

"Jesus Christ, sir," cried out Foster.

Waters exclaimed, "Mr. President, don't—"

"Shut up, just both of you shut the hell up!" roared Cox. "Now, anyone attempts to stop us, Larry, you can escort my *body* back to D.C. and explain to everyone there how you tried to protect me by driving me *insane* enough to blow my own brains out!"

He motioned to Jane. "Get out, Jane." He looked back at Foster. "I'm going in that building with my wife. We will be in there for no longer than a few minutes. And there will be no electronic surveillance or listening devices on that structure. The kidnapper was very clear on that. When we're done then we will leave, get on this chopper, and fly back. Then my niece will hopefully be released and every single one of you will forget that any of this happened. Am I *clear*!"

The men didn't speak; they just continued to stare at their president with a pistol against his head.

The silence was finally broken by Waters. "Sir, if you insist on doing this, you have to do one thing."

"I am giving the orders here, *not* the FBI!"

Waters glanced at Jane. "It was something that Sean King told us, ma'am. Something he found out. You trust him, right?"

She slowly nodded.

"Then you have to do exactly what I'm about to tell you. Will you both do that?"

"If it means we can go in that building over there and get this done, yes!" said the president.

A few minutes later Jane, her long coat drawn around her, and the president climbed out of the chopper. When the HRT squad saw the president with a gun in hand they did something they ordinarily would never do. They froze.

"Mr. President?" said the squad leader with a quizzical look.

"Get out of my way!" yelled Cox. The squad leader, a veteran of two wars and countless gun battles with homicidal drug dealers and assorted nutcases wielding big guns with no regard for human life, nearly jumped a foot off the ground. With his path clear to the house, Cox took his wife's hand and they walked on. Reaching the small porch, they looked at each other once, and then stepped inside.

82

The First Couple stood looking down at Tippi Quarry as the machine inflated her lungs, the oxygen seeped into her nose, and the monitor recorded the jumps of her heart and the status of her other vitals.

"Over thirteen years she's been like this," said Jane. "I had no idea."

The president studied her. "I don't remember her, honey, I swear I don't. She has a pretty face, though."

When he said this she moved slightly away from him. He didn't seem to notice. "Tippi Quarry?" he said inquiringly.

"Yes."

"In Atlanta?"

"That's right. At the PR firm that helped handle your early Senate campaign launch. She was a volunteer there, fresh out of college."

"How do you know all that?"

"I took the trouble to find out. I took the trouble to find out about all the ladies you seemed so interested in back then."

"I know I put you through hell." He looked back at Tippi. "I don't remember having any contact with her at all."

"That's no doubt why no one ever put the two of you together. But you *did* have contact with her. Something that even surprised me. I found you two together in our hotel room. She was screaming for you to get off her, but it was too late. You'd already finished. It took me hours to calm her down while you were lying in a corner passed out from too much gin and not enough tonic."

"Why didn't the police come, then? Are you sure it wasn't consensual?"

"She didn't phone the police because I finally convinced her what a mess it would be if the incident became public. That it was only her word against yours, she was in *our* hotel room, and that I couldn't testify against my own husband. You were on your way to the Senate and possibly the presidency. She was a young woman with her whole future ahead of her. A future that could be ruined if something like this came out. If people thought she had instigated the sex. Tried to take advantage of your position. Tried to trap you somehow. I was very persuasive. I even told her that it was a disease you had. I painted a very sympathetic picture."

"Thank you, Jane. You saved me. Again."

She said coldly, "I hated you back then. I hated you for what you did to her. And to me."

587

"Like you said, it was a sickness. I've changed. I worked through it. You know that. It never happened again, did it?"

"It happened one more time."

"But I didn't force myself on that woman. And after that, there was no more. I worked hard at it, Jane. I cleaned up my act."

"Your act? Dan, this wasn't a case of leaving your underwear on the floor. You forced yourself on that poor woman."

"But I never did it again. That's my point. I changed. I moved on."

"Well, she sure as hell didn't have the chance to move on."

The president suddenly thought of something. He looked wildly around the small room. "You don't suppose there are any recording devices in here, do you?"

"I think the man has all he needs. Even without this poor woman."

"What do you mean?"

"I mean Willa."

"What about her?"

"She's your daughter. And he knows it."

The president, his face pale, slowly turned to look at his wife. "Willa is my daughter?"

"Don't be stupid, Dan. What, did you think that Diane Wright was just going to go away when she got pregnant?"

Cox put an arm against the wall to steady himself. "Why the hell didn't you tell me this before?"

"What would you have done if I had?"

"I . . . well—I—"

"Right. Nothing, as usual. So I came in and cleaned up yet another mess."

"Why didn't she just have an abortion?"

"And end up like her?" said Jane, motioning to Tippi. "And it's not quite as easy as you think, Danny. I contacted her. Told her that it would be okay. That I understood what had happened and didn't hold it against her."

"How did it happen?"

"Apparently you picked her up, I believe in a bar. You must have been extremely charming to convince her to have sex that quickly. Or perhaps it speaks to the class of woman you were attracted to."

He put a hand to his forehead. "I don't remember any of it. I swear."

"So you don't remember Sean King bringing you home?"

"King? Sean King? He knows?"

"He found you in the car with her. And he's never said a word about it to anyone."

"So that's why you befriended him?"

"That was one reason, yes."

He looked sharply at her. "Were there other reasons?"

"Don't you even dare ask me that."

"I'm sorry, Jane. I'm sorry."

"Wright called me back about a month later. She'd missed her period. Then she'd found out for sure that she was pregnant. She was certain you were the father. She hadn't had sex with anyone else. In fact, you were her first, she said. I believed her. She didn't want any money or anything. She was just scared, didn't know what to do. Much like Tippi Quarry. Tuck and Pam were living in Italy at the time. She had gotten pregnant, but had miscarried. She didn't tell anyone other than me and Tuck. And the fact was that the baby was yours, even if you had it by a woman other than your wife. I couldn't just let it go to a stranger, because I knew Wright wasn't going to keep it. It was still your blood. I made an arrangement with Wright, and eight months later she traveled to Italy. I met her there. When the baby was delivered I took it to Pam and Tuck. When Pam came home later everyone just assumed the little girl was hers."

"You kept all that from me?"

"Considering what you've tried to keep from me over the years, I'd say I have a lot of ground to make up."

"But why all this for—"

"For a baby you got by screwing another woman? Like I said, she's your blood. She's *your* child, Dan. One of us had to take responsibility for it. And that one was me. It's always been me!"

"You never told them? Tuck and Pam? That Willa was mine?"

"How could I? Go up to him and say 'Oh, by the way, dear brother, this is Dan's bastard child. Would you like her?' And Diane Wright never met Pam or Tuck. She just assumed I'd lined up someone to take the baby. I never wanted her to know Willa's new identity for obvious reasons. But Sean King found out that Pam only gave birth to two children. That's why I had to keep the kidnapper's letters from everyone and try to cover things up."

"I don't understand."

"If they found out Willa was adopted, people might start digging, Dan. Like your political enemies. They could locate Diane Wright, maybe figure it out. Tie you to having sex with her and me arranging her baby, *your* baby, to go to my brother. There is no spin you can put on all that. Your career would've been over."

"I see. I am very fond of Willa," said the president. "I always have been. Maybe I sensed a connection with her."

"She's smart and good and sweet. And I would do anything to get her back safely."

The president looked at Tippi. "But we had nothing to do with *her* ending up like this."

Jane wiped her eyes with a tissue. "I did. She called me in a panic when she found out she was pregnant. She couldn't tell her parents, she said. They wouldn't understand. She also didn't want to carry it to term. I couldn't blame her since you forced yourself on her. Abortion was the only option. I couldn't have her go to a hospital or a real physician. Something might have come out. Her parents might have been contacted. It had to be done quickly and quietly. I knew of someone who could do it. I even drove her there and dropped her off. I paid for the procedure and gave her money for a cab home. The idiot obviously botched it. I . . . I never knew that this had happened, though. I never followed up. I guess I never wanted to follow up. I just wanted to forget all about it."

"A tragedy all around," the president said numbly, still looking down at Tippi.

"We should do this," Jane said. "And then get out of here. And get Willa back."

"Honey, if Waters is right about what he told us in the chopper, then we won't be getting Willa back."

"What do you mean?"

"He wants to kill us. This Quarry fellow. He may try to do so when we leave here."

"How can he? We're surrounded by an army. We're always surrounded by an army."

"I don't know, but if that was his intent all along? He'll certainly try."

"So what are you saying?"

"That we need to focus on us surviving this. If there is an assassination attempt and it fails he'll know about it. He'll kill Willa, if she's not already dead. But then he'll also try to reveal what happened. We have to be prepared for that. We have to concoct an alternative. Whatever proofs he might think he has, I know my people can counter them. He's just one man. I have an army of spin masters."

"He may be only one man, but look what he's done so far."

"That doesn't matter. It only matters how it ends. Now let's do what Quarry asked us to do and get out of here."

They stood in front of the bed and held hands.

Jane spoke first. "I'm sorry, Tippi. I never intended for this to happen. I'm truly sorry."

The president cleared his throat. "I hope you will forgive me for what I did to you. I . . . it's not enough to say that I don't remember, or that I wasn't myself. It was my responsibility. And I'll have to live with that for the rest of my life. I'm sorry too, Tippi. Deeply, deeply sorry."

Jane lightly touched Tippi's hand. The president started to do the same thing, but then apparently thought better of it and withdrew his fingers.

They turned to the doorway.

The HRT squad was a few feet away, Foster, Waters, and the Secret Service team right behind them, all poised to act on a second's notice.

★

In the bunker Carlos clearly saw the couple on the monitor.

He punched the single button on the remote. This caused two things to happen simultaneously.

The left side of the doorjamb was blown out as a nearly two-inch-thick metal door hidden in the cavity of the wall there sprang forth, powered by a hydraulic propulsion system concealed in the wall behind the lead sheathing. This action sealed the First Couple in the room.

Then, inside the room, there was a hissing sound. Around the perimeter of the interior were holes carefully precut into a metal lining underneath the subfloor. This was what the HRT drill had hit, not the cement, but a *second* subfloor hidden away in a cavity of the foundation. Inside this cavity were a series of connected metal cylinders containing nitrogen gas. They had been hooked to the splitter cable Quarry had run up through the PVC pipe in the foundation, and then triggered by the remote. The gas rose up through the holes in the metal and then passed through the narrow gaps in the floorboards. The tanks were under great pressure and deployed their contents with force. Soon the small space was filled with nitrogen gas.

Nitrogen occurs naturally, but it also depletes oxygen and in certain circumstances can be lethal. Humans exposed to unsafe levels of the gas don't feel any pain. They lapse into unconsciousness quickly and without really realizing what is happening. They are never aware that in a very few minutes they will suffocate as the oxygen is displaced. For this reason countries that were rethinking bringing back the death penalty were looking at deploying nitrogen in a gas chamber because it worked so quickly and painlessly.

They would do well to have studied Sam Quarry's model, since the man from Alabama had built the perfect execution chamber disguised as a shack.

Tippi's life support system included an oxygen converter and oxygen tank that together fed a mixture of pure and room-mixed oxygen into the ventilator trach tube and from there into her lungs. The mixture was very carefully calibrated, only now there was no oxygen left in the room. And the amount of pure oxygen coming from the tank wasn't nearly enough to make up the difference. In her terribly weakened condition, she expired almost immediately. The monitor screeched this result as she flatlined. Her hell on earth was finally over.

Outside, the frantic HRT squad and the Secret Service team were deploying every tool they had to get the door open short of opening fire or detonating a bomb, either of which could kill the people inside. They attacked the metal door and the walls, only to find welded metal under the boards. Men in suits next to men in fatigues clambered onto the roof with axes and chain saws but their efforts were blunted by heavy shingles and sheets of metal screwed down into thick wood. The little house was nearly impenetrable.

Yet they never gave up on their assault. Eight minutes later, using power saws, sledgehammers, a hydraulic battering ram, and pure sweat and muscle, they managed to knock down the metal door. Five men rushed in and then immediately rushed back out gagging from the lack of oxygen. Other agents donned oxygen masks and ran inside.

When they came out a few seconds later, Carlos, watching on the monitor, cursed. The president and the First Lady were pulling off their oxygen masks with attached small cylinder tanks that Jane had carried under her coat. They had been given to them by Agent Waters acting on the tip from King after he'd discovered the extra nitrogen gas cylinders in Quarry's basement and deduced what they might be used for.

Foster and his men ran to the First Couple and escorted them so rapidly back to the chopper that neither the man nor the woman's feet seemed to touch the ground.

"Are you all right, Mr. President?" asked Foster anxiously after they were safely inside the chopper. "We'll need to get you and the First Lady checked out medically."

"I'm fine. We're fine." He eyed Chuck Waters.

"Good call. We put the masks on as soon as the gas started coming in."

"That was Sean King's doing, sir, not mine. But even then, I didn't think the gas would be in that house. We thought it was all clear."

"Well, I'll have to thank Mr. King." He glanced at his wife. "Again."

A pale Foster added, "If I suspected for a second that the place was booby-trapped like that, sir, I never would have let you go in."

Cox slipped the gun from his waistband and handed it back to Foster. "Well, I really didn't give you a choice, did I? Whoever put that thing together was extremely clever. From the sophistication of the plot, it seems that a well-funded terrorist organization was behind this. And my stupid antics really put you between a rock and a hard place, Larry. I'm sorry."

Foster's face reddened. It was rare for a president to apologize to anyone, much less a Secret Service agent.

"Apology accepted, Mr. President." The two men shook hands.

As the door to the chopper slammed shut, the president said, "We need to get back to D.C. pronto."

"I couldn't agree more, Mr. President," said a relieved Foster.

"And your niece?" said Waters.

"After what just happened, there seems little hope of her still being alive. If their goal was to kill me, they obviously never intended to release her."

Jane Cox let out a sob and covered her face. The president put a supportive arm around her. "But we must continue to do everything we can." He looked around the interior of the chopper. "We must not give up hope. But we must also prepare for the worst. Those bastards tried to kill me and my wife today, but they failed. America will never give in to evil like this. Never. They can keep trying to get to me, but I will never let them win. Not on my watch."

Every agent on the chopper looked at Dan Cox with immense pride, forgetting that a few minutes ago he'd been a raging madman with a gun pressed to his temple, more worried about being re-elected than getting his niece back. He had bravely walked into what turned out to be a trap in order to save his niece. And now, having barely escaped death, he was being supportive of his wife and rallying the troops. That was some serious street cred that U.S. presidents typically never earned.

Before they lifted off it was decided that, under the circumstances, the Coxes should not travel on the same chopper together. Jane was shuttled off to the second chopper with six agents and a couple of

HRT members, while the bulk of the firepower and Agent Chuck Waters stayed with the president. Two agents remained behind to deal with the local police and Tippi Quarry's body.

83

Quarry threw down the SAT phone and with a scream of rage he raced back inside the mine.

Watching from their cover position Sean said, "He doesn't look very happy."

"I think he just found out the man isn't dead."

"What are you two talking about?" asked an attentive Gabriel. "What man?"

"Gabriel, how well do you know the interior of the mine?"

Michelle broke in. "Sean, no!"

"Michelle, we can't go in there blind."

"He's just a kid."

"There may be another kid in there too."

Gabriel spoke up. "I'll go. I know the place real well. I want to go in there. I can talk to Mr. Sam."

Sean said, "He wants to go."

Michelle looked at Sean and then at Gabriel's pleading face.

"Michelle, we don't have much time. You saw Quarry tear in there."

They scrambled over some more rocks and

sprinted to the mine entrance. The door was not a problem because Quarry had not bothered to shut it.

They raced inside, guns and flashlights out.

Within a few moments they disappeared into the darkness.

"Daryl!" screamed Quarry. "Daryl!"

His son appeared from out of the darkness. "What is it?"

Quarry could barely speak. He could barely think.

He clamped a big hand on his son's shoulder. "Carlos called. It didn't work. They got out."

"Shit! We're screwed!"

"Oxygen masks," Quarry muttered.

Daryl looked angrily at his father. "What we gonna do now, old man?"

Quarry turned and raced down the passageway. Daryl lumbered after him. Quarry unlocked the door to Willa's room and threw it open.

One glimpse of his enraged face and Diane Wohl started stumbling backward. "No, please. Don't. Please!" she was shrieking.

Willa looked confused. "What's going on?"

"Don't kill us!" screamed Diane.

Willa jumped up and started to back away. Quarry and Daryl moved forward.

Quarry was breathing hard. "They're alive. They're alive! Dammit!"

"Who's alive?" cried out Willa.

Quarry knocked the table aside, threw the chairs across the room. Willa raced to Diane, who was back as far as she could go in the corner.

They both screamed as Quarry grabbed them and started pulling them toward the door. "Come on!" He yelled, "Daryl!"

Daryl grabbed Willa and lifted her off the floor.

"Please, Mr. Sam, please." Willa was crying so hard she could barely speak.

Diane had let herself go limp and Quarry ended up dragging the woman across the floor. When they got out to the passageway, he stopped and listened.

Diane was still screaming and he said, "Shut up, woman. Now!" She didn't.

He slipped a pistol from his belt and placed it against her temple.

"Now," he said very firmly.

Diane fell silent.

Willa was in Daryl's arms. When Quarry looked up he found her staring at him. And his gun.

"Did you hear that, Daryl?" said Quarry.

"Hear what?"

"That."

It was the sound of footsteps pinging off the mine walls.

"It's the police," Quarry said. "They're here. Probably a whole damn army."

Daryl looked stonily at his father. "So what you wanta do now?"

"I wanta fight. Take as many of them with us as we can."

"Then I'll go get us something to fight with."

Daryl handed Willa off to Quarry. Right before his son hustled off down a side shaft, Quarry grabbed his arm and said, "Bring the switch."

Daryl smiled maliciously. "We gonna take 'em down, Daddy."

"Just bring it. But give it to me."

"You still giving the orders, huh? We ain't never getting out of here alive. Gonna be like old Kurt. Nothing but bones."

"What is he talking about?" cried Willa.

"Just go!" Quarry snapped at his son.

"I'll go, all right. And then I'll be back. But my way, old man. Just this one time. This one *last* time. *My* way."

"Daryl—"

But his son had already vanished into the dark.

More footsteps headed their way.

"Who's there?" roared Quarry. "I got hostages!"

"Mr. Sam," cried out a voice.

"Gabriel!" said a stunned Quarry.

Michelle had not been quick enough to stop Gabriel from yelling out to Quarry. Now she put a hand over his mouth and shook her head.

"Gabriel!" yelled Quarry. "What you doing up here?" Silence. "Who's you with?"

Quarry knew there was no way the boy could have gotten up here on his own. They had him. They had escaped the little house. Tippi was dead. And they had Gabriel. And now they thought they had Sam Quarry. Well, they had thought wrong. His rage swelled. All those years. All that work. For nothing.

"Who is it?" Willa said in a quavering voice, her arms around Quarry's thick neck.

"Hush up now."

"It's that boy you talked about. Gabriel."

"Yeah, it is. But somebody's with him."

Quarry nudged Diane with his foot. "Get up, quick."

Diane rose to her feet and with Quarry gripping her arm they fast-walked down the passageway and turned a corner.

"Please let us go," wailed Diane. "Please."

"Shut up, woman or I swear . . ."

Willa said, "Don't hurt her, she's just scared."

"We're all scared. They never shoulda brought Gabriel up here."

"Mr. Quarry!"

They all froze at the sound of this new voice.

"Mr. Quarry. My name is Sean King. I'm here with my partner, Michelle Maxwell. Can you hear me?"

Quarry remained quiet and stuck his gun into Diane's side to make her do the same.

"Can you hear me? We were hired to find Willa Dutton. That's all. We're not the police. We're private investigators. If you have Willa, please just let her go and we'll leave."

Quarry still said nothing.

"Mr. Quarry?"

"I hear you," he called out. "And you'll just walk away if I give her to you? Why do I think there's an army of police waiting right outside?"

"There's no one outside."

"Yeah, you got no reason to lie to me, do you?" Quarry pulled Diane farther down the passage.

"We just want Willa, that's all."

"We all want a lot of things, but we don't always get what we want."

Sean's next words froze the older man.

"We've been to your house. We saw the room. Gabriel showed us. We know what happened with your daughter. We know all about it. And if you let Willa go we'll do everything we can to help the truth come out."

"Why you wanta do that?" he cried out.

"It was wrong what happened, Mr. Quarry. We know that and we want to help you. But we need Willa safe first."

"Ain't no help left for me. Ain't nothing left for

me. You know what I tried to do. It didn't work. They'll be coming for me now."

"We can still help."

Sean had reduced the volume of his voice so that Quarry would not know that they were on the move, that they were growing closer.

"You don't want to hurt a little girl," Sean said. "I know you don't. If you had, you would've already done it."

Quarry thought quickly. "Where's Gabriel? I want to talk to him."

Michelle nodded at the little boy.

"Mr. Sam, it's me."

"What you doing up here?"

"Coming to help you. Don't want to see you get hurt, Mr. Sam."

"I appreciate that, Gabriel. But them folks with you, listen up, Gabriel and his ma had nothing to do with this. It's all me."

"We found the letter you left," said Sean. "We know. They're not in trouble."

Gabriel said, "Mr. Sam. I don't want anybody to get hurt. You or that girl. Would you let her go and then me and you can get on back home? Maybe we can go in the plane, like you promised."

Quarry slowly shook his head. "Yeah, that'd be real good, son. But I don't really see that happening."

"Why not?"

"Rules, Gabriel, rules. Thing is, they don't apply

to everybody. Some folks break all the rules and . . ." His voice trailed off.

Sean said, "Mr. Quarry, will you please let Willa go? And Diane Wohl too? You have her too, right? You don't want to hurt them. I know you don't. You're not that sort of a man."

They were close now. Sean and Michelle could feel it. They motioned to Gabriel to get behind them.

"Mr. Quarry!"

Quarry felt Willa clinch his neck tightly. As he looked at her, he suddenly thought he saw another little girl there whom he'd loved with everything he had and that he'd left to perish in a house of his own making. The fellow was right. Quarry was not that sort of man. At least he didn't want to be.

"All right. All right. I'll let 'em go."

He set Willa down and knelt in front of her so they were eye to eye. "Look here, Willa, I'm sorry for all that I done. If I could take it back, I would, but I can't. See, I lost me my little girl 'cause of what some folks did. And it just ate at me, made me something I never wanted to be. Can you understand that?"

She slowly nodded. "I guess so," she said in a tiny voice. "Yes."

"When you love someone you got to be prepared to hate too. And sometimes the hate just wins out. But you listen to me, Willa. You might have a real good reason to hate somebody, but you still got to let that hate go. 'Cause if you don't it'll just tear you apart your whole life. And even worse than that, it won't leave no room for any love to get back in."

Before she could say anything he spun her around to face away from him. He called out, "She's coming toward you. Just her. Walk, Willa. Just walk toward their voices."

"This way, Willa," called out Michelle.

Willa looked back once at Quarry.

"Just go, Willa. Go on. No looking back." He knew when she found out about her mother that the grief would change her entire life. She would hate Quarry and she should. He just hoped the little girl had listened to his words and wouldn't let that hate ruin her life. Like it had his.

She hurried down the passageway.

Quarry called out, "How'd you find me out? Was it the writing on the woman's arms? The Koasati stuff?"

Sean hesitated before answering. "Yes."

Quarry shook his head. "Shit," he said quietly.

"Now Diane Wohl," called out Sean when Willa reached them safely.

Quarry glanced over at the woman and nodded. "Go on."

"You won't shoot me in the back?" she said, her voice quivering.

"I don't shoot people in the back. But I might shoot 'em in the front if they give me reason to." He pushed her forward. "Go!"

She raced down the mineshaft, but turned back to yell, "You bastard!"

But it was drowned out by another scream coming their way. It was like the cry of Johnny Reb during the Civil War right before they attacked.

"Look out!" yelled Michelle a second later.

"Daryl!" cried out Quarry, who'd recognized the source of the first scream. "No, boy! NO! Gabriel's here."

Daryl was hurtling down a shaft with an MP5 in one hand firing away.

"Get down!" said Michelle. She pushed Willa behind her and fired back.

Sean ducked down as a wall of bullets sailed over his head.

Caught in the middle, Diane Wohl took multiple MP5 rounds to the torso, nearly cutting her in half. As she fell, the woman looked back toward Quarry, her mouth half open, her eyes wide and wild. And accusing. She sank to the hard floor awash in her own blood. This mine would be her tomb.

"Sons of bitches!" roared Daryl, who'd dropped his empty clip and shoved in a fresh one, scattering shots all over; bullets ricocheted off walls, the ceilings, and the rock floor. It was like they were trapped in a lethal pinball machine.

Quarry jumped forward. "Daryl, stop! Stop! Gabriel . . ."

If Daryl heard him he wasn't listening to his daddy

anymore. This was apparently what he had meant by "his way."

He dropped the overheated MP5 and pulled out twin nickel–plated semiautomatic pistols and walked forward, sending walls of fire ahead of him. When they were empty he slapped fresh mags in and blasted away. When the triggers clicked empty he pulled a shotgun from a long leather holster strapped to his back, racked the weapon, and opened fire anew. The big-bore weapon blew large chunks of rock off the walls and sent lethal shards spinning off.

A few moments later Michelle leapt up as Daryl was reloading the ten-gauge and nailed him with a round at chest height.

"Shit!" she exclaimed as he merely staggered back after his armor absorbed most of the impact. "When am I gonna learn to aim for the damn head."

Sean opened fire too, trying to keep Daryl pinned down. But the man seemed unafraid of dying. He reloaded and fired off blast after blast from the ten-gauge, laughing and cursing as he did so. At one point he screamed out, "Is this what needs doing, Daddy? Huh? Your boy's right here for you, Daddy."

Realizing that they simply couldn't match the firepower arrayed against them, Michelle screamed, "Gabriel, Willa, run!" She pointed behind her. "That way!"

Gabriel grabbed Willa's hand. "Come on!"

They ran off.

"Shit!" Sean grunted in pain a few seconds later.

Michelle looked up from where she was reloading, and saw him hunched over holding his arm where one of the rock tailings had ripped across it.

"I'm okay," he said, grimacing.

They couldn't see him in the darkness but Daryl was now holding something far more terrifying than even an MP5 at close quarters. He had a small box with a toggle switch.

"Hey, you Feds, let's all go see Jesus," cackled Daryl.

"Don't!" Quarry collided with his son right as he flipped the switch. Daryl went down hard. Quarry's momentum carried him past his son and he rolled into and then over a pile of fallen rock.

There was a moment of silence and then the first charge went off. The force of the nearby explosion roared down the constricted tunnel like a runaway train, pushing suffocating smoke and jet-propelled debris ahead of it.

Daryl stood just in time to take the full brunt of it. A large flying rock severed his head completely from his shoulders. Quarry was mostly shielded from the blast by the pile of stone he'd landed behind. He rose moments later on shaking legs hacking up mine dirt.

Quarry barely glanced at what was left of his son and then hurried down the shaft. He found Sean and Michelle where they'd been blown down the tunnel and helped them up. "Run!" he exclaimed. "Next one's gonna go only about ten feet from here."

They ran as hard as they could. When the next blast detonated, the ceiling of the mine collapsed right behind them. The concussive force knocked them all off their feet again. Michelle tried to get up, but she screamed out in pain and grabbed her ankle. Quarry bent down and with his great strength picked the tall woman off the floor and slung her over his shoulder all in one motion. An instant later a huge chunk of rock struck right where she'd been lying.

"Move, move," he yelled at Sean, who was just ahead, holding his wounded arm. "The next one's gonna go."

As the three clambered over the pile of rubble, in the smoke and confusion they didn't see Gabriel and Willa huddled far down a side shaft, where they had retreated after the ceiling here had almost caved in on them.

Moments later a third charge went off, and the mountain did another heave. More parts of the rock ceiling gave way and thundered down.

Finally, they reached the entrance and were through it. Quarry set Michelle down and stayed bent over, heaving like a spent marathoner.

Michelle held her ankle and stared up at him. He was covered with dirt and coal dust, and with his wild white hair and sun-ravaged face he looked like a survivor of some sort of holocaust. And in way he was. They all were.

"You saved my life," she managed to gasp.

He eyed Sean and saw the blood pouring down his arm. He ripped off one of his shirtsleeves and fashioned a rough tourniquet above the wound. As he drew back, Sean saw the lines burned into the man's arm. He looked questioningly at Michelle. She'd seen it too.

Sean suddenly became as rigid as a statue. "Where're the kids?"

Quarry and Michelle stared all around.

She called out, "Willa? Gabriel?"

Quarry, however, was already looking at the mine entrance. "They're still in there." He turned and raced back through the door just as another explosion rocked the mine.

Sean jumped up to follow.

"Sean, don't!" yelled Michelle as she clutched at his arm. "Don't go back in there. The whole mountain's about to come down."

He pulled her hand free. "I was the one who got Gabriel to go in there. I promised his mother I'd bring him back."

The tears were streaming down Michelle's dirty face. She tried to say something but it wouldn't come out. He turned and ran toward the mine.

She pulled herself to her feet, tried to go after them, but collapsed, grabbing her fractured ankle.

Quarry was ahead of Sean and moving fast with the energy of panic. But Sean ran like he had never run before and quickly caught up to the older man.

They both screamed out, "Gabriel! Willa!"

To his left, they heard something. They turned down that shaft just as a charge leveled another part of the mine. Everything was creaking and groaning with sections of rock giving way. Soon, even without any more explosions, it all was going to go.

They found them, huddled together next to a mound of collapsed ceiling. Sean lifted Willa up while Quarry grabbed Gabriel's hand and headed back. They sprinted to the entrance.

Another charge, not more than fifty feet away, knocked them all down again. They sat up sputtering and spitting up dust, eardrums screaming, their bodies battered to near physical failure. Getting to their feet, they somehow staggered on. The entrance was in sight. They could see the shaft of daylight. Sean suddenly ran harder than he ever had, holding Willa tight against his chest. His heart felt like it was going to burst with the effort.

Then they were through the entrance and Sean put Willa down. "Run, honey, run to Michelle."

The little girl sprinted toward Michelle, who had managed to stagger up by holding on to an outcrop of rock.

Back inside the mine, Quarry, always so sure-footed, but now fatigued beyond belief, tripped and fell over a chunk of rock. Gabriel stopped and turned back.

"Go, Gabriel, go!"

Gabriel didn't go. He came back and helped Quarry up.

They ran right at the door. Right at the sunlight. The Alabama sky was beautiful, the sun rising high and warming.

Sean was heading back in. He saw them. "Come on," he roared. "Come on." He grabbed Gabriel's hand, pulled the boy along.

Michelle and Willa watched from a distance. In the darkness of the shaft they could make out the images of the two men and the boy running with all they had left.

"Come on!" screamed Willa.

Michelle added, "Sean, run!"

Two feet.

Then one precious foot.

Sean cleared the entrance.

The last charge detonated.

A flood of dirt and smoke poured out of the mountain as the mineshaft completely collapsed.

When it finally all cleared away, Sean King lay sprawled on his back covered in dirt and rock.

On top of him was Gabriel, still breathing.

However, there was no sign of Sam Quarry. He was still in the mine, under tons of rock.

84

Dan Cox had been educated at some of the country's best schools. He'd been successful at just about everything he'd attempted. As president he was as well versed in foreign policy matters as he was in domestic issues. There weren't many holes in his intellectual armor. Yet with all that, the people who knew the First Couple well would have agreed, at least in private, that Jane Cox was probably smarter than her husband. Or at least more cunning.

As she was flying over rural Alabama in a chopper she demonstrated the validity of this opinion. Dan Cox's plan would not work, she decided. This matter could not simply be spun, or blamed on terrorists. There were things they didn't know, that they simply had to know, to make an informed judgment about what to do.

She stared out the window of the chopper and saw the large house down below. She had been looking out the window all this time, in fact. This was the first home they had passed. The chances were very good, she felt, that whoever owned this house also owned the building she had almost died in. She pointed to it.

"Who owns that property?"

A young agent glanced past her, out the window. "I don't know, ma'am."

That was the other thing that Jane had subtly orchestrated without seeming to. Larry Foster and Chuck Waters were flying with her husband. She had banished the veteran Aaron Betack to that chopper as well. She had done it simply with one penetrating look, and the man had fled to the safety of Marine One. She had done the same with Agent Waters. The security detail she had with her was relatively young. The two HRT members were just gun jockeys. She knew how to deal with them.

"I want to go to that house."

"Ma'am?" said the confused agent.

"Tell the pilot to put down in front of that house."

"But my orders—"

"I've just been through a terrible ordeal. I was almost killed. I don't feel very well and I want to get off this chopper before I throw up. Do I make myself clear? Because if I don't I will take it up with the president when I get back to Washington and I am sure he will make it very clear to your superiors."

The HRT guys glanced at each other but didn't say a word. They just stayed hidden behind their big guns. The other agents arrayed around the First Lady stared at the floor of the chopper, unwilling to make eye contact with the woman.

The agent next to Jane said, "Walt, take us down to that house."

It landed a minute later and Jane stepped off the chopper and walked toward Atlee.

The young agent sprinted ahead of her. "Ma'am, can I ask where you're going?"

"I'm going in that house, get some water, and lie down for a bit. Do you have a problem with that?"

"No, ma'am, of course not, but let me just get the place checked out first."

She looked at him disdainfully. "Do you really think there are criminals or terrorists hiding inside that old house?"

"We've got protocols to follow, ma'am. Just let me check things out."

Jane simply marched past him, forcing the team of agents and the HRT snipers to rush ahead of her and build an impromptu protection bubble around the woman.

The door opened and Ruth Ann stood there with a kitchen apron on. When she saw who had just pressed her doorbell, her mouth gaped.

"May I trouble you for some water and a place to lie down, Miss—" Jane said.

When Ruth Ann found her voice she said, "I'm Ruth Ann. You, you come on in, ma'am. You just come right on in. I get your water."

After fetching a glass, Ruth Ann started to leave, but Jane beckoned her to remain in the small front room.

Ruth Ann sat down across from her looking about as nervous as a person could look without actually passing out.

Jane said to the detail leader, "Can you wait out in the hall? I believe that you're making our friend here extremely nervous."

"Ma'am," the agent began.

"Thank you," she said, turning away from him.

"Do you live here alone?" Jane asked after the agent had retreated into the hall.

"No, ma'am. I live here with my son. And Mr. Sam. It's his house."

"Sam?"

"Sam Quarry."

"I know that name. He has a daughter, doesn't he? Tippi?"

"Yes, ma'am. She ain't here right now. I don't know where she be." Ruth Ann looked as though she wanted to run out of the room, but she just sat there picking at her apron with her stained, work-hardened fingers.

"Has anyone been by to visit you lately?"

Ruth Ann looked down. "I . . . uh."

Jane reached over and put a gentle hand on the woman's bony shoulder. "I didn't come here by accident, Ruth Ann. I know things, you see. I know about Sam. I wanted to come here and try to help him. Help you. And your son. Is he here?"

Ruth Ann shook her head. "He done gone off with those folks."

"Folks? What folks?"

"Man and a woman."

"You knew them?"

"No, they just showed up here early this morning."

"Really, you just let your son go off with complete strangers?"

"I . . . he wanted to. They with the government, like the police. And Gabriel say he wants to go help Mr. Sam out. And Mr. Sam, if he done something wrong, I don't know nothing about it. Gabriel neither." A tear plunked down on the stained apron.

"I'm sure, Ruth Ann. I'm sure. So these people came here. Did they tell you their names?"

"Man say his name . . . King, that's right. King."

"Tall, good-looking man? The woman was also tall, brunette?"

"You know 'em?"

"They're actually friends of mine. What did they want here?"

"They looking for your niece. I told 'em we ain't know nothing 'bout that. And I swear to God, ma'am, we ain't."

Jane said soothingly, "I believe you. Of course you didn't."

"And then Gabriel he was all fired up wanting to show 'em that room."

"Room?"

"One down in the basement. Mr. Sam got stuff in that room. Stuff on the walls. Pictures and writing, whole bunch of stuff. It had your niece's picture on it. Gabriel showed me. She a pretty girl."

"And King and his friend saw this room?"

"Oh, yeah, they was in there a long time. They got real excited."

"Can you show me this room?"

"Ma'am?"

Jane stood. "I'd really like to see it."

They went downstairs, Jane ignoring the protests from her security detail. They reached the room. The door was unlocked. The detail chief insisted on at least making sure no one was lurking inside.

"That will be all you do," she said sternly. "Don't even turn the lights on. And then come directly out."

It only took seconds to make sure the room was empty.

Jane turned to Ruth Ann. "Do you mind if I go in alone?"

"Go right ahead, ma'am. I ain't want to go back in there."

Jane closed the door behind her, flicked on the light, and looked around.

She started at one end of the room and kept going until she reached the other. With each photo, each line of writing, a name, a date, a description of an event, memories, awful memories came flooding back to her.

"He raped me, Daddy," she read off the wall, when she'd gone back to the beginning of the piece of history built on these walls. She slid a chair to the middle of the room, sat down and continued to stare at this story. At *her* story.

She looked in the file cabinets, but they were mostly empty.

She only teared up once, when she saw the photo of Willa looking down at her. She had not been entirely truthful with her husband about Willa. She had wanted Willa to stay in the family because that would always be a secret that she could hold over Dan Cox. Her husband was a good man for the most part, but unpredictable. She was sure there would come a time in their marriage, after they left the White House, when such leverage would be very useful to her. It had been an intoxicating notion to know that the president of the United States was actually less powerful than his wife. Yet over the years she had come to love and care about Willa. She wanted her back.

She had to confess admiration for Sam Quarry's skill and tenacity. It really was an amazing accomplishment. After what had happened today there would be an investigation, of course. That was a real problem, but not an insurmountable one.

Her husband's charmed streak would continue. Jane knew exactly what she had to do. And in accordance with her efficient nature, she set about methodically to do it. It was just another time where she had to pick up the pieces. Just one more time.

Her husband would not be remembered this way. She stared at the wall. He *had* changed. He didn't deserve *this*.

And neither do I.

When you had clawed your way to the level the Coxes had, you lost all individuality. You were no longer him or her. You were *them*.

Five minutes later she came out and shut the door behind her.

She looked at the lead agent. "I want to go back to D.C. immediately." She turned to Ruth Ann. "Thank you for your hospitality."

"Yes, ma'am. Thank you, ma'am."

"And everything will be fine. Don't you worry."

They hurried up the steps and out of Atlee.

The chopper lifted off seconds later. It set a heading to the northwest and the pilot hit the throttle. They were soon out of sight.

Ruth Ann closed the front door and went back to work in the kitchen. A few minutes later she smelled something funny. She walked from room to room trying to figure out what it was. She finally ventured down the stairs, hastened across the passageway, and arrived at the door to the basement room. When she touched the doorknob, it felt warm. Puzzled, she pulled it open.

It was at that moment that the fire set earlier by Jane Cox using paint thinner, rags, and a match hit the pressurized oxygen cylinders, igniting them. The explosion rocked the old plantation house to its bones. The flame ball that rocketed out the open door gushed over Ruth Ann, incinerating her. The woman didn't even have time to scream.

By the time the fire was noticed and help called in, it was far too late. By the time the volunteer fire department arrived, there was hardly anything left of Atlee.

Later, Sean, Michelle, Willa, and Gabriel pulled down the long drive in the SUV. When they saw what was going on, Gabriel jumped out while the vehicle was still moving and sprinted the rest of the way.

"Momma! Momma!"

Michelle gunned the engine and they sped up. Gabriel was running so fast he reached the ruins of the house at the same time. As they were climbing out of the SUV, the little boy had already dodged past the firemen and was wading into what was left of the house.

Sean raced after him. "Gabriel!"

Michelle ran up to one of the firemen and flashed her ID. "Did you find anyone? A black lady?"

The man looked at her solemnly. "We found . . .

some remains." He looked over at Gabriel, who was clawing through the rubble trying to find his mother.

Michelle turned and ran toward them. She stopped as Gabriel sat down on the ground, sobbing and holding something. As Michelle edged forward she saw what it was. A burnt rag. As she drew closer, she saw it was more than that. It was the remains of an apron.

As Sean and Michelle tried to soothe the little boy, Willa walked carefully through the piles of wet, smoky wreckage, sat down next to him in the dirt and filth, and put her arms around him.

He glanced over at her. "It . . . it was my ma's."

"I'm sorry," she said in a quiet voice. "I'm so sorry, Gabriel."

He looked at her, his face twisted in anguish. But he nodded his thanks and started sobbing again. Willa wrapped her arms more tightly around him.

Sean glanced at Michelle. "I never thought it would be his mother who was in danger," he whispered to her.

"We had no way of knowing. Do you think this is something Quarry did somehow? Erase all the evidence?"

"I don't know."

Sean and Michelle stood back and watched the two kids sitting there, one supporting the other. It was clear from their expressions that they were thinking the same thing.

Willa didn't know it, but she was going to be experiencing this exact same grief. And neither one of them had the heart or courage right now to tell her.

Even before the last timber fell into the smoldering depths of the inferno and the old Quarry home ceased to be, Jane and Dan Cox were just landing at Andrews AFB.

Jane had told her husband what she had done. He praised his wife for her quick thinking and gave her a kiss. Despite the likely loss of their niece, the First Couple rode back to the White House with their spirits higher than they had been in a while.

They really had survived, one more time.

85

The country rejoiced at the safe return of Willa Dutton. It was all made far more poignant and indeed bittersweet by the loss of the young girl's mother. Willa was America's courageous little lady now, yet they had not seen much of her, because her family was shielding the bereaved girl from much of the media scrutiny.

An obviously relieved Dan and Jane Cox consistently mentioned it on the campaign trail, and asked both the public and the media to respect the privacy of the grieving girl.

If Willa was the number one story, a close second was the attempted assassination of Dan Cox by persons as yet unknown, though the investigation was ongoing. While he only would speak briefly and modestly of the ordeal himself, his staff made sure that the public knew how brave he and the First Lady had been, risking their lives to try and get their niece back and foiling the plot of what most of the country thought was the work of terrorists trying to kill their president.

He was so far ahead in the polls now that even the

opposition openly acknowledged the impossibility of winning the upcoming election. Jane had never been more popular. She had appeared on the covers of a number of magazines and had made appearances on all the major news and talk shows. For those who knew her well, while she seemed the same physically, still radiant if thinner, there was something different about her. A certain light in the eyes that was no longer there.

Sean King and Michelle Maxwell had also been brought into the national spotlight, however unwillingly. After the president and Agent Waters had mentioned what they had done to foil the assassination plot, they had been inundated with press inquiries, to such an extent that they both had moved and taken up residence at an undisclosed location.

They had briefed Waters on what had happened at the mines. And about Diane Wohl being in there along with Daryl and Sam Quarry. Attempts were being made to excavate the mine collapse. Yet it was becoming rapidly clear that any evidence that might have been in there was going to stay in there.

When Waters questioned them as to Quarry's motivation to do all this, they had claimed ignorance.

Sean's arm and other injuries were healing and Michelle had gone from crutches to a boot on her foot. Gabriel had miraculously suffered no serious physical injuries. However, the emotional impact of losing his mother and his home had taken its toll.

Sean and Michelle had discussed what to do about him.

"We can't just stick him in foster care," she said.

"I don't want to do that either. I want to find him a great home with a great family."

"I don't think anything will be great for him for a long time," said Michelle. "No matter what sort of family he ends up with."

"Do you think we could take care of him for a while?" he finally suggested.

"We? We live in separate places. We're not married. And with our occupation, being gone half the time, they'd never let us have custody of him."

"We can try."

Michelle had thought about this and then squeezed his hand and smiled. "We can try. At least for a while."

And with help from the FBI and the White House, Sean and Michelle received emergency temporary custody of Gabriel Macon after it was quickly determined he had no living relatives. There would be future legal hoops for them to jump through, but for now Gabriel had a place to stay and people to look after him.

Sean and Michelle had traveled down to Atlee once more a few days after Gabriel had become their ward. They hadn't taken the boy with them because there was nothing left for him down there. Gabriel was staying with Michelle and Sean was at a townhouse provided by the Secret Service.

The FBI was still on site, investigating what little remained of the plantation house, and also the site where the First Couple had almost died. And where Tippi Quarry *had* died.

The FBI had privately marveled at the skill and ingenuity with which Sam Quarry had put his murderous plan together. Sean and Michelle had learned that a cavity in the ground near the building where the First Couple had almost died had been discovered. There was a TV monitor inside this bunker along with a pair of binoculars, a remote control, and other equipment and provisions. If anyone had been inside there, he or she was long gone.

Sean and Michelle suspected it was either Carlos Rivera or Kurt Stevens but had no real proof.

"He built basically a gas chamber for Dan and Jane Cox," said Sean, as they stared at the little house.

"And he killed his own daughter in there."

"More like euthanasia," replied Sean. "After all those years."

The most important issue remained unresolved for the pair. What to do about what they'd learned in the basement at Atlee.

"Everyone's dead," said Sean. "Quarry. Tippi. Ruth Ann."

"Maybe we should just let it go," voiced Michelle. "It'll drag Willa and Gabriel back into all this."

"And rip the country apart," added Sean.

"But then Cox gets away with it."

"I know. But maybe that's better than the alternative."

They drove back to the ruins of Atlee. One of the HRT squad members securing the area approached them.

"Read about you in the paper," he said. "Wanted to thank you for what you did for the president."

"No problem," Sean said without much enthusiasm while Michelle said nothing. Both were thinking about the president of the United States in a light far different than the HRT guy was, even if they had decided to do nothing about it.

He nodded at the ruins. "Looked a lot different the first time I was here."

"You were here when it was still standing?" asked Michelle.

He nodded. "I was riding on a bird with the First Lady when all that shit went down. She made us put down here. Said she wasn't feeling well. Went inside, met up with some black lady. Think she was the maid. They talked a bit and then the First Lady went down to a room in the basement. Insisted on it, in fact. She was the only one who could go in. She did, and then she came out later and we hightailed it home."

Sean and Michelle stared over at the rubble.

And then Atlee burned down.

86

The invitation came two days after they returned from Alabama.

The White House looked beautiful in the soft light of a late summer evening. They had dinner in the First Couple's private quarters. The president wasn't there. Jane had invited them. After the meal was done they sat in the living room with their coffees the butler had brought in. For a few minutes no one spoke. Sean and Michelle sat there tensely while Jane did not make eye contact.

Finally, Jane said, "We've certainly come a long way."

"How's that?" asked Sean.

"Finding Willa, getting things back on track. I can't thank you enough for what you did. If not for you, the president and I would be dead. And so would Willa."

"Sam Quarry's dead. So is his son. And Tippi Quarry. But then you knew that. And a little boy named Gabriel lost his mother. And Diane Wohl? We knew her as Diane Wright. The woman who was screwing your husband in the car in Atlanta? You remember her, right?"

"Please don't be crude, Sean, there's no need for that."

"So Willa lost both her mothers. That's a real tragedy."

"You have no proof that Pam was not her mother."

He pulled some papers from his pocket. "Actually, I do. They're DNA results. They show Diane Wohl is or was Willa's mother."

Jane set her cup down, touched a linen napkin against her lips, and stared at him. "I asked you here to make an offer going forward. Not to wade through the past."

"Why do you feel the need to do that?" he asked, while Michelle looked on in silence.

"Because I know you went to that house. I know you saw that room."

"Oh, you mean at Atlee? The place that burned to the ground right after you left there? The same fire that killed Ruth Ann?"

"I was deeply sorry to hear about that."

"You met Ruth Ann, didn't you?"

"Briefly, yes. She seemed like a nice woman. I'm glad we were able to help you two gain temporary custody of her son."

"What, you couldn't think of another way of getting rid of the evidence? Other than burning the house down and killing the woman?"

Jane looked at him with an impassive expression. "I have no idea what you're talking about. When I left the house it was perfectly fine and so was she. You can ask anyone who was with me. And you are growing dangerously close to something you shouldn't go near, Sean."

"Now, is that a threat? Because even threats against nobodies like me are actionable."

"Would you like to hear my offer?"

"Why not? We came all this way."

"What's happened is regrettable. All around. Without going into detail I will tell you that all of this has been difficult, complicated. For both me and the president."

"Yeah, good thing it was so simple for the Quarry family. They just had a lifetime of misery because of what your husband did."

She ignored this interruption. "For the good of the country I am asking that you not raise any issues that might embarrass the president. He's a fine man. He's served his country with distinction. He's been a wonderful father."

"And why should we look the other way?"

"In return, I can assure you that no action will be taken against you for breaking into my brother's office and stealing his files. His confidential files, some of which I understand had to do with classified national security issues. This is a very serious matter indeed."

"I was working a case. On your behalf."

"That of course would be up to a court to decide. But I never told you to break the law. In addition, I've done a little digging on my own, and it's come to my attention that you also threatened Cassandra Mallory, allegedly blackmailing her. I believe that Ms. Mallory will also allege that you made improper sexual advances to her in her home to which you gained entry under false pretenses while she was in a state of undress."

"Little Miss Cassandra doesn't scare me at all, Jane."

"I also discovered that Aaron Betack apparently broke into my office and took something from my desk. And I think the facts will show that he did so at your behest. Not only will Agent Betack's career at the Secret Service be over but the three of you could go to prison."

"If you can prove it, go for it. But getting back to the list of your wonderful husband's accomplishments, I think you left one out."

"Which one?" she said coldly.

"Being an adulterer? That one get lost off your little checklist somehow?"

"And how about being a rapist?" said Michelle.

Jane rose. "You have no proof of anything. So I strongly suggest that you keep such ludicrous accusations to yourself unless you want to find yourselves in very serious trouble. He is the president of the United States. Show some *damn* respect."

"Respect for what?"

"I don't care what lies you might have seen on those walls in that house, you have no right—"

Sean cut her off. "What we saw on those walls was the *truth*. You knew it too, and that's why you burned the place down. And we have every right, lady."

"*First* Lady," she said.

Sean rose too. "When did you stop caring about the truth, Jane? When did it stop mattering to you? After the first cover-up? The second? Did you just convince yourself that it was always somebody else's fault? Or that he'd come around one day, take some pills, and it would all be better? The past, the hurt, just wiped clean? That a guy like Sam Quarry would just walk away, let it go? Like everybody else had? Because your husband was such a rising star? Because he'd make such a great president?"

"You can't know what it's like to be here, in this house. To always having to be on. To never once letting your guard down. Knowing that the smallest mistake you make will be broadcast all over the world."

"Hey, nobody twisted his arm. Or yours."

"I've worked too damn hard—" She broke off and dabbed her eyes with a cloth.

Sean stared at her. "I really thought I knew you. I thought I respected you. I thought you were real. It was all bullshit, wasn't it? All smoke and mirrors. Just like this town. Nothing behind the curtain."

"I think it's time for you to leave *my* house."

Michelle stood next to Sean.

He said, "Fine. But just remember one thing, *Jane*. It's not *your* house. It belongs to the American people. You and the hubby are just renting."

87

The newspaper business sucks, doesn't it, Marty?" said Sean loudly. "Nobody wants to wait for the paper anymore. They can get it all online all the time. Even if it's all made up."

It was midnight. He and Michelle were standing next to a support column in an underground parking garage in downtown Washington. The man walking toward them stopped and then chuckled as Sean and Michelle stepped out into the wash of light from the overheads.

Sean shook hands with Martin Determann and introduced Michelle to him.

"What business doesn't suck right now?" said Determann, who was short, with thick, graying black hair and a loud voice. Sharp eyes danced behind slender glasses. "And asking people to take the time to read and actually think about stuff? Heaven forbid."

Sean grinned. "Nobody likes a whiner, Marty."

"So why all the clandestine stuff?" He looked around at the empty garage. "I feel like I'm in a scene from *All the President's Men*."

"Think your own Deep Throat will help you sell a few more papers?"

Determann laughed. "I'd prefer a Pulitzer but I also keep an open mind. Hey, maybe I can ghost-write your autobiography. What with all the ink you two have gotten lately, we could probably sell it to some publisher for seven figures, easy."

"I'm not kidding about the Deep Throat thing."

Determann turned serious. "I was actually hoping you weren't. What do you got?"

"Come on. This is going to take a while."

Sean had rented a motel room a little north of Old Town Alexandria. They headed there.

"So how do you two know each other?" asked Michelle as they drove on the George Washington Parkway alongside the Potomac.

Determann clapped Sean on the back. "This guy represented me in my divorce. Unknown to me, my ex was a cokehead who burned through my savings, cheated on me with the UPS driver, and actually had the nerve to poison my goldfish. And she still wanted half of everything I had when I caught on and filed to kick her out of my life. By the time Sean was done with old Ursula she got zip. I even got her dog. Which was a good thing, because he always liked me better anyway."

"I think Marty is exaggerating my accomplishments, but even though he sometimes stretches the truth, he's a helluva reporter."

"But still looking for that first Pulitzer." He eyed the large and packed accordion file Sean had beside him on the seat. "Is it in there?"

"You're going to find out soon enough."

They got to the room. Sean closed the door behind them, took off his coat, and said, "Let's get to it."

They methodically went through all the photos that Michelle had taken at Atlee as they filled Determann in on everything they had found out, from the AWOL report to the story Quarry had built on the walls in the basement to their near deaths in the mines.

When they got to the part about the First Lady burning down the house and killing Ruth Ann, Determann said, "You're screwing with me!"

"I wish we were."

Sean also showed him all the files he'd taken from Atlee that contained some of the background details on Quarry's hunt for justice.

Determann took copious notes and asked many questions. They ran out for coffee and drank it down as the hours drifted by. As the sun came up they went out for some more caffeine and breakfast at a restaurant in Old Town. While eating they kept going through it as the smooth waters of the Potomac sat in front of them and a jet lifted off from the nearby airport and soared across the sky. Back in the room they endured too much secondhand puff from the chain-smoking reporter and kept plowing through what they had learned and also what they suspected. By the time they were done the sun was high in the sky and it was past time for lunch.

Determann sat back and stretched. "Can I tell you that this is the most amazing shit that I have ever heard?"

"Don't suck up," said Sean in a joking tone. "It's unseemly."

"No, really, I mean this makes Watergate and Monicagate look like teepeeing a yard after a high school football game."

"So you believe us?" asked Michelle.

"Believe you? Who could've made this stuff up?" He motioned to the photos and pages of notes spread over the table. "And it's not like it doesn't come without proof."

He lit another cigarette. "But what I don't get is, why kidnap Willa? I mean, she is the niece and all, but how could they be sure that the president would go along? It wasn't his kid after all. No one could really blame him if he'd ducked that one."

Sean pulled out another file he'd taken from Quarry's records. They had purposefully withheld this part of the story from the reporter until he'd asked that question.

"These are the results of DNA tests that Quarry

had done. These on Pam and Willa Dutton's blood. And then this one on Diane Wright. Quarry penciled in the names under each test result."

"Diane Wright aka Diane Wohl," said Determann, who had proven a quick study, and had a strong command of the story and principal players already.

"Right."

"But why a DNA test?"

"It shows that Diane is Willa's mother and Pam isn't."

Determann took the papers and studied them. "Call me stupid, but I'm not following you, Sean."

Sean explained about what had happened in that back alley in Georgia nearly thirteen years ago, the first time he'd told anyone other than Michelle. Loyalty to Jane Cox had caused him to keep his silence. However, loyalty had its limits and he had reached his with the First Lady. He had told Sam Quarry back in that mine that he wanted to help the truth come out if he let Willa go. The man had kept his part of the bargain, and while Sean had initially decided to keep quiet, after he'd found out what the First Lady had done at Atlee he intended to honor his promise to the dead man.

Determann sat back and took off his glasses. "Then Senator Cox with Diane Wright on top? Nine months later out pops Willa? She's his kid? Jesus. And then what he did earlier to Tippi Quarry? What a prick!"

"That's exactly the part of his anatomy that he couldn't seem to control," pointed out Michelle.

Sean picked up a photo that showed the image of a sour-looking man in his late forties. "And Quarry found out that Jane Cox knew the butcher who performed the abortion on Tippi and ended up cutting into an artery. The police found her in the basement of an abandoned building, probably where the scum dumped her after he realized what he'd done. He'd lost his license to practice medicine because of drug and booze problems, but he was still open for business for his old friends."

"And no regular doc or hospital because Tippi might spill what had happened? Or people might start asking inconvenient questions?"

"Exactly."

Determann sat forward and studied the papers. "But no one checked the president's DNA?"

"If they did, it would be a match."

"Well, they have the man's DNA on file. Maybe this story will prompt one more test to be run." He started scribbling notes down but stopped when Sean put a hand over his. He looked up with a questioning expression.

"Marty, can I ask a favor?"

"After giving me the story of the century? Yeah, I think I can spare one."

"I don't want you to write about this part of the story. About Willa."

"Come again?"

Michelle spoke up. "Willa's lost her mother. The woman who actually gave birth to her is dead too. We just think it would be too much. It wouldn't be fair to put her through all that."

"And you have plenty enough without it," added Sean. "Including very compelling circumstantial evidence that the First Lady torched a house and killed an innocent woman to cover up her husband's misdeeds. But you're the reporter, so it's your call. We won't make you withhold it."

Determann looked uncomfortable. "You think Jane Cox intended Ruth Ann to die when she burned down the house?"

"I hope she didn't. But I guess no one other than her knows that. I do know that Willa has been through enough."

Determann nodded and reached out a hand to Sean. "Deal."

"Thanks, Marty."

Determann said, "It's a great story, Sean. And I can completely understand why you both would want the truth to come out."

"But?" Sean said warily.

"But it's going to rock this country to its soul, man."

"Sometimes you have to, Marty. Sometimes you just have to."

88

Willa sat across from Sean, Michelle, and Gabriel with her hands in her lap and her head turned downward. They were at a house that Tuck had rented about a mile from their old one, which was up for sale. None of them wanted to go back there to live. Tuck sat next to his daughter, one arm protectively around her.

"I'm sorry that your ma died," Gabriel said, not looking directly at Willa. He was dressed in a new white polo shirt and blue jeans and he held a new Atlanta Falcons ball cap that Sean had bought him to replace the one he'd lost in the fire. He had one hand in his pocket, his fingers curved around the only thing of his that had survived the fire: the Lady Liberty coin that Sam Quarry had placed on his nightstand before he'd departed Atlee for good.

"I'm really sorry about your mom too," Willa said. "And you were very brave in that mine. I don't think I'd be alive except for you."

Gabriel glanced sideways at Sean. "He pulled me out. I sure wouldn't have made it without Mr. Sean."

Willa looked around the interior of her temporary home before gazing back at Gabriel. "He had a daughter. Her name was Tippi."

"Yep. She was real sick. Mr. Sam let me read to her."

"Jane Austen, he told me."

"Did he talk to you a lot about her?" Sean asked Willa.

"Not a lot, but I could tell he thought about her a lot. You just sort of know." She glanced at her father. "I tried to get away once. I almost fell off the mountain. He saved me. Mr. Sam grabbed me right before I fell."

Tuck fidgeted a bit. "That's all in the past, Willa. You don't have to think about it anymore, sweetie. It's over."

She fiddled with her fingers. "I know, Dad. But part of me—" She leaned forward. "He lost his daughter, didn't he? He lost Tippi?"

Michelle and Sean exchanged a quick glance. "Yeah, he did," he said. "But I believe your dad's right. You probably shouldn't think about it too much."

Tuck eyed Gabriel. It was obvious that the man was not entirely comfortable with anyone associated with Sam Quarry being in his home and around Willa, even an innocent little boy. "So he's staying with you guys. How's that working?" His tone clearly implied that it would not work at all.

"It's working just *great*," said Michelle firmly. "We've enrolled him in school up here for the new year. He graded into algebra even though he's only going into seventh grade, and his foreign language skills are off the chart," she said proudly.

"Spanish and Native American," added Sean.

"Well that's great," Tuck said insincerely.

"It is great," Willa said, eying Gabriel. "You must be really smart."

Gabriel shrugged. "I'm okay. Got a lot to learn, and everything up here is . . ."

"Different?" said Willa. "I can help with stuff like that."

Tuck gave a hollow laugh. "Wait a minute, honey, you'll be plenty busy yourself. I'm sure Mr. King here can take care of the boy."

Michelle looked at Willa. "But thank you for asking, Willa. That was very sweet." Now she looked directly at her dad. "And who knows, you two might become really great friends."

Later, Tuck drew Sean and Michelle aside while Willa showed Gabriel her room. "I can't tell you how much I appreciate what you did. The things that Willa told me happened. God. It's a miracle she survived. That any of you did."

"You probably don't want to hear this, but it was Sam Quarry who went back in that mine and really saved Willa. If he hadn't done that, she wouldn't be here."

Tuck's face reddened. "Yeah, well, if the asshole hadn't done any of this, Willa would never have been in that mine and Pam would still be here too."

"You're right. Have you talked to your sister much?"

Tuck scowled. "Not too much. Dan wanted to take Willa on a little tour with him on the campaign. But—"

"But you thought it seemed a little too *exploitative*?" said Michelle.

"Something like that, yeah."

"The kids really need you now, Tuck. So you might want to let your partner David Hilal run the show for a while." He paused. "Just stay away from his wife."

Before a surprised Tuck could say anything, Sean put a hand on the man's shoulder and added, "And if you go anywhere near Cassandra Mallory, I'll cut it right out of your pants, you son of a bitch."

Tuck chuckled briefly before realizing that Sean was deadly serious.

As they were walking to their car later, Willa rushed outside and ran up to them. She handed them three envelopes.

"What's this for?" asked Michelle.

"Thank-you letters, for all you did for me."

"Honey, you didn't have to do that."

"My mom said you always write thank-you letters, and besides, I wanted to."

Gabriel held on to his envelope like it was the most precious thing he'd ever been given. "That was really nice, Willa. Thank you."

She looked up at them, her eyes so large they seemed to envelop her entire face. "I hate Mr. Sam for what he did to my mom."

Gabriel immediately looked down and stepped back.

Michelle said, "I know, sweetie. I don't think he meant for her to get hurt, but it was still his fault."

"But right before he let me go he told me that if you ever love you have to be prepared to hate too. I guess he meant if someone hurts somebody you love you're going to hate them. It's just natural."

"I guess so," said Sean a little uneasily, unsure of where this was going.

"I think Mr. Sam loved his daughter."

"I think he did too," Michelle said softly, rubbing at her left eye.

"He did," said Gabriel. "No thinking about it."

"And because someone hurt her, he hated them."

"That's probably right," said Sean.

"But then he said you always have to let the hate go. Otherwise it'll just tear you up inside. And it won't let any love back in." She looked at Gabriel when she said this. The two children held this gaze for several long moments.

"I think Mr. Sam was right, Willa. For both of

us." A tear plunked down on Gabriel's new shirt, while tears slid down Willa's cheeks.

Michelle turned away while Sean took several quick breaths as Willa looked up at them with her wide, sad eyes.

"So I'm not going to hate him anymore."

Now Michelle let out a sob and took a step back, trying to hide behind Sean, whose eyes were tearing up.

"Okay, Willa," said Sean in a hoarse voice. "That's probably a good idea."

She gave all three a hug and then ran back inside.

Sean, Michelle, and Gabriel just stood there for a while. Finally, Gabriel said, "She's a good friend to have."

"Yes she is," said Michelle. "Yes she is."

On Election Day, Dan Cox, bolstered by his heroism and the dramatic return of his beloved niece, won a second term to the White House by one of the largest margins of victory ever seen in American presidential elections.

Two months after the inauguration, Martin Determann, who had worked day and night on nothing other than the story of a lifetime, published a nine-page exclusive in the *Washington Post*. Determann had wisely piggybacked on all the years-long work that Sam Quarry had done, but had brought to it a professional investigative journalist's eye and, more importantly, solid proofs. His story was backed up by facts and sources so meticulously cultivated and catalogued that every media outlet in the world immediately picked up on the story and did their own investigations, uncovering even more well-hidden secrets from Dan Cox's past.

And Determann *was* nominated for a Pulitzer Prize.

The results of all this created a groundswell of fury across the nation against Dan and Jane Cox. So much so that on a gloomy day in April a disgraced and humbled Dan Cox addressed his fellow Americans from the Oval Office and announced that he would resign the presidency of the United States at noon the following day.

And he did.

89

A month after Cox's resignation Sean and Michelle once more visited Atlee.

Tippi Quarry had been buried beside her mother in the graveyard of a nearby church. Based on evidence that Sean and Michelle had given as to the time of Sam Quarry's death, his estate had passed to Ruth Ann Macon under the terms of the will that Sean had found in the basement, since Quarry's death had preceded hers, if only by an hour or so.

And that meant that Gabriel, as her only living descendant, inherited Sam Quarry's property. Sean was working on the legal part of all this with a lawyer licensed in Alabama. They were planning to sell the two hundred acres to a real estate developer who was willing to pay a price high enough that Gabriel would have no problem paying for college and with quite a bit left over.

After they finished meeting with the lawyer and representatives of the developer they were walking back to their rental car when a voice reached them.

"Hello?"

They turned to see a man with brown skin, shoulder-length white hair, a wide-brimmed straw hat, and a heavily wrinkled face. He was standing by where the porch to the house had once been.

"Hello, back," said Sean. They walked over.

"Are you Fred?" said Michelle.

Fred nodded as he moved toward them.

"I'm Michelle, this is my partner, Sean."

They shook hands and then surveyed where the plantation had once stood.

"Did you know Sam?" asked Fred.

"A little. I suppose you did?"

"Good man. Let me live on his land. Brought me smokes and the Jim Beam. I'm going to miss him. I'm going to miss them all. I guess I'm the only one left now that Gabriel isn't living here anymore. I had two indigenous staying with me, but they moved on."

"Koasati?" she asked.

"The lost people, yes. How did you know?"

"Lucky guess."

"I hear the property is being sold. Are you involved in that? I saw you meeting with some folks."

"That's right. But Gabriel told us about you and we've made provision that you and your Airstream will still have a place here."

Fred smiled grimly. "I doubt that'll matter."

"Why?"

He coughed deeply. "Doctor says I've only got a few more months left. Lung thing."

"I'm sorry," Sean said.

"Don't be. I'm old. I'm supposed to die." He put a small hand on Michelle's sleeve. "Would you like to come back to my trailer for a beer? It's close by here. And my Airstream has never seen anyone as beautiful as this young lady."

Michelle smiled. "How can a girl refuse an offer like that?"

They sat inside his little trailer and drank a bottle of beer each and Fred regaled them with stories about Sam and Gabriel and life at Atlee.

"You know, I could always tell that Sam was unhappy. He tried not to show it, but he was an unhappy man."

Sean took a swig of beer and nodded. "I think you're right there."

"Sam had great respect for our culture. Asked me lots of questions about it. Our symbols and rituals."

Sean sat up. "Fred, I saw a mark on Sam's arm one time." On the layer of dust on a rickety table in the trailer, Sean drew it out and spoke as he did so. "Four lines. A long one intersected by two perpendicular ones at each end, with a short one in the middle."

Fred was already nodding before he finished. "I told him about that. You see, in Native American culture that is the mark of spiritual protection. It's not Koasati, but another tribal language. Not sure which one. Anyway, the left line means *winyan*, or woman. The right mark stands for *wicasa*, or man. The long center line stands for the *wakanyeza*, or innocent children."

"But what does it mean?" asked Sean.

"It means it's the responsibility of the parent to always protect the child."

Sean looked at Michelle. "Thanks, Fred. That really clears it up."

On the drive back to the airport, Michelle said, "How do people like Jane and Dan Cox go as far as they have?"

"Because she's strong and tough and will do whatever it takes. And he has the gift of making people want to root for him. A real people person."

"So that's all it takes? God help us."

"But it all comes with a price, Michelle."

"Really?" she said skeptically.

"Knowing that one day it could all come crashing down."

"That doesn't seem to be enough of a price to pay, sorry."

"Trust me, his resigning the presidency was just the beginning. They're looking at a few decades of depositions and trials. And they'll be real lucky if both their butts don't end up in prison."

"We can only hope they're not that lucky."

They drove on for a few more miles before Sean

reached in the backseat and slid something out of his briefcase. Michelle, who was driving, looked over at it.

"What's that?"

"The file you threw in the Dumpster the night you broke into Horatio Barnes's office."

"What? How?"

"I came around the corner in time to see you chuck it. I got it out and dried it off. I haven't read it, Michelle. I would never do that. But I thought you might want to have it."

She glanced down at the pile of papers. "Thanks, but I don't need it. My dad and I already worked it out."

"So you already know what it says?"

"I know enough, Sean. I know enough."

After they landed in D.C., Michelle drove her SUV out of the airport parking lot. Thirty minutes later they were at Michelle's apartment. They had decided that Gabriel would stay at her place for now, but Sean would be an equal caretaker.

Tonight, though, Gabriel was sleeping over at none other than Chuck Waters's house. The FBI agent had six kids, three of them near Gabriel's age, and the veteran and sour-faced federal cop had shown that he had a very soft heart for children and had taken to Gabriel immediately. The agent lived out in Manassas and over the last few months Gabriel had gotten to be good friends with all the Waters kids.

Sean thought Chuck was secretly recruiting the highly intelligent Gabriel for a career in the FBI once he finished college. However, Sean had set Gabriel straight on that. "You gotta aim higher than the FBI," he'd told Gabriel as the two of them and Michelle were having dinner one night.

"Higher how?"

"The Secret Service of course," Michelle had answered.

Michelle dropped the car keys on the kitchen counter. "Help yourself to a beer. I'm going to grab a quick shower and change into some fresh clothes. Then maybe we can get some dinner."

"I'll give Waters a call and check on Gabriel." He smiled. "This dad thing isn't so bad."

"Yeah, that's because you missed all the sleepless nights and dirty diapers."

Sean opened a soda and sat down on the couch and called Waters. Gabriel was doing great, the agent said. When Sean talked to the little boy the happiness in his voice confirmed this. As he put the phone down Sean heard the shower turn on in Michelle's bedroom. He tried to watch TV but the plot of the crime drama he happened on was so flimsy and uninteresting compared to the events he'd just lived for real that he turned it off. He sat there with his eyes closed, trying to forget much of what had happened over the last months, at least for a few seconds.

When he opened his eyes, he noted that Michelle had not come back. He glanced at his watch. Fifteen minutes had gone by. He could hear nothing from the bedroom.

"Michelle?"

No answer. "Michelle!"

He muttered a curse, rose, and looked around. With all the crazy shit they'd been involved in, who knew? He pulled his pistol and slowly made his way down the short hall. He flicked a light on by hitting the switch with his elbow.

"Michelle!"

He eased open the door to the bedroom.

A small light was cast from the adjacent bathroom.

He said in a softer voice, "Michelle? Are you okay? Are you sick?"

He heard the hair dryer start up and then he sighed with relief. He turned to leave, but then he didn't. Sean just stood there, looking at that crack of light from under the bathroom door.

A couple minutes later the hair dryer turned off and she came out wearing a long thick robe, her hair still damp. It wasn't a sexy number like the one Cassandra Mallory had worn. Michelle was completely covered up. Not a trace of makeup. And yet to Sean, there was no comparison. The woman he was looking at was the most beautiful person he'd ever seen.

"Sean?" she said in surprise. "Are you okay?"